Mystic Chords

William J. Ridley

BILLU, Inc

Acknowledgments

After *Mystic Chords* was designed and roughly drafted, many kind and talented individuals helped bring it to its final form:

Early readers: Kevin Fitzpatrick, Mary Regina, V.S.P., Jack and Iris Campbell, and Sylvester Turbes, provided vital advice and encouragement. Walter Kurtz suggested repairs for flaws detected by his expert, scrutinizing eye. Family members and friends flattered and suggested improvements that lifted the fledgling author's flagging spirits.

Special thanks are due our daughter, Marie, whose creative editing refined, illuminated, and enlivened the narrative and helped embellish and decorate the finished model. And loving Lucille, who endured the daily anguish and noise of construction, yet provided essential faith throughout, contributed gentle insights, and survived to pronounce the novel worthy.

Those readers who do not agree with Lucille's assessment should hold the author alone responsible for its shortcomings.

Clarifications and Distinctions

The following listed events are historical. Other events in this novel are creations of the author.

Governor Ramsey/Agent Galbraith meeting with Sioux.
Steamboat Fannie Harris' Minnesota River trip.
Incident between Sioux braves and settlers at Acton.
Selection of Little Crow as Sioux Spokesman.
Sioux attacks on Fort Ridgely and New Ulm.
Governor Ramsey's appointment of Henry Sibley as Commander.
Battles of Birch Coulee and Wood Lake.
Events at Camp Release, including Sibley's "prairie court."
Execution of 38 convicted Sioux warriors at Mankato.
Minnesota First Regiment involvements, including:
    Training at Fort Snelling.
    First Battle of Bull Run.
    Bivouacs at Camp Stone, Harper's Ferry, and Alexandria.
    Battles of Antietam and Gettysburg.
    Deactivation of Regiment in Washington, D.C.

The following listed individuals and their actions are historical, though their thoughts and words are the author's creations. All other characters in the novel are fictional.

Abraham Lincoln, President of the United States.
Union Officers: Generals George Meade, Winfield Hancock, and John Pope and Colonel William Colvill, Captain Andrew Messick, and Lieutenant Timothy Sheehan.
Confederate Officers: Generals Robert E. Lee and Thomas Jackson.
Alexander Ramsey, Governor of Minnesota.
Henry Sibley, Commander, U.S. forces in Minnesota.
Thomas Galbraith, Indian Agent.
Little Crow, Mdewakanton Sioux Spokesman.
White Spider, Little Crow's half brother.
Cut Nose, Little Shakopee, and Gray Eagle, Sioux war chiefs.
Little Paul, Spokesman for Western Sioux tribes.
Andrew Myrick, Trader.

Prologue

Saint Paul, Minnesota
October 26, 1941

The crisp breeze tugged at David's jacket as he stood on the bluff surveying the panoramic view of Saint Paul. The scene was highlighted by the copper-green dome of the Cathedral, the gold-leafed State Capitol, and the granite-gray First National Bank tower, structures that proclaimed in stone and marble the forces of Church, State, and Commerce that shaped Minnesota's past and present. Along the near bank of the Mississippi River shining steel rails stretched westward as lifelines to communities from the heart of the nation to the Pacific.

At the sound of her approach, he turned to greet his aunt, a regal figure moving along a path between twin Norway pines. Only close-cropped silver hair and weathered, graceful hands betrayed her years. She wore a heavy wool, emerald-green shawl that heightened the gray-green of her lively eyes.

"Great birthday party, Aunt Virginia. You must be pleased."

"Oh yes, David, I've been so blessed."

With his arm around her frail shoulders, they relished the pastel-hued sky surrounding the retreating sun. "Eighty-four beautiful, productive years, dear lady, and I trust many more ahead."

Her sparkling eyes met his, then looked away. "Eighty-four years is a generous span." She briefly savored the southwest horizon. "I've always enjoyed this scene at day's end. Reminds me of my mother who seemed to feel eternity in sunsets."

"Is that what you feel, too?"

"No, she was far more profound and spiritual than I, David. Sunsets remind me of the beauty of this area when I was a child. Pristine, barely trodden. The Indians revered the land and blended into it. They dreaded the flood of settlers, knowing their way was doomed. You'll recall one of their sayings, 'Only the rocks are forever.'"

"You were raised during exciting times."

"Yes. Extraordinary events visited on ordinary people who rose to meet the challenges. They prevailed because of their beliefs, personal qualities, and determination, attributes we'll always need as a people. I trust we modern Americans have the same will and purpose."

"You don't doubt it, do you, Aunt Virginia?"

"No, I don't. Still, it might be an opportune time to remind ourselves of the price our people paid to provide us with all that we take for granted today." She held up a gold disk suspended on a delicate chain from her neck. On its surface five embedded emeralds glittered. "You know the significance of this heirloom of course. One stone for each of our five family members who emigrated from Ireland in 1857. Their story was like those of thousands of others from many lands."

The temperature had dropped noticeably. She shivered but continued. "I saw everything with a child's eyes, but I listened to tales told by my mother and my uncles over the years."

She turned away and led him along the path toward the back entry. "I need your help, dear nephew. With your contacts and associations in the literary community, you can identify an author for me to write our people's story. I will commission a book to capture and preserve the memories of those times and people."

"Wonderful idea. Several authors come immediately to mind."

"I'm countin' on you. Now let's discuss it further over a final toast to my birthday. You'll remember that I keep some 'Irish' for special occasions."

They entered her Summit Avenue home, removed outer garments and proceeded to the living room. She placed her hand on a hand-hewn, oak rocking chair facing a massive fireplace. Above the mantel hung a painting of a small log cabin at the base of a hill adorned in vivid fall-colored foliage. She poured an inch of amber contents from a decanter into low-ball glasses and raised hers to the painting.

"To our people, David, and our first Minnesota home, the cabin on the Cottonwood River."

She reached down to open the lid of a battered cedar chest. "I have my mother's precious journals and hundreds of family letters that are available to the author, and I'll share my personal remembrances. I have never related the details of what happened to my mother and me during the Sioux Uprisin'. Though I was only five, that experience remains vivid to this day."

"The telling may be painful for you, Aunt Virginia."

"Perhaps, but also rewardin'. I want you to convince our author that the story will be best related in the form of historical fiction. Excellent historical studies have been published, but they are read mainly by scholars and by students as assignments. I want this book to have broader appeal. Fiction, but based on events as they happened and as seen through the eyes of the participants. The author need not embellish the occurrences of those turbulent times. The truth far surpasses what any writer of fiction could create."

"You're asking for a great deal, sweet lady, but I'll find the right someone."

Her face was slightly flushed, and her eyes shone as she spoke with a voice that seemed to come from a distant place. "I know you will. It will be the tribute those people deserve and may help to preserve their precious legacy."

She sighed, rose, brushed her nephew's cheek with her fingers, and glided the few paces to look out the French doors at the last faint light. She turned and smiled. "As I neared this birthday, it occurred to me that I am almost exactly half as old as our nation. Think of it, David. Roughly 'four score' years from the Declaration of Independence to the Civil War and now a second eighty year span to the present. Only God knows what is in store for America in the next eight decades."

"I'm not worried. America has always met every challenge."

"True, but never doubt that forces relentlessly seek our downfall. As I pondered the future I was moved to re-read several of President Lincoln's speeches. A melodic phrase in his first Inaugural Address reminded the people of the secedin' states that strong bonds tied all Americans. He stated his belief that the 'mystic chords of memory . . . would yet swell the chorus of the Union.' Were Lincoln alive today, he would remind us that those mystic chords must never be permitted to fade away. Let this book be our contribution to that everlastin' chorus."

David nodded but could find no words to respond on the level of her heartfelt plea. She reached the foot of the staircase, turned, blew him a soft kiss and began her ascent. He stepped to the landing and watched her as she slowly climbed and until she disappeared into the darkness above.

Mystic Chords

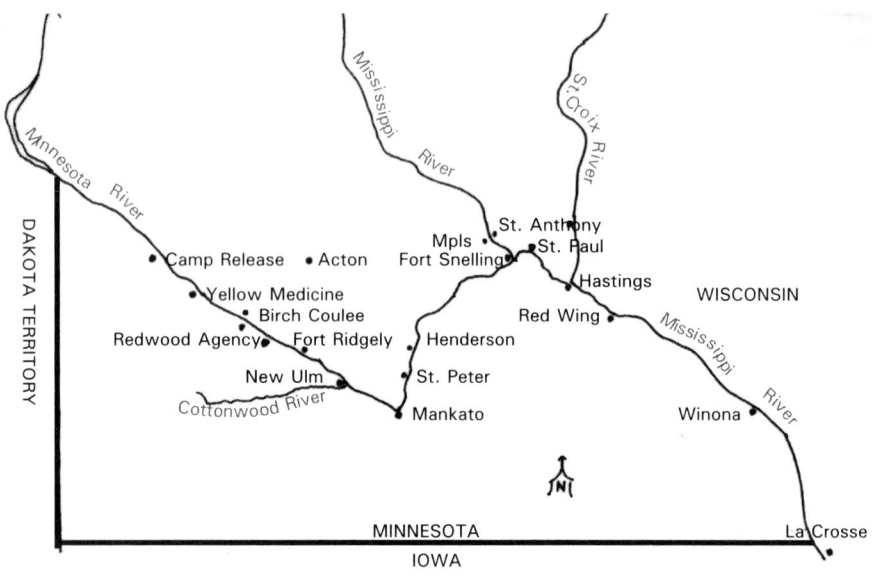

PART I

Transplanted

October 1860 to August 1862

*. . . The mystic chords of memory, stretching from every
battlefield and patriot grave to every living heart and hearthstone
all over this broad land, will yet swell the chorus of the Union. . . .*

Abraham Lincoln
First Inaugural Address

*. . . from a thousand breaking hearts, there comes this wailing cry:
Torn from the home that has sheltered us, home of our joys and fears,
Thrust from the hearth where the laughs and songs gladdened us many years,
Homeless we wander tonight, under the moonlit sky . . .
England may break the Irish heart, but its spirit will never die.*

Anonymous

Chapter One

Suland

October 26, 1860

To the Indians it was *ptanyetu sotuzu*. White men called it Indian Summer. It spoke of welcome warmth before cruel cold, balmy breezes before blinding blizzards, last glimpses of color before the gloomy black and white of Minnesota winter.

A bald eagle rode the upcurrents westward, patrolling its domain of undulating hills speckled with forest-framed lakes and striated with countless streams and creeks that drained into the Minnesota River. Brilliant sunlight heightened the purples, whites, and yellows of lingering wildflowers under a high sky, cloudless except for a dark purple rim at the northwest horizon.

Detecting a discordant intruder, the eagle descended to investigate but quickly judged the rude objects to be neither threat nor prey. The predator lost interest, elevated and drifted toward its lower range.

The squealing train of ox carts stopped at the edge of a pond where riders dismounted and unyoked the beasts to let them drink and graze. The train leader spurred his mount to the crest of a ridge where he stopped to view the scene to the northwest. After a moment, he doffed his cap, ran a hand through thick black hair and mumbled aloud, "Mère de Dieu, what a spectacle!"

The scene was dynamic, yet harmonious. Countless waterfowl of varied size and plumage energized the area above, upon and around a long, narrow lake and surrounding marsh. The airborne were only a fraction of the total population. Open water surfaces were covered with bobbing, feeding itinerants. Like a great army formed from separate states and corps and regiments, each species dis-

1

played its unique identity within the grand array. Thousands of disparate voices blended in a vibrant chorus that sang the message of imminent migration.

The enthralled Frenchman's lips curled in a gentle, loving smile. He spoke aloud again. "I am pleased to share this moment with you, mes amis."

Sunlight reflected off a rising band of white waterfowl. Awkward at takeoff, they quickly gained grace in full flight.

"Sweet Jesus, it is the trumpeters."

The giant swans cleared the lake and banked to the south, ever elevating. Their arc took them over the resting ox carts into a southeastward swing, where they accelerated and seemed to waggle their rumps disdainfully at the distant, advancing cloud bank.

The rider turned in his saddle to follow their flight. "You are so beautiful and fortunate. I, Alvin Milette, will stay here and toil and endure the snow and ice and bitter blizzards. My nose will be bitten by frost. My feet will become brittle. My blood will thin, and I will shiver in the night. But you, my shrewd ones, will frolic in the warm southern waters with your friends and kin. You will savor succulent meals, remain warm through the winter, then return in your leisure to the sweet breezes of spring. You are magnifique! Bon voyage and bonne chance!"

The trumpeter swans settled into a steady downwind rhythm. Their panoptic vision revealed a widening river meandering through a broad valley, heavily treed from the ridges on the north to the rising hills on the south. The water and the sand beaches were barely discernible through the canopy of elms, willows, and cottonwoods. A few settlements, isolated farms, and Indian villages appeared along the tributary streams and increased in number as the migrators flew on.

The flock traced the river to near its south nadir at Mankato, then swung northeast to follow its sharply altered course. Steady flight carried them by daybreak to the mouth of the Minnesota where it joined the Mississippi below Fort Snelling. They had flown more than two hundred miles of Minnesota River Valley since leaving the prairie lake.

As the swans funneled the few miles east through the river gorge, they were startled by the harsh sounds of bustling Saint Paul. The wary flyers veered to the southeast to realign with the bending Mississippi that soon served as the border between Minnesota and Wisconsin. Just north of LaCrosse their tranquility was disrupted by a whistle-blowing, bell-clanging, stern-wheel steamboat struggling into the surging current. The swans elevated slightly, contemptuously dismissed the puny craft, and swung their determined eyes back to their true course.

Maurna Murnane Russell leaned against the steamboat's upper deck railing, shielding her eyes. Peeking out of a gray bonnet, her rich auburn hair framed a rosy-cheeked, oval face, featuring gray-green, sparkling eyes. Beside her, a gangly young man with similar eyes and rust-colored hair scanned the sky to the west and excitedly fixed on a dazzling sight.

"Aunt Maurna," he shouted, "look out there a little to your right. A flock of white geese. Headin' south. See 'em?"

Her eyes followed the aim of his arm. "Oh, Pim, they're majestic." She lifted a white-bonneted child and aimed her at the sight. "You see them, Ginny?"

"I don't see anything, Mama. Where? Where?"

"Show her, Pim. Hurry now."

Pim lifted his little cousin and pointed. When she saw the high flyers, Ginny cried, "Oh, so pretty. Do they see us, Mama?"

A stocky, middle-aged man laughed appreciatively and spoke to the child. "Pretty they are, my little one, but I must inform you that those are not geese. They are far too large and long-necked to be geese."

"What are they then, Mr. Campbell?" asked Pim.

"Those are swans, Pim. Trumpeter swans they're called. Name comes from the bugle sound they make. Too far to hear them now. They're on their way to their wintering grounds near the Gulf of Mexico and won't be back until spring."

His angular wife, Iris, spoke up then. "Oh, how it is to live with such an expert, on everything. Forgive my husband for correcting you, children, but his enthusiasm sometimes overrules his diplomacy."

Angus Campbell laughed, "Oh, Iris, you know you can't embarrass me. I'm too insensitive."

Maurna quickly inserted, "No need to be embarrassed. We are grateful to you for helpin' us learn. We have so much to discover about this new country."

"You can learn a great deal from traveling," Mr. Campbell declared.

Maurna answered. "Perhaps, Mr. Campbell, but 'tis enough travelin' that we've done to be wishin' for more. We're anxious to settle in. Our journey's been long and tirin'. Winter or no, we just want to put down for a good while." Three years in America had barely diminished her Irish lilt.

"Spoken as one who has never experienced a Minnesota winter," warned Angus. "Soon you'll be wishing to join the swans."

The railings were crowded on both levels with passengers and off-duty crew enjoying the sunshine and the sights. The hills and gorges on both sides of the river revealed a radiant spectacle. The basic color was gold in shades from pale lemon to deep copper punctuated by showy red and orange maples and white-skinned, black-freckled, yellow-crowned birch. Olive-hued willows and burgundy sumac rimmed the shoreline. The balmy weather had given clinging leaves a temporary reprieve, and the overall effect was primeval glory as it had been for thousands of years.

Maurna and the children continued to converse with the Campbells. The relationship, begun on the train out of Chicago, had grown to mutual fondness. Three-year-old Ginny had been the catalyst, delighting the older couple with her chatter and antics. The two families had exchanged histories and current plans. The Campbells had prospered in the dry-goods business in Baltimore and later expanded to Philadelphia and Chicago. Their latest venture was a store in St. Paul where they would reside for as long as needed to help their youngest son, John, build the business.

Maurna had in turn told the Campbells about her family. She and her husband, two brothers, and a nephew had fled oppression and famine in Ireland in March 1857. Her husband's older brother, Bernard, who had left Ireland eight years earlier and established himself near Harper's Ferry, Virginia, had welcomed them and helped them get situated.

The five had built a small log house on Bernard's property and settled in. Her brother, Joseph, and husband, Timothy, had found work on the railroad. Their first child, a daughter, was born a few months after their arrival, but their new life had been cruelly wrenched when her husband died just before Christmas 1857. Joseph had persuaded the others to pool their earnings and buy a small farm in Minnesota.

"Everything we have is committed to this move," Maurna confided to the Campbells. "We're not without misgivin's but intend to do whatever it takes to make it a success."

As the boat passed Winona, Pim pointed to the high bluffs and asked, "Is the Minnesota River Valley as pretty as this, Mr. Campbell?"

"Not as spectacular but equally as beautiful, I'm told," he replied. "I've not seen it myself, but I've heard tell that it's the Garden of Eden or close to it."

Veiled with a few fleecy clouds tainted in pastel shades, the sunset was glorious. Breezes diminished. Voices became more subdued. The full moon and prominent stars eased into view in the darkening sky that obscured the encroaching cloudbank. Indian summer, so welcome, so magical, so short-lived, was embraced and cherished as a loved one about to depart.

As they said good night, Angus commented that the boat would travel over one hundred miles while they slept, and by morning they would be within thirty or forty miles of Saint Paul.

Maurna had paid a precious four dollars for a tiny stateroom for their long night on the river. A porthole allowed fresh air and a beam of light in as Pim settled on a blanket between two cots and soon joined Ginny in slumber. Maurna lay awake. As her anxieties and fears increased in the darkness, her thoughts returned to Ireland and to her husband in a cold grave in Virginia. She wept silently. So far from our origins. Half a world away. Oh, Tim, I miss you so much. We're not even half way across this huge land. So vast and overpowering. So easy to be swallowed up.

As the boat paddle-wheeled through the October night Maurna rose, lit a candle and extracted from her satchel a wine-colored, leather journal and a well-worn letter. She opened the journal and began to read the first entry.

Maurna's Journal
March 22, 1857

This journal is a gift of my dear mother who has wisely suggested that I keep a record of our activities beginning with this most critical change in our lives. I will attempt to enter events at least once per week.

Oh, the wrenching of the heart! It tears at the central core to leave the families behind. To face the unknown, to journey so far, to bid farewell to loved ones, to no longer have a place. Aye, that is the worst of all. To no longer have sunken roots, familiar faces, places, and objects, a refuge called home. Will we ever find another so dear as Cork? Harper's Ferry, Virginia, is to be our new home. Timothy's brother seems to be contented there with his American wife. But will we be? Will it ever be home to us?

Just as so many other Irish mothers' and fathers' hearts have been broken, our good parents are in terrible agony to see us away. They understand but can barely endure the loss. To give up one's children must be the greatest sacrifice the Good Lord can demand. Much of our own pain is a reflection of what we see in our parents' eyes. Will we ever see them and Ireland again?

May God watch over them and us and help us find our place in the new land. I so fear the ocean voyage and the great hardships ahead. But nothing for it, we truly have no other course. We are more fortunate than most of our emigrating countrymen. Bernard and Mary will be there to greet us and help us get started.

Foreboding, frightening and so final is our decision to depart. But once begun, we must abide, meet the vicissitudes head on, and trust in His divine will.

She rested the book and recalled the agony of their departure and the indignities, sickness, and near despair they endured during the long voyage. Joseph's wariness had served them well by protecting them from parasitic passengers and crew members. Tim and Ben, though less aggressive, backed up Joseph with their cool courage, and even little Pim stood tall when it counted. Despite the memories of miseries endured, she smiled when she recalled the demeanor of her four "men." Gentle Timothy, angry but well-intentioned Joseph, ebullient Ben, and budding Pim. Four true princes. She smiled again to herself. My rocks. My emeralds.

After a difficult crossing, they had endured two weeks of quarantine on Grosse Isle in the Saint Lawrence River. Finally released, they had journeyed to Albany, New York, where Bernard had met them to bring them to Harper's Ferry. They had arrived in Virginia in the spring of 1857 and within a few weeks had completed construction of a log house on a corner of Bernard's property.

She opened the journal again and paged ahead selectively until she stopped to read the entry from June 6, 1857.

Maurna's Journal
June 6, 1857

If all goes as expected, our child will be born in November. Please God, let this dear one be born alive and healthy and live a full life. Timothy is so pleased. The child was conceived in Ireland and will be born in America. What a true wonder it all is! A symbolic bridge between the two lands? If the little one survives, it will be a hardy child. Imagine an ocean crossing already and not yet born!

Timothy is feeling poorly. We saw so much sickness during the crossing and on Grosse Isle. People died by the hundreds. God watched over us through it all.

I worry about dear brother Joseph. Along with Tim, he has taken work with the Baltimore and Ohio Railroad, working on a crew that maintains the tracks and roadbed. He is so sad and angry and has not been himself since the loss of his adored Nell. (Little Pim was but a sprite of four at the time.) I'm afraid Joseph has taken to the drink again. I know he hates feeling dependent and is anxious for us to get a home of our own. A farming man clear through, he'll not be satisfied until he gets to the land again. I worry about the way he ignores Pim, who worships his father and desperately needs his love and approval. I know Joseph loves the lad dearly, but he seldom displays his affection.

It is amusing to have people constantly asking how Pim got his uncommon name. We have called him Pim all his eleven years and forget that to strangers the name sounds odd. When we tell them it's for the initials of Peter Ignatius Murnane, they smile and understand.

Brother Ben has learned from Bernard about carpentry. Since Tim and Bernard are older than Ben, he refers to both of them as "uncle" rather than the unwieldy "brother-in-law." He is impressed with Bernard's skills and admires him in every way. I think Bernard has become almost a father to Ben who lost his own when so young. Father Curran, the Harper's pastor pushes at Ben about the priesthood. We are almost sorry that we spoke with him about Ben's possible religious vocation. Ben is confused, and the more he is pressed, the more he resists. Father Curran may be unwittingly driving him away.

She skipped ahead to an entry for October 28th.

Maurna's Journal
October 28, 1857

Oh joyful day! A gift from God and His precious mother. A new life! A precious daughter, whole and beautiful. Born at sunset on October 26, 1857. Squalling and healthy from the first breath. Timothy is ecstatic, the happiest and proudest man on the globe. After the heartbreaks of our three stillborn angels, we are finally blessed. Oh, thanks be to God! We will christen her Virginia Ann in honor of our new home state and for her great-grandmother Ann Russell. Baptism will be on the first Sunday that Father Curran is available.

One disquieting note in the midst of our happiness. Timothy cannot shake his malaise and seems to be worsening. He hasn't been able to work for a fortnight, and I sense that the doctor is more concerned than he lets on. Please, dear Jesus, we need him. I cannot imagine facing life without him. Surely he will be all right, now especially with a fresh, bright life lighting up our world. Bernard presented us with a lovely, thoughtful gift to celebrate Virginia's birth. He built a magnificent new oak rocking chair with brass hardware and a needlepoint seat cover. He said a new mother should have a rocker for her babe. Ben helped him make the chair, and Mary created the needlepoint seat cover. We will treasure it forever. I am so blessed to be surrounded by so much love and warmth.

She paused, looked up at the porthole and tried to see even beyond. Her eyes slowly filled with tears. She knew what the next journal entry included and hesitated to read the words that described that fateful day near Christmas 1857. She steeled herself, opened her eyes and made out the words of the journal entry that followed.

Mystic Chords

Maurna's Journal
Christmas 1857

Most years, December 25th is the day of joyful celebration of Jesus' birth. Not so this year. On December 20th, beloved Timothy passed away from the fever that has been working up on him since our stay on Grosse Isle. We thought we had escaped the contagion, but Timothy began to show its signs soon after our arrival in Virginia. It eventually ravaged him. He was reduced day by day until toward the end he became but a shadow. Never a complaint from him through his entire ordeal. Only once did he break down with me to berate himself for failing his wife and newborn. As if he ever could or would! No thought for himself, only concern for us. Joseph said that he was a man who knew how to live and also how to die. Timothy passed over while in my arms and with the name of Jesus on his sweet lips. God rest his beautiful soul.

We miss him so much. Even tiny Ginny seems to be looking for him, sensing her great loss. The little babe will never know her father. Sometimes I am overcome with grief and longing and near despair, but I know that I must carry on for Ginny. And also for Pim and Ben and Joseph. We began our quest with five. We rejoiced in our wondrous gain in October. We grieve achingly for our tragic loss in December. We are again but five.

Her tears had stopped. She rose, walked to the porthole, breathed the crisp air, watched briefly the moonlit shore, then returned to take up the journal again. Paging ahead, she passed over the remainder of 1858 and most of 1859.

Maurna's Journal
Christmas 1859

Can it be two years that Timothy is gone? His spirit still exists in me . . . and in our daughter. What a delightful little leprechaun is she. Auburn hair, the Murnane gray-green eyes, the Russell turned-up nose and freckles. So full of zest and bright as a new copper coin. She gives my life real purpose.

All of us are well. Joseph is putting away what wages he can, attempting to fulfill his dreams of purchasing land. The dear man has taken the pledge to not drink and is staying with it. I'm so proud of him. Ben makes a few dollars on woodwork projects that Bernard passes on to him. Pim is fourteen, can it be believed? And even he earns some coins doing odd jobs and hiring out.

Joseph continues to agitate for a farm of our own. Bernard says that land around Harper's is not to be had except at terribly inflated prices. It will take years to save enough to buy Virginia land. Ben is of an age where he may be moving on to create his own life. I will do whatever the men decide unless it would be detrimental to Ginny. We can't remain wards of Bernard and Mary. They've been kind and generous, but our pride will not tolerate the situation much longer. By this Spring, we must decide our course and act. God help us! And may He watch over dear Timothy.

Maurna recalled that Joseph had made an exploratory visit to Minnesota in the Spring of 1860. He and a friend with similar land-buying interests had read circulars describing good lands at reasonable prices in the new state. After they inspected several available pieces of land, Joseph favored a small farm near Stillwater, but had insufficient funds. To preserve his dwindling dollars, he earned wages in a lumber mill in Saint Anthony Falls, upriver from Saint Paul, and continued his inquiries. Advised to investigate the Minnesota River Valley, he looked at several farms and settled for one that he described in a letter dated July 3, 1860.

Dear Maurna, Ben, Pim, and Ginny,
 I trust everyone is well. I am healthy and in an excited state. I have found our home! At least it will become our home once we apply hard work and pay the amount owed. It is not much now but the potential is unlimited for a fine farm in a beautiful setting. There are good neighbors, friendly and welcoming. (Some Indians around, too, but don't worry. They are peaceable and harmless.)
 Forty acres of rich soil, about half under cultivation, the remainder to be broken. A rude, but sound, cabin was the former home of the family who are selling half their original eighty acres to us. They have bought eighty adjacent acres. Their new house is about two miles upriver. The owner is a widow who farms with her father and three sons, the oldest about Ben's age. They seem fine people and are offering a reasonable price and fair terms. She says she'll sell us a milk cow and let us use her work horses when they can free them from their own needs. Until we can buy our own.
 My plan calls for taking possession in October. The owners will harvest the current crop, then the land is ours. I will pay her sixty dollars now, another forty dollars in October, then the remainder in the fall of 1861. That means I'll have to keep earning into spring. I'm asking Ben to come out now to use his carpentry skills on the cabin to get it ready for the three of you to come out mid-October. (Remember, you have to get here before the rivers freeze up in November.)
 I know it's sudden, but it's what we need to do. This area is bustling, and folks are pouring in. Prices will rise, and we'll never be able to afford the price if we wait. There's a village called New Ulm, six to seven miles downstream on the Cottonwood River.

The valley is beautiful. The opportunity is here. I couldn't be more optimistic, and I truly believe that it's meant to be our home.

> Best wishes and love to all,
> Joseph

Maurna put down the letter and recalled how Joseph's news had struck her. She was at first fearful and full of foreboding and saddened to think of leaving Timothy behind. Also, she was appalled at the descriptions she had heard of the frontier, the primitive living conditions, the savage Indians, and the scarcity of law and order. She acknowledged her ignorance of the situation, however, and hoped that her fears would be exaggerations.

Ben set out for Minnesota three days later, commenced work on the cabin immediately, and wrote Maurna a glowing description of the farm and area. His positive report had reassured her.

She turned back to her journal to read the entry written the evening before they had departed for Minnesota.

Maurna's Journal
October 20, 1860

Tomorrow we leave for the new state of Minnesota. Once again the unknown. Not as difficult as leaving Ireland. Maybe each move gets easier. At least Joseph and Ben are there to greet us. Pim is excited but he doesn't really understand what we will be facing out in the wild. I don't guess I do either, but I've plenty misgivings. We're getting farther from Ireland and our origins and having to try to put down new roots again. What's ahead for little Ginny and for Pim, for all of us for that matter? Will this finally be home or just another stop along the way?

Joseph's resolve and excitement are heaven-blessed. We all need to support him. Ben's sold on Minnesota. He's sensible and seems to have adjusted just fine. But then, it's always easier for menfolk. They just don't hardly notice the important things. They go about their business, and where they are doesn't seem to fret them much. A warm bed, abundant food, a little tobacco, and some game to hunt or fish to catch and they're happy. The making of a real home takes more doing than they ever dream of.

We'll miss Bernard and Mary and will never be able to repay them. Mary is so kind and good and Bernard is made of the same fibre as his dear brother Timothy. I hope and pray that we won't be seeing the two of them for the last time tomorrow.

Long journey by rail and then by steamboat on the Mississippi River. I'd hoped to never see another boat, but at least on this one the shore'll always be in sight. Must switch trains five or six times before Chicago and then on into LaCrosse, Wisconsin. Hundreds of miles before we sleep in a warm bed again. But thousands have done it before us.

Best to bed and a good night's sleep. I said my goodbyes to Timothy at his grave site this afternoon. Holding Ginny in my arms and with Pim there, too, I wept my prayers over him. We must go on. Home is ahead for us out there somewhere.

Maurna closed the journal and snuffed the candle. Eager to be reunited with Joseph and Ben, she prayed she would have the courage and strength to support her family in their new venture. Her most urgent prayer was that Minnesota would be a permanent home for the Murnanes and Russells. She fell asleep intending to be fresh and positive in the morning when she would meet her brothers and have her first look at Saint Paul. As Indian summer came to an end, their new life was about to begin.

Chapter Two

Pig's Eye Landing

After breakfast, Maurna, Pim, and Ginny bundled up and ventured onto the nearly vacant deck. The northwest wind was fore-running the cloud bank that now covered the northwest quadrant. The stern-wheeler had transported them into territory where the foliage had diminished considerably. The hardwoods were nearly denuded, stark and barren against the background of slopes bedecked with fallen leaves. The bluffs, though not as high as those near Winona, were impressive in the brilliance of the early morning sunlight.

A distance ahead, the river appeared to divide, one channel continuing on, the other angling to the left. Before she could frame the question, Angus' familiar voice provided the answer. "The great Mississippi veers more northwest here, my friends. I'm glad I got here in time to help you discover it," said Angus.

They returned his smile and that of Iris, who said, "Good day to our fellow travelers."

"And to you, Mrs. Campbell. How much farther to Saint Paul?" asked Maurna.

"Approximately thirty river miles. With the stopover in Hastings and about two hours from there, we should be in Saint Paul . . . let me see. . . ." Angus pulled out his pocket watch.

Iris bent to read the time. "You've not the eyes to see it without your spectacles, Angus. It's near 7:00 A.M."

He laughed. "I was bluffing, but you caught me out. We should arrive in Saint Paul between 10:00 and 10:30 if we experience no delays."

By 9:00 warmly clad and breakfasted passengers were on deck enjoying the scenery. They were startled by a sudden deep voice booming from above and behind. "Hear ye, Hear ye." All turned to view a gigantic crewman on the pilot deck wearing a red stocking cap and a grin. "I have the good Captain's permission to guide you with my voice over the last few miles to Saint Paul. We wouldn't want you to miss several points of interest. If you're familiar with this stretch, just ignore me. Those making their first approach deserve to be informed. May I proceed?"

The passengers cheered and turned to gaze up-river as the baritone went on. "Now I may be a bit exaggerating in calling Minnesota paradise, but only a little. We've been a state just over two years, and the proof of it's attractiveness is the number and quality of people who are coming here to live. The state stretches 400 miles from north to south and 200 miles wide and is blessed with abundant game and forests and fertile soil, as well as thousands of lakes and streams. The air is pure, the beauty unspoiled, the politics mostly uncorrupted (so far), the climate, except for a few nippy weeks in dead of winter, is magnificent. In fact, the winter months are just uncomfortable enough to cause even greater appreciation of our fresh springtime, balmy summer, and unparalleled autumn. But most of all, opportunities abound. There are no limits here. You can be whatever you set out to be. People help one another and pull together. You'll feel that spirit the moment you arrive."

He paused for a moment to shift gears a bit, then went on. "The beautiful Mississippi valley you have seen since LaCrosse was once the domain of the Sioux and Winnebago Indians. They have deeded all but reservation lands in treaties with the government. The Chippewa tribes live to the north of Saint Paul. Now, on your right a few miles ahead, will come into view a large body of water just off-channel. It's called Pig's Eye Lake and carries with it some history. The lake is named after one of Saint Paul's first citizens, an old French trapper named Pig's Eye Parrant. One of his eyes was opaque white, hence his name. He staked a claim on the east bank of the Mississippi, set up a grog shop and served his few neighbors, some local Indians, and river travelers. He was run off by the territorial marshall but not before the emerging settlement had become known as Pig's Eye Landing. Fortunately, a Catholic priest built a log church that he named Saint Paul's and the leading citizens decided to change the name from Pig's Eye Landing to Saint Paul. Aren't you glad? Going to Saint Paul seems more dignified than to Pig's Eye."

Laughter from the assemblage provided another pause. The riverman was thoroughly enjoying his own performance and hastened to continue.

"To your left on the high bluffs is an area called Kaposia, that was home base for many of the Sioux tribes until the Treaty of '51 when they were moved onto a reservation about 100 miles west along the Minnesota River that stretches out to the Dakota border. From Kaposia west the land is hilly prairie sprouting grasses that cover rich, fertile soil. The land all the way to Canada is forest, both hardwoods and conifer. There's so many lakes that the Indians refer to the country as the "land of sky blue waters."

"To your right again, ladies and gentlemen, I call your attention to the bluffs just to the east of where the river makes a wide turn. The elevated land is called Dayton Bluff, an area of old Indian burial mounds thought to be the resting places of tribes that inhabited these lands thousands of years ago. And now, please cast your eyes around the bend of the river to the east bank, and you will see the fair city of Pig's . . . excuse me, Saint Paul, rising up the terraces. The impressive building in the background is the state capitol. When you dock and step off on shore, remember you walk the ground that Pig's Eye once claimed. I doubt he'll be there to greet you, but many others will be. Again, welcome to paradise and may your stay be long and prosperous."

They cheered his performance and took his suggestion to look around the bend. Sprawled on the hillside was the largest community in the state, the embryo town that was the hub of a fast growing area. A single wooden bridge spanned the Mississippi to a scattering of buildings on the west shore. Packet boats were tied at the landing. A cheering, waving throng awaited their arrival.

For over a week from Harper's Ferry, the newcomers had experienced delights of vivid color, and virtually unspoiled beauty. Now their eager eyes fell on an ugly, gouged wound on the landscape. Nearly treeless, the terrain was cluttered with paint-faded, frame buildings and houses arranged in a scattered melange from the water's edge uphill to the north and west. Ugh, thought Maurna, litter and mud and crude shacks. Oh, dear God, is this to be our lot? It's as barren as the treeless hills of Kerry.

A wider view, however, brought her some relief and hope. The background beyond the capitol building and to the west displayed hills, bluffs, and cliffs adorned with heavy woods growing out of rich grasses and thick underbrush, all appearing to be as yet untouched by ax or saw. And the scene was dynamic. Carts and wagons rattled in all directions. Hundreds of citizens moved with vitality and purpose. A raucous crowd demonstrated.

The captain incessantly blew the whistle during the half-mile approach. Maurna, Pim, and Virginia searched the crowd of faces for Joseph and Ben. Most of the greeters were bundled in leather or wool garments topped with an eclectic display of colorful headgear. All ages, male and female, shabby and elegant, intoxicated and sober, Caucasians and American Indians. As the boat docked, the steamboat officers ordered the crowd to draw back. A narrow path was grudgingly formed to allow the passengers to disembark.

No sign of Joseph or Ben. Maurna realized that since she had been out of communication with her brothers for nearly a month, something might have occurred to prevent their appearance. Her imagination instantly created the possibility of accident, or illness, or worse. Mercy, she thought, such a disagreeable place, with only strangers about, and me with two children to watch over and all our belongings.

Iris Campbell sensed Maurna's concern, placed a comforting hand on her shoulder, and said kindly, "Maurna, don't fret, your men will be somewhere in the crowd. Just stay with Angus and me. Hold on to the children's hands now so you don't get separated."

Maurna silently blessed her, and linked to Ginny and Pim and in the wake of the Campbells, they were jostled toward the gangplank. As they stepped onto the landing, a welcome voice sounded from deep in the crowd, "Maurna, Maurna." She felt an instant rush of relief.

Pim spotted Ben and began bellowing, "Ben, Ben, we're all here. Hello!" He shouted to Maurna and Ginny, "See him up there waving? There, by the tall man in the red cap. He sees us!"

Pim lifted Ginny to see her uncle, but she failed to locate him. He put her down and held her hand and Maurna's as they followed the Campbells. Suddenly they were face to face with beaming Ben who hugged each in turn, slapped Pim on the back, laughed and whooped. Ben carried Ginny as they moved off towards the village. At last free of the crowd, they all hugged again.

Maurna asked, "Glory be, Ben, is it always this frantic at the landin' of a boat?"

Ben smiled. "They tell me that at this time of the year, each boat may be the last one 'til spring. Last mail 'til the dog sled trips up Military Road."

Pim asked, "Is my father on the way, Ben?"

"Joseph will be along tomorrow, Pim. He's not free from the sawmill until later tonight. He said to greet you and express his love and his eagerness to see all of you."

As Maurna introduced Ben to the Campbells and was telling him how kind they had been, a short, red-faced young man inserted himself. "Mother, Father, so sorry to be late. Welcome. Did you bring with you the change in weather?"

Angus countered, "I was going to accuse you of ordering the clouds and cold to remind us of what's ahead. This is our son, John, Mrs. Russell. John, the young men are her brother, Ben, her nephew, Pim, and this tiny flower is pretty Virginia, her daughter."

Iris Campbell suggested, "John, we'll give these folks time to get reacquainted, have their dinner and rest a while. Then perhaps you can show them the town. They'll only be here for a day or so. We can't let them go on upriver without seeing Saint Paul up close."

"I'd be delighted, Mother." He turned to Maurna. "We've only been here for a year ourselves, so my touring may be less than adequate. But we'll cover the major attractions."

"Our home is yours while you stay, Mrs. Russell. We have sufficient room for all," Angus declared.

Ben quickly responded. "Oh, what a nice offer, you have become good friends. But I have rented a room for tonight."

Maurna looked from John to Angus to Iris, shook her head and exclaimed, "Such generosity! We'll accept the tour offer, but decline the lodging if you don't mind. Please know how much this welcome means to us."

Angus said, "We'll leave you now then, Mrs. Russell. We'll be expecting you for supper. We're old folks, you know, and will welcome the rest this afternoon." He bowed to Ginny who responded by kissing him and Iris.

Maurna, Ginny, and Pim followed Ben back down to the vacated landing. Tied to the far end of the platform was a wooden flatboat half-filled with an oil cloth-covered cargo. Ben told them he had purchased supplies in Saint Paul because they were less expensive than in New Ulm.

In a few moments, Maurna identified her two trunks and her crated rocking chair. Pim and Ben quickly loaded the items into the flatboat, covered the load, and tied it down. Ben then poled the boat around the steamer, tied it to the packetboat, and leaped aboard. He spoke briefly with a crew member who nodded and handed Ben a slip of paper.

Ben assured Maurna that their goods were safe. "For a dollar they will allow us to tie up to the packet and be pulled along up the Minnesota River. They will also watch over our boat and property 'til Monday mornin'. Let's be gettin' to some hot dinner and bringin' me up to date. I've been alone so long, I've got a lot of talkin' built up."

They talked and laughed their way up the hill to the Merchants Hotel where they wolfed the savory fare as if they hadn't eaten for days.

Maurna gave Ben news of Harper's Ferry and letters from Ireland and recounted events of their journey.

Ben tried to describe the farm, the cabin with its additions, and the pieces of furniture he had built. "I'm not as good at describin' as I am at buildin', Maurna. Two more days and you'll see it yourself."

"Oh, Ben. I'm so anxious to be there and settled. The way you describe it already makes it sound like home. And don't be worryin' about what it looks like . . . we're only lookin' for three assurances. That it be safe, that it be warm, that it be ours. The third condition is the critical one. We've been guests and borrowers enough for a lifetime. We will finally have a place that's our own."

The tour of Saint Paul proved that Angus' son, John Campbell, was more knowledgeable than he had let on. He showed them the Capitol building and its spacious grounds, then downtown shops and the Campbell store on Seventh Street, and hotels, taverns, and warehouses near the river. "A bad fire destroyed thirty businesses earlier this year. All rebuilt now though."

He drove them to the old log structure on Bench Street that was the original Saint Paul's Church founded by Father Lucien Galtier and later used as convent and school by the Sisters of Saint Joseph when they arrived from Saint Louis in 1851. John told them that during the typhus epidemic of 1853, the nuns converted the structure into a hospital where they performed heroic service.

He stopped the carriage at Fourth and Exchange Streets across the way from a building labeled County Jail. "Until now I've shown you and talked about positive and promising aspects of Saint Paul, but I will now add one unpleasant episode. In March of this year across from where we sit there was a public hanging. Hangings are not uncommon in our town, but on this particular occasion the condemned party was a woman."

Maurna inhaled noisily. "They hanged a woman? What on earth had the poor soul done?"

"Yes, Mrs. Russell, a woman who was accused and then convicted of poisoning her husband. Thirty-six years old she was, a lady named Ann Bilansky. Maintained her innocence until the end but was hanged in front of more than 4,000 folks this past March. Quite an event it was."

Ben hastily commented, "Why not a woman, Maurna? Guilt is guilt after all."

Maurna was aghast. "Even the Brits didn't hang women, Ben. Least as far as I ever heard. Poor creature, and exposed to a mob. How awful!"

John summed up. "The judge said only that justice will be meted out to each citizen in true and full measure. Hard to argue with that standard. Welcome to the frontier, my new friends."

"'Tis a lovely home you have, Mrs. Campbell. You must be cozy even in the cold months. Is the Minnesota winter as cold as people say?" asked Maurna as they toured the Campbells' two-story brick home.

John Campbell's wife, Beverly, nodded. "It certainly can be, Mrs. Russell, and it is long. Toward March one becomes anxious for it to ease, but snows have been known to fall even into May. We've lived through only one winter here, but it was memorable, and I don't relish the onset of another. The worst hardship is the icing up of the river, shutting us off from cities down the line. Only occasional dog-sleds come up from LaCrosse with medicines, emergency supplies, and the mail. We newcomers burrow in and wait for spring. More experienced residents find ways to get about and don't pay winter much mind. Except for blizzards. Everyone respects blizzards."

"Blizzards?"

"Yes. Blizzards are nearly indescribable. They come up sudden and can do great harm to people and animals caught out with no shelter. The snows come hard-driven by howling winds that decrease visibility to zero. And they can come on so quickly. We observed a blizzard last winter from the warmth of our home, and it was frightening to see. We thanked God to be under sturdy roof and prayed for those who weren't. Blizzard may be a new word to you, Mrs. Russell, but one that will become a part of your vocabulary here in Minnesota. Beware!"

Ginny, who had fallen asleep in her mother's lap, was carried to the couch in the parlor and covered with a blanket. Talk continued into the evening about local matters and about the upcoming national election. Angus and John both seemed well-informed.

Angus led off by saying, "If the Republicans win, the folks in Philadelphia and Chicago think that the southern states will rebel. To them the owning of slaves is the big issue, and they're afraid that Mr. Lincoln will work to end slavery. Says that isn't his intent, but the people of the south don't believe him. Whoever's elected, it won't matter much to Minnesotans."

"Don't be so sure about that, Father," John argued. "The country is getting smaller the way people can travel in such a hurry these days."

Iris terminated the conversation by saying, "I think that John is right, dear husband. The Mississippi flows through both the north and the south. We can't have two separate countries. We've been countrymen for almost one hundred years. If they let the women settle it, we'd have peace for sure, right Maurna and Beverly?"

Angus blew out the candle and lay down beside Iris. "Nice people, those, and that precious Ginny, what a beauty she will grow to be."

Iris answered, "She'll have to go some to equal her mother's classic features, gorgeous eyes, and dignified bearing. But, I fear so for Maurna and little Ginny. They seem so delicate and frail and gentle. To have them subjected to that lonely life on the prairie with its harshness and crudity. No one around but rude settlers and Indians. It's a life of bare survival."

Angus scolded her. "Ach, Iris, you are being pessimistic and unfair. She won't be lonely. She'll have around her two brothers, a nephew, and a darling daughter. She'll have neighbors who know how to share and help one another. It's their code. And since when can you judge the inner strength of a person by looking at them? I don't see her as frail, but lean and strong. I don't see her as delicate, but refined, an essential distinction. Yes, she is gentle, but that is a trait often closely associated with patience and quiet determination. No, Iris, Maurna will abide and not only survive but thrive. She'll be the anchor for her family. The inner fiber can be seen in her eyes. Her strong faith will sustain her, too. Don't fret for Maurna, dear wife. She is the kind who will build this country. Mark my words. Now, to sleep, old woman. You lie next to a tired old man."

She smiled, grateful for the strength and optimism that he never failed to provide. She reached over and touched his cheek.

"Old man is right," she whispered sweetly as she snuggled up to him. "When you were younger, sleep wasn't the first thing on your mind when you came abed."

Joseph joined them just before noon. He looked fit, his thick black hair extra long and a new beard sprouting untrimmed from his squared jaw. He was full of hope and optimism. "Pim, you'll be taller than your old father, you keep growin'. You'll love the farm, and Ginny'll have acres to play on and beauty in every direction. And wonderful folks all around us. Friendly, eager to help. And the soil is so rich and ready. There'll be no famine here. And no selfish landlords. Ben tells me he's expanded the house and added a bedroom and a plank floor to keep out the cold. I only regret that I can't be with you 'til April. Can't leave the sawmill when I can save another forty dollars. But I'll be there for plowin' and clearin' and plantin' and honest to God proper livin' from then on, I will."

They celebrated the brief reunion with a grand dinner at the Merchants Hotel. Joseph winced at the cost of forty cents each and twenty cents for Ginny but made sure they all got their money's worth. They reminisced, laughed, joked, made plans and received countless admonitions and instructions from Joseph about what needed doing at the farm and how to deal with the snow and cold.

"Be sure you provision well, Ben. Don't forget candles and matches, and soap and medicines and lots of blankets and buy a big scoop shovel for the snow and be sure you have enough wood chopped and laid by and be pullin' the flatboat up out of the water so it doesn't freeze in, and keep the chimney cleared. A fellow at the sawmill says when it snows heavy, pack it tight clear around the bottom up against the house. Bankin' they call it; keeps in the heat of the house. He said also that there's usually one or two thaws and the roof better be tight or it'll leak in somethin' awful and...."

"Slow down, dear brother, that's enough to take us two winters to complete," broke in Maurna.

"Is the roof gonna' leak, Mama?" asked Ginny.

In the laughter that followed, Maurna replied, "No, I don't think so, darlin'. Ben'll see to that."

"I just wish I could be there. It's frustratin' to be so close by and all helpless to do my share," commiserated Joseph.

"You've done more than your share with the bulk of the earnin' and bein' without family and comin' out alone ahead of us," soothed Maurna. "And Ben livin' as a young bachelor these months. We're grateful to the both of you."

Joseph then talked about the purchase agreement and the payment terms. He added that he hoped to expand the farm north and east. "Need land for Ben and Pim eventually. There's more than 100 acres between us and the Rivard's place as yet unclaimed. Owned by the state." He told them about the Koukkaris. Rose Koukkari had lost her husband six years before in Missouri. Soon after, she had sold their place and came north for the great opportunities in Minnesota. "Fine sons, she has," he concluded.

Ben then reminded Joseph of the Lundes in New Ulm whom he had come to know quite well since arriving. "They're fine people, too. Mr. Lunde helped me select the best woods for the room addition and the flooring. And his son, Tony, came out to the cabin to help for a few days. Between Tony and Ox Koukkari, I've made two good friends already."

Joseph said, "Good for you," and then asked Ben if he had come downriver by flatboat alone.

"No, big brother, I didn't come alone. And yes I came by flatboat. There's always somebody lookin' for passage into Saint Paul. I just let the Lundes know when I'd be leavin', and they spread the word I'd carry a passenger for free if he'd do the polin'. One of Mr. Lunde's apprentices was leavin' to go to Chicago for a bride. He poled. I steered. Worked out fine."

"Where you got it tied up? I'd like to see what kind of boat you built."

"Only a few steps down to the dock. Want to walk down and look at her?"

Pim joined them, and they set off, while Maurna got herself and Ginny ready for bed. Once outside, Joseph asked, "Any Indian stirrin's you've heard about, Ben? Lots of talk at the mill about it."

"Only talk. Some grumblin' by both traders and Sioux. Sioux claim they're not gettin' their due. Promises not bein' kept. Traders say there's no pleasin' them. Who can sort out who's right? There she is, Joseph." Ben pointed to the boat. "Built exact as the Koukkari's boat, board for board. Ox showed me theirs for a model. Watertight and steers good. Carries a good load, too."

Joseph looked at the boat and the cargo and seemed pleased. He re-covered the goods and they started back.

"I'll be leavin' before you folks are up in the mornin'. Got a hitch on a wagon leavin' for Saint Anthony. I'll be out to the Cottonwood as soon as the ice breaks. I want both of you to know how much I think of the way you stepped in to do what needed doin' to get the house ready and the ladies here safe. I'll never forget it."

"Our home, too, you know, and our future maybe. Glad to do it. We had enough of Harper's. 'Tis us who are grateful to you, big brother, for steppin' out and providin' the initiative. This family is on its way, I'm thinkin'," Ben said.

Joseph threw an arm around Ben and the other around Pim as they strode back. Maurna and Ginny were asleep. The two brothers quietly lay down on either side of Pim and were soon dreaming of waving grain and plump potatoes.

Chapter Three

To the Heart of the Valley

The packet boat departed Saint Paul precisely at 7:00 A.M. Their flatboat rode alongside. Maurna was uneasy about the portage of "every item of cutlery, dinnerware, cooking pots and utensils, clothing, and personal belongings that we have in the world," but was assured by crew members that the load was secure.

They moved upriver through a gorge for several miles to the mouth of the Minnesota River. Above them on the west bank reigned Fort Snelling, an imposing presence that had been a source of comfort to settlers for more than twenty years. The packet docked briefly to drop off mail and board a young lieutenant, then circled Pike Island to enter the main channel of the Minnesota River, cutting southwesterly into a hill-shouldered valley. John Campbell had informed them that, eons ago, the valley had been the bed of the River Warren, which in turn was a remnant of the glaciers that had formed the topography of the region. It was difficult to imagine a river wide and deep enough to fill such a broad expanse.

After quick mail drops at the villages of Belle Plaine and Henderson, they were provided a simple lunch in the small dining area. Lieutenant Ames introduced himself as he joined them at table and to their inquiries responded that he had been stationed at Fort Ridgely since June of 1859. He described Fort Ridgely and the soldiers' life there as routine and frankly "rather dull." The fort's purpose he said was to provide protection for the settlers. "We have our Fort Ridgely, a few miles north of New Ulm, to keep an eye on the four Santee Sioux tribes and a few Winnebago. Then there's Fort Abercrombie on the Red River at the Dakota border to see to the western

Sioux, Fort Ripley 100 miles up the Mississippi to protect against the Chippewa, and of course, Fort Snelling remains the main control point. The Indians respect our strength and don't challenge it."

Ben asked, "How many Indians around here, Lieutenant? I've heard anywhere from a few hundred to thousands."

"Nobody knows for sure, but there's estimated to be around 10,000 Sioux between New Ulm and Fort Abercrombie up on the Red River. There's two agencies, one just west of New Ulm at Redwood, the other about thirty miles upstream at Yellow Medicine. There are four major Sioux tribes, and each of those is divided up into smaller villages."

Ben was curious about the chiefs. "Do they have one big chief and a bunch of smaller ones or how does that work?"

"Chiefs with the most power are the ones with the most followers who come live in their village. They can't hold them there though. If an Indian wants to leave to go to another village, he's free to go. Between New Ulm and the Redwood River there are six villages. Chiefs don't talk much with one another, being rivals more than friends or allies. Strange society it is." Sensing that his comments were exceedingly negative, Lieutenant Ames softened his words. "Most Indians seem peaceful enough. There's good ones and some not so good, same as other folks. They just want to be left alone, except for collecting what's due according to the treaty terms. Can't blame them for that. Some traders cheat them out of money and provisions. There's good and bad traders, too, I guess."

Ben tried to ease concerns Maurna might be generating. "Our place is on the Cottonwood River west of New Ulm. We probably won't see much of them where we are."

"Don't count on that," said the Lieutenant not sensing Ben's intent. "They roam the countryside. Lots of folks think that being on a reservation means they stay there all the time, but they're free to go anywhere, except on private property. Reservation boundaries are for keeping whites out, not keeping redskins in. Whites can't build a house or farm on Indian land or hunt or trap there. That land is for Indian use only."

After Lieutenant Ames excused himself, they returned to the aft deck to "watch the country go by." Ginny constantly asked how much farther they had to go.

"Been a long journey hasn't it, darlin'?" asked Maurna. "You've been such a good traveler. Just a little while more now."

Pim seemed confused. "That soldier said the Sioux have a whole kettle full of chiefs, all with their own ideas. Seems a strange system to me, Ben. How do they ever get all the Indians to do something or to agree on anything?"

"They probably don't, Pim. That may be why they've been losin' ground all these years. Their way gives 'em a lot of individual freedom, but not much over-all strength or unity. Some of them even have more than one wife. Did you know that?"

Maurna chuckled. "One wife's more than most men can deal with, I'm thinkin'. Wonder how those wives get along. Must get pretty noisy in those tepees from time to time."

As they left Mankato, the Captain announced that New Ulm was the next stop. Since they would not arrive until after sunset, their first clear view of the townsite would be in the morning. Oh well, thought Maurna, everything usually looks better in the morning.

It was nearly dark as they neared the settlement, but huge flaming torches reached out from the dock to light their way to the landing. The Captain whistled their arrival and maneuvered carefully in the gentle but capricious current until they bumped to a halt.

As they stepped ashore, they saw lights up the bank at several levels and a few low storage buildings and small warehouses near the dock. Wagons and carriages were lined up to take on passengers and goods. Maurna silently thanked the Lord for delivering them safely, then said aloud, "There'll be no more railroads or boats in our lives for a good while. I've had my fill; how about the rest of you?"

Pim smiled acknowledgement and Ginny asked where they were sleeping.

Ben answered for Maurna. "We'll be stayin' with our friends, the Lundes, and then tomorrow we'll be in our own snug home, little one."

"Ben, you didn't tell me we'd be someone's guests. I must look a fright."

"Oh, sis, this is the frontier, not the big city. Don't be so fussy."

She scolded him. "Ben, you know little about the ladies, I'm thinkin'. A woman is a woman wherever she is and sensitive to the appearance she makes."

A stout voice was heard from up the slope. "Ben, I'll be there in a minute. I have to wait in line."

"We'll unload while you wait, Tony," Ben hollered. To Maurna he said, "That's Tony who's anxious to be meetin' all of you. Pim, let's see to our flatboat while he waits to bring up his wagon."

Ben and Pim had just finished unloading when a wagon pulled up. A young man came bouncing onto the dock halooing Ben and smiling his welcome. Ben shouted above the noise of the crew, "Tony Lunde, meet my sister Maurna Russell, her daughter Ginny and my nephew, Pim."

Tony's grin widened. "At last, the long-awaited ones." He bowed to Maurna and said, "Mrs. Russell," then turned to Pim, shook his hand vigorously and said, "and Mister Murnane." He solemnly patted Ginny's head, bowed and intoned, "Miss Russell. Welcome to all of you. When Ben described you to us, I thought he was exaggerating and that you'd never live up to the notices. But he did not do you justice. Miss Ginny, you are spring in late October."

Ben laughed. "Maurna and Ginny, you are now under the spell of the fastest talkin' woman charmer in the valley. Even if you don't feel well when you meet him, you soon will. He's got a silver tongue, so watch yourselves."

Maurna went along. "'Tis never a crime to lift people's spirits, Mr. Lunde. The world could use a bit more charm and will applaud you for it. I will have to caution Ginny though to beware of sweet-talkin' young gentlemen."

"From the look of her, Mrs. Russell, I predict that she'll be the charmer and will break hundreds of hearts in a few years," chuckled Tony. "But Pim is the greatest surprise. Ben, you said he was your little nephew. He's taller than I am and nearly up to you. And some growing years to go yet. I'll be talking nice to this one, I'll tell you."

"Anything happenin' in town?" asked Ben.

"You know nothing ever happens in New Ulm, Ben. Have to go to Mankato for excitement. Just another dull day here until you folks landed to brighten our shores. But let's be getting loaded up and take a run up to the house to meet the other Lundes. A decided improvement they'll be over the family representative you've met."

Maurna noted Tony's handsome, bony face, framed by rich and wavy black hair and small, tight-set ears. Coffee-brown eyes shining under thick lashes and brows, a wide and slightly upturned nose, a tanned and smooth complexion, and a smile that flashed white, even teeth completed the portrait.

"He's pretty isn't he, Mama?" asked Ginny.

They howled and Tony blushed. "Oh, she's shot me down like a mallard duck with one little arrow. I'll never recover from this."

Maurna was still laughing. "Ginny, dear, you never refer to a man as pretty. They take great discomfort from that word. It's the curly hair I think that inspired her comment, Tony. She's from a long line of straight-haired men, and also women, I'm sorry to say."

They clambered aboard the wagon that Tony turned up a steep slope to a first level and then up again and in amongst a cluster of frame shops and warmly-lighted homes. Turning into a street of commercial buildings, they passed a two-story frame structure with lanterns illuminating a sign that read

Dakota Hotel. Tony pointed ahead and said, "The first log cabins were built here in '55. We don't build much with log anymore. All the new buildings are frame lumber. There's talk that some of the newer ones will be brick." They pulled up beside a two-story frame house, ablaze with welcoming light.

Through the front door, a lantern-carrying, middle-aged couple were emerging, followed by a young woman whose long brown hair featured bouncing curls to her shoulders. They all wore the Lunde smile, already a decided family trait that Maurna noted.

Tony stepped forward. "Maurna, Pim, Ginny, let me introduce you to my parents and my sister, Abigail."

Mrs. Lunde came forward, clasped Maurna's hands warmly and said, "Welcome, Maurna. I am Belle and this is my good husband, Ansgar, and our daughter, Abigail. We are so pleased to finally meet all of you." She smiled sweetly, and Ansgar stepped forward to add his welcome. Abigail curtsied gracefully.

Maurna spoke for her group. "'Tis our privilege to meet the Lundes. Ben has spoken glowingly of all of you. We want to thank you for your many kindnesses to him. It has been lonely for him, but you have eased that with your hospitality."

"Thank you, my dear," said Belle. "Ben has deserved every bit of it. But come in, come in, it's chilly out here. We'll warm you with some coffee and chocolate for the youngsters." As she led Maurna, she whispered, "Your daughter is adorable. Such eyes and pretty features."

They were soon seated around the preset dining room table. Under the light of the candle chandelier, they had their first clear view of one another. Maurna noted the strong family resemblance with Tony favoring his mother and Abigail her father. Ansgar appeared to be about fifty. Crowned with wavy gray hair, his large-featured, florid face wore a pleasant and warm expression. Tightly bunned chestnut hair framed Belle's fleshy, unwrinkled face. Better light confirmed the handsome impression Tony had made. His square jaw with deeply clefted chin connoted strength and a hint of pugnacity, though his twinkling eyes and impish smile belied that impression. Nearly as tall as Tony, Abigail was just snuggling up to womanhood. At fifteen her features were not fully formed, but indicated promise of delicate beauty.

The Lundes managed to extract from Maurna, with minor contributions from Pim and Ginny, everything they wanted to know about the Murnanes and Russells that Ben had not already told them. Maurna was eventually able to shift the conversation to the Lundes and New Ulm.

"You've come to a unique settlement," Belle began. "A community like no other, and not by accident. If you understand its background, you'll more likely appreciate its good points. Ansgar knows the history better than I, and since he's not German can give a less biased description. I am German clear through, Maurna. Maiden name was Deutsch. Ansgar is a rare mix, half Norwegian and half Swede. He loves to talk about New Ulm, so refill your cups and sit back for your history lesson."

Ansgar laughed and began, "You will note, Mrs. Russell, that I do not speak until invited by my wife. I would not attempt to compete with her."

Maurna made a request. "Please excuse what I promise will be my last interruption, but I ask you to please refer to me as Maurna. We are to be friends, and Mrs. Russell is too formal for a friend."

"Gladly, Maurna, but only if I am Ansgar to you." At her smiling nod he began again. "The village of New Ulm is still an infant. Less than five years of existence, yet great strides have been made, as you will see for yourself tomorrow. The community was founded by individuals seeking freedom from tyrannies. All of the founders were immigrants from Germany who fled Europe's political oppression and religious persecution. Most of them were Turners, an organization that believes in sound bodies and independent minds, advocates free-soil principles, and opposes temperance and prohibition. In other words, they sought self-determination and full kegs of beer." He laughed at his own attempt at humor, took a sip from his cup and continued.

"Some people call the Turners free-thinkers. Others call them hardheads. They sought escape from city life and went off to seek a virgin site. To make a long story short . . ."

Belle burst in. "To make a long story short, Ansgar, would require someone else to do the telling."

Despite the laughter, Ansgar retained his poise and went on, "My helpmate, Maurna. Isn't she delightful? Well anyway, a small group was commissioned to seek a site and, after searching in Wisconsin and Iowa, finally were led to this gorgeous valley in the fall of '55. They suffered during that winter and only survived because of the assistance of a few trappers and the generosity of the Sioux. Some of the party decided on a site west and north of here they called Milford. The majority felt that this site, where the Cottonwood River empties into the Minnesota, would be preferable. Word was sent back to Chicago and Cincinnati, and people began to arrive. In '56 a commune was established to purchase land and establish a community-owned sawmill. Originally all clergy and lawyers were prohibited. Churches were also forbidden. By '57 when we arrived, there were twenty-four log houses and a general store."

Belle relieved Ansgar. "We moved here because we felt it would be a better place to raise youngsters than Chicago. My brother, Hermann, talked us into joining his family and heading west."

She paused and Ansgar continued. "My trade of carpentry was in demand for the building that was planned. We arrived in the early fall and have watched New Ulm grow to a village of 600 people and over 200 buildings. There is no longer communal ownership of any kind, and you'll see tomorrow that we have churches and even a few lawyers. We have a small core of free thinkers who ridicule religion and politics, but most citizens, including Turners, show none of the original intolerance. We are on our way to becoming a normal, sound village with freedom and opportunity for all. We are proud of New Ulm and intend to make it attractive for anyone who wants a prosperous, orderly life."

"Good gracious, Ansgar, we're Irish Catholics. Will they be throwin' us out?" asked Maurna half seriously.

"Heavens, no, Maurna," Belle answered. "A good many Germans are Catholic. Luther didn't convert them all you know. In fact, they're in the process of building a Catholic Church as we speak. Ansgar, correct me if I'm wrong, but aren't there more Catholics here now than any other denomination?"

"I believe that's true, dear wife."

Pim asked, "How about the Indians? Do they have their own religion?"

Tony contributed. "All the churches try to convert them, but most Indians believe in their own God. A few have converted, not many."

Quickly joined by Abigail and then by Maurna, Belle began to clear the table. "Sit still," she said to Maurna, who began to rise, "you're the guest here."

"I was taught by my mother not to be a sittin' guest, Belle. I want to help."

When the three women were alone in the kitchen, Belle whispered, "Maurna, call Ginny. We'll make a quick tour of the house and show you where you'll be sleeping. Ben will be in Tony's room, and I thought Pim could take to the couch in the parlor. All of you must be exhausted from all your traveling."

"How thoughtful. Thank you," said Maurna and went to get Ginny, who was becoming noticeably heavy-eyed.

Belle whispered to Abigail, "Such nice-looking folks. Love to hear that accent, too. Lovely people."

"Yes, and Pim's a fine-looking young man himself. He has a dignity about him. Well bred, all of them," commented Abigail.

Belle smiled to herself and thought, Abby, you would notice the male near your own age, wouldn't you? You're your mother's daughter, that's sure.

With the promise of an early rise and a tour of the town in the morning, they were led to their beds. Ben made a point of seeing Belle alone to thank her for their hospitable welcome. He thanked Tony, too, just before they dropped off to sleep.

"The families took to each other well, Ben," said Tony. "Mighty fine people you spring from."

During breakfast the view to the south revealed a high ridge of hills framing the settlement. A few snowflakes fell as Tony led them on a walking tour up the street past the Dakota Hotel to Turner Hall, a spacious lodge used for meetings, gymnastics, dances, theatre, and church services. From the terrace, the river view was spectacular down to where the Cottonwood River emptied into the Minnesota.

After completing the tour, they made their departure. Tony reminded Ben of the hazards of the Cottonwood River Trail and warned him to be especially careful at the ford. Ben assured him that he would have the borrowed team and wagon back by 9:00 A.M. the next day. They left their flatboat secured at the landing to transport them back upriver after returning the Lunde's rig. At last they were off to their home on the final short leg.

Maurna sat in front with Ben. Pim and Ginny reclined on straw mats in the wagon bed. The Cottonwood Trail led south up and over another terrace, down and through a valley to a ford about a mile from the village. As they entered the wooded area by the river, they heard muted voices and looked up to see an elderly, stooped Indian standing barelegged in the rushing water. The old man wielded a long, sharply pointed pole for spearing fish. A few yards up the bank sat an old woman holding a bundled infant. Ben stopped and shouted hello. The woman looked away. The Indian shrugged, stepped aside, smiled a toothless grin, and waved them through.

"Any fish?" asked Ben.

The old man shrugged again and smiled.

"He must not speak or understand," said Ben and began to traverse the rock-bottom ford. The horses did not shy at the water, but Maurna rose in her seat and held on for dear life. Ben laughed and eased across, waving his hand at the old Sioux as they went by. They scrambled up the hillside trail to emerge on the open prairie where flat terrain, covered with golden grasses, fell away to the south. They turned onto the rutted road and after four or five miles of bumpy travel, Ben pointed to his left along a trail that he told Maurna led to the Rivard farm. He noticed a whisp of smoke to their right above the tree line. Alarmed slightly, but not indicating concern to Maurna, he told her that in just a few turns of the wheels they would bend in off the trail to descend part way down the slope to their farm yard. As he left the main trail, he informed Maurna that the turnoff to the Koukkari place was two miles farther down the road.

"Just around the next bend, you'll see the top of our house through the trees. Up above the ridge on your right. You can already see the smoke from the chimney. See up there? See, Ginny, Pim?"

Maurna had braced herself for this moment and knew that Ben would be reading her face. She had warned herself not to expect a house like the Campbells in Saint Paul or the Lundes in New Ulm. "Yes, I see it, Ben. Look up there, Ginny. See the smoke?"

When they passed over the ridge, Ben stopped the wagon so they could take in the full effect. A high, wooded hill rose in the background of a log cabin set on the bank a few yards above the river. The front porch faced south out over another low ridge. Both sides of the river were well-wooded, mostly elm, cottonwood, and birch. A worn landing area was cut into the river bank, revealing a sandy shoreline.

Ben released the team and eased them up near the porch. He recognized the wagon near the shed and sighed in relief. It came as no surprise to him, but Maurna jumped when they heard a deep voice from near the shed holler. "Welcome to your new home!"

Maurna looked up into the deep blue eyes of a giant young man who stood in front of the shed with hands on hips and a wide smile and wholesome face, partially hidden beneath a cascade of yellow hair.

Ben shouted, "Ox, you old hound, how did you know when we'd be gettin' here?"

"Didn't know, just guessed. Been here a couple hours. Did a little work around the place. Thought you might not want to be coming to a cold house."

Ben helped Maurna and Ginny off the wagon and introduced Ox. Maurna thanked him, saying, "How thoughtful of you to think of buildin' up a fire for us. Is it Ox you want us to be callin' you or do you prefer your given name?"

"Mrs. Russell," he laughed, "Ox ain't the prettiest name, but I guess it suits me. When you hear my real name, you'll understand why I don't complain about being called Ox."

As they stepped toward the entry, Ox stopped them. "I won't be going in with you, Mrs. Russell. Woman ought to see her house without anybody looking on. I'm to wagon on home to get Ma. She and Will and I'll come back here after an hour or so. Grandpa and Rob will come over another time. Ma's so curious she can't wait to meet all of you. Said it wouldn't be fitting for her to be here when you arrived, that you'd want some time to yourself. But before I leave to get her, would you come with me out to the shed? Got something to show you."

Though Maurna was anxious to see the interior, her good manners compelled her to follow the others and long-striding Ox in the direction of a low shed built part way into the hillside.

"Her name's Johanna," said Ox as he pointed to a white-faced black cow whose sad brown eyes looked up at their approach. The beast sounded a low, drawn-out moo. "She's saying hello," chuckled Ox.

"What an ugly, handsome beast," exclaimed Ben.

"Ain't she though? Ma says you'll need milk for little Virginia and for the rest of you, and butter, too. She says your brother and her had made Johanna part of the business deal, and you might's well have her now as later. She's all milked 'til tomorrow. Hay's there for her, too."

"How kind and thoughtful," enthused Maurna. "I'm so eager to meet your mother. And the others, too."

"You won't need to wait long. I'll go fetch her. Be back in a couple hours. Ma baked some cookies. She'll bring them over. Said you should brew some coffee, and her nose will bring us right to it. See you in a little bit."

"Ox, thanks for everything and for bein' here. Coffee'll be ready." Ben shouted after him. They turned back to the house.

"Well, big sister, shall we go in?" smiled Ben.

"Lead on, good sir, we'll be in your wake."

Holding Ginny's hand, Maurna felt the warmth and noticed the odor of new wood. Her eye detected the white curtains on the side windows and guessed who they had come from.

The long, narrow room revealed a stone fireplace at the far end, two windows, two drape-covered side doorways and a large iron stove near the back wall. A rectangular table with side benches and a wood chair at either end dominated the back half of the room. Other benches were arranged along the side walls. Just to the right of the entrance, stood a tall, deep wardrobe with a drape front. They pulled off their outer garments and hung them on dowel pegs inside the wardrobe.

"Oh, Ben, it's lovely," enthused Maurna as she stepped into the center of the room. "So roomy. What a beautiful fireplace." She stepped toward the fire and stood before its warmth as she looked back at them standing near the front door. "Oh, Ben, I love it."

As Ginny ran to hug her mother, Ben explained, "There's a bedroom on each side, one for you and Ginny and the other for the men. I'll put real doors on them when I've the time. The drapes give privacy in the meantime. There's a pantry, a storage room and a washroom by the back door. See the oak shutters? Those can be folded across the windows and barred. I'll make more chairs and tables when we see the need."

"Really nice, Ben," said Pim.

Maurna's eyes were moist. "Just beautiful work. Joseph will be so pleased and proud of you. Come on, Ginny, let's look at our bedroom." They crossed quickly and stepped through the drape. "Oh, Ben, how homey." Two narrow frame beds, a large wardrobe and a low dresser nearly filled the room. An undraped window was cut up high in the wall. Maurna and Ginny crossed to the other bedroom that boasted a single narrow bed and a two-level bunk.

"Pim, you bein' the youngest get stuck with the top bunk. But not until Joseph gets here in the spring," Ben said.

"How clever of you, Ben. A way to use the space well. My, but I have a talented brother."

A narrow opening around the left side of the fireplace led into a spacious room designed for washing and firewood storage with a back entrance.

Maurna sat on a bench and brought a handkerchief to her eyes. "I've been anticipatin' and fearin' this moment for weeks. I confess I've been dreadin' what we might find. I should have had more faith in my brothers. Forgive me, Ben. I can't tell you how pleased I truly am. Ginny, you and I will make a real home of this place. Ben, you've done a remarkable job. Not just skill went into it. I can feel the love expressed in every board. Thank you from the bottom of our hearts."

Ben beamed. "You mean you'll stay, ladies? First bit of women's work is to make a pot of coffee. We've got visitors comin'. While you're brewin' the coffee, Pim and I'll start unloadin'."

They heard the wagon rattle into the yard. Maurna saw Ox's broad back as he reached for a tiny, bonneted lady wrapped in a blue shawl. Rich chestnut hair edged the bonnet and terminated in a tight bun at the nape of her neck. Stepping toward the porch, she raised deep-brown eyes to meet Maurna's and began a sweet smile that grew with each step of her approach. Ox shuffled beside her and made the hurried introduction. "Mrs. Russell, let me present my mother, Rose Koukkari."

Rose closed the short distance and embraced Maurna warmly. "Welcome, dear lady, we've looked forward to your arrival for ages it seems." She stepped back and looked up at Maurna. "The family resemblance is amazing. I'd have been able to spot you in a crowd."

"Your welcome is so appreciated. Only a very kind, understandin' woman would know what it means to us," responded Maurna.

"And this is Pim, Joseph's son, and little Virginia," interjected Ox.

Rose pulled her eyes from Maurna's, went to Pim and shook his hand. "And welcome to you, too, young man. You look a great deal like your father." She moved on to Ginny. "And you, little sweetie, are especially precious, since we have so few of us to deal with the males around us."

Rose turned and teased. "And let me introduce my son, Will, who's wanting to get at the cookies he's carrying." They smiled and greeted Will who blushed and grinned.

Ben had waited in the background until the introductions were completed, then held the door open. "Even Minnesotans ought to know enough to come in out of the cold. Come in, come in, the heat's awastin'."

Maurna took Rose's arm as they entered with Ginny tucked between them. "It seems odd to be welcomin' a lady who's house this used to be, Rose. It's my understandin' that this was your home when you first came to this area."

"Yes, that's true, though we didn't build it. I bought this place from a woman who lost her husband and their dream soon after they had built the cabin and settled. You're actually the third owners, and the house is only five years old."

"Sure hope it'll be a long time before the fourth one," said Ben.

"Aye to that," echoed Ox.

Ben strode to the stove. "Time to taste the coffee. Smellin' it for long enough." Rose uncovered the platter of cookies and placed it on the table.

There was milk for Ginny and Pim. Ben and Maurna took coffee. The Koukkaris all filled glasses half with milk, half with coffee. "The Finnish way," said Rose, and they settled on benches around the table.

"The curtains, Rose. Your doin' I'd wager," said Maurna.

"Thought you'd appreciate them, Maurna. Just some spares I had. Nothing makes a house look quicker a home than curtains. Truth is, they used to be on those same windows when we lived here. Didn't fit the new place. Been in a trunk for over a year now."

"Overwhelmin'," enthused Maurna. "I've never been anywhere where people have been more thoughtful. A wonderful couple on the steamboat, their son and his wife in Saint Paul, the Lundes, and now Ox and Will and you. Are all Minnesotans so considerate and welcomin'?"

"I'd say yes, Maurna, true of Minnesotans, but true of pioneering people everywhere. Folks who have gone through the transplanting and remember how difficult it was and want to help ease things for newcomers. It's contagious. You'll do the same for others and then their turn will come. I hope people never lose the custom. The Rivards welcomed us special, and the Lundes and others, too."

Ben was enthused. "And Tony and Ox helpin' me with the house, and the suppers I've had at the Koukkaris and the Lundes. No way to thank enough for all of the kindness."

"Easy to thank, Ben. Just be good neighbors. That's all anybody expects for thanks," said Ox.

Ginny inserted, "Sure is a lot of thankin' goin' on!"

Through the laughter, Rose said, "Ginny's right. Enough with the thank-yous. Let's do some real talking. Maurna, the chances to talk with another woman out here are seldom. I've got so much gossip built up I'm 'bout ready to burst. Ox here brings news from New Ulm once in a great while, but he doesn't know how to make it into satisfying gossip. Three-word sentences is the most I ever get out of him."

Ox teased back. "Oh, Ma, you usually only stop talking long enough for me to slip in but three words."

"I can still reach up high enough to paddle you, big boy," countered Rose, then grew serious. "Maurna, I'd like you to take a little walk with me while there's still daylight. We'll bundle up good. Bring Ginny if you like but no men allowed."

Rose led Maurna and Ginny out past the shed and started up a lightly worn pathway through the trees and up the hill. The summit permitted viewing in all directions. A spreading oak that still retained its copper leaves dominated the east side. Rose turned to the west and waited for Ginny and Maurna to come up beside her.

"You can see for miles on a clear day. The whole valley spreads out in front of you. It's my favorite place in all the world. When we lived over here, I seldom missed a sunset from this very spot. I'm ever at peace in this special place. Close to God in His heaven. You'll learn to love it yourself, I'll wager. Your brother, Joseph, fell in love with the view. I think he made up his mind to move here when he saw the future from this hill."

Maurna surveyed the scene. The great breadth of the valley was on display. To the limits of her vision the open vista stretched westward. Rolling hills, predominately prairie, but showing occasional patches of woods and cultivated pieces. Prominent were ravines, defiles, gullies, and undulations left untouched since their haphazard formation by the glaciers and currents of the great River Warren. Powerful, thought Maurna, timeless. Inspires a feeling of permanence. The temperature was dropping as snowflakes descended softly. She felt winter's inexorable onset, portending drab, confining months. But on that hill, at that moment, Maurna felt a warm glow. She knew without a trace of reservation that Joseph had been guided by the hand of God to this good place and these remarkable people. Her hand held Ginny's, and she reached with the other for the hand of Rose.

Back at the house, the women did most of the talking. Rose extracted news of Joseph and when he was expected in the spring. She invited them for Thanksgiving. "There's talk that they'll select a date for the Thanksgiving holiday all over the nation. One thing's settled. It'll be a Thursday in November." Rose was set to teach at the Redwood Indian Agency for eight weeks during January and February and talked about the program. Maurna showed Rose the handsome rocking chair and told her its story. Maurna then offered supper, but Rose would not permit it. She signalled the Koukkari's departure by saying that Will was anxious to be going because the cookies were all eaten. "Pa will be fretting for his supper, Maurna, and I'm a little too old to be getting scolded. Best be off." They left for home in the early darkness.

Maurna came back in from the porch drying her eyes. "I'm sorry to be showin' my tears. Please, don't misunderstand, they're tears of relief and joy. I'm so happy to have that long journey over with and the feelin' of a place for us. Our own beds to lie on, our own food to cook and eat. And friends. Rose seems like a sister already. A woman is not a roamer by nature. We need to settle in. I just love our house. Sure it's plain and simple, but it's also clean and snug. Ginny and I will brighten it up, wait 'n see."

Ben embraced her and said softly, "When Joseph gets here in the spring, we'll be a family again, complete and whole. We'll make do here, Maurna. Hard work for sure, but we'll be workin' for ourselves to build a future. It feels so good to have all of you here. I'm not much good all alone. Got a taste of it. Didn't like it. Welcome home."

Maurna hugged Ginny, then Pim, dried her eyes, and started making supper. "Early to bed tonight. Lots to do tomorrow."

Chapter Four

Thanksgiving

Ox pulled in at dawn, stomping inside with a rush when Pim opened the door. "Right brisk out there, Pim. Tickles the nose. Winter may be coming soon."

Pim was incredulous. "You mean it's not here yet?"

"Just joking, Pim. But it will get a whole lot colder than this."

"Sit for some coffee, or would you want milk instead?"

"Too cold for milk, Pim. Hello there, Mrs. Russell, Ginny. Ben around or still soft in bed?"

Maurna approached with a warm smile. "Mornin', Ox. Ben's out cuttin' firewood. Probably heard your wagon and be hurryin' inside. Coffee's hot. Want it the Finnish way as your mother calls it?"

"When it's this cold, I take it heavy on the coffee and light with the milk, Mrs. Russell. 'Bout three-fourths coffee, if you will." He sat and warmed his hands by the stove.

"Everyone fine at your place, Ox?" Maurna asked.

Before he could answer, Ginny asked, "Is your real name 'big boy,' Mr. Ox?"

They all roared with Pim laughing the hardest. Ox recovered and asked, "Why do you think that, Ginny?"

"'Cause I heard your mother call you big boy and thought it a funny name."

"Oh, honey, his mother was teasin' him when she called him that," chuckled Maurna.

"Well then, what is his real name?" persisted Ginny.

Thanksgiving

"Might as well get it over with," said affable Ox. "I'll tell you, Ginny, if you promise to never call me by it. Understand now, I'm not ashamed of it. Just don't like it. My father's name was Toivo," which he spelled for them. "He named me Oskar, with a K. Both are common names in Finland. When I was a little mite and I tried to say Oskar, it came out sounding like oxcart. After a while the cart got lost but the Ox stayed."

"Ox it will be," said Maurna. "Now drink your milk, Ginny, and offer friend Ox here some bread and butter."

Ben burst in and headed straight to the stove. "Mornin', big boy," he cajoled.

Ginny scolded Ben. "His name's Ox, not big boy."

"Guess that settles it for good and all," laughed Pim.

Ox put down his glass and got up. "Best be on our way, Ben. Weather's a little uncertain this time of year. Always allow more time, case you need it. We'll be back before dark, Mrs. Russell. Got your list in your head, Ben? This time of year we need to think ahead. Don't know when we'll be able to get into town again. Lots of room in the wagon."

"Maurna wrote out a list for me. Take care of the ladies, Pim." Ben pulled on his mittens and tied his scarf over his chin. "Bring in some of the wood I cut, will you?"

Maurna cautioned, "Take care of yourselves. I'll have supper for both of you. Here's some bread and cheese to take along. It's cold but at least will fill you up."

Ben grabbed the food and the young men breezed out. Ben started to mount the wagon when Ox held up his hand. "Got something to do before we leave. Won't take long." He pulled out a length of rope that he threw over his shoulder as he headed up to the shed. He tied the end of the rope securely to the front post support, then headed back toward the house playing out the hemp as he moved along. Curious, Maurna threw a shawl over her shoulders and stepped out on the porch. Ginny and Pim watched out the window.

"What on earth?" asked Maurna as Ox came up to the porch.

Ox reached up with his knife to cut a notch into the porch post. He allowed some slack, cut the rope and tied the cut end to the post. He tested the tension and seemed satisfied.

Finally, he explained. "We all do it for safety sake. It'll guide you if you slide your hand along it when a blizzard gets to blowing. Believe me, blizzards deserve respect. This rig has been known to save lives. To finish the job, Ben, cut a short piece of rope to make into a loop that'll slide along the main rope, then leave a handle hanging down for Ginny. She can't reach it as high as it is."

"That's the second time I've been warned about blizzards, Ox. They must be frightful."

"Believe it, Mrs. Russell. Everything turns white. Lose your directions real fast. Let's be off, Ben."

They jumped on the rig and Ox steered the team in a tight circle that led to the rutted path. Maurna glanced at the blizzard rope and shivered. She shook her head in wonder and went back inside to the warmth.

Rose had invited them to share the Koukkari bounty. Ox came to collect them for the winding, two-mile jaunt to their home situated on a low hillock back from the river and cleared of trees for thirty yards on all sides. The log-sided and peak-roofed structure featured a low porch across the south-facing front. A barn and several smaller sheds were set near the trees on the north and east sides. The approach ran down a slope from a ridge and up through a swale.

Maurna wondered about the barrenness of the immediate grounds. Apparently reading her mind, Ox remarked that they had cleared the trees from around the house to provide close-up, handy garden space that would receive direct sunlight, and so anybody approaching would be obliged to cross open ground.

"You mean Indians, don't you, Ox?" asked Ben.

"Maybe. Never know. Better to be ready for trouble than unprotected."

"But, Ox," said a concerned Maurna, "we've been assured that the Indians are peaceable. Did we not hear the truth of it?"

"No worry really, Mrs. Russell. Hasn't been trouble for years. We're extra careful is all. Grandpa's the one who insisted. He's got a long memory of what happened to his people back in Ohio years ago. Despite his feelings, he insists we befriend the Sioux. He's convinced that they should have been more friendly to the Indians in Ohio."

Rose's voice interrupted from the front door. "Come in. It's cold out there."

They stomped the snow off their boots and stepped into the warmth and savory aromas. The hearth fire was crackling, the table was set with lighted candles at either end and the pots and kettles were hissing a chorus of promise. Rose introduced them to her father, Pa Kotelnik, a wiry little man with a warm smile even though half his teeth were no longer present to contribute. Nearly bald, he sported a speckled gray-white beard. Wide red braces hung from his narrow shoulders over his wool shirt and pulled up his trousers nearly to the middle of his chest. He wished them a happy Thanksgiving, put on his coat, and went quickly out the door. "I'll take care of the horses, Ox," he shouted as he slammed the door.

Rose's chortle was partly embarrassment and partly affection. "Please understand, Maurna, Ox isn't lazy, but Pa'd have scolded him awful if he hadn't left the team for him to take care of. He thinks he's the only one can handle horses proper. He says that horses are like people. They work better when they're fussed over a little."

"Makes sense to me. Let me help you, Rose. Just tell me what you need done."

"Later maybe, Maurna. Just a couple things to do here, then I'll show you around. Sit down a minute."

Will and Rob burst in, slamming the door behind them. "Ma, Grandpa near run us down. Didn't even see us." complained Will.

"Keep your eyes peeled, Will. You know your Grandpa. Boys, meet Mrs. Russell and her daughter, Ginny. You already know Ben and Pim. Maurna, you remember Will who ate all the cookies at your house? The other rascal is his brother, Rob."

"Hello there, boys. Pleased to meet you, Rob."

"Pleased to meet you, too, Ma'am and Ginny," responded the shy Rob.

"Kick those boots off, you two," scolded Rose as she came into the parlor. "Come on, Maurna. You too, Ginny. Let's do a quick tour."

She showed them the kitchen with its new wood stove and oven and the maple cupboards built over the sink and an indoor pump. "Being on a hill, we had a long dig for a good well. It's sure handy to have the pump indoors." Next was her bedroom and Pa's on the other side where she lifted a trapdoor to show the root cellar below. "Ox told me Ben built you one of these when he set in the new floor. Great idea. Handy in the winter. Keeps potatoes and vegetables just right." They climbed a ladder to the loft that covered the back half of the house. Three narrow cots and two three-drawer dressers covered most of the floor space.

"Ox, Rob, and Will sleep up here. Having a loft saves widening the house for more bedrooms, Maurna. Most of the new houses in New Ulm are two-story now. Lofts waste some heat, but we made sure to insulate real thick. Cozy house. Even on the coldest days."

"Love your curtains, and your furniture is grand, Rose. That bureau in the parlor is just lovely."

"That was my mother's, God rest her. The bureau and the painting over it are all we have left from those days."

"Havin' their things helps keep them alive with us, don't you think? Pieces of the past. Few more years we will be, too, Rose."

"Heavens, Maurna, it'll come soon enough without talking about it. We've got lots of good years left."

"You're right, Rose, no kind of talk for a holiday of Thansgivin'. I'd say we have a great deal to be thankin' the Lord for, settled as we are."

"Only get better, Maurna, only get much better."

The dinner included roasted wild turkeys, mashed potatoes, bread dressing, gravy, corn, beets, hot rolls, berry preserves, and rich pumpkin pie. They gorged themselves and between mouthfuls raved about the quantity, variety, and flavor.

"That pie is far and away the best I've ever eaten, Rose," enthused Maurna. "Must have that recipe."

"If she doesn't get it, I will," chuckled Ben.

"Have another piece, Ben. You too, Pim. Lots to go around. We're supposed to fill up extra today. Sure, you can have the recipe, Maurna. I got it from Mrs. Letelier at the Redwood Agency. She's a mixed-blood, wife of one of the traders. Sioux women can cook pretty good when they take the time to do it."

Ox changed the subject. "Ben, you see where Ramsey was elected our new governor? Republicans been trying to get in power. Finally made it. Don't know much about Ramsey, but folks say he works hard at bringing settlers into the area."

Ben nodded. "I heard he's a go-getter all right. We need more folks out here to build up the area."

"Mixed feelings about that Ramsey," Rose said. "Back in '51 he was the one got the Sioux to sign their land away. That's the treaty where the Sioux were given ten miles out from the Minnesota River on both sides all the way up to Big Stone Lake. Over a million acres. Besides the land settlement, the Indians were supposed to get gold money every year in June. Called annuities. Trouble is, the Indians claim they never see it. Most don't want to be farmers. Rather hunt and trap. That's always been their way. We're trying to change them to suit ourselves."

"Come on now, Ma," said Ox. "You and I both know they'd be better off farming. Not enough game left for them to live off."

"Maybe so, Ox, but can you blame them? Nobody would tell you or me to do something if we didn't want to. Hard heads like us. Well the Sioux have some hard heads, too."

"Nobody harder headed than the Irish," said Pim.

Maurna suggested patience. "Nothin' good ever happens overnight. 'Specially if it means change. The young Indians might be trained to be farmers, and then in years to come, it'll become their natural way. Just takes patience and time to change."

"Funny you should say that," said Ox, "but it's the young braves that are the most hard-headed. Sibley got along with the Sioux because he knew them from the old days. This Ramsey seems to want to push them faster. Hope he knows what he's doing."

Rose spoke again. "That's not the election we should be worrying about, Ox. Lincoln is the one that scares me. Not because of him, but because all those crazy Southern big mouths hate him so much."

"He said he isn't against them keepin' the slaves they've already got, just doesn't want any new states to have 'em. Seems fair," commented Ben.

"Not that simple, Ben," said Ox. "Sure, they can keep the ones they've got. But the Southerners worry that new states coming in without slaves will mean more states without slaves than with 'em. The southern states would be outvoted."

Rose's voice betrayed her feelings. "They should be outvoted. Slavery's ugly, unjust, and against what our constitution says. No human should be somebody's property. Saw enough of it in Missouri."

Maurna agreed. "We didn't have slavery in Ireland, but the landlords controlled the people so they had no voice in their own doin's. Not outright slavery, but bad enough to drive thousands to places they could be free."

Pa Kotelnik became agitated, and finally burst forth. "Seen it in one form or other all my life. Strong beating on the weak. Using them for their own greed. Saw darkies whipped, families sold to different buyers and split up. Ever see a mother lose her child that way? Worst thing you ever see. Same in the old country. Slovaks and Czechs killing one another, Poles and Ukranians. That's why my people came to this country. To be free. The darkies didn't even choose to come. They was dragged here kicking. This country's the last hope in the world for real freedom. If this Lincoln don't do something about it, we'll end up no better than the rest of the world." He was near tears and got up from the table to go put on his coat. Just as he went through the door, he leaned back in and added, "Paper founding this country says that all men are created equal. Well, maybe, but some of 'em don't stay that way long, do they?"

"Pa gets upset," Rose explained. "His parents were bad oppressed in Europe. Any time freedom's the topic, Pa gets worked up."

"My brother Joseph's like that, too," Ben said emphatically. "He'll fight like a wildcat when it comes to bein' free. He carries a lot of hard feelin' for the Brits. Guess we all do."

Pim had been intently listening, then voiced his concern. "Some say the Indians are as bad treated as the Irish farmers, Mrs. Koukkari."

"Truth to that, Pim. Some troubles they bring on themselves, but most is due to breaking of the treaties. President Lincoln will be appointing a new Indian Agent. Hope he's a man that has some understanding of the Indians. I agree with Maurna. Give it time. I see hopeful signs at the Agency. Some of the young ones are learning to read and write and maybe think a little different."

Ox changed the tone. "Kind of serious talk around here for a holiday. We've got a lot of good things happening, too. Lots to be thankful about. New friends and neighbors. Good harvest in the barn. New land broke and ready for spring. We're all healthy. Let the politicians worry the problems."

Ben quickly agreed. "The Murnanes and Russells sure have been fortunate. When Joseph gets here this spring, we'll be all set. We made a long, hard move and got settled in a good home. Lot of our thanks are to you Koukkaris and the others who have made us feel so welcome."

"Nothing you wouldn't have done," said Ox.

Pa pushed open the door, shook off the snow, and came over to the table wearing a sly grin. "Saw some Indians down by the river. They was hunting and had 'em two skinny rabbits. Got to thinking about those stories about those Pilgrims and the first Thanksgiving. Remembered, too, about the Sioux custom of sharing whatever they've got with one another. Not a bad custom. So fill up two big heaping plates of dinner. We got us some company."

He went back to the door and gestured. A Sioux boy and man came in, looked at all of them, and the elder smiled. Pa closed the door, took their outer blankets, and led them to the table. "This here's Gray Coyote and his son Little Horse. Thought you might want to wish them Happy Thanksgiving."

It was late afternoon in mid-December and already dark. A vigorous wind blew the loose snow past the window in ghostly gusts.

Ginny was standing with her arms upraised, being fitted for a dress, and her mother was kneeling, pinning the hem. Ben was reading, and Pim awling holes in his belt. The eerie sound at first seemed far away. All of them heard it and looked from one to the other. It sounded like the whine of a child and was repeated, slightly louder. Pim moved to the door, slowly undid the latch, peeked outside, and looked down into appealing brown eyes. Then he saw the blood.

"Oh, poor fella," he said as he went out and onto his knees.

The others crowded around. Pim picked up the creature and carried it in to place it by the fire. Without a word, Maurna went for a bucket, soap and water and a clean rag. The others were down on their knees. Ginny reached out to touch the rich brown fur. "His foot's hurt, Mama, he's bleedin'."

"I know," said Maurna and began to gently wash the front right paw. "Heat some water, Pim, it's stubborn to get off."

Pim sprang to obey. The animal whimpered under Maurna's touch, but licked her hand and flip-flopped its tail.

"Such a beauty you are. Hurry, Pim, the warm water will soothe. Just warm's enough, not hot."

The dog was a mixed breed, about fifty pounds, mostly brown with white on the front and under, and on the paws and face. The snout was long, the eyes huge. It was thick-furred, indicating it was accustomed to being outside.

"Is it a boy or girl, Mama?" asked Ginny.

"All boy, darlin'," responded Maurna, immersing the wounded paw into the water. The dog winced but acquiesced.

"Where'd he come from do you s'pose?" asked Pim.

"Hard to know," said Ben, "wonder how he hurt that paw?"

"Will he be all right?" asked Ginny.

"Should be." said Maurna. "The cut's not all that deep. Poor fella's in pain though. Don't think a bone's broken."

"I'll get some scraps. Maybe he's hungry," said Pim.

"Look's like he's more thirsty than hungry. He's drinking the water, but the soap he doesn't like." Pim brought a dish of water that was lapped up in seconds. "Gracious, we got a drinker on our hands, we have," chuckled Maurna.

The dog pulled his paw from the water, rolled on his side by the fire, and looked up at them wagging his tail.

"He looks like he's gonna be fine," said Ben.

"Can we keep him? Can we?" asked Ginny of no one in particular.

"We can tonight for sure. He's not goin' far with that foot. He'll decide if he stays or not, don't you think, Ben?" asked Pim.

"In the end it's their decision, 'less you tie 'em. Never did like to see a dog tied up. If they want to stay, hard to send 'em away. If he doesn't like where he was, he'll stay. Simple as that. We'll just see what happens."

"If he stays, he'll have to have a name," commented Pim.

"No sense wastin' time on that 'til we see if he wants to stay," said Ben.

Ginny curled up and patted the dog's neck and ears. His eyes had already won them over. He stopped the licking, closed his eyes and went to sleep.

"Would you look at 'im?" Pim marvelled. "Looks like he's already decided to stay. We better be thinkin' about a name at that. Could be we've got another member of the family."

"Just remembered somethin'," said Ben. "Tony Lunde says the Indians have a lot of dogs. Fact is before they had horses they used dogs to pull their gear. Could be he's an Indian dog. Tony says the Indians sometimes kick and beat dogs, even eat 'em. Might be he got tired of bein' kicked."

"Better not kick one in front of me," vowed Pim.

"That's bad," said Ginny solemnly.

"I don't s'pose they all do it," noted Ben. "Some white people treat dogs cruelly, too, you know."

"Nobody will be bad to this one, will they Ben?" asked Ginny.

"Not if we can help it, darlin'."

"Who would eat a dog?" questioned Maurna.

"Indians," said Ben disgustedly.

Soon after, they blew out the lamps. The dog rested close to the fire.

Ginny was up before daybreak. On her approach, the dog's tail wagged in welcome, the eyes soft and greeting. She sat on the floor with him until Ben came out to stir the fire.

"Seems content, Ginny."

"Can we keep him, Ben? He's so nice and gentle."

"We'll see if he wants to stay. He's welcome far as I'm concerned."

Pim and Maurna emerged. Pim went straight to the dog. "He sure slept sound. Not a peep out of him all night."

Getting slowly to his feet, the animal tested his paw gingerly and limped slowly toward the door.

"Oh don't let him out, Pim, he might run off," cried Ginny, walking after the dog. "Please, Ben, keep him inside, please."

"Now, Ginny, nature's callin' to him, and he wants to answer. Glad to see he knows to go outside. He probably won't run off but we've got to find out. Good a time as any." Ben unlatched the door.

The dog looked up at him as if to say thanks and stepped onto the porch. He sniffed the air, looked around, limped slowly off the porch and turned toward the shed. Ginny and Pim ran to the side window to watch. Ben came up behind them.

"What's he doin'?" called Maurna.

"He's doin' what all dogs do. He's checkin' out the territory. He just caught a wiff of Johanna. He's headin' right for the shed." said Ben.

At a trot he approached the shed, slowly poked his head around the wall and kept his long tail down low. After a moment, the tail started to flop side to side, and they heard a loud, contented moo. The dog disappeared into the shed, tail wagging.

"I believe they just declared mutual friendship," Pim exclaimed.

The dog trotted jauntily out of the shed, circled the yard, and headed for the front door. Ginny let him in. Ignoring all of them he sauntered over in front of the fire, lay down, and began licking his paw. His thumping tail told the story.

Ginny giggled in relief. "He likes us. He's goin' to stay, isn't he, Ben?"

"Looks like, Ginny, looks like. But you never know how long. He'll judge us over a few days, and if we meet his approval, he'll condescend to stay with us. Big of him, don't you think?"

"Yes, I do," said Ginny seriously.

Ginny went to the dog and sank down in front of him. "Mama, we've just got to give him a name. What should it be?"

"I don't know darlin'. We'll think of somethin'."

Pim said, "Dog's coat is the exact deep brown color of whiskey. Let's call him that."

"Whiskey? Doesn't seem right, not in this house. What do you think, Ben?" asked Maurna.

Ben thought a minute, "Well, Maurna, Pim's right about the color for a fact. Seems to me we shouldn't be afraid of the word."

Pim enthused, "Come on, Aunt Maurna, it seems right."

"Tell you what," said Ben. "How's about makin' him a downright Irish dog and satisfy Pim at the same time by using the Irish word for spirits. Let's call him Poteen, what do you say to that?"

They all agreed, and Poteen became a member of the family.

Maurna's Journal
Christmas, 1860

Such a glorious Christmas. Best by far since the tragic year when we lost Timothy. God keep him, and may he rest in peace.

We had the most wonderful surprise on Christmas day. Joseph appeared unannounced. A deep growl from Poteen, Ben opened the door, and there was Joseph's beaming face. He bellowed Merry Christmas, Ho! Ho! Ho!, and was hugging us and laughing and dancing around like a madman. He brought gifts for each of us, but the real gift was himself, dear man.

Complimentary he was about the house, Ben's carpentry and the work of the rest of us to clean and brighten the place. He opened his sack and took great pleasure in giving a gift to each of us. And we didn't have one for him. He dismissed the notion by saying his gift was being with his family. A red bonnet for Ginny, a hunting knife for Pim, deer skin mittens for Ben, and a green wool shawl for me. He said he bought the gifts in a general store in Saint Anthony Falls.

We talked into the wee hours with first Ginny and then Pim drifting off to bed along the way. We told Joseph about how kind and good people had been to us. Joseph always loved dogs, took immediately to Poteen, and said it was a good safety measure to have him around.

Then he went to the bottom of his sack and took out an object that put instant fear in Ben and me. He pulled out a jug of whiskey and held it up with a big grin on his face. He carried it to the shelf above the window, ceremoniously kissed the jug, placed it up on the ledge, stepped back and bowed to it. Ben and I thought he'd lost his sanity. But he reminded us it was the second anniversary of his taking the pledge to drink no more. Swore he hadn't had a swallow of alcohol in that full time and repeated his pledge for the rest of his life. The jug was corked tight, and he placed it atop the window as a reminder. He forbade us to touch it, even to dust it. He wants the cobwebs to grow to it as proof that it was never opened. Our relief was total.

With very little sleep, we were up before dawn, having arranged with the Rivards for a ride in their roomy wagon to Christmas Mass in New Ulm. After, we had a full dinner topped off with the pumpkin pie that Rose had showed me how to fix. Plenty for all, and Joseph said he was anxious to get back to this kind of cooking.

We talked and reminisced all afternoon. The toboggan rides on the back hill freed Ginny and Pim from our adult talk, and the time passed quickly, knowing Joseph would be leaving before dawn. Just at dusk, Poteen growled and raced for the door. And then we heard the loud and enthusiastic, if not artistic, singing of Christmas carols. We rushed out the door and looked upon a scene I shall never forget.

Holding lighted candles and standing in a semicircle were Rose, Ox, Will, Rob and Pa Koukkari, Adrien and Bernadette Rivard, and their daughter, Carole, standing with a young man we didn't know and the three Rivard sons, Claude, Lionel, and René. Pim and Ginny ran to them but were sent back to stand with us on the porch. They caroled us for fifteen minutes. Of course, we joined them in the singing. I had tears in my eyes the whole time, and I noticed even Joseph and Ben were fighting back the growing mist. It was so much beyond just being neighborly. We had the feeling of being accepted, welcomed, and even loved. And did we feel love for them in return.

When the singing stopped, they mingled with us, and we met the young man, Clement LaChance, who the Rivards announced would become their son-in-law. Carole was beaming.

We found out later that Rose had concocted the caroling scheme with the concurrence of Bernadette. Joseph was an added surprise for them, especially for Rose, I'm thinking. The Rivards met him on the ride to mass in New Ulm, but the Koukkaris were unaware that he was home until just before the concert.

We invited them for refreshments, but they refused, saying there were too many of them. Bernadette said they had all been refreshed already, just by seeing the looks of surprise and joy on our faces. Rose told Joseph that he was an extra pleasure they hadn't expected. They left us speechless and full of gratitude. As their wagons pulled away, they

Thanksgiving

waved 'til out of sight, and we heard the sound of carols gently fade away.

If we live someday in a mansion and have millions of dollars, we'll never have a happier Christmas or feel warmer towards our friends and neighbors. Christmas evening 1860. God bless them all forever.

Chapter Five

Insights

When Ben heard that Ox would be traveling to the Redwood Agency to bring his mother home, he sent word that he'd appreciate a ride as far as New Ulm. Ox stopped at the cabin at daybreak, and Ben hopped aboard.

"When we went to our first mass in New Ulm, we introduced ourselves to Father Vogel, Ox. After services, I handed him a sealed letter that had been originated by Father Curran back in Virginia. I suspect the letter includes information about our family and introduces us to the pastor. Before he even read the letter, Father Vogel asked me to stop by for a talk. I promised him I would."

Ox chuckled, "If he's like our preacher, he'll be asking for a contribution. Seems like those religious folks are always short of money. But who isn't, eh Ben? You'll have plenty of time for your talk. If I know Ma, she won't be near ready when I get back to Redwood. I'll be about five, six hours out there and back."

Ben's talk with Father Vogel started off well enough. After extracting some family history, the priest referred to Father Curran's letter. The message urged Father Vogel to encourage Ben's potential vocation to the priesthood. Though his tone was soft, the priest's eyes betrayed his intense desire to pursue the matter to a conclusion. "Ben, Father Curran feels quite certain you have a vocation. There is no higher calling, and it mustn't be ignored."

Ben chose his words carefully. "Father, I don't know what my feelin's are for sure. I've talked it over with my sister, tryin' to get help in sortin' them out. I need more time to decide."

"Benedict, others can't make the decision for you. No one is sure at your age. You must experience the life. You owe it to God and to yourself to find out directly by beginning the training. Mrs. Russell is surely in favor, isn't she?"

"Yes and no, Father. Nobody has a stronger faith than my sister, but she also believes the decision must come from me. Besides, she feels strongly that some of us Irish are too easily influenced by people in authority."

Father Vogel's eyes flickered, betraying, Ben thought, the priest's awareness of this generally held belief about the Irish.

"It has been my experience, Benedict, that all young men need a push to jar them into making a decision, especially one of this magnitude. I don't think it is peculiar to the Irish."

Ben's eyes met Father Vogel's. He hesitated, but decided to confide circumstances that his instincts and family loyalty had kept unrevealed to non-family members.

"Father, I know the priesthood carries with it the promise to keep secret what a person reveals. This isn't the confessional, but I would ask you to honor my request that what I am about to tell you is confidential."

"You can depend on it, Benedict."

"Father, a few years ago in Harper's Ferry, my older brother, Joseph, was a heavy drinker. Nearly every week when he came home from work, he would be flushed with spirits and surly in the bargain. His son, Pim, bore most of the burden, but we all were included. We knew that he was simply trying to ease his sorrow. Father, the man had suffered two years of prison at hard labor, and his wife had died while he was there."

Ben studied Father Vogel's face, but the priest maintained an interested, non-judgmental countenance.

"The problem continued for more than a year. After a public scene, my brother was arrested, bringing shame on all of us, includin' my uncle Bernard and his wife. When Joseph came home after three days in jail, he was more penitent than usual. The evenin' was spent in near silence. The young ones and I finally went to bed, but I was awakened by the voices of my brother, my uncle, and my sister. I opened the door a crack so I could hear.

"Understand, Father, Bernard is Maurna's brother-in-law who came over to America before we did, then sent money for our fares across the Atlantic. So, he had some right to speak. He told the story of his own departure from Ireland in '49 and the difficulties he had in gettin' established in America. The main reason he gave for havin' left Ireland was hopelessness.

He blamed the English landlords for the situation and for the despair. But, Father, he then said somethin' that I had never heard before. It sounded strange comin' as it did from an Irishman. Bernard said that the English and the land system were the cause of the problem, but that the reason for the Irish condition was a basic character flaw in the Irish themselves.

"Bernard stated that many Irish after centuries of conditionin' have convinced themselves that blame for their status resides with their oppressors, not with themselves, that they take comfort in believin' they are victims. They've become passive and content with a little to eat, some socializin' with their own kind, close family life, a drink, a dance, and a poem. He went on to say that their attitude is understandable given the conditions in Ireland, but he said that many immigrants brought their passivity with them to America. Over here, my uncle said, ambition is rewarded. He told Joseph that he had only himself to blame if he didn't succeed. He urged my brother to throw off his Irishness and resolve to work hard at savin' money and bein' ambitious, if not for himself, for Maurna and the children. He added that Joseph had the intelligence, the good health, and the strength of character to make a real good life for all of us."

Father Vogel spoke to the short pause in Ben's narrative.

"Ben, your uncle must be a very perceptive, wise man and skilled in stating truths in a positive, kindly manner."

"Bernard's words hit my brother just right, Father. Joseph meant it when he told Maurna and Bernard that from that moment he pledged to never drink again. He told them that every spare dollar would be put into a fund until we had enough to buy our own place. Well, we now own that place, Father, but we need to work together to make it a success. Joseph has done his part and more. We came here to build a home. My obligation to help is clear. My life will have to wait."

Father Vogel waited a moment, walked over to the window with his back to Ben. "In other words, Ben, God can wait."

Ben shook his head in amazement at the response, then said in a sturdy voice, "The God I wish to serve would not expect me to abandon my family, Father. I feel certain of that."

Father Vogel was still looking out the window when he heard the door softly close behind him.

Maurna had not heard the wagon approach, but Poteen's barking preceeded a familiar, welcome voice. "Maurna Russell, you in there? Put the coffee on. You've got high-class company."

Grinning, she barely beat Ginny to the door, threw it open and stepped onto the porch to greet Rose, Ox, and Ben. "I sometimes think you favor the coffee over the residents, Rose. How've you been? You surely have two handsome escorts." She and Rose hugged.

"Handsome men around me, Maurna. Been that way all my life. Ginny, you're taller and prettier every time I see you. You been behaving yourself, young lady?"

"Of course." Ginny was patting Poteen, whose tail was flop-flopping his welcome.

"Seems like a good mutt you've got there, Ginny. Friendly fellow. Well, Maurna, I just spent some time gabbing with Belle Lunde. Being at the Indian Agency, I miss out on all the gossip. You hear anything from your good-looking big brother, Joseph?"

"Not since Christmas, but he's not much for writin', like most men."

As Maurna poured the coffee, Rose looked around at the improvements made since January. Ben and Ox gulped their coffee and hurried out with Ginny.

"Maurna, you're a wonder with what you've done here in such a short time. The place is real inviting and home-like."

"Thank you, Madame, but I didn't do it all myself. Even Ginny is learnin' and contributin'. Come look at the sleepin' rooms. Got some things to show you."

She showed Rose new coverings, quilts, and curtains that brightened both bedrooms, and a new dress for Ginny. "I'll be startin' on some men's shirts as soon as I finish the sheetin' work. Then maybe a dress for myself for Easter."

"Lordy, you really do sew up a storm . . . and such workmanship. Wish I'd have learned to sew the way you can."

"Oh, anybody can learn, I'm thinkin'. Just takes time and patience and some practicin'."

Rose shook her head. "I don't mean to sound disagreeable, but I think you're underestimating your talent. I could never be as good as you, if I worked at it a full lifetime, and being an old woman, I haven't enough lifetime left."

"Oh, nonsense, you're a vital woman yet, Rose. Don't be talkin' 'bout my good friend that way."

When they were seated, Rose became solemn. "Bad trouble, Maurna, with these southern states seceding. And all because of that damnable slavery. Pardon my language, but I hate it so."

Poteen barked and ran to the door wagging his tail. Pim entered, brushed off his cap and stomped the snow from his boots. As he took off his coat, Rose turned to him and said, "I've heard buffalo stampede quieter than you, Pim, for a fact."

Pim laughed and approached the table. "That son of yours called Ox isn't exactly a ballet dancer himself, Mrs. Koukkari. Will or Rob either. How are you, Ma'am?"

Rose chuckled, delighted at the repartee. "An Irishman is never without a quick reply is he? Maurna, you tell your nephew, touché."

Pim looked stupefied. "Two what, Mrs. Koukkari?"

Rose roared. "Don't mind me, Pim, that's just the only French word I know. Means you gave me a right smart response."

Pim smiled. He didn't know what she was saying, but he wasn't going to pursue it.

"We've been talkin' about the southern states leavin' the union, Pim. Lot of talk in town, Rose says."

"How many states is it now, Mrs. Koukkari?"

Ben, Ginny, and Ox came in and shed their garments. Rose restated most of what she had told Maurna. When she paused, Ben repeated a few comments he had heard some men make in New Ulm about teaching those southerners some manners.

Ox said in conclusion, "Don't know what anybody can do if those states want to go their own way. It's like a young man wantin' to leave home. If he really wants to go, awful hard to stop him short of killing him. Bad solution either way. Maybe President Lincoln will have some answers. That Buchanan sure doesn't seem to."

"Think it might come to actual fightin'?" asked Pim.

"Hope not," Ben replied. "Americans against Americans would be pretty stupid. Beginnin' to sound like Ireland, eh Maurna?"

Chapter Six

Spring at Last

Poteen howled as he sprinted off the porch in the direction of the ravine. Pim and Maurna rushed out the front door and were greeted by grinning Joseph, seated on a buckboard led by two exhausted brown horses. As they ran to him, he held up his hand to stop their charge.

"Your carriage, Madame," he intoned in mock formality.

"Oh, Joseph, it's you we want. The carriage can wait." Maurna reached to pull him down, then hugged him fiercely. Pim shook his father's hand and the three of them formed a hand-held circle and danced an Irish jig with Poteen barking at their flying heels. When they finally stopped, they were out of breath and laughing like crazy.

"What do you think of my new purchase?" Joseph asked proudly, pointing at the team and wagon. "Got the outfit in Mankato. Made a little extra wage at the mill. We can't be without a way to haul and travel. Can't lean on Rose and her family forever."

Examining the rig, Pim said, "Pair looks sturdy enough. Need to build a higher box for the wagon. How old the horses?"

"Horses are as old as the seller claims, Pim. No way to know for sure but their teeth say five or six. Bought the whole durn package at a livery in Mankato from Henri Cossette. Says he knows Rose and Ox and is related to the Rivards. Hearin' that I didn't think he'd be likely to cheat me. Already named the two horses, I have. Meet Pat and Mike."

They all hooted.

"They look grand to me, big brother. With the winter behind us and now a means of travel, I feel like a bird, free and chirpin'."

Ben and Ginny had seen the wagon enter the yard and came running as fast as Ginny's legs could bring them. She flew into Joseph's arms, and he swung her up and around. When he put her down, she gave him a big hug and kiss. "Can't be our little Ginny, can it? So tall. Prettier than Ginny, too."

"It's truly me, Uncle Joseph."

Ben stepped up and quick-embraced his brother. He looked him square on. "Seems awkward to be welcomin' you to your own home, brother."

By this time Maurna was crying. "First time we're all together since Harper's Ferry way over a year ago, 'cept for that day in Saint Paul last October and a few hours at Christmas. Joseph, you'll not recognize the house with what Ben's added and the furniture he's built."

Poteen led the way, warming to Joseph right away. Joseph held Ginny by the hand, and his other arm circled Pim's shoulder. "Remember how to unharness a team, do you, Pim? We'll have to add on to that shed to get 'em stalled proper. Would you mind tetherin' them to the shed posts. Give 'em a little slack and some water. We'll rub 'em down and feed 'em later on."

Pim turned to the task with a nod. The others watched him for a moment, then entered the house.

Joseph was pleased with the improvements since Christmas, and especially impressed with the trapdoor that could be bar-locked from the inside. He nodded his head in approval as Ben replaced the lid. "Fits so tight you'd never see it, if you didn't know. To make it even better hidden, we might ask Maurna to make a rope rug just a little bigger than the trapdoor, then nail it to the cover. Nobody'd ever know it's there, and the rug would make a handle to lift it up with. What do you think, Ben?"

"Good idea, Joseph. You must be well rested; you're thinkin' well."

"Ben, I'm proud of your work. I hardly recognize the place as the one I remember Rose and Ox showin' me. And it's so sparklin' clean." They moved out to the kitchen and Joseph added, "Maurna, you're a wonder. I honest to God feel I'm home for the first time since Cork. The four of you have done a beautiful piece of homemakin'!" As he choked up, he walked over to the window to hide his face. "Pim's comin' back in. Let's meet him and walk on up the hill. For six months I've been dreamin' about lookin' out over the valley from up there. When we see that view, I'll know I'm home for sure and for the rest of my life."

Nobody welcomes spring more than beleaguered Minnesotans. In late October through early November, the obvious signs of winter begin to appear, but the onset is gradual, and people are distracted by the preparations and feasting after harvest and at Christmas. In January they brace themselves for the onslaught, anticipate the worst, and often have their expectations met. About the middle of March nature teases with intermittent warm, balmy days that lift hopes and expectations and generate premature thoughts of spring. Disappointment invariably follows with renewal of heavy snows, cutting winds, depressing overcast and enervating cold. The capricious weather often spans mid-March and into April, lifting spirits one day, dashing them the next. To many it is the most exasperating period of the year.

But when spring arrives, glorious days bequeath a surge of energy, optimism, and joyful exuberance. Brilliant wild prairie flowers, budding trees and bushes, and thawing soil blend their aromas to perfume the gentle southern breezes. The frost sinks into the earth about the second week of April, and creeks and streams swell with the melt and rush to their widening mouths. Clouds, fleecy again, yield to the urgency and separate, allowing the sun to warm the land. Animals leap forth in renewed industry, digging, foraging, squealing, frolicking, procreating and building. Birds, new arrivals as well as hardy winterers, chirp and chorus joyful messages.

People's attitudes awaken, too. Camaraderie increases, torpor evaporates, and hibernators re-emerge. The elderly feel their bones thaw and their limbs move more fluidly, and children dash wildly in the open air. Everyone opens doors and windows and shuttered minds. Lovers of all ages experience the rush of exhilarated hearts. All savor the feelings of renewal. Minnesotans earn their springtime and gleefully collect their due.

Three with such exhilarated hearts were returning from Mankato after a Saturday excursion. They had spent the day with the Cossette twins, Lucie and Louise, and several of the girls' friends. Tony and Ox were smitten with the twins. When Ben asked Ox which of the two he preferred, Ox responded, "The one that Tony doesn't take." The two pretty young ladies were cousins of Carole Rivard, who had introduced them to Tony and Ox.

Tony was enthused. "What did I tell you, Ben. They're so pretty they ought to be outlawed. Always happy and laughing and oh, the sweet smell of 'em. Makes your nose tingle. Makes other parts tingle, too."

But the subject most on their minds was the news about the Confederates' shelling of Fort Sumter. They wondered whether more states would secede.

Ox was sure the South was determined to fight to the death. "That South Carolina got the whole South stirred up. They sure are a mouthy bunch."

"Let 'em go, I say," said Tony. "Who needs 'em? They need us more'n we need them. They want those darkies so's they have cheap workers. The green dollar's the main reason."

"They claim it's more than that," Ox responded. "Want nobody in Washington telling 'em what they can and can't do. Guess I can understand that feeling."

"They sure hate President Lincoln," commented Ben. "He walked into a polecat fight, didn't he? No way he can stop it."

Tony said, "My father heard an interesting bit of news last night. Seems that Governor Ramsey happened to be in Washington when Lincoln put out the call for troops. He rushed right over to the Secretary of War's office, met with the man and promised 1,000 Minnesotans to defend the union. Seems that Lieutenant-Governor Dennolly had already signed the order. Ramsey confirmed it and that made Minnesota the first state to pledge soldiers. Ramsey's real proud. 'Course you can bet he won't be one of the thousand."

They chuckled at that one, then Ox said, "Alex over at the feed store says we'll be fighting the South before it's settled."

Tony laughed. "That'll keep us out, Ox. We're lovers not fighters."

Joseph, Maurna, Rose, and Adrien Rivard had attended a preliminary session to inform everyone of the provisions of the new Homestead Act permitting individuals to claim up to 160 acres at a minimal charge per acre as long as they agreed to work the land and improve it over a five-year period.

On the ride home, the neighbors discussed the opportunity. Adrien, Joseph, and Rose had already decided to stake new claims. Rose said she intended to extend westward along the Cottonwood and maybe a piece on the north side of the river. Joseph favored a stretch along the river toward the Rivard property.

Adrien agreed. "I'll meet you there, Joseph. We'll close it off to anyone trying for a piece between us."

"Great," said Rose. "Adrien, you and I each have three sons and Joseph's got Ben, Pim, and Maurna here to consider."

"What an opportunity," Joseph crowed. "Can you believe it, Maurna? Told you this was the place to come."

Maurna smiled. "Five years is a long commitment, Joseph. Lot of things can change. Just look at the past five. Ireland to Virginia to here. Hard to know where five more'll bring us."

"Aw, Maurna, five years'll fly by. Besides if it doesn't work out, they can do no more than throw us off. We'll still have our own forty. But that won't happen. We'll make it work."

Adrien warned Joseph and Rose about claiming land on the north side of the Cottonwood. "I'd be cautious, I were you. The east boundary of the Sioux reservation isn't far from there and there's still argument with the Indians just where their treaty land begins. Might be you'd claim it, then lose it to the Indians."

"Guess you may be right, Adrien, might not be worth the risk at that," commented Rose.

Joseph got very heated on the subject of the Sioux. "Damn Indians got enough land all the way up to Big Stone Lake. How much do they need? They don't do anythin' with it anyway. Just sit on it and wait for the annuity money. They've got the best land now all along the river."

"Oh Joseph, be fair," said Maurna. "They have rights, too. The government already took their land north and east of the Minnesota and left them only that ten-mile strip. It's little enough, I'm thinkin'."

"Don't agree, little sister, they've no right to it if they don't use it."

"They do use it in their own way. Not our way maybe, but they've a right to use it the way they want. Let 'em be, Joseph. Besides, more and more of them are takin' to farmin' all along."

Rose laughed to ease the discomfort that was growing. "You two will never come together on that subject for sure. You're both right and wrong at the same time. I know we need to use the land, build it up, make opportunities for people. It'll help this part of the country prosper and bring in more people. But at the same time I think I understand the Indians when they say that we run off game, destroy the beauty, and push them out of the way. They were here a long time living with it the way it's been for hundreds of years. It's their home. Sure wouldn't like anybody pushing me out of my home. Would you, Joseph?"

"'Spose not, but it's not possible to destroy all this beauty. It'll be here forever."

"Hope you're right," sighed Rose.

They dropped off the Rivards and proceeded to the farm where Joseph asked Maurna and Rose to climb the hill with him. At the crown, they tried to see through the openings in the foliage where Joseph was pointing.

"A nice chunk along the river that's wooded, then south on the prairie towards the Rivard's. Good land. I've looked at it many times goin' into New Ulm. What do you think?"

Rose paused waiting for Maurna, then commented. "Seems a good choice Joseph." She turned to the west and led them over to that side. "Love that land across the river, but Adrien's right. Might lose it to the Indian claim."

Joseph spread his arms and extolled, "Look up that valley. Prettiest sight on God's earth. The whole white race couldn't destroy that beauty in a thousand years. Isn't just the Indians that love it."

Chapter Seven

Answering the Call

It had become ritual. Whenever a private conversation was in order, the involved parties climbed the hill. When Ben and Joseph sauntered off, their nonchalance did not fool Maurna. She watched them out of sight, then tried to put it out of her mind.

Ben's request for a private session had been no surprise to Joseph because Maurna had asked him whether he thought something was troubling Ben. He was not aware of a problem, but he, too, had noticed Ben's preoccupation. "Maybe the priesthood thing again or maybe he's fallen in love, Maurna, who knows?"

The brothers stood side by side as an awkward silence stretched. Ben's reluctance to begin was obvious. Joseph looked out over the river and ravines to the west and waited. Finally trying to ease the situation, he said, "Ben, might's well fire your rifle, it's sure primed and loaded."

Ben relaxed a little and sighed. "That obvious is it? Don't quite know how to begin, brother. Never easy to bring bad news, I guess."

Joseph turned to him and smiled. "Won't get any easier by waitin'. Just go ahead and pull the trigger." He turned his eyes back to the valley.

"Ox and Tony and I been talkin' and workin' up on somethin', Joseph. Last week we met and talked about the war out east. Talk led to action. We went to Fort Ridgely to see the regular army folks and try to get some answers. Lieutenant Ames told us Minnesota promised the government 1,000 men, and they'd be signin' up volunteers soon. Tony and Ox were ready to sign on right there and then. They've made up their minds to go, Joseph. Said they wouldn't miss it for anything."

While he waited for more, Joseph's mind spun. He considered the implications and thought of the family's needs. He put himself in Ben's position, knowing he wanted to go with his friends. What young man wouldn't? But he also knew Ben would feel guilty about leaving all the work of the farm to him and Pim. As difficult as it was, he knew the response he had to make.

Still facing west Joseph spoke very slowly. "Ben, we have to take circumstances as they lay out. Some duties conflict with others, and we're forced to choose. You have a duty to your family and to your country. I expect that young men all over America are havin' to sort out what they should do just 'cause some damn fools stirred up this secession business. Ben, you do what you think is right. Simple as that, but only you can decide it. We'll not starve to death without you. Pim's near bein' a man. He can step up. So what I'm tryin' to say is, do what your mind and heart and conscience tell you. Do what's right as you see it, but do it for the right reasons. What others think is their problem."

Ben absorbed the words for a moment, then said, "I'm feelin' ashamed that I was reluctant to speak with you. You're an amazin' man. You get riled up and feisty over little things, but on important matters, you're as solid as granite and wise as a coyote. Part of me says stay and help the family. Another part says go and be part of this big event. Might be the biggest one in my lifetime. Truth is, I want to go. Not even sure of all the reasons why, but the overall feelin' is to go. Most people say it won't last long, be over by end of summer. If that's true, better go early or not at all. We could be back by harvest or at worst by Christmas."

"Don't know that anybody can predict how long, Ben. That part will play itself out based on things people can't guess. That's not the important thing anyway. The right or wrong of it is what counts. That wisdom you talk about comes from our heritage, Ben. Use it when you make your decision. One other thing to remember. You've already done a hell of a lot to build up this place. Just know that we won't think you're lettin' us down. Hell, Ben, I'd like to go myself if I was free to."

"Joseph, it means a lot to me your takin' it this way. I'll never forget you for it. Part of my wantin' to go is for the adventure of it I s'pose. But also to go with Ox and Tony. I don't want to someday be regrettin' havin' missed it. It's excitin' thinkin' about it. That must be part of the Irish heritage, too."

"Truly it is, Ben. It also offers an escape from the dullness and monotony of everyday livin' and postpones other decisions you have to make at your age. You see it as an adventure with the crowds cheerin' and the bands playin' and the ladies throwin' kisses. Excitin' to think of the places you'll be seein' and the people you'll be meetin'. It'll be all that, Ben, but it'll also be other things, if it comes to true warfare. There'll be times you'll wish to God you'd never seen the army. But, still and all, if you survive it whole, there'll come a day when you'll be glad and proud that you were part of it. I envy you. I truly do."

"I understand what you're sayin', Joseph. Funny it is that the excitin' parts submerge the miserable ones in our thinkin'. My heart says go, and seems to be overrulin' my head. Bothers me, too, that you're back only a month and we're splittin' up again. Maybe when we get this war over and done, we'll have some years to make up for it. I'll still contribute what I can from my pay and send it on home to help out. We get $11.00 every month. Wouldn't know how to spend that much on myself."

"You know that our best goes with you, Ben. You and Ox and Tony look out for each other. You'll need your friends, and they'll need you to make it through. Now let's get back down to the real reckonin', the hardest part you've yet to do. You have to tell Maurna. Don't envy you that. I'm a coward; I'll be out in the shed."

"Don't blame you for missin' that."

Maurna saw them descending the hill, two solemn faces, set in the Murnane rigidity. Her heart suddenly felt heavy.

She was a great white ghost, an enormous wide-beamed lady. Her name was *Fannie Harris*. When seen on the broad Mississippi she was unremarkable, but emerging from the misty dawn on the upper Minnesota, she appeared monstrous. She looked like an elephant in a wash tub, uncomfortable and out of place. Bells clanging, whistles tooting, the 200-foot stern-wheeler rode high on the flooded waterway apparently seeking tie up at New Ulm. She'd had a hard journey, been ripped by overhangs and bounced off narrow banks and rocky bends. Her gingerbread decorations had been rudely ripped off, except for a remnant dangling from the upper deck molding. One stack had been sheared off, the other tilted thirty degrees. A major portion of the forward upper deck had been wrenched away as if by a giant's grasp, and the bow cabin was gouged open to the elements. The vessel looked as if it had survived damaging hits from an enemy battery. *Fannie*'s cosmetics were rudely smeared, but she proudly went forward to meet the challenge.

The mission was critical. The U.S. Government was prepared to pay for all damages to the vessel as it traversed the flooded, twisting Minnesota River to reach Fort Ridgely where it was to load the Sherman Battery of Light Artillery for transport to LaCrosse, Wisconsin. From LaCrosse, the Battery would be carried by rail to Washington, D.C., to aid in the defense of the threatened Capitol.

At the landing in New Ulm, the crowds grew at the news of the river giant's appearance. People streamed from their homes, businesses, schools, and nearby farms. Indians and settlers swarmed to the river banks to view the spectacle. No vessel like *Fannie* had ever been that far upstream, and the excitement built into a festive event.

As the craft approached New Ulm, she paused as if unsure of her welcome. A frantic conference was conducted on the damaged bridge. Bells rang out and the *Fannie Harris* began to back away toward midstream. A huge groan from the gathered crowd generated a gesture from the captain, who thrust his hand forward upriver. Shouts rang out from among the crowd. "She's heading for the fort." "To Ridgely." "She'll tie up by the fort."

The throng disentangled and ran for any available conveyance to follow upstream. They were drawn to the unprecedented occasion like iron filings to a magnet.

Twelve miles farther on, the *Fannie Harris* tied up below Fort Ridgely. Loading the battery began immediately under the combined direction of its commander, Captain John Pemberton, and Captain William Faucette of the steamboat. The complex operation consisted of maneuvering mule-drawn wagons down a precipitous slope to the landing and across heavy planks onto the vessel. Cannon, caissons, battery wagons, ammunition stores, and horses were loaded by soldiers and the boat crew working at a frantic pace through the afternoon, into the evening, and through the night. The night work was lighted by lanterns, torches, and bonfires.

The entire operation was witnessed by a mix of interested spectators. Approximately 800 Indians ensconced themselves on the prairie plateau near the fort. Most of the eighty resident employees of the Redwood Agency and the agency missionaries sat in a group. Over 1,000 settlers including residents of New Ulm, Milford, and settlements along Birch Coulee and Beaver Creek congregated on both sides of the river to observe, speculate, eat and drink and wonder.

The removal of the battery of six-pound cannon caused concern among those aware of the growing discontent among the Sioux. Inquiries were made to ascertain what military force would remain at Fort Ridgely after the big guns were gone. Rumors spread that 100 soldiers and a few cannon would stay.

The watchful Sioux comments were limited to low mutterings and guarded discussions. The chiefs were each surrounded by adherents but were not observed communicating with one another. Consensus might ensue, but only after a great amount of posturing and debate. Undoubtedly the impetuous young braves looked upon the departure of government firepower as highly significant.

The fully loaded *Fannie Harris* blew her whistle several times and backed away. The remaining four cannon saluted her with a series of loud booms. The throng cheered lustily as the stern-wheeler turned in the treacherous current, faced downstream, and eased into her return trip. She was riding low under the weight of the battery but appeared to be well balanced and controllable.

Ahead was Saint Paul and then LaCrosse, more than 400 treacherous river miles, four days of hard steaming. She was part of the new war effort and moved out proudly to do her duty. The critical Sherman Battery would arrive in Washington, D.C., eight days later and play an integral role in the Battle of Bull Run. The beleaguered *Fannie Harris* would go into drydock repair at LaCrosse, recover from her ordeal, and bring her owners $8,000.00 in gold as payment for the unprecedented run to Fort Ridgely and back. Her epic journey was a once-in-a-lifetime experience for her crew and the spectators. The distant, embryonic War Between the States was brought closer to Minnesotans by the historic *Fannie Harris* run. For the first time, they felt directly involved.

Tony, Ox, Ben, and René Rivard were ready to leave for Fort Snelling. More exhilarated than apprehensive, they were anxious to be a part of an event they could only imagine. Young men north and south were charged with a surge of energy and resolve that they were unable to comprehend, let alone attempt to articulate. It was an irresistible movement, built and fed by rabble rousers, abolitionists, pro-slavers, unionists and states rightists, newspaper editors, and ordinary patriots. The young men of the Minnesota Valley were caught up in the fervor. Slavery and states' rights and other reasons were to most of them vague concepts. To take part in a unique adventure was reason enough.

Twelve additional recruits would set out with them on wagons for Mankato to board the packet to Fort Snelling and formal enlistment for ninety days. They hoped to become members of the Minnesota First Regiment but had been told that if the 960-man First was filled, they would help form the next regiment. Their training would begin at Fort Snelling.

Rose and Will accompanied Ox to pick up Maurna and Ben for the ride into New Ulm. Joseph, Pim, and Ginny said their good-byes at the front porch where Joseph reassured Ben that all would be well until he returned. Joseph and Pim shook Ben's hand, and Ginny gave him a tearful hug and kiss.

Belle Lunde insisted on providing the boys their last home-cooked meal. Ansgar poured a touch of wine and made a toast, "If I were young enough, I'd be going with you." The dinner took longer than planned and forced them to run for the wagons parked in front of the Dakota Hotel. Belle pulled Ox and Ben aside at the last moment after Tony had already hopped aboard.

She turned her back to the wagon and spoke directly to Ox. "Ox, you've pulled Tony out of many scrapes. You know how impulsive he can be. I'm asking you to please watch over him. You and Ben have good heads and calm temperaments. I'll be grateful forever. And take care of yourselves and each other." She broke away and stood in the background with the other ladies to watch the wagons away.

There were shouts of "Be sure to write" and "Keep your heads down" and "Give those Rebs what they got coming" and "Good luck" and "God speed" as the wagons followed the blaring German band down the main street to the bridge over the Cottonwood. The people lined both sides, applauding and tossing flowers. Many women wept, but the men stood proudly. Children chased until their parents ran to drag them back.

All of them needed the comfort of good friends. Gathered at the Lundes, not much was said for several minutes. Belle served tea. Handkerchiefs were in heavy use, and eyes were downcast.

Belle finally whispered, "They're so young and full of life and so unaware of what they'll be facing. And Tony is such a rascal. Always leaping before he looks. Since a baby, he's been like that. I fear for him so. For all of them." She broke down and covered her face with her kerchief.

Rose sought to lift the gloom. "Belle, we raised those boys right and true. Have faith in them. Two kinds of faith. One in God that he'll watch over all of them. Two, faith in what we put in them. What's there will come out. They're good young men, and not fools. They'll take care of each other. You'll see."

Bernadette Rivard agreed. "Rose is absolutely right, Belle. They're not little boys any more. Sure they're country lads without much worldly experience, but they've been gorged with common sense. Those boys'll do fine."

Maurna asked, "Ansgar, how long do you think before they'll be back?"

"Hard to say. Some say weeks, some others think months or years. Hard to say." He looked out over the garden area and spoke in a low monotone. "One thing I do know, if it lasts more than a few weeks and comes to real battles, they'll become men in a hurry. The naive fellows you waved off this morning will see things that'll change them for life. They'll see places and parts of the country that will open their eyes to possibilities that would have never occurred to them. They'll meet people of all kinds, many like they've never met before. The experience will stretch their knowledge and open their minds. What they've been taught will be compared with the standards of others, and their principles and morals will be tested. It will pass before their eyes so fast they'll have little time to absorb it and sort it out. War is a lifetime education in a short time and is for better or worse even more than marriage is. They'll come back harder or softer, kinder or more harsh, with stronger or weaker faith, with more or less ambition, with greater or less love for their fellow man. Only one idea that's for sure, they won't ever be the same."

By the time the New Ulm area recruits arrived at Fort Snelling, rumors were floating freely. Some had foundation, but most did not. They were going to Washington within three days. They'd ride the river to Saint Louis, then capture Memphis and New Orleans. They were all going into the cavalry. The rumor they most feared was that Minnesota recruits would be assigned to home-state duty to replace regular army troops at local forts. The men complained that they didn't enlist to stay home. They wanted to go where the fighting would be and that "sure wasn't going to be Minnesota."

    Meanwhile, the training was ongoing and constant. Drills, marching, calesthenics, musket firing, cleaning weapons, guard duty, mess duty, cleaning barracks and grounds. Drill, drill, drill.

He was the regimental drill sergeant. His name was Leroy "Sarge" McMahon, a thirty-six-year-old lumberman son of a lumberman father, born in the woods of Maine. As a child he had performed odd jobs around the lumbercamp and, by age fourteen, had become a full-paid lumberman. The only body fat he carried was in a small pot protruding over his belt. Six feet and two inches of bulging muscle, he had thinning brown hair, and one ear that sagged a bit lower than it's counterpart. Ice blue eyes, a jutting chin, and a nose that had encountered a hard object conveyed formidable pugnacity.

    Shortly after his tour of duty in the Mexican War, McMahon had been asked by his employer in Maine to transfer to Minnesota to take on the task of training local, fledgling lumbermen. He had married a pretty half-Chippewa maiden and settled in a cabin he built by hand on the rocky banks of the Saint Croix River just south of Taylors Falls. He dearly loved straight whiskey, hunting and fishing, his two daughters, his wife, and orderly ranks in the recruits he drilled. Tough as jerked beef, he browbeat his troops, drilled them in the hottest part of the day, in rain storms, before dawn and at midnight. "Battles aren't all fought on nice days between ten and two in the afternoon, don't you know? Huh? Huh?"

He had been elected sergeant because of his distinguished experience in the Mexican war as an eighteen-year-old infantryman. He had only one comment about his military career. "I either did things right or I was damn lucky. To survive, you better have one or the other. Havin' both is best."

When McMahon got his first look at the New Ulmers, he leered and shook his head. "My Gawd. I didn't think those rebels had a chance in hell to win this war 'til I saw this bunch. How in Gawd's name can any mortal man be expected to make sojers out of this scraggly bunch? Huh? Huh?"

They were marched countless miles within and around the Fort Snelling compound. The recruits feared him, worked their arses off for him, and learned from him. He told them he had only two goals. "One, to kill enemy sojers. Two, to save as many of your arses as we can while doin' number one."

Tony, Ox, Ben, and René stuck together like motherless cubs. They had been told they would be kept in the First Regiment, but not necessarily in the same company. Full strength would constitute around 1,000 men with subdivisions by company, squad, and special units such as artillery and commissary. All of them opted to stay in the infantry to enhance their chances to remain together.

Two other recruits gravitated to their foursome. Will, the tall, lean, slow-moving son of a widow school teacher from Red Wing, told them that he joined up to "get away from Ma and all the other women plaguing me. They just can't leave me alone and I don't know why. I know I'm handsome, intelligent, and well-born, plus I'm experienced at makin' them happy, but you wouldn't think that'd be enough to cause them to throw themselves at my feet the way they do."

His slightly hooked nose, thick black unruly hair, broad forehead, squinty, close-set gray eyes, and languid frame didn't add up to handsome, but his manner was fresh, and he was full of fun. When his full name was read at muster with all the slow deliberate sarcasm Sarge McMahon could generate, the whole company fell down laughing. Sarge strung out all seven syllables as long as he could. "William Shakespeare Cosgrove." He became "Shakey" for the rest of his service.

Sarge had a good time with other names. He called the three New Ulmers Oskar KooKoo Ree, Thunder Thor Lunde, and Insane Murnane. And then he called the name of his clerk, Parker Wordsworth Henderson, an overweight, soft-muscled, eighteen-year-old from a settlement of Swedes near Lindstrom. The lad was five feet six, narrow of shoulder and broad of hip with a rather prominent posterior. When Sarge remarked that Henderson reminded him of a pudgy woodchuck, he became "Pudge" from that moment on. Sarge made him clerk because he was bright, could handle numbers, and could read and write. It was never mentioned, but Sarge had never been observed either reading or writing.

Camaraderie grew and cemented during the rigorous training. The State of Minnesota conferred upon members of the regiment black, loose-fitting pantaloons, red flannel shirts, and floppy black felt hats. Many recruits had brought their own rifles, a few had pistols, and most carried a knife affixed to their belt. Only the officers were permitted sabres or long swords.

Washington requested that the First Minnesota up its enlistment period from ninety days to three full years. Three months was considered sufficient at the outset, but second thoughts about the defiance of the Confederacy precipitated the request. The change caused many recruits to reassess.

At parade the next morning the men were called by name. They had been instructed that a "yea" response volunteered the individual for three years with papers to be signed later. A "no" response was tantamount to an automatic discharge. After discussing the matter thoroughly the night before, Ox, Tony, and Ben responded with resounding "yeas." Crestfallen René declined, saying his father would never forgive him if he were away from the family work that long. He left for home humbled and deflated.

Ox, Tony, Ben, and their new friend, Shakey Cosgrove, replaced four men from Company F, the Red Wing Volunteers under Captain William Colville. While they were awaiting official acceptance, the Company F sergeant asked them why they had chosen the Red Wing company. Ox replied, "We want a company with enough openings so we can stay together." The sergeant responded to that by saying, "We Red Winger's are a bunch of river rats that know how to fight." Tony laughed and said, "We're three river rats, too. Just a different river is all." Cosgrove said his reason was simple, "I'm from Red Wing myself." The acceptance of the four into Company F became official on May 23.

Chapter Eight

Whisps of Smoke

Indian Agent Galbraith requested a council meeting with the Mdewakanton Sioux at the Redwood Agency. With the venerable Chief Red Owl as their spokesman, over one hundred braves attended. Governor Ramsey had agreed to accompany Galbraith to show the Indians that the State of Minnesota was concerned about their situation.

Ramsey opened the proceedings with a brief speech. "I come here representing the good citizens of the State of Minnesota to speak with the people of the great Dakotah Nation and to bring you greetings from our people. I come to give the Dakotah the assurance that the terms of all treaties with the federal and state government will be honored. We want eternal peace with your great nation and to live in harmony forever with our good neighbors, the Sioux. The Mdewakanton tribe of the Dakotah are leaders among all the Sioux and have great influence with all other tribes. We look to you to show good faith with us and for you, also, to honor your promises under the terms of the treaties. Agent Thomas Galbraith is a good and hard working man who will be fair and work with you to resolve any problems that arise. He is very interested in justice for the Dakotah people and in bringing you satisfaction in your business with the government. He will distribute among you the annuities monies that come from the White Father in Washington. The newly chosen White Father, Mr. Lincoln, though busy with a big war, has not forgotten the Dakotah. The monies promised you under the treaty will be enough for all of you to feed your families and to help you become self-reliant by learning white man's ways of living. We look forward to growing brotherhood with the people of the great Dakotah nation."

When he was certain that Governor Ramsey had completed his address, Chief Red Owl rose and began his response in a cracking voice that betrayed his advancing years and declining health but left no doubt about his conviction. He reached back for reserves of strength to speak firmly. "The Mdewakanton are pleased with the words of Governor Ramsey and the best wishes of the people of Minnesota. The words show respect for the Sioux . . . but the actions of the government are not respectful, only the words."

The old chief proceeded to vehemently harangue the governor and agent. During his long speech the audience of Indians displayed approval by nodding and uttering supportive sounds.

Chief Red Owl listed grievances compiled through the spring months, including complaints about the management of the Redwood Agency and alleged violations in the distribution of treaty payments. He accused many of the traders of dishonesty and thievery. The chief addressed Agent Galbraith directly, indicting him for causing dangerous dissention among the Sioux by pushing too hard and too fast the policy of converting to white men's ways. Agent Galbraith and Governor Ramsey were left with no doubts about consensus among the Mdewakantons regarding their complaints.

Chief Red Owl further charged that serious treaty violations had occurred when white settlers cut timber and hay, planted crops, and squatted on reservation lands to the east of Redwood. "The Great Father in Washington has plenty of land elsewhere which he can give to these whites," he declared in a rising voice. "We demand that they stay off our land as the treaty promises. The Sioux want no whites to settle on Indian reservation lands. These whites give whiskey to our young braves who kill cows and other livestock. The government then pays the people who lose animals out of Sioux annuity. Not fair! Must stop! Also white farmers on other side of river are in the path of braves who wish to go to Big Woods to hunt. Trouble will come if whites interfere with hunters." He folded his arms, signalling that he was finished speaking.

The meeting concluded with no substantive issues resolved. Agent Galbraith assured the attendees that he would investigate the complaints and speak with them later about solutions. The Indians filed out, obviously not pleased with the results.

"Time is on our side, Governor," reminded Galbraith, "in a few weeks food will become more available from early harvests and ripening berries. By August when the wild rice and corn are ripe, their bellies will be full again and they'll settle down. We have until next spring to make more progress with the farmer program, and then we will have the June annuities as incentive. The President and Congress have more to worry about than a few Indians. Their problems will have to take a back seat to preserving the union and punishing the rebel states."

Ramsey responded. "Much of what you say is true, but it is important to keep the Indians from causing trouble. We can't have adverse publicity. Fear of the Indians is endemic among easterners considering moving to the state. More myth than reality as you and I know, but nonetheless sufficient to dissuade many of them if unpleasant incidents occur. It is imperative that we keep the braves under control."

"I agree, Governor, but it will be a juggling act. I will give them enough to keep them from any organized effort. In the meanwhile I will continue to promote the benefits of conversion. Many prominent chiefs are converted or considering it."

"I'm not so sure the conversion policy is workable or even a good solution over time, Galbraith. I know on the surface it appears beneficial but looking down the long road, I'm not so sure. The Sioux lands under treaty are valuable if owned and developed by whites. They will fill the state's coffers and build the business climate. We gave the Sioux some of the most fertile country in the state. Should have moved them farther out and away. Some day they will have to give up those lands. Too valuable for them to keep. Obviously I don't want to be quoted, but just keep it in mind. By the way, Tom, I need your assistance on another matter. The First Minnesota lads are training at Fort Snelling for transfer to the east and as you know I have promised the Secretary of War several additional regiments. I want you to assist me in recruiting young men from this area to fill up those rosters."

"I have already begun, Governor. We are in the process of forming a group called the Renville Rangers that will be given cursory training and then sent on to Fort Snelling for official enlistment. The war is without question our highest priority."

"Excellent. I'm most encouraged. I would like to have another discussion with you in the fall. The Indian concerns will be minimal by then, and we can give our full attention to the war."

"I am confident that the worst is behind us, sir. The Sioux are like unruly children who merely have to be slapped down from time to time. They'll simmer down. Don't worry."

The two officials shook hands, feeling good about the mature, businesslike way they had managed an awkward meeting.

Later on the packet, Ramsey asked James Seymour for his impressions. Seymour, Ramsey's long time aide and counsellor, who in private spoke as an equal with the governor, was a man of perception and good judgment. "Alex," he responded, "I watched those Indians closely during the whole session and I saw genuine conviction. I've heard they have serious divisions within the tribe, but I'm not so sure after this morning. I'd dearly love to hear what they are saying to each other. It's hard to know where their boiling point lies. They are convinced they have been wronged. Frankly, I'm uneasy. I don't trust the situation. Galbraith referred to them as children. Well, maybe. But they are children well versed in the use of weapons, and their eyes told me they wouldn't hesitate to use them."

Chapter Nine

Running of the Bulls

A courier arrived at the fort at 10:00 P.M. to relay the orders from Governor Ramsey to Colonel Gorman. A few moments later the troops were startled by a roar from headquarters and the sight of their officers laughing and hugging one another. They soon learned that a message from Washington had ordered the entire regiment to report there immediately. They were going to the war in the east to defend the nation's capital.

Preparation sped up. The news spread fast throughout the state. Food, gifts of blankets, knives, bibles, and hundreds of pairs of socks were sent from every hamlet.

The steamers *War Eagle* and *Northern Belle* were at the landing below the fort at sunup to board the troops, who were barely settled when they docked and disembarked at the upper landing at Saint Paul. They displayed their newly-honed marching skills to the thousands who lined the streets. Tony told Ben that there'd never been that many pretty girls in one place before in the history of the state. A band led their march through town and down to the lower landing where they quickly reboarded. The music was deafening, handkerchiefs waved, tears welled, and the Minnesotans were off to the wars.

Trains from LaCrosse and Prairie du Chien carried them to Chicago where enormous crowds cheered every step of their march to another station to reboard for the trip through Pittsburgh to Harrisburg, Pennsylvania. Through Illinois, Indiana, Ohio, and Pennsylvania, every whistle stop displayed mobs of bombastic well-wishers. The soldiers' importance in their own eyes grew by the moment. "Let us at those Southerners," Shakey shouted. "With people behind us like this, there's no way we can be beat. War'll be over before you know it."

Orders awaited them in Harrisburg to proceed directly to Washington where they arrived on the evening of June 26, to another rousing welcome. The First Minnesota briefly encamped on Capitol Hill until their removal to a bivouac just outside Alexandria, Virginia. Each was issued a Springfield rifle and training was recommenced. After all, the Confederates were only a few miles away out there in the Virginny Hills.

Ben commented that he could hardly believe he was back in the state of Virginia after only one year. He told his friends Shakey and Pudge, "I have a little niece who was named Virginia because she was born here." Shakey thought for just a moment and said, "Golly, Ben, she's sure lucky she wasn't born in Massachusetts."

Sensing that their first battle was imminent, McMahon felt it was time for a fervorino. Near sundown he gathered companies "F" and "G," put them at ease, and told them to sit on the grass and "listen good." Lieutenant Spencer looked on in approval. Sarge looked over the group of just under 200 raw, young soldiers and knew it would be his last look at some of the upturned faces. "Not a one of you has been in a fight like you're gonna see. You been trainin' and drillin' and learnin' to be sojers for 'bout six weeks and you're a sight better'n when you first come, but no way are you ready. No way anybody can get you ready for the first time somebody starts shootin' at you. No more band music and wavin' ladies and puffed up big talk. All a sudden your hide's on the line and the hides of your friends. Shells blastin', minié balls whistlin', smoke, screamin', confusion, and blood. Blood, boys, maybe your own. It ain't pretty to see. No tellin' how any one of you will act when it starts. I've seen the toughest talkin' men fold up and try to hide or run. I've seen sojers scared-to-death goin' in, stand up and battle like they've been doin' it all their lives. You can talk big and tell yourself what you'll do, but you just don't know. Believe me, you don't."

He paused and strode back and forth. Close to 400 eyes were concentrated on him, not a sound could be heard. Lieutenant Spencer, as inexperienced as the troops, was hanging on Sarge's every word. Sarge stopped, put his hands on his hips and began again.

"Your best bet is to try to remember what we've taught ya. Your trainin' is the best thing you've got on your side. You been bitchin' and moanin' 'bout all the drillin' and marchin' and shootin', but now's when all that takes on some meanin'. Discipline is the sign of a good unit. Army preaches discipline all the time. Ya get sick of hearin' the word. But when the iron starts flyin', it's the one thing makes a sojer. Yer feet may want to run, but yer head has to stay in charge. Unit discipline saves lives and whips the enemy. But unit discipline comes down to each sojer's self-discipline. Each man is responsible for his own arse, but he's also responsible to those around him. If one man cuts and runs, he puts those around him in more danger. So remember. When the fur is flyin', you stand your ground 'til ya hear an order to move. If each sojer stands up to it, then the whole unit does, and maybe the whole Union line. One break in the chain weakens the whole line. Don't be the weak link. Depend on yer trainin, yer officers, and each other. Simple as that. Discipline."

Sarge let his message sink in for a moment, then asked, "Any questions?"

A voice came from the rear rank. "Sarge, you think the Reb's'll break?"

Sarge liked the question. "Those Rebs are just the same as you and me. They been trainin' and waitin' and talkin' 'bout how they're gonna run us like stampedin' cows. But lemme tell you somethin', they're just as full of doubts as you. Most of 'em ain't never fought a battle neither. Their women sent 'em off to war same as ours did, people cheerin' all along the way, but that cheerin' don't help much when the artillery starts boomin' and the grape shot starts churnin'. No answer to yer question, Private Lawson, except to say those Rebs are the same as us. 'Til it starts, they got no idea what'll happen."

"More of us than them, ain't there Sarge?"

Sarge thought that one over. "Don't know that anybody can tell us who's got more. But I can tell you this, more don't always count for winnin'. Mexicans had us outnumbered lots of times, but we won 'cause we had two big advantages. We had better discipline and better leaders. Officers may be a pain in the arse sometimes, pardon me, Lieutenant, but their plannin' and maneuverin' with their troops can make a real difference. Seen it many times. Good officerin' really helps win."

"McDowell know what he's doin' you think, Sarge?"

"Must know or he wouldn't have the job. Whether he's as good as Beauregard, we'll soon find out. Ain't only the top officer that makes the difference though. Once the battle starts, those under him have the field. Decisions made all the way down through the majors and captains and lieutenants and even sergeants count high. One or two bad decisions by any of 'em can change things fast. Ain't just McDowell, it's all of 'em. And remember this. Those officers are only as good as their decisions and the way their troops take orders and do their jobs. Small as you think your part is, don't let it be the one that fails. Now, before we break up, ya been hearin' rumors just like me. There's been two skirmishes, one at Blackburn's Ford and the other at Mitchell's Ford over that little stream called Bull Run. We're just a few miles from the Reb army. Just a matter of time 'fore we gotta test each other, see who's better. So get yerselves ready. And 'member what I said. Discipline, hold yer ground for those around ya and fer yerself. Ya do that and the whole army will do good. Comin' soon now. When it does, good luck to ya."

They were dismissed and broke up into small groups around fires. They remained subdued, most of them thinking about what Sarge had said. Shakey broke the near silence with a statement that more or less said what each was thinking. "You know, that old McMahon's been stomping our rear ends something fierce, but maybe he's been doing us a favor, getting us prepared like."

Ox agreed. "He's been hard on us, but I think he takes some pride in what he's been able to get us to do. Remember back at Snelling when he told us he had only two reasons for working us hard? Kill the enemy and save our hides. Think he means it, don't you?"

"Yep," said Shakey.

"Gotta listen to somebody that's been there. Crazy not to," Tony commented.

"Sure sounds like it's goin' to be soon. We'll know a lot more once we've had a taste of it," said Ben. "Better sleep on it, may have nightmares afterwards."

"You dream the way you choose, Murnane. I've got my own dreams to keep me warm," laughed Lunde.

At dawn, Union artillery fired the first rounds. The First Minnesota was positioned to the left of the New York Zouaves and their red flannel shirts made them appear to be part of the red-uniformed New York unit. After the initial charge, the whole line came to an abrupt halt. Colonel Gorman screamed an order calling to the regiment to quick march behind the Zouaves to their right to extend the flank. As they cleared the New Yorkers, they were greeted by Rebel artillery positioned behind a wooded patch, 200 yards to their front. During that march across the front of the enemy, the Minnesotans were cut up by shells zeroed in on their line of march. Two men from Winona were blown to pieces in front of Ox, who stepped around the crater and kept going. Ben, Tony, and Shakey sprinted past the carnage and kept double timing with the line. Once positioned, they knelt to fire a unit volley into the woods. The shielded Rebel infantry returned the fire into the flattened-down, but exposed Minnesotans. A few men broke, then more, then half a company. The Rebs were coming at them out of the woods, and the New Yorkers on their left were already gone. The whole regiment sprinted back about 200 yards over the low crest of a hill where Lieutenant Messick rallied them. Formed on line, they crashed a volley into the Rebs as they charged over the crest. From then on they fired, fell back, fired, fell back, and kept reasonable order. The Rebs closed with them in hand to hand fighting on two occasions. Those in the confines of their own little part of the battle had no way of knowing that the Union advance all along the line had taken a huge chunk of ground, been repulsed, fallen back, and was now in full retreat.

The First Minnesota fell back nearly to Centerville where the Rebel pressure eased, and they were able to regroup under Colonel Gorman and await orders. They knew they hadn't won, but they had no idea yet that the rout was total. They received orders to proceed to Alexandria to set up defensive positions. The survivors marched with mixed feelings. They didn't think they had done too badly considering their position, but they didn't like being part of a defeated army. And they had seen lots of Minnesotans fall. Sarge had been right. Blood. A friend's blood. Not your own, this time. But blood spilled. Men wounded and dead. The war had indeed begun.

That night they sat around the fire sucking boiled coffee that tasted bitter. Sarge joined them. They hadn't talked much before he came, but joined in after he opened it up.

"We got whipped pretty bad, boys. We got outsmarted and then whipped. Told you about leadership. Theirs was smarter than ours this day, 'cept for one bad decision they made toward the end of it. They had us if they'd kept on comin'. Might a had Washington, the way we was split up and wanderin' around. They got cut up, too, but they shoulda come on. Hope they live to regret it."

"Where are they now, Sarge, anybody know?" asked Ben.

"They fell back. Seems they're content to just brag and talk like they won the war. I got a feelin' they'll eat those words one day. But, they fought good, better'n we did."

"Don't like losing, Sarge, we should have done better. Can't blame it all on McDowell. Just like you said. A few run, the others follow." said Shakey.

"If ya don' like losin', Cosgrove, then the best cure is to not lose next time. Minnesota boys did all right considerin'. Better'n most, I'll say that. Damn fool officers got us caught out there without cover. Lot of good men went down. Stupid! Fallin' back was all we could do when New York folded up. Went back with good order, though. Good discipline after the

Lieutenant stopped those first runners. Discipline of that retreat saved lives, it did. We'll do better next time."

"How 'bout casualties, Sergeant McMahon?" asked Pudge who had remained behind the lines and felt left out.

"First Regiment reports are forty-seven killed, 107 wounded, thirty-four missing out of the whole regiment. Those numbers may change. Just preliminary. Too damn many, but considerin' where they put us, lucky it wasn't more."

Tony tried to relieve the feeling of loss a little. "Rebs lost a lot of men, too, didn't they, Sarge?"

"Hell of a lot. Probably as many as we did. Both sides got beat up pretty bad. Lot of casualties for nothing really gained." Ox was staring straight ahead, still shaken. He hadn't spoken until now. "I can see his face. He was coming right at me with his bayonet. I fired from the hip, didn't have time to even aim right. His face just disappeared in blood and bone. Jesus, God in heaven, I'll see that boy's face 'til my grave."

"Him or you, Ox. Regret it if you like, but you're here and he ain't," encouraged the Sarge. "Nobody can hurt that boy none now, Ox. His war's over."

Unfortunately their war wasn't over. The Union army fell back around Washington to regroup and to defend the capital. The Confederates encamped near Warrenton, Virginia. The two armies had enough of each other for a while.

Chapter Ten

Camp Stone, Maryland

President Lincoln was justifiably concerned about the potential danger to Washington. He immediately cashiered General McDowell and appointed George McClellan, a thirty-four-year-old West Point graduate who had achieved recent successes in minor battles in western Virginia. General McClellan impressed nearly everyone with his organizational skills, and the troops under his command appreciated his attention to their needs. In a few weeks, the new Commander established a "picket fence" of defensive strongholds around Washington, improved supply services, demanded incessant drilling of the troops, and remade the army into a legitimate fighting force. With pay in their pockets, fresh uniforms, and weapons and supplies at their disposal, the Union soldiers regained their confidence to take on those "bragging Rebels" again.

One of the "pickets" in the fence around Washington was a Union force placed in defensive position a few miles from Edward's Ferry, thirty miles upstream on the Potomac River. Regiments from Massachusetts, New York and Minnesota comprised Camp Stone's Division. Confederates were established just across the Potomac near the town of Leesburg, Virginia.

The two forces engaged in minor skirmishing and nuisance sniper activity but in the main drilled, prepared and waited. The Minnesota boys settled into their new surroundings with renewed hope and purpose. The countryside was lush, the climate delightful, and the locals were generally supportive of the cause. Their food, supplemented by fresh fruit and vegetables, was satisfactory and enhanced by delicacies sold by sutlers assigned to the camp. Military duties were light and passes were made readily available for visits to Rockville and Washington.

Ox, Tony, and Pudge were free on a twenty-four hour pass. Sightseeing in Washington, they sauntered around in the area of Willard's Hotel. Soldiers were everywhere, in and around the taverns, small groups strolling, a few with women on their arms. The streets were alive with a mix of types. Staggering drunks, businessmen, the prominent and the wealthy, loose women on parade, ruffians, thieves, and far too few policemen. Nearly every narrow lane leading off the main avenues offered lively dice games that the beleaguered police tolerated unless violence ensued.

It was by chance that the three Minnesotans happened along just at dusk. Hearing deep groans, loud cursing, and thudding sounds emanating from a semi-dark alley as they passed, they investigated. Barely visible a few yards into the shadows appeared five men clubbing a soldier slumped against the wall. One was kicking the victim in the ribs when Ox rushed at the attackers and shouted at them. "Get away from that soldier!" Tony and Pudge had no choice but to follow their impetuous friend. The muggers stood their ground and turned their attention to the onrushing Ox as their victim slid noiselessly to the mud in the lane.

Ox plunged into the five with Tony and Pudge in close support. The thugs gave, as well as took, heavy blows until the sound of a shrill policeman's whistle near the entrance to the alley put them to flight. Wearing a few minor bruises, the three Minnesota soldiers caught their breath as the two policemen came up.

"See here, what's the trouble? You boys raising a ruckus? Who were those men who ran off? Disturbing the peace you are? We'll have to take you in!"

Ox protested. "The peace was well disturbed long before we got here, sir. We was trying to stop those folks from beating on this soldier here. Had him five against one, kicking him when he was already bad beat."

The officer turned his attention to the prone, motionless victim, face down in the mud. He checked the pulse, then rolled him over onto his back. "Soldier boy. Head's cut. Took some hard blows. Let's drag him out where there's some light."

They helped the officers carry the dead-weight soldier to the end of the lane where the light from the street lamp revealed the bloody, pulverized face. Pudge spoke first in disbelief. "My God, it's Sarge, Ox."

Their sergeant was in bad shape. Eyes puffed closed, head wounds dripping blood down his neck and under the collar of his torn shirt, mouth swollen and bleeding. One policeman pressed near the wounds to staunch the flow as the other dashed off shouting about getting an ambulance.

Tony was still shaking. "They might have killed him, Ox. Good thing you rushed at 'em. They hurt him bad as it was. Wonder what he did to get the bastards after him like that. Nobody deserves what they was doing to him."

Sarge began to moan. His head rolled from side to side, until the policeman reached down to hold it. "You boys know him then, do you?"

"Sergeant in our regiment, sir. Don't know him real well, but well enough to know he didn't deserve what he was getting from those five heroes. Thing is, he's one of ours. First Minnesota Regiment, officer. What'll they do with him? Hospital near here? We got to see to him, sir. We take care of our own." Ox was angry, but he was also concerned about Sarge's condition and status with the law.

"Ambulance lads will decide where they take him. Looks bad enough for a hospital to me. May have more busted than what shows. He's lucky you boys came along. Those crud was after his money. Lot of that happening with alone soldier boys. They know the troops got their pay in their pockets or they wouldn't be in town. You soldiers should never wander around alone. These scavengers are on the lookout for you. Take your life for a few coins."

The ambulance arrived and Sarge was rushed to Providence Hospital. They followed along to see that he was identified properly and to find out about his condition first hand. After a half hour wait, the doctor emerged and spoke to them. "Patient is in bad shape, but will recover. Cracked ribs, broken forearm, numerous lacerations and a concussion. We don't think that the shattered ribs punctured a lung, but can't be sure. We'll send along an official report to the Regiment, but it won't be delivered for two or three days. I suggest you inform his unit so he won't be listed as missing."

Ox asked the doctor to take good care of their friend, and the soldiers hurried back to camp. The regimental first sergeant shook his head and mumbled, "That old buzzard ought to know better than to go it alone like he did. No fool like an old one. We'll take care of it, Koukarri, and thanks for seeing to him like you did."

Ten days later Ox, Tony, Ben, Pudge, and Shakey were given a couple of hours to visit Sarge. They found him propped up, still in great pain, but buoyant and anxious to be released. He was harassing the nurses and other patients when they walked in. He spotted them coming. "Well now, what more could a man ask? KooKoo and Thunder and Shakey and Insane and Pudge. What a bad hand of poker you five make." A teasing grin split his swollen face.

"How you getting along, you old army mule? Hard-headed as you are, the bad guys probably broke their hands on your skull," teased Ox.

"You didn't look so tough lying in the mud in that alley, Sarge," added Tony.

"Well, whoever they was, they're lucky Old Sarge had a drink or two in him or I'd of wiped 'em out. Takes cowards to go five on one. Like to get a hold of them one or two at a time, I would. See who goes to the hospital then."

"Best not take anybody on for a while, Sarge. Even one at a time," said Pudge.

Sarge looked away and turned to the side. His words were awkward, and not what he wanted them to be, but nevertheless he tried to say thanks. "What you boys did in that alley, policemen told me. Sarge won't forget. Took guts what you did. Grateful I am."

"Nothing you wouldn't have done for us, Sarge. Glad it worked out the way it did. You going to be good as new?" asked Ox.

"Physical, I'll be just fine. Few more days. My head needs examining, though. Shouldn't have been off by myself. Ought to know better, like the Colonel said. He was in to see me along with Lieutenant Messick."

Tony laughed. "Only way to get officers to talk with you is to get your head stove in."

"Real nice to me they was. Wished me well and back on my feet. Colonel said he had bad news though. Had to bust me to private. Couldn't have a sergeant actin' like I did, he said."

"Can't believe it, Sarge," said Shakey. "You a private? Won't seem right."

"Right kind of you to say so. I probably made some enemies. Had to shape you up fast. Green as spring grass when you come to the army. Not bad lookin' troops now, I do say so myself. Be a pleasure to soldier with you. Be proud to. Hope you can be in our company, Sarge," said Ben. "We could use some experience around us."

Gradually a rivalry developed among the regiments, especially between the New Yorkers and the Minnesotans. Mostly good-natured, the interplay gradually fostered mutual respect and appreciation. Curiosity about the lifestyles each group led at home generated exchanges that helped dispel misconceptions. The New Yorkers had imagined the ways of Minnesotans to be primitive and uncultured and were surprised to learn that they actually read and conversed intelligently, lived in houses, and weren't under constant Indian attack. Minnesotans in turn had pictured New Yorkers huddled together in rat-infested slums, breathing foul air, and under constant attack by one another. The New York troops called Minnesotans "rubes" and were labeled "slummers" by their rivals.

Friendly contests were concocted to test which state's men were superior. Champions were selected by the respective regiments to compete in shooting, wrestling, bare-knuckling, running in sprints and longer distances, and in various ways to measure strength. When neither state emerged a clear-cut winner, a special contest was devised and rules agreed upon that were intended to settle the issue. A champion from each regiment would compete under the following conditions:

Each contestant would pull a railroad hand car up a grade of spur track for 150 yards from a dead start. Each would make three alternating trips with the car loaded down with as much weight in rocks as he could load. The rocks hauled the full 150 yards would then be weighed and the cumulative three-load total calculated. The man who pulled the highest total weight would be the winner. Each trip was to be completed within a time limit of fifteen minutes. To build suspense, the weight total at the completion of each run would not be revealed. Only Captains Donovan of the Thirty-fourth New York and Wilson of the First Minnesota would know the run weights and they would be sworn not to give any indication until the contest was over.

The eager New Yorkers' pride and joy was Karl Kirkegaard, a bull of a man with powerful shoulders, enormous biceps, and gnarled, bulging thighs. He was a gentle man, but determined not to let his comrades down.

Sarge was the Minnesotan's first choice, but he refused, saying that he might make one good run but a younger man would have better endurance. Ox was the alternate choice. After assurances that he would not be censured if he lost, he consented. Pudge became the wage-recorder.

Ben, Tony, and Shakey talked strategy with Ox. All agreed that the contest would be won not by brute strength alone, but also by good calculating. They argued over the amount to be loaded for each run.

Ben opened. "Ox, it appears to me that Kirkegaard may be overall stronger but you may have him on endurance."

"How can you tell? He looks strong enough to pull a train."

Tony inserted, "Listen to a little guy who has to think to survive. I calculate that you should pull less weight each time 'cause you'll be losing strength from the pull ahead of it."

"Maybe, but how'll we know how much to take the first run? Could be we'll overestimate and ruin him for the next two," said Ben.

Shakey spoke. "Let's fix up a pad to put on each shoulder to soften the rope cutting down. No rule against that, is there? Case they haven't thought of it, we'll keep it hid 'til just before he starts out."

"Good idea, Shakey. You're thinkin'," said Ox.

"Knee pads, too, in case you go to your knees."

"Good Lord, if I do that, I'll never get up anyhow."

"It'll still feel better when you come down."

"Why not? How in hell did I get into this mess?"

"You ought to feel honored, representin' the regiment," teased Tony.

"Feel free to replace me, Tony, honor and all."

Kirkegaard won the coin toss and chose to pull last so he could study the weight taken on by his rival. Pudge was taking last minute wagers at a table off to the side.

Ox stripped himself to the waist and when he strapped on the jerry-rigged shoulder and knee pads, the New Yorkers scoffed and called him a softy. Ignoring the catcalls he loaded carefully, selected the bigger, flatter pieces for the edges and then filled in with smaller stones. Satisfied, he walked to the head of the cart, took up the rope, and strained into the pull. To the delight of the New Yorkers who fell all over each other in noisy glee, the car did not budge. "Double my bet." "Contest's already over." "Minnesota can't pull its own weight," they howled. The Minnesota rooters cheered him on, "Come on, Big Ox. Pull, big man, pull. They're laughing at us. Pull."

Ox's second effort barely overcame inertia, but he got the rig moving. He turned off his mind and focussed on one step at a time, his concentration becoming so absolute that he didn't hear the noise, feel the heat, or suffer the pain. They had to stop him at the finish line or he would have overrun the scale. He looked up, dropped the rope, and began to unload. The Captains quietly noted the amount.

Ox headed for a grassy patch to lie down, but Tony shouted in his ear. "No, no, Ox, you can't lie down. Come on, walk your muscles or they'll tighten up. Believe me, I know."

"Easy for you to say, you squirt, lemme just rest a minute."

"A minute will do you in. Walk down to the start, then lie down. Come on, big guy. Lot of money on you, you know."

They helped Ox back to the starting point where Kirkegaard was piling on large rocks with very little effort. Knowing he had loaded more than his competitor, he grabbed the rope and set off at an easy pace. Kirkegaard appeared hardly winded at the crest, off-loaded onto the scale, and marched confidently back to the starting point.

Ox staggered to the rock pile and piled a load about one-third less than his first run. He managed his pull to the crest, and unloaded onto the scale with over a minute to spare. During his walk back, he suffered the jibes thrown at him by the New Yorkers.

The second Kirkebaard pull was uneventful and almost effortless. The Dane again made sure his load was larger than Ox's and enjoyed the acclaim he received on his journey to the top. He felt unbeatable and nearly dropped the rope to acknowledge the applause. He unloaded and hurried down the slope to put even more pressure on his opponent.

Ox was angry and offended by some of the personal remarks he had heard delivered by a few New Yorkers, but if the truth were known, he was more hurt by the lack of good cheer from the Minnesota group. I'd sure like to show those bastards, he thought. He leapt to his feet and converged on the rock pile and loaded carefully, actually exceeding the amount of his first effort.

The crowd stood silent, noting his optimistic load and respectful of the spirit of competition it represented. Ox lunged viciously at the rope and set off. It was a superhuman effort, rewarded by a suddenly reinvigorated Minnesota crowd. Ox looked to neither side, hardly faltered, finished, off-loaded, and strode back down the incline with his head held high, acknowledging not at all the cheers ringing in his ears. He knew it wasn't enough, but it was all he had to give. He swallowed a pint of cold beer without a breath and reached for another. With a wave of his hand he shooed away Shakey and Tony and Ben and a few others who approached. They respected his wishes and backed away.

Kirkegaard was the man of the hour. Never in his uneventful life had he ever experienced anything like the adulation he was receiving. Applause first heard can be very heady. He played to the crowd, became an entertainer. He estimated that even a half load would be enough to win, but had learned to love the "oohs and aahs" of his admirers and couldn't resist placing a load that would get their attention. He set a load about half the size of Ox's last, and, for an exclamation point, selected a huge, round boulder that he struggled with but finally lifted onto the car.

The crowd rewarded him with what he sought. They cheered lustily knowing that the huge boulder would put him far over the top. He bowed ceremoniously and began the pull. He barely got it started and moved along slower than either of his previous passes, but was enjoying every moment. His head was up, his eyes sparkled, his muscles strained. His smile grew with each step. The New Yorkers shouted, pushed up to the tracks, and followed directly behind the car, laughing and tumbling and spraying water and other liquids on each other and on their champion.

Within thirty feet of the crest, Kirkegaard faltered, then regained his rhythm. The excited crowd got too close and one of the New Yorkers was pushed against Kirkegaard who staggered to his knees. The Minnesotans' hopes were suddenly renewed. They jeered and taunted Kirkegaard unmercifully.

Infuriated at the interference the big man roared in anger and thrust upward to regain his feet. The jerk of the rope caused the boulder to topple off the car onto the track. Kirkegaard's forward momentum was suddenly increased by the lessened weight and he again fell to his knees creating a slight slack in the rope. The car continued upward a few feet then started back down. Kirkegaard, bent backwards, wrenched his shoulder, but managed to stop the car. Bleeding from the knees but frenzied in his determination, he raced back, lifted the boulder with a remarkable effort, and replaced it on the edge of the car. Leaning against it, catching his breath, he realized that as soon as he removed his weight from behind the car, it would start rolling back down the slope and he'd be unable to stop it.

Knowing that his time was running out, he calculated that even without the boulder he had enough total weight. He rolled it off the car, rushed forward, grabbed the rope and dashed off to unload. The Great Dane, as they were now calling him, descended to the starting point and went directly to Ox to shake his hand, sat down next to him, chugged a mug of beer, grinned, and said, "I don't know who won and I don't really give a damn. We showed 'em a couple of men today, Mr. Large."

Ox chuckled and said, "I'm sure you won. You're the strongest I've ever seen. We'll never hear the end of this from you New Yorkers. They'll pull our chains 'til the end of the war."

Kirkegaard leaned over and whispered in Ox's ear, "Don't let 'em . . . I'm actual from Pennsylvany."

Seeing the two laughing like a couple of idiots, the crowd thought they must have lost their minds.

Captains Wilson and Donovan came down the hill with all the importance of those who own vital information that no one else has. The crowd gathered. Captain Wilson stated, "Our congratulations to two mighty fine competitors. What do you say, men, a lusty hurrah for both of them."

The crowd, filling fast with beer, cheered 'til they were hoarse but then shouted, "Who won?" "Lot's of bets to be paid off, Captain." "Who's the big winner?"

"Gentlemen, we are the captains, and it is in our power to name the winner, 'cause we're the only ones who know. Both these boys are winners. How can anybody call either one of them a loser?"

A few chorused, "But somebody won, Captain. A lot of money is riding. We got to know so's we can settle."

The Captain held up his hand. Silence fell.

"Yes, men, one of them outdid the other . . . " He paused. "Now I know there's lots of money bet, but we're going to leave it up to all of you to vote by voice. One of these men hauled a total of three pounds more than the other. Three measly, stinking pounds. I don't think it's enough difference to make one a winner and the other a loser or enough difference for you who bet to win or lose money. If your voice vote agrees, I'll call it a draw, all the money will be returned, and no one will ever know from us who actually won. Now if you agree, let's hear it loud and clear!"

There was a brief pause, then a rumble began, then a lusty cheer arose that deafened any detractors. The captain quieted them, held up the sheet of paper that recorded the run weights, lit a match and burned it. They cheered again and the crowd broke up, the wagerers heading for the table where Pudge was set up for business.

Pudge had paid back all but a dozen or so betters when a New Yorker named Frank Haney identified himself and requested four dollars that he had bet. Pudge quickly checked for his name, didn't find it, then checked again. He looked up at Haney, trying to remember him making a bet, recalling there'd only been a few who'd bet more than two dollars. When he told Haney there was no record of his bet, the man cursed Pudge and had to be restrained by others in line. Pudge told Haney he'd finish with the others, then check again. Haney waited sullenly a few feet away. Pudge asked the next man to carry a message to Captain Wilson requesting that he come over to help settle the dispute.

The captain arrived just as Pudge was finishing with the last man and handing back the last dollar from the box. It had all come out exact except for the four dollar claim. The captain asked Pudge to explain the situation as he beckoned Haney to join them.

"Captain, I kept these records as accurate as can be. The only explanation I can think of, sir, is that somehow somebody figured a way to claim Haney's money, though I can't imagine how."

"Bullcrap," hollered Haney. "You dumb lard butt, you screwed up or else stole the money for yourself."

"Not true," countered Pudge.

Captain Wilson intervened. "Private Haney, you'll watch your crude use of language and control yourself so's we can get to the truth of the matter here. How do we know that you bet the money? Was there any one with you to verify it? Any other proof?"

"My word, Captain. That's all I need against his, that's all I need."

Pudge said, "I don't honestly recall the man, sir, but there was so many it could be he's telling true. Not many bet as much as four dollars. I just don't know."

The captain thought a minute. "There may be one way to find out. Haney, step away for a minute while I talk with Private Henderson."

When Haney was clear, the captain spoke low. "Remember now, there were two separate times you took bets. Once in the morning by the mess tent. Then later by the starting line. You and I counted the morning money together, and it checked to the dollar. You took in about half again as much after that you told me. Now, we'll ask Haney when he made his bet, and if he claims that it was in the morning, he's lying. If he claims later, maybe he's got us."

"Whatever you say, sir."

Haney was beckoned over, and the captain put it to him straight and fast. "Haney, bets were made at two different times in two separate places. We want to know from you where and when you laid your bet."

Haney looked from one to the other and hesitated, a pause that spoke volumes to the captain and Pudge. Belatedly Haney remembered the bet line he had seen. "This morning over by the mess tent, that's where. I 'member now."

The captain looked him straight on, then over at Pudge, and said, "Come on Henderson, I don't like to be seen in the company of a liar."

Mail call was a much anticipated occasion. Reading a letter from Maurna, Ben sat on a log next to Pudge. Tony, Shakey, and Ox had wandered off for a little privacy and didn't notice when Pudge swiftly left the area. But Ben had heard the sharp intake of breath and observed the sagging shoulders as Pudge disappeared into the woods. He assumed that Pudge had received disturbing news and wanted to be alone. He made a quick mental note to watch for his return.

Ben finished Maurna's letter and digested the news. Everyone was healthy. All of the folks from miles around had attended the gala wedding of Carole Rivard and Clem LaChance. Maurna said she felt privileged to make the wedding gown. The young couple would reside at the Rivard home after a brief honeymoon in Saint Paul. Good for them, thought Ben, two fine people who deserve each other. Maurna went on to say that the potatoes were abundant and "as plump as we've ever seen" according to Joseph. Ben could hardly be unaware of the irony. The humble potato seemed to have become a major factor in their existence again. Bane in Ireland, bounty along the Cottonwood. Could be I'll be a farmer after all, he projected. Oh, well, plenty of time for decidin' that later.

Ben waited half an hour before following after Pudge. The path became more faint and winding as he penetrated the woods. He heard soft sobbing before he saw him. Approaching quietly, he saw the young man's back shuddering in spasms. Ben paused, unsure, then strode forward noisily to give Pudge a moment to compose himself. "Can I help, Pudge? Need someone with you, friend?"

Pudge's head came up. The sobs were choked off. The shuddering stopped. "Never needed one more."

Ben sat next to him, but refrained from eye contact. Waiting, he looked out over the placid canal. The silence lengthened as Pudge struggled for composure. His lips opened to speak several times, and then suddenly the words tumbled out, one over another, garbled, anguished, despairing.

"My best friend in the whole world, Ben. Gone! Dead of fever! Only nineteen years old and already gone. My sister, more'n my sister, my twin. Best person I ever knew. Won't ever be the same with her gone. Best of all the Hendersons by far. God, how I'm going to miss her." He broke off, stood, pulled his kepi low over his eyes, folded his arms across his chest and took several deep breaths.

"Penelope and I were born late, Ben. My father was fifty, my mother in her mid-forties. They thought they were through with having young'uns, there being seven before us. My oldest sister was already married and gone, then there was six brothers, all big Swedes like my father. My twin was always frail and sickly. Had a club foot, too. But a special, loving creature right from first breath. My father just went on like we never really happened. Mother was kind and good to us, but she feared my father, like we all did. Penny and me, we stuck together, looked out for each other. My brothers all modeled themselves after my father, even took up his attitude toward Penny and me. Laughed at me, ridiculed me for being weaker than them. But Penny stood up for me, looked them in the eye and shamed them. God gave her a frail body, but a big, big heart and real courage. She was my strength, and my one true friend. I've lost my soul mate, Ben. Why'd God have to take her? She hardly knew life at all. And what little she knew was . . . . "

Ben had never felt so inadequate. He walked over, put his hand on Pudge's shoulder and gently said, "I've never lost anybody that close to me, so I won't pretend to know how you feel. I 'member when my sister lost her husband, how low we all felt, but he wasn't as close to me as your twin was to you. Try to think of her as happy now and as still watchin' over you. She'll always be with you, Pudge. You've been wronged by your people, but that can either destroy you or make you stronger. Live strong for her, Pudge, and for yourself. That'd be her wish for you."

Ben paused and waited for Pudge's eyes to meet his. "Remember this, too. You've got real brothers here in the regiment, good men who will go to the wall for you, as they know you would for them. I'm truly sorry for your loss, Pudge. Only consolation I can offer is my condolences and my friendship."

Ben squeezed Pudge's shoulder and began to head slowly away. Pudge's voice stopped him. "Ben, I appreciate your words and your friendship more than I can say. Ask you for a couple of favors though. Don't want the others to know about my family troubles. And pray for my sister, Ben. I'll ask her to watch over you, too. If God don't listen to the likes of her, He don't hear anybody, Ben."

Tony and Shakey were plying Sarge for some of "the expensive learnin'" he had gained during his previous tour with the army.

"I was a young buck full of vinegar in those days. Learned some things the hard way. Had some fun learnin' though."

Tony pursued his main interest. "Girls are a problem, Sarge. Except when we're parading, they shy away from soldiers. Durin' the parade, they wave and smile and stir us up with their pretty smiles. After the parade though, when you try to approach 'em, they run quick behind their mothers. About the only ones that'll talk to a soldier are the ones that hang around loose on the streets."

"Stay away from that kind, boy. There was two fears when we was in Mexico, the water and the women. Between the two, more boys got laid low than all the guns of Mexico combined. Here the water's all right, but those kind of women are just as bad. They carry around nasties you want nothin' to do with, believe me."

"Understand that, Sarge. But how does a soldier get next to the decent ones? Like Tony says, they run and hide soon's you look at 'em," Shakey complained.

Sarge looked at the two, wondering if he was ever that young and naive. "Boys, the only place you can go where the decent ones go is church. That's where some of my friends used to meet the nice ones. Got the preacher to introduce 'em proper after the service or at one of their social affairs. Works, sometimes, but it's slow work. Waste of time to try to do any regular courtin' and try to be a soldier, too."

"Sounds hopeless, Sarge, the one's you can have, you don't dare touch. The others you say are a waste of time. No wonder soldiers drink so much," moaned Tony.

Sarge laughed and laughed. "Never heard it put more plainly, Tony. You talk about the decent girls that are out of reach and the dirty girls you don't want to touch as if they's the only kind there is."

"What else is there, Sarge?" they chorused.

Camp Stone, Maryland

"Well, I don't want to be the one leadin' you astray, but there is one other type. In fact probably the best kind of woman for soldiers on the move."

"Which ones you mean, Sarge?" asked Shakey.

"Why the professionals, gentlemen. They make a business out of what you're discussin' here. The oldest profession they call it. They stay clean at the better places. Kill business if they don't. Fact is, when you clowns saved my hash in that alley, I'd just come from one of their establishments. Now I hasten to add that I haven't paid for such services since I been married and that's a fact. Why was I there then? Something about the atmosphere to do my drinkin' that I take to. Besides, I still like bein' around 'em and talkin' with 'em. Enjoy it, I do."

"Where is this place, Sarge?" asked Tony.

"Boys, you make it sound as if they's only one. Why when you walked into town tonight, you probably passed twenty of 'em. Some say there's more whorehouses in Washington than there is regiments in the Union Army. Wherever they's a lot of men, you can bet the business ladies'll be there."

"Sarge, take us on over. Just want to see what one looks like. Educational it'll be," begged Shakey. "Be an old man before I see one."

"Education is it? Worst excuse I ever heard. Place I went to is three blocks from the White House. High class place. Friend of mine in the Fourth Pennsylvania introduced me to the madame, a fine woman named Mai Montplaisir. Pretty French name translates to Mount Pleasure. She's a great gal, knows how to make a man feel comfortable."

A short walk later they went up a flight of stairs with Sarge leading the way. Two brutish bouncers looked them over as they entered a long room with a mahogany bar down one entire length. The space was crowded with low tables and a row of booths on the side opposite the bar. Four bartenders were working furiously to keep up with the demand. Low laughter and humming conversations mingled with the clink of glasses and bottles and a slow working fiddle at the far end. A sweet waft of perfume came floating behind a quick spurt of cigar smoke.

Approaching them was a voluptuous woman in a low cut, gold, full length gown, wearing makeup like a cake carries frosting and yellow hair piled two feet above her forehead. About two inches over five feet, she must have weighed well over 200 pounds. Her round face was handsome, though, with delicate features and kind, welcoming eyes that said she liked herself and expected others to like her, too. She rolled up to Sarge and offered him her ring-infested hand to kiss. "My old Minnesota buffalo. Good to see you back among the healthy, McMahon. Way you talk, I never thought a mere five men could put you down."

"They sneaked up on me, Mai. I ever see 'em again, you'll be readin' 'bout 'em in the obits. Meet two of my young troops from the great state of Minnesota without which the North could not possibly win this war."

"Your modesty is no doubt your greatest charm, McMahon," she laughed.

"This is Cosgrove and Lunde, a couple of boys makin' their first ever visits to an establishment such as yours, Madame Montplaisir."

"Welcome, boys, you don't look old enough to be on solid food yet, but being in the army makes you welcome. Take a booth over there by the wall. I'll send a pretty one over as soon as you get seated. I'll join you later when I get a minute. You boys have a good time now. Need anything you just call for Mai." She spun away, leaving Tony and Shakey open-mouthed.

They could see clearly that nearly every table was occupied, mostly with soldiers, but also a sprinkling of well-dressed civilians. Costumed young ladies with tiny waists and not so tiny, exposed bosoms were spinning through the narrow aisles with trays of drinks. A few of the hostesses were seated at the tables, flashing smiles at the patrons. There's more feathers on display here than in the whole Sioux nation, Tony thought to himself. They got situated just as a pert young miss splashed up to their booth. "Gents, what's your pleasure?"

"Three of your tallest and coldest, darlin'. Busy night for you?" asked Sarge.

"'Bout like usual. By the way, I'm Samantha, should you be inquiring." She smiled provocatively at Shakey and Tony, then swung herself gracefully and wiggled away, knowing their eyes were following her. After about six steps, she pivoted 180 degrees, smiled back at them, spun again and headed for the bar.

Both were instantly in love. They would have fought a duel over her. Sarge had to practically strap them to the booth, as he held his mirth in check.

"You ever see anything like that, Shakey?"

"Ain't nothing like that in Red Wing, you can bet on that."

"She seems to like us Sarge," said Tony.

"Hate to dampen your risin' enthusiasm and doubt your irresistible charm, Lunde, but she does work on commission you know." Sarge was enjoying himself immensely.

"What do you mean?" asked Shakey.

"Percentage of her back room business. She gets a part of what's paid. Old Mai gets the rest. That smile you boys got was just promotin' business for her pocketbook. Nothin' personal at all."

"Back room business you say? You mean she's one of them?" asked Shakey. "So pretty, why's she do that? With looks like hers, she shouldn't have to."

"Money, boys. That's what she's all about, what all this is all about." His sweeping gesture took in the whole room. "She makes more in one night than we make soldiering for a month or more. Mai's gettin' rich, too. Money's what makes the world turn on its axis, boys. Time you learned that."

"Business looks good, Mai," he said to the bouncy Madame as she sat down next to him. Her bracelets covering both forearms settled down just after she did.

"Always good, McMahon. Men need distractions with this dirty old war goin' on. Makes 'em forget for a while. You boys like anything you see, you just let Mai know. And you, McMahon, you still on the women wagon, are you?"

"'Cept for you, darlin', nothin' here to make ol' Sarge change his mind. By the way, Mai, I spotted a man over yonder looks familiar. That one there with the two soldiers three tables over. Know him? Can't place him."

She squinted into the crowd to locate the man Sarge described. She raised up a little, then smiled and said, "That's George Stanley, Sarge. Don't know where you'd know him from unless you've been in jail recently. He's a police Captain with the D.C. constabulary. Comes in nearly every night. Bachelor fella. Oh, I forgot. You did have some business with the police lately didn't you?"

"That's where I saw him. One of the police that come to see me in the hospital. Tried to get some description of those five that jumped me. I was sort of groggy when they came. That's where I saw him though. Police feel right to home here, eh Mai?"

"Lawdy yes, even get senators in here from time to time. Mayor come once himself."

Tony and Shakey kept looking from Mai to Sarge. Sarge had said something about getting an education. Education may not have been the right word for it, but they were certainly learning. Shakey finally blurted out a question he just couldn't hold back. "You mean all this is all right with the police and the law? They don't even try to shut you down?"

Mai chuckled knowingly. "Where you from, boy? Course not. 'Sides we've got 'em bad outnumbered if they tried. Good business for everybody, son. The money reaches lots of different pockets. No trouble from the law, not since the war. After the military, our kind of business is the biggest one in D.C."

Tony was struggling not to reveal his lack of sophistication. "Heard about some of this going on in Saint Paul, Shakey. Never been there myself, but heard about it."

"How big a town is Saint Paul, son?"

"'Bout 10,000 people or better last I heard."

"That many folks you can bet your blue britches it's going on. More'n one place, I'd wager."

Saying she had to circulate, she left them to move from table to table, booth to booth, talking a few minutes with each group. Occasionally she would wave her hand to a pretty hostess and a few minutes later one of the gents would push back his chair, saunter casually to the back, push aside a beaded curtain and disappear into the darkness beyond. One going through the curtain would sometimes have to step back to allow another to pass coming back into the room. Traffic was steady.

They drank their beers and ordered another. Sarge watched his two young friends study the scene and knew what was going on in their minds. Their backgrounds and home training were struggling with their natural temptation. Sarge even guessed which would win in the end, and that they were getting close to a decision. He shrewdly made it easier for them to resolve the dilemma and to ease his own conscience.

"Boys," he said from his reserve of worldly wisdom, "I want you to do old Sarge a big favor and put his mind at ease. Get up with me now, and we'll walk out of here, head back to camp and see another day. If you want to come back here another time, you just decide for yourselves, like every man has to do. But for my peace of mind, don't do anythin' about it tonight. I brought you here as untainted lads. You leave the same way you come, only a little more worldly wise. If you come back on your own, then it's on your own head. Now let's get on back to camp."

They looked at him feeling both disappointment and relief, then nodded and followed him out the door. They were anxious to get back to camp and contribute their new knowledge to Ben, Pudge, and Ox.

At year's end, the Confederate and Union armies were in winter quarters gearing up for the campaigns expected in spring of 1862. In the interim, recruits and replacements enlarged both commands, and the skills of the soldiers were enhanced via drills and maneuvers. The Rebels were supremely confident in their military prowess and exaggerated superiority; the Yankees were not yet in a position to do any bragging, but they were most anxious to quiet the humiliating echoes of Bull Run and Ball's Bluff. Both armies were girding for a struggle to the death. Fall of 1861 would be the last breathing spell for the divided Union until Appomattox.

Camp Stone, Maryland

Maurna's Journal
February 1862

    I cannot speak of my growing sadness to anyone. The others need to look upon me as strong, and I must not fail them. But I am at the lowest point of my life with the exception of when we left dear Ireland and the day when I lost Timothy.

    There must be few places on God's earth as desolate and isolated as rural Minnesota in the dead of endless winter. We are shut in with stale, dry air and hardly a view out of frost-laden windows. If we could see out, there would be nothing to look upon but leafless trees, heavy gray skies, and the suffocating snow and ice. The only disturbances in the snow are our little pathetic paths to the shed and the tracks of small animals who have somehow adapted to survive in this harsh tundra. Even those marks are quickly erased by the ever constant, howling winds and drifting snows. Birds are scarce and seem never to sing. And the cold! I could never have imagined cold so fierce. The lungs scream in agony. Everything is hard and brittle to the touch. Frightening, painful cold. Last winter was brutal, but we were told that it had been milder than usual. I should have known what to expect this year. But one must experience it, the imagination cannot match the reality.

    The days are seldom sunny and even when they are clear, the hours of light are so brief that we eat breakfast and supper in total darkness. There is little talk among us since we are so constantly together. Joseph senses the gloom and tries to spark our moods, bless him. Pim takes Ginny up the hill for tobogganing when the cold abates, but that has been seldom. Since the New Year we have been to New Ulm but once. We have not been to mass since Christmas and miss its comfort. We miss Ben's vitality. God keep him from harm.

    Joseph and Pim keep busy with their trap lines and have accumulated quite a number of pelts they will sell in New Ulm. The funds are critical since Joseph says we lost our chance to sell a few bushels of surplus corn that he was counting on. The Sioux tribes who were depending upon corn are in desperate straits. How those Indians have learned to survive these cruel winters in their flimsy shelters is beyond my understanding. Hardy people!

    When Rose returns in a few weeks, I must take her into my confidence and get her good counsel. She has endured many winters in this isolation and has apparently learned to cope. I suspect another reason she spends part of the winter teaching at the Agency is to break the monotony of the winter months. She is very wise and understanding.

    I must put on a good face. I pray to Jesus for the strength to endure and for the self-control to disguise my true feelings. Spring seems an eternity away. I was raised on the belief in the values of faith, hope, and charity. In the past my emphasis had always been on faith and charity and I had never given much consideration to hope. I now take new meaning of the word and begin to understand its status. Hope is merely the opposite of despair. For the first time in my life, I can acknowledge the possibility of despair.

    I recall a private moment with Timothy, just before we departed from Ireland. In attempting to allay my apprehensions, he read a line from the Roman poet, Horace, who wrote, ". . . they change their skies but not their souls who cross the ocean . . . ." Please, Dear Lord, let it be so!

Chapter Eleven

Blizzard Guest

Joseph panicked.

"Good God, Will, can you believe this? We have to get back home fast."

Joseph and Will Koukkari were in New Ulm when the low roiling cloud bank plunged into the valley. The light suddenly dimmed, the wind began to roar and swirl, and the snowfall increased. In a few moments, the ground snow being carried by the shrieking winds combined to reduce visibility. The force of the wind drove cutting ice pellets horizontally, and the temperature fell by forty degrees in less than twenty minutes.

Will noticed people pointing to the northwest and rushing to shelter. With Joseph he sprinted for their rig and they set out. They covered less than half a mile when all became white, giving them no choice but to turn back. The howling wind made even shouting futile. Feeling their way to the stable near the Dakota House, they unhitched the animals, and led them to shelter. They would spend the next two days and nights within their quickly chosen refuge.

The blizzard struck along the Cottonwood with even greater force than in town where buildings provided some protection. The force of the sudden gusts rattled the windows, startling Maurna and Ginny. "Good heavens, what is that, Pim? Dear God, the trees are bendin' half over and it's near dark as night. What's happenin'?"

Pim and Ginny were beside her at the window. "'Tis a storm for sure, a wild wind and the snow is fallin' fast. I'd better get out for more firewood. No tellin' how long it's to last," said Pim.

"Oh dear me, be careful. It's so dark and all. Is Poteen about? Take him with you. Animals can find their way better'n we can. Pray that Joseph and Will aren't caught without shelter."

"Poteen is outside. I'll get the wood and milk Johanna, and pile her up some hay. Wish I had done it before this storm struck. Keep calm. I'll not be long."

Poteen was at the door, ears flat and looking to get inside. Pim could barely make out the darker shade of the shed. He grabbed the toboggan by the rope and that reminded him of the line that Ox had attached to the porch. He gripped the lifeline and made his way to the shed where he serviced Johanna and gave her a reassuring pat on the rump. The cut logs were already covered but he dug out a healthy load for the toboggan and added the milk, and a shovel. Except for a faint light in the window, he could not see the house. His lungs barely able to tolerate the cold air, he followed Poteen and slid his hand along the guide rope. As he shouldered open the door, Maurna and Ginny reached for the milk and a few logs.

"Never would I have believed it," he said in awe. "Man nor beast could live long in that wind and cold. Thank God for Ox's rope."

"Drink some coffee, Pim. It'll warm you. We were frightened when we lost sight of you. How will we survive this, Pim? Dear Lord, it's the blizzard they've been tellin' us about. Now that I've seen one, I'd sooner not see another. Have we enough wood? It'll go fast in this cold, I'm thinkin'." Maurna jabbered on as she only did when she was distraught.

"Mama, you settle down now, we'll be fine," said Ginny.

Pim said, "Would you be listenin' to her? Who's calmin' down who around here? And look at Poteen, the master of the house. He's as comfortable as if he was at the beach."

Indeed the dog looked content. Snout resting between his paws, ears flat, he signalled that as far as he was concerned, all was well.

They were amazed at the sudden ferocity of the blizzard as they watched the slicing crystals shriek by in the light from the window and the frost gradually ride up on the pane. Maurna started supper. Ginny lay down by the snoozing Poteen as Pim checked the stove, added a log, and took advantage of Maurna's absence to sit in the rocker. He closed his eyes.

Poteen's ears rose sharply. He growled, low and throaty, then rushed to the door, barking in rage. Ginny ran to Maurna who was looking at Poteen, then at Pim. Trying to calm the angry dog, Pim went to the door. "Back, boy, back!" The dog, hackles rising, backed off slightly. "Hold him, Maurna, I'll see what's out there." She grabbed the dog's collar but could barely contain him.

Pim threw the latch and opened the door a few inches. When the wind tore it from his hand, the dog went wild, straining forward, teeth bared.

Maurna held on. A person lay motionless at the threshold, unidentifiable, shrouded in a blanket, only an ear showing. Pim reached down and uncovered one side of the face. "An Indian, don't know if he's dead or alive."

"Drag him in, for heaven's sake."

Pim grasped the man under the shoulders and tugged, managing the inert form past the door. Maurna pushed it closed against the force of the wind. Poteen's piercing barks echoed in the small space.

"Let me see to him," said Maurna. Pim took charge of Poteen, yanking hard on the collar again and again. The barking reduced to low growls, but the hackles remained rigid, the stance square and ready.

"He's alive, but breathin' shallow. His hands are likely frost bitten and maybe his feet, too. Help me get him closer to the heat. Ginny get some water in two low pans. Pim, quiet that dog so I can hear what I'm thinkin'."

They dragged the Indian to the floor by the stove. Maurna placed a quilt on the floor. They rolled him onto it face up, and put a pillow under his head.

Maurna rambled. "Young man, about thirty. What's he doin' out on a night like this? Wonder if he was alone or got separated. He'd never survive out there. His lips and hands are blue, and look at those whitish spots. My good heavens, he's lucky he found the house. Must have seen the light in the window. Heat a bit of water now, Ginny. Rose told me to never put frost-bit hands into hot water, just warm or regular temperature. Hope she's right."

She placed a pan of water on either side of the man, immersed his fingers, and with a soaked rag gently rubbed his cheeks, ears and nose.

"Pim, take off his mocassins. See what his feet look like. We may need to soak them, too. Hurry now."

Pim did as asked and said, "Never saw a dog get so riled. Must be he doesn't take to Sioux."

Maurna added two more blankets. The Indian had not moved.

"I don't like him here to tell the truth, Aunt Maurna. I don't quite trust Indians. Can't leave a man out there to freeze, but I intend to keep an eye on him."

"He needs our help, Pim," said Ginny.

"I know, Ginny, and help we will." Pim responded. "But if I was in his place and him in mine, you can bet he'd keep an eye on me. Don't you think?"

"I don't know, I s'pose."

Maurna shook her head and suggested they all go about their business. "We've done what we can for the moment. Like all of us, he's in God's hands, poor man."

Poteen's eyes never left the Indian. The dog lay still, growling low, waiting, watching. After a while Ginny kissed them good night, then turned to their sudden guest.

"Good night, Chief Blizzard or whatever your name is, I'll pray for you tonight along with Ben and Joseph and Ox and all our friends. Night Pim and Mother."

"Night darlin'," said Maurna. Pim smiled and said, "Don't worry, little one, we'll watch out for him."

A few minutes later, the Indian began to mumble and stir. He spilled a pan of water before Pim rescued the other. Poteen was up and growling, ears up, eyes fixed.

Blinking in the light, the Indian squinted, rose onto one elbow, groaned and lay back. Eyes again closed, he touched his face gently. He tried to locate the dog, started to get up and grimaced in pain.

Maurna and Pim stood over him looking at his long stringy hair, lean hawk-like face, square jaw and thin lips. The white spots on his cheeks and ears looked like spattered paint.

Maurna met his eyes. "If you can hear me, sir, we have tried to ease your frost bite. We hope you are warm enough. If not, we will get you more blankets. We won't let the dog hurt you. We want to help you but don't know what else to do. Are you thirsty or hungry? Do you understand what I'm sayin'?"

For a few moments there was no response. The Indian focussed on Maurna, Pim, growling Poteen, and finally spoke. "Bad storm. Saw light. Lost. Separated from brothers. Storm that blinds. Storm that kills. Fire feel good. Thankful to you."

"Will you eat or take some water?" Maurna asked. "Or hot soup to warm you inside."

"Water be good. Soup help, too. Will try to sit up now." He rose to one elbow. Poteen growled, low and steadily.

"Dog not like Unktomiska. Dog not trust Unktomiska."

"Unktomiska? That is your Indian name?" asked Pim. "What do the white's call you in their tongue?"

"Unktomiska called "White Spider" by whites."

Maurna chuckled. "White Spider it shall be." Then she smiled and said, "Though I don't usually like spiders in our house."

White Spider looked at her with lips drawn tight. He saw her smiling, then he smiled, understanding. Then he laughed. "This Spider not make web in house. My woman no like spider neither."

He looked carefully at his fingers, then his toes and touched the tip of his nose, his cheeks, and his ears. "Frost not take hold. More time in cold, lose fingers, maybe toes, maybe life. Hope brothers find shelter, build fire."

He limped to the table, slurped soup and drank the last remnants from the bowl, then several dippers of water.

"Food good. Hungry from long day. All Sioux hungry this winter. Some die. Many sick. Cutworms eat corn, not Sioux. Bad times!"

Maurna's heart went out to him. "Oh the poor little children. Can't you get food from the government? They are supposed to provide food for you."

"Traders give Sioux food only if Sioux give trader pelts or gold. No game left. Whites drive them away. Traders get Indian gold, not Sioux."

Pim had heard enough. "We will hear more of what you say tomorrow. Sleep here by the fire. Aunt Maurna, you go on to bed. I'll clean up. Poteen and I will stay up for a while."

White Spider rose, nodded his thanks to Maurna, and moved to his place on the floor by the fire. He lay down, covered himself in blankets, and closed his eyes. "White Spider thank lady and young man. Not know their names to use."

"I am Maurna. The little girl you haven't seen yet is called Ginny. Pim is the son of my brother, Joseph, who lives here, too. He'll be here when the storm is over."

"Maurna . . . Pim . . . Ginny . . . Joseph," mumbled White Spider, as he drifted off to sleep. "Strange white names."

Pim pulled Poteen by the collar and followed Maurna to her bedroom. He whispered to her, "Don't worry. With Poteen and me guardin', he'll not take a step without us knowin' of it.

"I'm not worried, Pim. He seems peaceful enough. Why would he want to hurt us? He seems genuinely grateful. With Poteen watchin', you can go to sleep in peace yourself. Good night, my dear."

Pim blew out the lamps. The only light was the glow of the fire. The Indian's snoring sounded like the whistle on the *Fannie Harris*. Pim stayed awake as long as he could but he needn't have worried. Poteen slept not at all.

White Spider stayed through the next day and night. When the wind finally decreased, he said he could travel. He had talked freely, answered all their questions, and had given them interesting insights into the lives of the Sioux.

To their questions he responded that he was "thirty summers and two. I am Mdewakanton Sioux, live in village of Chief Little Crow, across river from Birch Coulee near Redwood Agency. Have wife and two little sons. No daughters. Had same father as Little Crow. He was Chief Big Thunder. Dead now."

Maurna asked him again about the traders. "I understand that most of the traders have Indian wives. Why are they so difficult for you to deal with?"

"Have Sioux wives, yes. But not good to Sioux, most traders. Want gold. Take annuity monies. Say we owe them. Sioux see no money. Traders take. Galbraith side with traders and farmer Indians, not hunters like Little Crow and White Spider."

"Farmer Indians?" asked Ginny.

"Yes, little lady. Government try to make Sioux be farmers. Want us cut hair, dig in soil, grow corn and squash. Farmer Sioux get food from Galbraith. Hunter Indians don't want land tore up or trees be cut down. Land belong to all people. Hunter brothers call farmer Indians Dutchmen. They not share with hunter brothers. Galbraith want all Sioux be Christians. Not have own Great Spirit."

"Do you think there will be trouble between the Agent and the Sioux?" asked Pim.

"Yes trouble. Sioux hungry. Annuities come June. Sioux need gold for food. Winter bad and spring be hard until gold in June. Trouble come if Agent not give Sioux gold."

White Spider was candid, but polite and gave no offense to any of them, except Poteen who never warmed to him. Ginny was fascinated with his stories and legends and plied him with questions that he never tired of answering. Over and over he referred to Ginny as his "little lady."

White Spider left after a good dinner. When he thanked all of them, he said he would never forget their kindness.

Pim's trap line territory included the wooded land on either side of the Cottonwood for a mile upstream toward the Koukkaris and several miles in the other direction along the river toward New Ulm. During the winter months his line was fairly productive. Snares caught mostly cottontails, grouse, and gray squirrels, while his traps yielded weasels, mink, squirrels, muskrat, the rare beaver, and once a small bobcat.

He encountered young braves from time to time who were neither hostile nor friendly, simply nodding and quickly passing on. He often wondered what they were really thinking. He felt no resentment for their incursions into "his territory," feeling that it was as much theirs as his. Occasionally one of his traps would be sprung with droplets of blood on the jaws, but no animal in the trap. He suspected that the Sioux robbed his trapped game, but since he had no proof, he kept quiet about it. The hide and fur man in New Ulm had told him that the Indians were not happy that the whites hunted and trapped along the Cottonwood, but Pim had no intention of being driven off.

In the fall he used the shotgun to harvest ducks and grouse. Hunting for meat, not sport, and being conscious of the cost of powder and shot, he shot the ducks on the water where he could often hit more than one per shot. Through it all he had learned from Ox, then from Will and Rob, how to shoot and stalk game. He studied the local animals and their patterns of behavior. Thoroughly enjoying his solitary sojourns, he often reposed in secluded ravines and glades when the weather was fair. He learned to remain quiet to observe the animals and birds and to watch the eastward soaring clouds through the canopy of overreaching limbs. Envying them their lofty view and their opportunity to travel over the countryside, he joined them on imaginary journeys that recalled the vast country they had passed through on their way west from Virginia.

He vaguely recalled the green hills of Ireland, but with no longing or regret because the memories included a great deal of sadness, poverty, and hunger. Harper's Ferry and the Shenandoah Valley were fresher in his mind. He intended to return to Virginia someday, but only as a visitor, for he truly loved Minnesota and believed it to be the grandest place on earth. His future was here in this valley and on this land.

The good feelings about his new life he attributed to the change in his father. As a lad he had known Joseph as a bitter, angry man, burdened by shame for his prison time and filled with resentment and grief for the loss of his wife. Pim felt early on that his father associated him with his bad fortune and tried hard to win his favor and love. Perhaps too hard. Having no memory of his mother, Pim transferred those feelings to his Aunt Maurna. His Uncle Timothy had been more father to him than had his own. Observing that Timothy's death had impacted Pim heavily, Joseph finally understood that his son needed his love. From the day of Timothy's funeral Joseph had attempted to let Pim know that he had a full time father again.

Their relationship had mended and held promise to become what they both wanted it to be. Though he felt very good about his father's renewed affections, he retained a bit of wariness, lest he be hurt again. He respected Joseph for giving up the drink, honoring his pledge, being a strong decision maker, and building the future for all of them. He felt that the changes showed his father's true character. Joseph was still quick to anger and had an overbearing nature and deep stubborn streak, but had mostly mastered his temper and learned to consider the opinions of others.

All in all, Pim was content. He was busy learning how to live successfully in Minnesota and enjoying the friendship of Will and Rob Koukkari. And then there was that pretty Lunde girl, Abigail.

Chapter Twelve

Abomination

The winter in Maryland around Camp Stone could not compare with the bitter conditions prevalent in Minnesota, except perhaps in the degree of discomfort and misery it caused the First Regiment soldiers. Cold rains, sleet, snow, and far below-normal temperatures plagued the Minnesotans whose shelters were not designed for nature's onslaught. Some of the men concocted creative furnaces out of barrels and pipes arranged in ingenious fashion; unfortunately, a few of them backfired and caused minor fires and a few harrowing escapes. Many of the more enterprising soldiers erected crude log huts to serve in lieu of tents.

January and February were a miserable finish to their five month sojourn at Camp Stone. When word passed in late February that they would at last be on the move, the troops were enthusiastic and relieved. Anywhere promised to be better.

Anywhere turned out to be Harper's Ferry. After being mud-marched to Adamstown, the division was loaded on a train that carried them to the river town of 5,000. The Minnesota Regiment bedded down in the empty armory and neighboring buildings where John Brown and his cohorts had been captured.

Ben was quick to arrange permission for a visit to the Russell farm. Accompanied by Tony, Ox, and Pudge, he surprised his aunt and uncle with an early morning visit. The Russells were thrilled to see Ben and to meet his friends. Since they arrived just after breakfast, Mary had plenty of time to prepare a noon meal. Ben, Bernard, and Mary exchanged information and news that each had received from Maurna's letters. Mary told Ox of the many flattering words Maurna had written about the Koukkaris. "Land sakes, that Rose must be quite a woman to impress Maurna the way she has. She loves all your family."

Ox responded, "The Murnanes and Russells are fine new neighbors that fit in like they've been there all their lives. 'Course nobody's been there very long, Mrs. Russell. Area was only Indians and trappers 'til about '55."

"The Lundes have come in for a lot of praise, too, Tony, for the way your family extended their welcome. Knowing our Maurna, I know she thanked you but let Bernard and me add our appreciation to you."

"Thank you, Mrs. Russell, very gracious of you to say so. Promise me you'll not say anything, but we think that Pim has taken special notice of my sister Abigail. Might be something interesting happening there."

Bernard smiled, "That Pim bears watchin', Tony, comes off as a shy one. Better watch that Irishman."

When asked, Pudge described the community of Swedish immigrant farmers near Lindstrom and how over the recent years the first settlers had lured more and more of their countrymen to the fertile and beautiful region north of Saint Paul. After speaking of his family's situation, Pudge surprised them when he said that he wasn't sure whether he wanted to be a farmer like his brothers. "They're all big fellows like my father. Not like me at all. Guess I might rather work with numbers some way or other."

"Good farmer needs to know his numbers, too, young man," commented Bernard. "Saves him from a mess of mistakes. 'Sides, farmin's a good life, keeps you humble."

After an enjoyable dinner the four took their leave. Mary and Bernard stood arm in arm on the porch to watch them down the road. Both willed that all would survive what lay ahead for them.

The Minnesota boys spent a few days on Bolivar Heights, then entrained for Washington. Their haphazard movements echoed the state of Union strategy. They spent one night at the Soldiers' Rest, another near the Capitol, then were boated to Alexandria. By March 27, they were back in camp in the Virginia countryside near where they had been before the Battle of Bull Run.

Sarge detested facial hair of any kind, whether a beard or mutton chops or a simple mustache. "It's a man's duty to do everything he can to not look like an ape. At our best, we come close enough as it is." He found a way to shave at least every other day no matter how trying the circumstances. As testimony to his obsession, he usually wore razor cuts on his chin and neck.

As he joined the group around the fire, the others were trying unsuccessfully to suppress their laughter. "What the hell's so funny, you hyenas?

You look like country hicks at a burlesque house, gigglin' like school boys. What's ticklin' you?"

Tony recovered sufficiently to explain. "Sarge, our Red Wing romeo has decided to improve his lady-catching appearance. You know, that rugged, manly look. Kind of hard to tell 'cause there's not much evidence, but Shakey's working on a mustache for himself." The group broke up, and even the irrepressible Shakey joined them.

"Jealousy is a painful thing to observe, Lunde," Shakey countered. "You are like that Fox and Grapes fable that Aesop wrote about. 'Member? The old fox jumped and jumped to get the grapes, but when he failed, he said he didn't want 'em anyway. Give your right arm to look mature like old Shakey's gonna look."

Sarge walked close to Shakey, bent over and squinted to see better. "Glad you tole' me, Lunde, can't see much sproutin' yet. Didn't you ever hear about the eleventh commandment, boy?"

"Eleventh commandment?"

"Yessir. Eleventh commandment states, Thou Shalt Not Cultivate on Thy Front Lip What Groweth Wild On Thy Rear End."

When the laughter had subsided, Shakey said. "Sarge, I got enough trouble with the first ten, never mind having an eleventh commandment to deal with."

"Speakin' of which, the Chaplain was lookin' for you, Sarge. Said he wanted to meet you," teased Ben. "Said he's heard of you, but never seen you."

"I've been preached at by experts from Texas to Maine, Murnane. Never did like messages that come second hand. God'll come get me when He wants me, I figure. No sense bothrin' Him, busy as He is. 'Sides, my little woman's prayin' for me up there along the Saint Croix River. He'll listen to her before me anyways."

Pudge got up, groaned, and said, "First time in my army career I'm happy to be going out on guard duty. See you fellows in a few hours. Keep the fire glowing. Maybe it'll be a higher level of conversation when I get back." He ducked the handful of gravel that Sarge pegged at him as he sauntered off.

New Yorkers Haney, McCarthy, and Jaworski had been drinking since noon. Their laughter had increased with their imbibing. Unhappily, the jug was empty. They had no money and credit was out of the question. "Got to get more liquor," said Jaworski, grinning in anticipation and barely able to stand. He leaned against a sapling that bent with his weight. The others were lounging on ponchos spread over the wet, cold earth.

"Got no money," slurred Haney, "and no prospects. Mights 'well sleep." He rolled over and fixed a blanket around himself.

Pudge descended the ridgepath, whistling softly to himself as he hurried out to relieve the guard on the far ridge. He'd in turn be relieved after three lonely hours. It gave him a chance to get off by himself, though, and he had plenty to think about. He heard the New Yorkers before he saw them and instinctively quickened his stride to hurry by. Unfortunately, they spotted him.

"Well, if it ain't that fat boy from Minny-soota. The one that cheated me out of four dollars and got me in trouble with the captain. Haney ain't forgot about that, lard butt. Haney never forgets. Look at that nice jiggling rear end. Can't be a man, gotta be a girl under there. Hurry along there, sweetheart. You don't want to be where there's real men. They might get ideas."

Their laughter enraged him but Pudge knew better than to stop or comment. He fought down the impulse to smash those dirty mouths. Keeping his eyes straight ahead, he strode on out of earshot but was already worrying about the gauntlet he'd have to run on his way back. The only other route to camp was up and over the ridge through heavy underbrush and a mile longer. The light was beginning to fade, and he prayed that the New Yorkers would be gone by the time he was relieved.

When his replacement arrived, Pudge asked him if he'd seen anyone along the path on his way up. The soldier replied that the only living thing he'd seen was a chattering squirrel that he'd pegged a rock at and missed.

Pudge was hopeful but apprehensive as he quietly descended the path to the creek bottom. Every few steps he stopped to listen. As he approached the critical area, he peered over some rocks. Two figures lay snoring in the grass along the stream. He crept slowly along the path, ready to instantly step off into the protection of the brush. Just past the sleeping pair, he suddenly felt on his neck the vicious grip of a hand that forced him forward, down to his knees and onto his face.

"Hyah, boys, I found me a prize. A little fat hog ready for butcherin'." Haney's hulk pressed down on Pudge, pinning him to the path and mashing his face into the wet turf. The other two arrived and were laughing down at him.

"Caught you a Minny-soota fatback, didn't you," mouthed McCarthy. "Juicy and ripe as can be. My turn after you, Haney."

Afterwards, they continued their assualt with words. Jaworski spat out, "You tell anybody about this and we'll kill you, you hear? You're a dead man if you breathe a word."

"And we'll know if you do, fat boy, we'll be able to tell by watching your friends. Any sign of their knowin', and we'll get you sometime when you're alone. You take my word on that." McCarthy was sobering quickly.

"He ain't gonna tell nobody. It's too shamin'. He'd never live it down. Now let's get on back to camp. You'll be all right, fat boy. The whores all say it gets easier every time you do it." Haney's laughter would echo in Pudge's ears for a long time.

When he was sure they were gone, Pudge rose to his knees, pulled himself up with the aid of a bush, and began to look for his clothing. Leaning against a tree, he managed to emit what started out as a soft prayer. "Dear God, why? What have I ever done to deserve this? Why? Why? Am I just dung?" Self-pity turned into rage. "Where were you, our refuge and our strength? Where? Preaching love and forgiveness? Thy will be done. I've lived by that creed. If this was your will, then damn your will."

His eye caught a silhouette against the dull sky. Hanging in silent testimony high on branches were his garments. He shook his fist at heaven and shinnied up the tree. The pain in his lower body was so severe he didn't notice the new gashes from the climb. He retrieved and put on his clothes, then immersed himself to the waist in the icy stream.

He stayed in the water as long as he could stand it, then crawled to shore and massaged his legs to regenerate circulation. He searched the stream bed until he found a sharp, jagged-edged rock. Determined to cover up the shame-filled episode, he repeatedly jabbed himself with the point of the rock, ripping his flesh through his clothes and splotching his backside with a mix of gravel and blood. Angrily slamming the bloody rock into the stream, Pudge began the pain-filled struggle back to camp.

Sarge brought the bad news. "Old Pudge got hisself hurt pretty bad. He's over at the hospital tent gettin' fixed up. Doc says he'll be laid up quite a spell."

"What happened to Pudge?" asked Tony.

"Said he was on guard detail and comin' back after he got relieved, he tripped on a root and fell off a ravine onto some sharp rocks. Landed hard and tore up his backside real bad. Tail bone and upper thighs were ripped wide open. Barely made it back to camp, bleedin' like a gut-shot buffalo. Doc says they'll be sendin' him to Providence Hospital. He's in lots of pain and clammed up. Feelin' foolish as well as hurt most likely. I was you, wouldn't try to see him 'til tomorrow when he'll be feelin' some better probably."

"Pore ol' Pudge. Must hurt like hell," commented Shakey.

"Pudge sure does get more'n his share. Got other news for you, too. More'n rumor this time. We'll be headin' down the Potomac to Chesapeake Bay and on down to the peninsula between the York and James rivers. Close to Yorktown where ol' George Washington stomped on that Britisher Cornwallis in the Revolution. Seems like we'll be goin' from there straight on into Richmond. That's the plan anyways. 'Course plannin' is one thing, executin' is another."

Ben thought a minute, then asked, "Won't that leave Washington undefended, Sarge? How do we know the Rebs might just rush on Washington if we leave the door open by goin' way down there?"

"General McDowell and his bunch will stay up there to stop 'em. He's got plenty men. Word is we'll have enough troops goin' down to that peninsula to get us on into Richmond."

"When we leaving, Sarge?" asked Shakey.

"Day after tomorrow. Some are already on their way. Ol' Pudge won't be going' with us though, you can bet on that."

"Maybe his fall wasn't bad luck after all," Shakey commented.

Chapter Thirteen

Portents

See the bumblebee, Uncle Joseph? Oh, there are two more. They light on the clover and buzz back and forth. Will they bite us, Pim? Aren't they pretty?" Ginny had brought corn bread cakes, a bucket of cold well water and a dipper to Joseph and Pim in the potato field.

Pim spoke a trifle condescendingly, "No, Ginny, they'll not bite you if you leave them alone. They mean you no harm."

"They drink from the clover, Ginny, then rush on home to turn the nectar into honey," advised Joseph. "You like honey, don't you darlin'?"

"But how do they make honey?" Ginny asked..

Pim responded, "The same way Johanna makes milk, Ginny. Johanna eats hay and turns it into milk. The bees drink nectar and turn it into honey. Nobody knows how it's done. Just the way God made things, I guess."

Joseph added, "The bees also gather things on their sticky feet and carry them from flower to flower. That's how big flowers make little flowers. Flowers are born and live and die just like people but there are always more of them because the bees carry sticky stuff back and forth between them. The bees have to carry it because the flowers can't fly from one to another."

Ginny laughed delightedly, "Whoever thought a flower could fly? Silly idea."

"Everythin' that grows, both animals and plants, has seeds, Ginny. Out of those seeds come the little ones that are born, grow up, and have seeds of their own. The experts call it the life cycle. They speak with great authority but actually know very little about the mystery of life. The bees probably know more than most of us, but they don't tell us." said Joseph.

"Maybe that's what they're sayin' when they buzz at us, Uncle Joseph."

He chuckled. "You may be right, Ginny. Listen closely to them, they may let you know their secrets."

"But you said animals and people have seeds, too, Uncle Joseph. How does that work to make little ones. Do the bees help do that, too?"

"No, darlin'. But Pim and I need to get back to work now, sweetheart. You take your questions to your mother. She'll be happy to answer you. In fact, I'd love to be there to hear her. You tell her I suggested that you ask her. And thanks for the cold water and cakes."

Ginny gathered the pitcher and cups and leavings in a basket and started away. She stopped suddenly, spun around and said, "You said that plants and animals all have little ones. Will Johanna and Poteen have babies, too?"

"Ask your mother, Ginny, ask your mother," laughed Pim.

Ginny giggled. "All right, I'll ask her. And you two, watch out for flyin' flowers."

Poteen's frantic barking brought Joseph and Pim dashing from the field. Joseph cocked his rifle as they charged through the ravine toward the back of the shed where Poteen had something pinned down. The dog was furious, teeth bared and making short charges, then backing off. Maurna and Ginny came running.

Joseph stepped cautiously around the corner of the shed. "Come out of there," he ordered. "Come out or I'll fire into the bush." No movement. "Come out, I said. Come out. NOW!"

An image appeared through the brush. An Indian, perhaps twelve years of age, came out slowly, his eyes wide, registering surprise more than fear. In his left hand he held a dead chicken. The boy looked steadily at Joseph.

"You little thief. You've got no right to our chickens. Throw down that chicken and go away."

The boy looked at him, then the others. Maurna started forward, but thought better of it. The boy dropped the chicken.

Joseph shouted again. "I see you here again, I'll shoot. Now get off my land. I hate thieves."

The boy stared, seeming more confused than hostile. "Not steal. Little ones hungry. Mother tell me go find food. Little ones need food. Not steal. When Indian have food, everyone eat."

Joseph was taken aback. Good God, he thought, he's a little one himself. Out to help feed his brothers and sisters. But I can't let him steal. He spoke but with a less strident tone. "Get off our land. Never come back. Stay away. Next time I shoot. Go, go to your village."

The young man straightened himself. "Land is for all people," he said, then turned to walk away.

Joseph's words stopped him, "Go away. Don't come back. But take your chicken."

The boy picked up the fowl and looked at Joseph. Smiling, he nodded to each of them and walked away.

Joseph lowered his rifle, shook his head, and turned to the others. "Well, what do you make of all that?"

Maurna approached him. "What do I make of that? I love my big brother very, very much is what I make of it." She gave him a hug that brought color to his cheeks.

"Stealin's bad, isn't it Uncle Joseph?," asked Ginny.

Joseph knelt to her and said, "Yes, Ginny, stealin's bad, but to him it is not stealin', I'm thinkin'. To him it's a way of providin' for his people. That's a man's job, Ginny. He's tryin' to be a man. Methinks he'll be one, too, some day soon. They must be awful hungry is all I can think."

Indeed the Sioux were hungry. In fact, many were literally starving. The blizzards of January, 1862, and the fierce cold that lingered into late March had brought near famine conditions.

Agent Galbraith rationed the stores and stubbornly continued to favor the farmer Indian families. By late spring, the desperate Sioux began to congregate near the Yellow Medicine Agency, pressuring Galbraith to provide flour, corn, and pork they knew were stored in the warehouse. The Sioux spokesmen suggested that the agent advance them credit against the annuities that would come due in June. Galbraith stalled, attempting to entice more Sioux to adopt the farmer culture.

Five thousand Indian men, women, and children gathered near Yellow Medicine. Indian lodges of bellicose young braves began to assemble. Harsh words were mouthed. Belatedly Galbraith became concerned and requested Captain Marsh of Fort Ridgely to provide a tempering military presence. Lieutenant Sheehan and 100 troopers were dispatched, but before they arrived the Sioux broke into the warehouse and confiscated barrels of flour and pork. The soldiers quieted the budding rebellion, but the circumstances remained within a spark of conflagration. Finally realizing the level of desperation, Galbraith called a meeting that included Sioux chiefs, several traders, and Lieutenant Sheehan.

During the meeting, a strong Sioux voice was resurrected. Little Crow, a Mndewakanton Chief whose influence had been diminished since he was party to and severely criticized for the loss of Sioux reservation lands, spoke forcefully and impressed the young braves with his persistence and adamancy. Agent Galbraith wavered under the verbal attack and begrudgingly promised release of more stores. The Sioux accepted his word, but Little Crow remained unsatisfied and challenged the Agent to provide food immediately at both Yellow Medicine and Redwood. Galbraith deferred to the traders' spokesman, Andrew Myrick, who ranted vehemently and concluded with a flourish.

The Sioux observed the anger in Myrick's face and his disparaging gesticulations but did not understand his words. A half breed interpreter translated. Myrick had disdainfully declared, "Unless they have gold, let them eat grass . . . or their own dung." When the Sioux comprehended the true meaning, they leapt to their feet in rage and had to be restrained by the soldiers. Galbraith attempted to temper the moment with more promises.

"Hello. Hello. Pim." Will's voice resounded from down by the river where he and Rob were tying their loaded flatboat. Maurna met them in front of the house.

"Hello there. What are you vagabonds doin' cavortin' around the countryside?" She put an arm around each of them and led them to the porch. "I'm bakin' bread. As if your noses didn' tell you that already. I'll cut you a few pieces and cover them with chokecherry jam. How's that sound?"

"Sounds great, Mrs. Russell. Pim somewheres around?" asked Will.

She busied herself at the work table and answered while she worked. "He and his father are out in the corn, I think. Why don't one of you fetch them? They'll likely be wantin' some bread once they smell it."

"I'll get 'em, Mrs. Russell," said Rob heading out the door. "Don't eat all the bread, big brother."

Maurna asked Will, "You been down to New Ulm for supplies? Hard work polin' back when the river's so low, isn't it? Your mother gettin' ready for the big festivities comin' this Sunday?"

"Yes, ma'am, hope the rain holds off. Though we could use some. Never seems to come when you need it, only when you don't. Lots of talk in town about the Indians, Mrs. Russell. Some blame the traders and the government. Others hate the Indians so much, they put all the trouble on them. Who knows who's right?"

Joseph, Pim, and Rob heard Will's last few words as they sauntered in.

"Howdy Will," said Pim. "I see you're fixin' to fill your belly as usual."

Joseph cuffed Will on the back and reached for a chunk of bread. "What's this you're sayin' 'bout Galbraith?"

Will repeated what he'd told Maurna and added, "People are divided about equal as to who's to fault. 'Pends on how you look on the Indians, I 'spect, more than it does on the facts of the matter. No matter, it's still getting out of hand."

"Lazy louts, lookin' for a handout. That's all most of 'em ever do. Sittin', smokin', drinkin' when they can get it. The ones that won't work ought to be run off out of the sight of hard workin' folks." Joseph's feelings about the Sioux were known to all present. Maurna put her hand gently on his arm.

"Simmer down, brother mine. What you say may be true of some of them, but they're badly treated, you must admit. God knows the government promises more than it delivers. I keep thinkin' of the women and little ones. Galbraith hasn't much to give them. Fault seems to lie back in Saint Paul or maybe farther even, back in Washington."

Will spoke up. "Fella in New Ulm claims they broke into the storage shed at Yellow Medicine and stole provisions. The younger braves are keepin' things stirred up. Big meeting a week or so ago 'tween the Indians and the traders. This fella said that Mr. Myrick, the trader at Redwood, refused to give the Sioux any more credit. Claims Myrick told the Sioux that they could eat grass or their own dung. Pardon me, Mrs. Russell, his words, not mine. That's pretty strong language to use on folks already riled."

"Good for him," said Joseph.

"Mother, what's dung?" said Ginny.

"Somethin' the world's full of, but it's not a word nice folks use. Don't let me ever hear you usin' it."

"I'm not too favorable toward Indians, but they ought to feed 'em if they said they would," said Pim. "Least ways they better do somethin' 'fore cold weather comes again."

Maurna changed the subject. "Enough talk of trouble, how about the doin's on Sunday? Your mother still wantin' to go into town Saturday afternoon and stay over for the parade and nonsense next day? Pim, Ginny, and I are to go in with her. Joseph will come on in early Sunday. That what she's still plannin', Will?"

"Last I heard, we'll be by for you Saturday after dinner."

"Tell her we'll all eat supper here Sunday. I've got beans, cornbread and a kettle full of venison stew. We'll fix up some bread puddin' to top it off. Tell her I won't take no for an answer."

Will and Rob rose to leave, "Thank you kindly, Mrs. Russell. We'll tell her. Should be a peck of fun Sunday. See you then."

Pim walked the two brothers to the landing. As they shoved off, Pim noticed that each had his rifle primed and loaded. Will caught his eye, lifted his rifle as they backed into the current, and said, "Don't go nowhere without these days. Recommend you do the same. See you Saturday, Pim."

Pim joined the others on the porch. Joseph said, "Plan sounds workable, though I hate to give up the work time."

"Oh, Joseph," Maurna sighed. "You need a little relaxin'. You and Pim have worked seven days a week since April. Only time you took off was a half-day on the Fourth of July. The work'll be there when you get back."

Pim agreed. "Need to see some folks and maybe laugh a little. Troublin' news about the Indians."

Joseph scoffed. "Nothin' gonna happen, Pim. Those Sioux are too busy fightin' among themselves and spittin' at the Chippewas to cause any trouble. Besides they know what'll happen to 'em if they get mean and do some real harm. Not to change the subject, son, but could your excitement about goin' into town have anything to do with a bit of fluff called Abigail?" He laughed and headed back towards the corn.

Pim ran after him. "She's a lot more than just fluff, Pa, a lot more. Come on, Poteen, can't lay around all day."

Maurna and Ginny watched them go. "What's fluff, mother?"

"Oh Ginny, I'd surely like to live in your world again for a little while. Fluff is a pretty bit of almost nothin', but the word doesn't fit young Abigail. The pretty does, but not the nothin'. She's somethin', that's for sure. Your cousin Pim sure thinks so, anyway."

The Harvest Fair had evolved over several years and generally occurred during the first half of August. Most folks began the Sunday with church service. Families made the journey to New Ulm for a day of foot and horse races, wrestling, shooting contests, knife and hatchet throws, and horseshoes. And there was food and drink in abundance.

Weather permitting, merchants displayed their goods outside. Clergymen frowned on Sunday commerce, but were mostly ignored.

After churches emptied, people lined the streets for the big parade. The ones in the parade outnumbered those watching. Anyone was welcome to join. A German band and choruses from the churches marched directly behind the honor guard from Fort Ridgely. The procession wound up and down the few streets at the whim of the officer in charge but gradually dissipated as marchers dropped out to join friends and kin.

Drinking was widespread. Teetotalers clucked their disapproval, but most people were tolerant and avoided confrontations. Young men circulated and inspected the crop of availables, looking and hoping. Young ladies did their own speculating, but gave the impression that they were really too sophisticated and proper for that sort of nonsense. Furtive, carefully delivered smiles, dimples, and fluttering eyes sought out and found their intended targets unerringly. Most prospects were recorded for future consideration since mothers, aunts, and grandmothers kept close watch.

Most contests were completed by noon. Participants and spectators drifted to grassy areas under the trees. The Murnanes, Russells, Koukkaris, Rivards, and their New Ulm hosts, the Lundes, congregated near the Catholic Church in an oak grove carpeted with goat-clipped grasses. Father Vogel mingled and sampled their victuals.

Rose and Maurna asked Claude Rivard about his sister Carole's condition and when she was due to deliver. Claude said the baby was expected "any time." His folks hated to miss the festival but didn't dare risk coming. Rose asked Claude to come over to inform her as soon as the labor started. "Just get word to us and we'll be there to help."

Conversations centered around news from Virginia. "They've been in some scrapes," Ansgar intoned. "Sure wish they'd get it over with. Was supposed to be over in three months. Now they're saying a year or more. Tony's got over the flu fever he had. He wrote that your Ox is up for some kind of medal for what he did down near Richmond, Rose. Fine young man that Ox. You must be awful proud, eh?"

Rose appreciated the praise. "I wasn't surprised when I heard about him. I wouldn't be surprised at what any of our Minnesota boys do. Ben and Tony are made of the same fiber. They'll do what needs doing, and take care of each other in the bargain."

"Robert E. Lee and Jackson are sure slippery," Joseph said. "Seem to be a step ahead of our generals. Maybe McClellan will give 'em a good whippin' one of these days. It's draggin' on way too long."

"Just bring our boys back safe and whole," Maurna inserted. "That's sure what I was prayin' this mornin'. Every mornin' and night for that matter."

Ansgar settled back against an oak. "Guess we ought to be worrying some about the Sioux right here at home. The agent needs to find a way to settle 'em down. Governor Ramsey sits in Saint Paul not doing a thing. Far enough away to feel safe I guess. He blames the federal government, and they pass it back to him. Not enough soldiers at Fort Ridgely to suit me."

Pim feigned listening but was more interested in Abigail. She stole quick glances at him from time to time, but when he caught her at it, her eyes fell away. A tiny smile, however, flickered each time. Gradually they drifted closer to each other and slowly increased the space between themselves and their elders. They began a whispered conversation just out of earshot. Their maneuvers didn't escape the notice of Maurna and Belle Lunde who exchanged knowing looks.

Suddenly a loud clamor erupted over by the town square. Ansgar and Joseph led the others as they hurried to see what was happening. It seemed to be another parade, not nearly as long as the first one, but definitely a parade. About forty drunken strutters pounded wildly on kettles while shouting and cursing at the top of their lungs. At the front of the pack a big man held a cross made of two birch saplings. Leather thongs held up a stuffed dummy that dangled from the cross arm. The marchers prodded the thorny weed-crowned dummy as they sang and shouted coarse epithets to taunt the Christian onlookers. The crowd, amused at first, began to respond in disgust. Some began to hurl back condemnations and threats.

"Who are they?" shouted Joseph over the din.

"Bunch of heathen, ignorant German farmers from just west of town. They love to provoke and pick fights and ridicule Christ and all He stands for." Ansgar's disgust was total.

"Taunting Christians is their favorite game," shouted Belle. "Every decent person despises what they do. Most Germans are fine Christians and ashamed of these people. That big oaf carrying the cross is their leader, Dolph Werner."

The paraders were nearly abreast when Father Vogel stepped out in front of them, hands up, palms forward. It appeared they might trample him, but were stopped by a shout from their leader. More sober than the others, Werner stepped up to face the priest. Father Vogel spoke clearly. "In the name of Our Savior, Jesus Christ, I demand that you stop this blasphemy. You've no call to foist your godlessness on the good citizens of this community." Despite his rage, he delivered his demand in a controlled voice.

"Oh, Father, it's advice and scorn for us, yah? Vee aren't free citizens in a free country? Vee can't parade our beliefs as vell as the Christian hypocrites? Protestants and Papists, you're all alike. Always preaching how other folks should live. Not your business how vee choose to live or vat vee believe. Out of the vay und let us zelebrate in our own vay. Jesus Christ verdamnt!"

Father Vogel stood his ground and maintained control. "You will not blaspheme, Dolph Werner. You will cease this crude display right now." The Lutheran minister, Ralph Zimmer, stepped up beside the priest to stand in support.

"Go to hell, Papist, and your Protestant friend. Take your Christ if you can stomach him, but don't force him on us. You give him da credit ven tings go gut. You never gif him da blame ven dey go poor. Jesus is a myth, a creation of church people yust to gif dem power over da volks who vork for dere livlihood. Vee zelebrate our sugsess and gut harvest today, not wit tanks to him but to our own hard vork. You and da Pope. Go kiss his perfumed ass, priest, but don't expect us to join you."

Joseph found himself squarely in Werner's face. He hadn't thought about it, just reacted. He stood six inches shorter and was fifty pounds lighter, but the German's weight advantage was mostly concentrated in a round, beer-fed pot belly.

"The good Father will get an apology, and nice and sincere it will be," Joseph warned.

Werner looked at Joseph in disbelief and laughed. His huge right fist caught the late-dodging Joseph on the side of the head and knocked him into the crowd. Werner immediately dove on Joseph as the crowd gave them room. Father Vogel helped to separate them.

"No, Joseph, not the way to deal with him. It's what he wants," shouted the priest over the din.

Werner, furious, rolled up his sleeves and spat at the priest, "Out of the vay, Papist, let him come. Vee zettle zis between uz. Christians not gut fighters. I zettle him, zen you or anyone elze who vants."

Joseph cooly demanded, "Apologize to Father Vogel and to the rest of us, beer belly."

Werner ran forward to deliver another blow, but Joseph was ready. He sidestepped the lunge that carried the brute into the crowd.

Werner screamed, "My fists vill deliver more zan apology, little man. Prepare yourzelf to eat zem."

Joseph smiled inwardly. Now what happens can hardly condemn me in anyone's eyes, he thought. He had learned to fight in Ireland and had perfected his techniques in many scrapes. He discovered after several early beatings that his best attributes were quickness and elusiveness and had further perfected them during the fights among rival factions of railroad work gangs. He had confidence in his ability and expected to thrash Werner thoroughly.

Werner lunged again but Joseph nimbly stepped aside, and his opponent sprawled at the feet of the crowd. The shouting grew in volume. Bets were being arranged, odds on Werner. The German again and again rushed wildly at Joseph with the same result, except that Joseph laid a cutting, slashing punch each time he lunged past. Werner began to show frustration and doubt as he rose for the fifth time. Wheezing and obviously winded, he angrily shouted, "Stand und vight like a man, you ducking coward." His only hope was to close with Joseph and squeeze the breath out of him.

"I'm right here in front of you, big bag of wind. Come ahead and eat some Christian knuckles. I'm going to beat the sausage out of you. Come on, bloated pig."

The master provoker became the provoked. Werner rushed again, enraged. The excited spectators closed in to make the ring smaller and smaller. The German swung a round house left followed by a straight right catching his adversary in the chest. Joseph had been counterpunching, but suddenly went on the attack. Slashing Werner with six quick jabs, he opened cuts around the nose and mouth and pressed in to deliver heavy, leveraged blows to the target belly. Werner lost his air and doubled over. Joseph deluged him with chopping, twisting punches that cut flesh and splashed blood on the nearest spectators. Werner's face resembled chopped sirloin. His teeth were either loose or knocked out. As he fell slowly to his knees, blood poured out of his eyes, ears and nose. He remained kneeling, but was unseeing and helpless. The crowd hushed.

Relentlessly, Joseph pursued the issue. "Your tongue is still whole, Werner. Use it. Repeat after me. "I will never again insult Jesus Christ or his followers."

Some of Werner's crew tried to intervene, but others held them back. Bets were being settled in the background.

Werner, still on his knees, wobbled unsurely. His chin fell to his chest, his legs splayed outward. He was barely conscious.

"You heard me Werner. 'I will never again insult Jesus Christ or his followers.' Say it now, loud and clear."

Werner tried to raise his head. His eyes were puffed closed. Blood dribbled from his swollen lips. The crowd waited, horrified, but fascinated. A strangled sound came weakly through the foamy blood on his lips. "I vill never again inzult Jesus Christ or his followers."

"Thank you, Werner, I'm sure at least Jesus will forgive you," said Joseph and pushed away through the parting crowd.

The people slowly dispersed. Joseph walked away with Father Vogel and Pim. After a few steps, he turned back. Werner's friends had left the loser to care for himself. Werner's wife began to clean off the blood and help him to his feet. Looking directly into Joseph's eyes, she held them a moment, then looked away. Joseph turned his back and followed after his friends.

The festive atmosphere was ruined. People gathered their gear, loaded their vehicles and headed for home. Maurna, Rose and Ginny rode off in Joseph's wagon on the Cottonwood Trail. The fight had upset all of them. Maurna tried to ease the strain.

"Interesting and a little ironic to have you defend the church and the Pope, Joseph."

He smiled to himself and said aloud, "Isn't it though? But you know, Maurna, I never have liked bullies. They always remind me of our former British masters."

"No more than the beast deserved," Rose said. "You spoke and acted for all of us, Joseph. It needed doing and it sure did get done! After all, Maurna, the man asked for what he got. That bunch is mean though, Joseph. Keep your eye out for them. They'll not take you straight on after what they just saw, but keep your eye peeled. That type finds forgetting hard to do. And forgiving they know nothing about."

Maurna changed the subject. "Rose, when are you going back to teach at the Agency?"

"Mid-January. I'll be there through February. They give me a little room and my vittles and lots of hard work. It's a good change for me and good for Pa and the boys to be on their own for a while. When Ox was home, he was getting to be a pretty good cook. Now Will is learning. They 'preciate me more when I come back after doing for themselves. Smart, huh?"

"Can the Indians learn anything or are we just trying to ease our consciences?," asked Maurna.

"Most of them can, only a few do. Got several youngsters doing real well. But they get a lot of ridicule laid on them by blanket Indians who try to shame them. For most of them, it's easier to just lay back and not try. They're sometimes their own worst enemies."

"Blanket Indians?" asked Maurna.

"That's the term used for those who won't try to adapt."

"White Spider called them hunter Indians. So Blanket and Hunter means the same thing then. Any hope the few will become prosperous and get the others to see it can be done?"

"Slight hope, maybe," said Rose, "but that'll take time. Probably more time than they've got. But you should see those few who work at it. Bright children, sweet dispositions. I teach them Rosie's three R's, reading, 'riting, and religion. Religion intrigues some of them. They like the manger story and Jesus talking back to his momma in the temple, and Joseph leading his family to Egypt. Some of them get baptized and all."

Joseph shot in a quick tease, "Baptized? More Protestants, that's all we need."

"Hah," scolded Rose. "Listening were you? You're as Christian as I am, Joseph Murnane. Protestants and Catholics fighting all the time. I'd be a Catholic as easy as a Protestant 'cept for one idea you're considering."

"What idea's that?", asked Maurna.

"How you folks can tolerate the notion that your pope is so perfect that he can't make a mistake."

"You mean infallibility. That will be only regarding faith and morals, not other things he does as a regular person," said Maurna.

"Humph, any time you tell a man he can't make a mistake, believe me you're asking for trouble."

Pim was already off-loading the Murnane purchases when they pulled in. "Claude went home in case that baby might be coming. He told me that Carole's husband would be over to get you two ladies as soon as the little one decides to come."

"After all that eatin', I'm needin' a good, crisp walk," Joseph said as he rose from the table. "Sun's gettin' ready to set."

Rose set down her plate and asked pointedly, "Would you walk alone, Joseph, or tolerate company?"

Over his shoulder as he walked onto the porch, he answered, "Whatever would please yourself."

Rose smiled conspiratorially at Maurna, picked up her skirts, and hurried off to catch up with the fast-moving Joseph.

"I'll come, too," shouted Ginny.

"No, you'll not, young lady. We've got cleanin' up to do and right now," quickly inserted Maurna.

Joseph and Rose emerged at the grassy crest and turned to the southwest. The sun hung low but still illuminated the full length of the valley. Serene, rustic, unspoiled, the scene rolled out before them. They stood silently side by side unwilling to break the spell. The aura was magical. Their sense of each other was acute. The moment stretched. Finally, she softly whispered as one does in church, "So beautiful. And still. God not only touched here, but I think he lingered a while. He must sometimes be amazed at his own creativity."

"Beautiful, yes. I've come to love it here. It has the feel of home that we've been seeking since leaving Ireland. I could ask for no more than this. But there's an overriding sense of loneliness that I feel when I stand in this place. This land will give and it will take away. Man's greed may tarnish this, too, someday, and that makes me very sad . . . and lonely." He dropped his hands to his side and sighed.

"Each of God's creatures is lonely, Joseph. Even in the midst of family and friends. Only He can ultimately relieve our yearnings and loneliness until we go back to Him. In the meantime, we must abide and seek comfort in our loved ones. Some more beloved than others."

Her bold statement had escaped and she couldn't retrieve it. He shuffled his feet and stared fixedly. Another moment passed.

"Rose is a beautiful name," he said.

She exhaled as noiselessly as she could, then recovered quickly.

"Aye, but only a name, Joseph. As they say, 'a rose by any other name would smell the same.'"

He chuckled. "Your quote is paraphrased too humbly. The actual quote is 'a rose by any other name would smell as sweet.'"

She glanced at him quickly. "It would be unseemly to speak of oneself as smelling sweetly."

He felt her glance and met her eyes. "Perhaps unseemly to you, but nonetheless very accurate."

She looked away out over the valley at the fast fading sun. "Why thank you, good sir. Your flattery is welcome and accepted."

He, too, looked off into the vista of diminishing light. "And well deserved."

His fingers brushed her hand. They remained silent, mining the last nuggets of the golden sunset. After a moment his hand cautiously, then gently enfolded hers. She leaned toward him and rested her head lightly on his shoulder.

PART II

Uprooted

August 1862 to December 1862

> . . . I am free as nature first made man,
> Ere the base laws of servitude began,
> When wild in woods the noble savage ran.
>
> John Dryden

> She has gone . . . she has left us in passion and pride . . .
> Our stormy-browed sister, so long at our side!
> She has torn her own star from our firmament's glow,
> And turned on her brother the face of a foe.
>
> Oliver Wendell Holmes

Chapter Fourteen

Detonation

The four young braves had raced the stolen team and wagon over the full thirty miles at breakneck speed. No longer inebriated, they began to realize the enormity of what had occurred and, wild with fear, burst into the village of Chief Shakopee near Rice Creek. They sought out Big Eagle, a sub-chief, and urged him to call together the soldier's lodge to inform the other braves of their encounter.

Eighty hunter braves gathered. The four instigators excitedly told of their clash with white people near the village of Acton where a man named Robinson Jones and four other whites had been killed. Afraid the government would send soldiers to arrest them, they begged their brothers for protection. The listeners suspected that all Mndewakatons would be blamed.

A few members saw the incident as a disaster that would bring swift retribution from the authorities; others, however, seeing in it a long awaited opportunity, called for immediate attacks on settlers and the Redwood Agency itself. Big Eagle advised them to contact their recently chosen tribal spokesman, Traveling Hail. Many young braves scoffed at his suggestion, saying, "Traveling Hail has become a farmer Indian. He is not the leader we need now!"

Militant voices began to prevail. "The whites can be driven from the Valley. They are weak now with few soldiers left to defend them. Thunder guns are gone away to the eastern war. They cannot stop us if we strike quickly and hard."

Shouting and arguing continued, but the majority favored immediate action. A brave shouted, "We need a strong Chief to lead us and be our spokesman." Various candidates were advocated, but one by one each was rejected. Finally because he had re-emerged as a strong spokesman and had remained traditional, Little Crow became their first choice. After sending messengers to the Yellow Medicine Agency to inform the Wahpetons, Wapakutes, and Sissetons of the developments, the militants hurried the six miles to the village of Little Crow. During the march, the animosity of the long-frustrated Indians built on itself, and their collective courage and resolution grew. "We will return to the ways of our fathers. We are proud hunters and warriors, not farmers. We will take back our lands and drive out the whites." Their determination increased with every step.

The shouting mob gathered before the small frame house of Little Crow. Rubbing sleep from his eyes, the chief emerged into the torch-lighted glare and quickly sized up the situation. He knew his people well, especially the young militants. Inscrutable, but listening carefully to the shouted demands and intentions of the warriors, he interpreted them in terms of tribal possibilities and personal aspirations.

Little Crow had been prominent in Sioux negotiations with government officials on many occasions. His father, Chief Big Thunder, a wise man whose followers had prospered during his long reign, had been the most powerful Mndewakanton chief during the 1830s and '40s. Little Crow had inherited the prosperous village, reveled in his enhanced status, and sought to expand his influence. He promoted marriages between his many half-brothers and sisters and members of the western tribes. The unions that ensued linked him with the Wahpeton, Sisseton, and Wapakute tribes and increased his influence among all of the Santee Sioux. He had ridden a crest of popularity and prominence until 1858 when he and several other chiefs were pressured into selling additional reservation land on the east side of the Minnesota River. The shrinking of their tribal territory had infuriated the Sioux and, when most of the blame fell on Little Crow, his stature declined.

Flickering light from the torches reflected off the wild eyes of the warriors who chanted and challenged Little Crow to join their cause and become their spokesman. They repeated the points that had been debated in the soldier's lodge, and declared their intention to attack the whites throughout the Valley.

Little Crow absorbed their taunts, then quieted them, and said, "I will not lead you in war. You have chosen Traveling Hail as your spokesman. Go talk to him!"

Several voices responded, "He is farmer Indian, not war leader. You, Little Crow, must be the one."

Little Crow then shouted, "You are full of the white man's devil water! You are like dogs in the Hot Moon when they turn mad and snap at their own shadows." He folded his arms imperiously, privately enjoying the moment and his rise in favor.

He tried to reason with them. "Sioux are only little herds of buffalo all scattered. The white men are like the locusts when they fly so thick that the whole sky is a snowstorm. You may kill one, two, ten. Yes, as many as the leaves of the forest, but there are so many that their brothers will hardly miss them. Kill one, two, ten, and then ten times ten will come to kill you. Count your fingers all day long and white men with guns in their hands will come faster than you can count."

A voice shouted, "White soldiers mostly gone to war in east. Not enough here to stop us!"

Little Crow responded coolly, "Yes, the whites fight among themselves away off to the east. Do you hear the thunder of their big guns? No, it would take you two moons to run down to where they are fighting, and all the way there your path would be among white soldiers as thick as tamaracks in the swamps of the Ojibway. Yes, they fight among themselves, but if you strike at them, they will all turn on you and devour you and your women and little children just like the locusts in their time fall on the trees and devour all the leaves in one day."

The braves continued to banter with him, challenging Little Crow to accept the role of spokesman.

"I think," a voice taunted, "Little Crow has become a miserable coward!"

The accusation shocked the throng into silence. They had dared to call him a coward. They watched him intently as he bent to a bowl held by his wife. He rubbed his hands together, blackened his face with powder and covered his head with a cloth.

Others took up the chant, "Coward! Coward!" They knew Little Crow could not let the charge of cowardice go unanswered. They watched and waited.

Little Crow moaned, uttered an anguished cry and appeared to be in great torment. His eyes rolled up, he grimaced and raised his arms heavenward. Through it all he rehearsed his next oration. His angry eyes flashed in the torchlight. He dashed his eagle feather headdress to the ground and spat out his words.

"Ta-o-ya-te-du-ta is not a coward, and he is not a fool! When did he ever run away from his enemies? When did he ever leave his braves behind him on the warpath and turn back to his tepee? When we walked away from our enemies, he walked behind on your trail with his face to the Ojibways and covered your backs as a she-bear covers her cubs. Is Little Crow without scalps? Look at his war feathers! Behold the scalp-locks of your enemies hanging there on his lodge poles! Do our enemies call Little Crow a coward?

He is not a coward and not a fool! Braves, you are like little children; you know not what you are doing."

He eyed them coldly, contemptuously. He allowed several moments of silence to prevail. Slowly raising his right arm, he spoke with an intense but saddened voice. "You are fools! You cannot see the true face of your chief; your eyes are full of smoke. You cannot hear his voice; your ears are full of roaring waters. Braves, you are little children. I say again, you are fools! You will die like the rabbits when the hungry wolves hunt them in the dark moon of January. Little Crow is no coward. But perhaps he is a fool, too. He will die with you!"

Streaked with jagged flashes of lightning, a black mass of roiling clouds descended from the northwest. The eastern sky, still cloudless, yielded faint dawn light that revealed the main compound of Redwood Agency, a cluster of brick, frame and log buildings that included sleeping quarters for the Agency staff. About a half-mile north and west, lamp-lighted windows of four recently constructed traders' stores indicated that owners and employees were arising or were already at breakfast, ready to begin the new week's work.

War Chiefs Cut Nose, Little Shakopee, and Grey Eagle led columns of nearly naked, painted warriors who moved silently to take up positions between the Agency and the isolated shops. The braves split into small bands, one surrounding each of the stores.

Suddenly from the bowels of the cloud mass a lightning bolt illuminated the scene and was quickly followed by a booming thunderclap. As if the thunder had been an anticipated signal, a startling crash of gunfire erupted. Without warning, bullets and arrows ripped into the stores. Devilish screams mingled with the roar of weapons as the vicious attack caught the inhabitants of the Agency completely unprepared and at the mercy of the attackers, braves who had little interest in mercy this day.

The shocking uproar brought many to the doors where several were cut down instantly. The Indians charged the shops, slaughtered a score of victims, and took ten women prisoners. In Andrew Myrick's store a clerk was killed instantly, but Myrick rushed up the stairs to his second floor quarters. Realizing his vulnerability, he abandoned his wife and children, climbed out a window at the rear and slid down a drain pipe, sprinting for the concealment of the woods. He was spotted, run down and recognized by several braves, including the brother of his abandoned first Sioux wife. His body was penetrated by six arrows and a rusty scythe. When his remains were identified later, he was found lying on his side with his terror-filled eyes locked open. His mouth was stuffed with tufts of grass.

Detonation

Recovering from their shock, agency survivors fled toward the Minnesota River ferry and escaped because the attackers failed to follow up their original onslaught. Confusion was rampant. The Indians were distracted by the goods and foodstuffs in the stores and sheds. They had suffered without for so long that they could not resist the plunder. Indian women who had remained on the perimeter during the attack began to converge. Their eyes moved faster than their hands, but in the end they missed little of value. The goods they acquired caused them no guilt or remorse, for nothing could compensate for what they had been denied.

Seated on a white pony near Myrick's store, Little Crow relished the early successes. His demeanor quickly changed, however, when he saw the initiative lost in his people's lust for booty. Spurring forward he shouted at Cut Nose to reorganize the warriors into concentrated attacks on the escaping agency personnel. Many braves reluctantly dropped their loot and rushed toward the ford. Along the way they slaughtered several Agency people who had concealed themselves in the brush along the river.

At Fort Ridgely, twelve miles away across the Minnesota River, Captain John Marsh was alerted by early escapees from the Redwood Agency. He immediately rushed toward Redwood with forty-three of his one-hundred man contingent. His bold action resulted in near total disaster. Anticipating the military response, Little Crow concealed his braves in ambush at the ferry crossing where they opened fire on the unsuspecting troop, killing twenty outright. In attempting to escape, Captain Marsh and several of his men drowned. The surviving soldiers frantically retreated to Fort Ridgely.

Small groups of rampaging warriors, many well fortified with Agency liquor, began to roam the area in search of vulnerable targets. Some sought out the despised German settlers at Milford. Others raced across the river to Birch Coulee and Beaver Creek. Up and down the valley, south and east beyond the Cottonwood and west and north beyond Yellow Medicine Agency, bands of maurauders struck. Within the first four days of rampage more than 500 civilian whites were slaughtered and more than one-hundred women and children taken captive.

Sundown on August 21, 1862, brought the first realization of the widespread killing that had begun at dawn on the eighteenth. The slain settlers and soldiers lay where they had fallen. Survivors were in hiding or seeking refuge by working their way toward villages or forts. Tales of horror and outrage began to trickle eastward. The most dreaded phrases in their vocabulary were being carried on the west wind. "Sioux on a rampage. Dakotah Indians on the warpath."

Chapter Fifteen

Crescendo on the Cottonwood

Monday was bread-baking day. During the hot months Maurna arose well before daybreak to do the sifting, mixing, and kneading preparatory to the baking that she began only after the family was breakfasted and off to their chores.

She was about to fire the loaves when the morning stillness was shattered by the noisy arrival of a wagon. She and Ginny rushed to the open door to see disheveled Rose scrambling from the seat. "Maurna, we're needed at the Rivard's. Baby's coming!"

Rose gained the porch and continued. "Clement came flying into our yard, all excited and panting. Poor lad could hardly talk. Soon as he finally got it said, he hurried back home from our place. Hope he doesn't crash that rig. Come on, Lady, get some things together. We got to travel."

Hand at her throat, Maurna exclaimed, "Land sakes, Rose, you scared us half to death. I'll throw some things in a bag." She turned to her daughter. "Ginny, run get the men. Tell them to hurry!"

As she tossed nightgown, fresh underclothing, hair brushes, and her sewing and knitting in a bag, Maurna asked Rose how much the young father-to-be had been able to communicate. "When did the labor begin? First babies often take longer, but not always. Is Carole all right?"

Rose, becoming more composed by the minute, chuckled. "He was stammering and as short of details as men usually are. Couldn't make sense out of most of what he was trying to say. Sounded like everything's normal, but first time fathers always make it the event of the century."

Joseph, Pim, and Ginny poured into the cabin, Joseph giving orders like a company commander. "Pim'll drive you ladies. Don't want you unescorted. Road's got deep ruts. He'll handle the team better. Pim, take your rifle! Never know."

Ginny quickly inspected Maurna's satchel and turned to her mother. "Shall I put my things in your bag?"

Maurna knelt in front of her and put her hand on a narrow shoulder. "Sorry to disappoint you, darlin', but you'll have to stay and be the lady of the house. Joseph will need you. 'Sides, we may be up all night birthin' that babe. We'll tell you all about it when we get back. Now, brighten that pretty face and help Joseph with the baking. There'll be no fresh bread for Pim and me today but rather a fresh life about to begin."

"Yes'm," mumbled Ginny.

Maurna turned to Joseph. "Ginny'll fix your meals. Lots of left-overs from last night. If the babe comes fast, we'll be back for supper. But if darkness beats the birth we'll stay over 'til mornin'. You 'bout ready, Pim?"

Rifle in hand, Pim responded, "Ready's can be."

"Got plenty bullets, Pim?" asked ever-worried Joseph.

"'Bout two dozen. Should be more'n enough."

Rose inserted, "I've brought my weapon, too, Joseph, and plenty experience using it. We'll be fine. Don't be fretting. You'll see us before you have time to miss us."

The three hurried to the wagon, sped out of the yard, and disappeared over the ridge line.

Joseph turned to his little niece. "Know you're disappointed, Ginny, but your mother is right as usual. May be a long session and you'd probably sleep through most of it anyway. Now, let's finish that bread bakin' and then come with me while I finish up some outside work. Then we'll come back in a little early and fix dinner together. All right, sweetheart?"

"Guess so, Uncle Joseph." She took a last look up at the ridge where the wagon had passed, sighed, and strode into the cabin.

Toward sundown Ginny ambled onto the porch where Joseph was relaxing with an after-supper pipeful. "Uncle Joseph, who says when babies come? Mother told me that God decides, but Mrs. Koukkari said the baby had decided to come."

Joseph chuckled and put his arm around her. "Your mother is right, Ginny, but Rose said that to bring us the good news that Carole's time has come. Her baby is movin' under her heart in such a way that a woman knows that it's time to bring it forth so all of us can admire it. Just an expression is all it is, Ginny. Birthin' is hard for the woman and that's why your mother and Mrs. Koukkari went on over to help. Pim escorted them so they'd be safe goin' and comin' back. I'd expect they'll all be home by mornin' with the news of a baby LaChance, and young Clem'll be struttin' like a rooster. A special time it is when the first born comes, Ginny."

"When will we see the new baby? I've never seen a newborn one."

"Soon as a week maybe if all goes well, Ginny. Now get on in and finish up, you hear?"

"Yessir."

Joseph mused on the events of the past few days. He had no regrets about the fight with Werner. I'm no great defender of the Church, he thought, but the likes of Werner have no business ridiculing the beliefs of others.

Other than that incident, it had been a grand time. Rose was in his thoughts more than he cared to admit. Fine woman, that. Seems more understanding of a man than most women. No great beauty, but handsome enough. Fire under that chemise, too, I bet. He smiled. Better not think about that too much. Old dried up juices may get to flowin' again. Well, what if they did? Who's to know but me, or her if I let on to her. Wonder what Maurna would think about Rose and me. And Pim. Have to think how things would look to him. He never really knew his own ma. He seems to like Rose and she likes him. Never thought I'd be thinking this way again. Forgive me, Nellie, I don't mean to be disloyal to your memory, but it's been a long, long time.

Poteen growled low and throaty, hair bristled along his back. "What is it, old fella? You hear something do you?" Joseph cocked his ear and after a bit heard them too, upriver, still a ways off, out past the river bend. Poteen was pawing at the ground, looking up at him and then back towards the noise. The dog's alarm worked on Joseph. All that recent talk about Indians was close to the front of his mind. He rushed into the house, told Ginny to be stone quiet and stay in the house. He grabbed his rifle, checked the load and stepped out onto the porch. "Shush now, Ginny, stay inside," he repeated and closed the door. The sounds were much closer, drunken shouts, off a ways but coming his way.

He saw them as they rounded the bend. Five braves in a flatboat. Probably stole that boat, he thought. Two in back with poles, one on each side, feet dangling into the water, one in front paddling. Drunk and still drinking. Are they wearin' paint on their faces? He couldn't be sure at that distance. They disappeared behind a bend.

He stepped forward above the bank leading down to his boat, held his rifle in full view, and stood stone-faced where they'd have to see him. He wanted to meet their gaze straight on, showing no fear. They came into view, war paint evident, voices at full volume. Poteen's barking alerted the braves, who looked up as they floated past, riding the easy current. Paddle and poles froze in their hands, voices hushed. They stared hard, then turned away. Just before the current carried them out of view, the one in the rear looked back. Then their laughing resumed.

Joseph listened for a moment as the sounds diminished, then sprinted for the house. Poteen spilled in ahead of him as he slammed and barred the door.

"Ginny, get some bread and a jug of water and a few blankets. Quick now. Run, girl."

As she sprang to action, he ran to close and bolt the main room shutters, then the bedroom windows. He barred the back entry, then looked out the peep hole to the north where the Sioux had disappeared downriver.

He watched a few minutes, then rushed back into the main room where Ginny was frozen in place. "What is it Uncle Joseph, what's the matter?"

"Ginny darlin'. It's some bad Indians. I'm not sure, but we got to get ready. Honey, I'm askin' you to do a hard thing now. You go down in the cellar and remain there as quiet as a mouse 'til I can be sure what's happenin'. You hear me child? Don't make even a tiny noise. They don't know you're here. They saw me, but not you. Now get down in there, girl, hurry!"

He lifted the trap door and threw the shawl and a blanket into the pit. He helped the weeping child down the ladder, then handed down the bread and water jug.

"Now, honey, you remember how to throw the board across to bolt the door?" She nodded. "Do it, Ginny, as soon as I close the door. I'll be seein' you as soon as they're gone. Don't be scared, I'm right here in the house."

He reset the trap door, not having the heart to look into her eyes as he shut out the light.

"Now set the board across, Ginny." She did. He tested it. "Good girl. I know it's dark down there, but it's safe. Stay still, now."

He quickly checked the back peephole, then out each side. Nothing. But he could feel them. The look in their eyes as they floated by . . . silent defiance . . . silent contempt. Poteen's growls confirmed his fears. Joseph raced between windows. Was that movement on the east side up beyond the shed? Might be I'm imaginin' things not really there, he reasoned. He had not milked Johanna, he remembered. What a time for a thought like that.

Those devils are quiet as death, he thought as he moved from shutter to shutter. They're probably surrounding the house. Nothing to do but to wait. If he didn't have Ginny, he could maybe slip away, but with her, they wouldn't have a chance. Dear God, don't let Maurna and Rose and Pim come back into the middle of this. Pim has his rifle, but they'd get taken by surprise and be helpless in a minute. Hope that baby is slow in comin'. Is that one of those devils under the bank by the river? Lots of shadows to fool the eyes. Won't be able to see much pretty soon.

His thoughts, fueled by adrenaline, flitted over the back of his mind. Settle down, he said to himself, keep your head. It's Ginny's life at stake as well as your own. If they rush, I may get two or three of them by the time they break in, but not all of them. How drunk are they? Will they try to burn us out? Even if they burn the cabin, Ginny might survive under there, but she might suffocate, too. Can't chance it. If they don't give up and leave, have to figure out some way to divert them. They might take a look and move on. Never know what they might do. 'Cause they don't know themselves 'til they do it.

No sounds. No movement. Time passed. It grew dark. Were they gone? Poteen padded to the front door, waited, growled low in his throat.

Suddenly Johanna bellowed out by the shed. Poteen leapt against the barred door. Joseph rushed to the east window to see them leading Pat and Mike and Johanna over the ridge. He poked the rifle at the opening and fired. He might have hit one of them, but couldn't see for sure as they stumbled out of view. They'll slaughter poor Johanna. The God damn brutes, they're more animal than she is. His hatred and frustration spewed out of his mouth until he remembered Ginny might be hearing him. He went over and spoke a few calming words down to her.

He realized for sure now they weren't just going to harass him and then move on. The act of stealing the animals committed them. They were in it now for the kill. He considered then the unthinkable, putting a bullet through Ginny's head, sparing her what they would do to her if they found her alive. She wouldn't feel any pain. But he dismissed the thought, knowing he couldn't pull the trigger.

He went over to the trap door and whispered, "Ginny honey, listen to me. I know its dark and you're scared. But you mustn't make a sound. No matter what you hear up here, don't unlatch that trap door. Until you hear me or your mother or Pim. You remember, Ginny, don't throw back that board no matter what you hear. Even if it's screams or gunshots. Don't open that door to anyone 'cept one of the three of us. You hear me, Ginny?"

"I hear, Uncle Joseph. Please, please not too long. It's wet and dark." Her voice was strong but full of fear.

"See you as soon as I can, Ginny."

He could reason only one plan that might work. He'd have to creep outside and try to scatter them. Keep movin' and pick them off one by one. If he got one or two, the others might panic and run off. At least he'd be doing something. Nothing harder than just waiting. If he could get into the brush on the hillside, he had a chance to surprise and maybe stampede them. He had to try. If they caught him outside, then looked in the house and found it empty, they likely wouldn't bother burning it down. The plan gave Ginny her best hope.

Through a slit in the shutter he saw the glow of a fire beyond the ridge and caught the aroma of cooking meat. "Bastards! Eating off Johanna." His rage was overpowering. He said a few more words to settle Ginny, then filled his pockets with ammunition, sheathed his skinning knife, and waited by the door for complete darkness.

"Dear God," he prayed, "I've been ugly, unforgivin' mean for many years now. I don't deserve forgivin' for myself, but please spare that dear child. Please guard her and keep her from those devils and what they might do to her. I've had my time. I've known love and received more of it than I ever gave or deserved. I thank you, God, for all your blessings. Just grant me that one final request. Let little Ginny survive unharmed."

He reached to unlatch the door, then stopped. Chuckling, he strode over to the cupboard, reached up, grasped the whiskey jug and brushed off the cobwebs. He pulled the cork with his teeth and held up the jug, addressing it in a low tone. "Old friend, I've shunned you for a while, but I need your help. You've never been more welcome." He took a long pull, swallowed, let it burn, took another short chug, and replaced the cork. "If I see the dawn, Dear Lord, I'll renew the pledge. If I don't, I guess it won't be time enough to be habit formin'." He put the jug back on the shelf and strode back to the door and the waiting Poteen.

After several calming breaths, he carefully released the lock. Poteen's manner assured him there was nobody waiting just outside the cabin. He hushed the dog, pulled the door open just a few inches, paused, and slipped out. Holding Poteen by the collar, he listened, waiting for his night vision to improve. Black as the hold of a ship. He noted low voices and firelight beyond the ridge as Poteen pulled him across the porch. "Lord Jesus Christ, Son of the Father, have mercy on me a sinner," he prayed. Funny how you never forget prayers, once learned, even if you don't say 'em for years. Remembering that some of the boards squeaked, he stepped off the porch. He could hear the braves clearly, though they seemed less boisterous. Content with full bellies, damn 'em!, he thought.

He crept toward the path leading up the hill where Rose stood so close with him just yesterday. If he could get to the crown, he'd be above them and have the advantage. He and Poteen moved cautiously, though controlling the agitated animal was increasingly difficult. Quiet, boy, his hand tried to convey as it patted the dog's hackles. They had progressed only part way up the hill when Poteen could contain his outrage no longer, wrenched free and veered off through the brush at full sprint. A primordial howl announced the dog's charge and crashing entry into the midst of the startled Indians. Joseph heard screams, vicious roars, several shots, a final defiant howl, then silence.

Hoping the braves would be distracted by the attack, Joseph abandoned caution, quickly gained the crest and looked down on the pillagers' camp. One, two, three of them, stood in full view in the glare of the fire with bloodied Poteen at their feet. In the background he saw Johanna's carcass and the tethered Pat and Mike.

Resolve conquered fear as Joseph edged over to stand beside the oak tree. Leaning against it to steady his aim, he picked his target, took a deep breath, held for a moment, then began to squeeze the trigger . . . .

The eight inch blade penetrated Joseph's right side under the ribs with an upward thrust into his heart that lifted him off the ground. He exhaled "Sweet Jesus," half-turned, and his brain registered its last image, a grinning, paint-streaked face that slowly dissolved in the enveloping blackness.

Chapter Sixteen

Lost and Found

Pa Kotelnik, Will, and Rob had been under siege since dawn in the barricaded house. Unable to sleep, Pa had gone to the barn well before first light to soothe a sick calf. While ministering to the beast, he had heard muted Sioux voices. He climbed out the hay loft door, let himself softly to the ground on the side away from the interlopers and circled to the far side of the house. Reaching the front door, he quickly entered and threw the bolt. He hollered "Indians!" to shock the boys awake while rushing to close and bar the shutters. Wild-eyed, Will and Rob dashed to assist him, asking questions as they moved. Each of them primed and loaded rifles as they talked.

"How many are there, Grandpa?," asked Rob.

"How do you know they mean us harm?," queried Will.

"Several, maybe six or more, who knows? If'n they didn't mean harm why was they sneaking? That answer your questions?"

"Guess so," said Will. "I'll watch by the front window. Rob you take the river side, and Grandpa, you take the barn side where you heard them."

Revealing his anxiety, Pa began to chatter. "Dawn's breaking, should be able to see 'em pretty good in a minute or two. They may not know we're on to them. Keep your eyes peeled, your life may depend on it. If they come at us, aim low and shoot to kill. No time for hesitation or mercy. If they come, it won't be for a visit. Sure hope your mother don't decide to come on home about now."

"Don't be firing at shadows now, Rob. Make sure it's an Indian before you shoot," advised Will. "They'll have to come across a fair piece of open space. I sure wouldn't want to try it if I was them."

"Saw some movement out by the barn, Will," whispered Pa. "Might be I should fire one shot that way to let 'em know we spotted them. Might be they'd think less about rushing us if they know we're ready for 'em. What you think, boys? Besides we got to get 'em out of here before your mother walks right into 'em."

"I think you're right. Let 'em know we're ready. All right with you, Rob?" asked Will.

"Fire away," shouted Rob.

Pa waited until he saw movement by the corner of the barn, then snapped off a shot that chinked away a piece of wood from the barn wall. The shattering sound reverberated in the confines of the house. They heard shouts and oaths from the direction of the barn. The warriors had received the message.

The sun was up. They watched and waited, sensing that the likelihood of the Indians rushing the house was diminishing with each moment. Rob shuttled between front and back while Will found cold biscuits that he brought to the others, then took his post again at the front. Two Indians came into view on a ridge 200 yards distant. Waving rifles over their heads in a taunting manner, they stepped from tree to tree, inviting the besieged to fire. Obviously drunk, they were enjoying their control over the entrapped farmers. The temptation to shoot was great, but Pa's words restrained their guns. The old man's anxiety increased as he was forced to make a difficult decision. Finally making up his mind he explained it carefully to Will and Rob.

"Boys, I've been thinking things out, and I've settled on what to do. Can't risk waiting no longer. Them devils look as if they're going to set up there and wait us out. We're safe here, long as we stay put, but we know your mother is due back any time now and she's gonna run right into their bloody hands. I've got to try to sneak out and get behind 'em on the prairie road to warn her back. Hate to leave you boys alone, but right now, you're safer than your ma. Can't just set here and let her fall into a trap. You understand, boys?"

Will spoke solemnly. "I've been thinking along the same lines, sir. But I'm younger than you and maybe could better bring it off. I might even be able to outrun 'em if they spot me."

"No, Will, you stay here with your brother. I've had lots of years. You got yours ahead. 'Sides, she's my daughter, my little girl. My job to protect her. Been doing it all my life."

Will's eyes were filmed with tears as he kept his face turned away from his grandfather. Controlling his emotions he said softly, "You always have said that a man's got to do for his people. Guess I never understood that before as I do right now, Grandpa. We'll try to cover you and be praying with all our might, eh Rob?"

"For sure, Grandpa, and be as careful as you can be. We love you, Grandpa. Good luck."

"You're fine boys and will be good men. I'm proud to be your grandfather." He hugged each of them, then went to the back shed door and peered out. "I'll leave you my rifle. It'll give you one more loaded gun if they come at you. Promise me that whatever happens you'll stay inside these walls. Don't get lured out no matter what you hear or see. Give me your word on that, boys."

They mumbled a reluctant promise.

"Hope they're all drunk and not watching the back. It'll take me a while to circle behind 'em. Stay alert and take care of one another. The great God has plans for you boys. Hope its a long, full life. I'll be seeing you soon." Pa unbolted the door and slipped out on the back stoop, heard the bar on the door refastened behind him, and crawled off towards the woods fifty yards away.

They had breakfasted late after the difficult birth. Young Carole had bled more than they liked, but seemed all right. Her new daughter was sleeping pink and shiny next to her mother and under the delight-filled eyes of Clement, Adrien, and Bernadette. Rose and Maurna had cleaned and straightened up the main room and accepted the gratitude of the Rivards.

Wearily they strode to the rig where Pim had prepared straw beds in the wagon. Their eyes thanked him as they climbed aboard. The return trip would take about an hour over the bumpy trail road. They propped up sacks for pillows and settled in. Though Pim drove the team slowly and carefully, the deep ruts ensured a bumpy ride.

Rose and Maurna talked of the birthing and the relief to have it done, with such a prize as the result. After a brief span of silence, Maurna glanced over and noted that her friend had fallen asleep. Smiling contentedly, she watched the clouds streaming east as they thickened and threatened to blot out the brightness of the day.

Maurna's thoughts drifted. She recalled the deep sadness of her three miscarriages during her early married years, the tears of pain in Timothy's eyes, and their fear that they would never have a live child. And she remembered the ordeal of the death of Joseph's wife, Nellie, and the child she was carrying. They're your children, too, Dear Jesus, why must these tragedies happen? Why do you permit them to be conceived and then allow the heartbreak and the pain? But I mustn't question. Thy will be done. You work in strange ways, they tell us. The clergy tell us not to permit doubts that will challenge our faith. But then why did you give us an inquiring mind?

Doubts came very seldom to Maurna, and she tried to dismiss them quickly, fearing that they might take root and contaminate her beliefs. She took too much comfort from her faith to risk losing the promise and consolation of it. Casting away the negative thoughts, she thought a brief prayer: "Thank you, sweet Jesus, for the beautiful child born to our friends this day and for the opportunity to help bring her into this troubled world. And thank you for this gorgeous day and for the good health of our family members and friends. And thank you for all your blessings, Amen."

She tried to doze off. Exhausted, but uneasy and inexplicably restless, she glanced again at her friend and envied her repose. Maurna recalled a recent conversation when Rose had introduced the sensitive subject of remarriage. Maurna had brushed off the question, commenting that she doubted any man would look at an old lady like herself. When Rose had laughed and asked her how old she was, Maurna had confided that she "had twenty-nine winters" and showed a lot of wear. Maurna had realized that Rose was leading up to something, more concerning herself than Maurna. She's pre-conditioning me about her relationship with Joseph, as if it wasn't as obvious as the sparkle in her eye.

Rose had persisted with the topic. Maurna had admitted to herself, but not to Rose, that the thought of possibly remarrying had crept into her mind only recently, but she had quickly dismissed it. No man could measure up to her beloved Timothy. She had felt guilty and disloyal and had deliberately dismissed the notion, but had told Rose that she could not imagine herself remarried, that Ginny had plenty of good male influence around her and that she, herself, had an abundance of love from her family and from all of their good friends. She had her dressmaking and her dream of creating grand gowns and other garments. No, she had concluded for Rose's benefit, she didn't consider remarriage even a remote possibility.

Rose had listened politely, but was obviously more open to the notion. She had stated that her husband was in the ground more than four years now. "He was a fine man and I loved him dearly. Still do, matter of fact. But life is a wheel. Each time it comes around, the view is a little different." Rose had concluded by saying she had thought about it some, just as an exercise of the mind, not of course with anyone in particular in mind.

Oh Rose, I love you like a sister, Maurna thought, but I'm not quite as unobservant as you think. She smiled as she looked over at her dozing friend. If Joseph is of a mind, she thought, he'd look far to find one better than dear Rose.

About a half mile from home, Pim noticed two raucous flocks of crows circling up ahead. They were agitated and rose up, then dove down toward the ground through the branches of the trees. Unusual behavior, he thought. Crows don't normally bunch up until late September. Might be the turbulent weather. Instinctively he hitched the reins and picked up the pace.

The heavier jolts stirred his passengers. Rose poked her head over the wagon box. "Getting near to home are we, Pim?" She lifted her head a little higher and declared, "Maurna, you can start to unravel. We'll be there directly." Rose busied herself, patting her hair in place under her bonnet.

She's getting ready to see Joseph, or rather for him to see her, Maurna chuckled to herself. She swept some loose hay from her skirts and stretched. "Birthin's are always special, aren't they, Rose? The beginnin's of life, so full of hope and promise. Carole had a hard time, but she's strong and will be up and around right quick. She looked beautiful, didn't she? Clement was a wreck, but so proud and relieved. He's a fine young man and loves her so. Pim, heaven's sake, what's your all-fired rush? You're goin' to wear out those poor creatures pullin' us so fast."

There was no response from Pim who stared up the trail. Just one more ridge to climb, he thought, and he'd be able to see down the ravine to the cabin. The cawing of the crows sounded a discordant chorus that disturbed him.

The first stark sign was the gutted carcass of Johanna lying just off the trail in low meadow grass beside charred logs. Blood was congealed, one whole hind quarter gone. Pim hollered, "Dear God" and leaned forward in a crouch, his hand reaching for the rifle on the floor of the buckboard.

Alarmed, the women rose up, holding on to the sideboards for balance. "Oh, Pim, whatever's happening?" shouted Rose over the loud screeching of the wheels.

As they came in view of the cabin they saw Poteen, eyes staring, throat slit, legs askew, blood over his entire upper half. They saw beyond him the front door ajar, the shutters closed, and felt the ominous silence. They leapt from the wagon, rushed across the porch and into the front room. A shambles. Clothing and pottery scattered everywhere, the whiskey jug smashed on the floor, blankets and sheets torn, and firewood flung about. Maurna rushed into the bedrooms, screaming, "Ginny, Joseph, where are you? Oh, Dear God, where are you?" Pim rushed outside and down to the boat landing. Maurna emerged from the bedroom and stood, struck numb. She was holding the bright red bonnet in her hands. Rose rushed out, over to the shed and past it. She had fallen as she climbed the path on the hill, searching frantically. Out of breath she reached the crest and froze. Starting as a low, heavy moan in her breast, her screams built in volume.

The screechings from above shook Maurna out of her trance. She rushed outside, met Pim coming up from the river bank, and raced toward sounds of anguish on the hill. When they broke through at the top, they saw Rose kneeling under the oak tree, fists clenched, huddled over a figure lying before her. Agonized moans emanated from deep within her.

Maurna fell to her knees beside her and beheld her brother Joseph, head layered with dried blood and his barely recognizable face cruelly lacerated. Maurna placed her bonnet over his face and took Rose in her arms. The dreadful moans continued. Standing above them, Pim looked away and quietly wept.

Maurna turned her head and said calmly, "Pim, we'll search the area for Ginny." They looked around the crest of the hill, then down by the shed and the river. After checking through the house again, they stood helplessly on the porch. Shock was giving way to painful reality.

Maurna spoke. "They must have taken her with them, Pim. God help her. We'll bury your father where he lies. Go get the shovel and bring a sheet and blanket to shroud him in." As she and Rose began the slow climb, Maurna said over her shoulder to the retreating Pim, "and a damp towel to clean him with, Pim."

On coming out of the cabin Pim stopped to pick up a stone that he hurled viciously at the crows on the ground picking at Poteen's body. The scavengers scattered, squawking.

They cleaned Joseph's face as best they could, wrapped his body tightly in a sheet, then buried him shallow under the shade of the oak tree. A few quick prayers and they descended the hill.

Rose got in the wagon, turned it around, and paused before leaving. "Maurna, I've got to see to my people. You and Pim can't stay here. They may be back. Your house is not strong enough. Start in to New Ulm. Stay near the road, but off it a little way so they won't see you. Hide until dark, then get into town. We may barricade at home. Our house is solid and we'll have plenty guns. We'll make our way to New Ulm when it's safe. You could come with me now, but I know you'll be wanting to find Ginny. God be with you." She was off in a rush, her jaw set firm, her eyes hard as granite.

Rose forced herself to shake off the horrible scene she had witnessed. Joseph dead. Ginny missing. She could not give in to grief and despair. Her sons and father became her only concern. She prayed to God with a fervor she had not felt for years. "Please spare them, Dear Lord."

As she rounded the last sharp bend in the road before her home came into view, she had to slow the pace to negotiate the unbanked turn. They emerged as ghosts from the brush beside the pathway and were on her before she could react. One brave dove between the animals to grab hold of the harness and reins. Another leapt into the wagon box. The drag of the Indian holding the harness straps slowed the horses to a walk. The reins were ripped from her hands from behind. She was yanked rudely from her perch and thrown heavily to the ground. Each of the nearly naked, painted Sioux grabbed an arm, lifted her to her feet, wrenched her arms straight out to her sides and dragged her through the brush to a campfire where four other braves were lounging.

She willed herself to silence and looked straight ahead, showing them no sign of fear or pain. Until her eyes fell upon her father. Pa lay spread-eagled, tied to bending saplings. Blood covered his bared chest and his torn groin. His legs splayed awkwardly, his mouth lay open, his teeth were clenched. His eyes were rolled back, his head was crudely scalped. Rose registered the gruesome sight, but was unable to withstand the shock. She recoiled and started a scream, but it aborted. Suddenly her pain and horror dissipated, replaced by a calm surrender that erased the anguish. Her mind could absorb no more. Her final dim thoughts accepted the inevitable that Will and Rob must be dead, too, or the Indians would not be so brazen near her home. If their lives had ended, let hers be over with, too. She lost control of her limbs and collapsed at the feet of her painted captors.

The braves commenced to taunt her, treating her as a toy, tossing her back and forth among them. They sought a response, but were thwarted. She had become a limp rag, a senseless creature. Her tormentors became annoyed and confused. No tears, or screams, or expressions of hate as they had expected. Angrily they stripped her nude, made obscene gestures, and derisory comments. They touched her all over, even her private parts, then withdrew their hands almost shamefully. They could not understand her peculiar behavior. Through it all her sparkless eyes met their gaze. She remained calm, non-judgmental, disinterested. Like a patient parent or teacher, she seemed to be waiting for their nonsensical behavior to end. Astounded, uncomprehending and becoming wary, the braves stopped their provocative antics and stepped back. One of the more daring tied her to a tree. They resumed their drinking, needing the infusion to screw up their courage. Mumbling among themselves, they glanced fearfully at Rose from time to time. They would deal with the crazy white woman later.

Maurna and Pim thoroughly searched the area before Maurna slumped resignedly on the edge of the porch, totally drained. Pim, searching by the river, suddenly came back in a rush, as if he had forgotten something. Sprinting into the cabin past Maurna, he fell to his knees on the bedroom floor and tried to lift the trap door. But it was locked securely. Locked from the inside! His heart pounded as he tapped the signal. Silence! He rushed outside, grabbed the axe and chopping wedge, sprinted back inside and jammed in the wedge. Prying upward, he inserted the blade and stepped on the handle for leverage. The trap door gave, then split and fell part way open. He reached inside to slide the board free. Light spilled into the cavity revealing the tiny form of Ginny curled on top of the flour barrel.

"Maurna, Maurna! Come quickly!" Pim climbed down the ladder to the dirt floor and went to the child. He put his face in front of her open mouth and felt her faint breath. He took her in his arms, tears running down his cheeks. He looked up at his aunt framed in the opening above him. "My father took care of her. She's alive!"

Chapter Seventeen

In God's Hands

Neither Will nor Rob spoke of their concern, but their eyes betrayed them. Pa had been gone more than six hours. They had no idea whether he had succeeded in circumventing the Sioux or whether he had been able to forewarn their mother. They only knew that the Sioux were still on the ridge where occasionally a drunken brave would show himself, brandish his rifle, and taunt. Will had fired at one of them, causing a swift retreat behind a tree, but apparently his slug had not found flesh. Soon after the gunshot, two laughing savages appeared on the ridge, displaying a form they held suspended by the arms in full view of the house.

"My good God, Rob," Will moaned. Rob raced to the window and shared the sight of their unclothed, bloodied mother hanging limp between the two braves, her chin falling forward on her breast, her hair hanging in strings to her waist.

"Filthy, rotten brutes," shouted the horribly shocked Rob who flinched as a shot rang out next to his ear. One of the Indians grasped his shoulder, dropped his victim, and fell to the ground. The other brave pulled Rose and his fallen companion back beyond the crest.

"You got one of them, Will. You hit him good!"

Will shook his head. "I was aiming at her."

Rob looked at his brother incredulously, then understanding slowly dawned, and he turned away so Will would not see his tears.

The braves were growing tired of the game. At first it was most enjoyable to humiliate the white woman and watch her suffer. But she no longer responded. She accepted every violation with neither pain nor shame. She did not express hatred or anger. One of the braves had recognized Rose as the Christian religion teacher at the Redwood Agency, ridiculed her God to her face and laughed at the idea of heaven and hell and of Jesus rising from the grave. When she looked through him, his frustration turned to rage. He jumped up and down before her, frothing and shouting, "You are Jesus lady. You preach Jesus to us. You say to us that Dakotah God is not true God. Only your Jesus true God. You tell us to live like Jesus. You say we should be like Jesus. Well now you be like Jesus. You die like Jesus."

Storm clouds moved in from the west in the early evening. Thunder rumbled and lightning streaked as the approaching cloud bank hastened dusk and melted away the last shadows. The boys made out only obscure movements on the ridge, dark images moving with feverish intensity. Lightning flashes intensified, thunder resounded, and light rain began. Suddenly a protracted bolt illuminated the scene for several seconds. The savages had lashed Rose's wrists to a horizontal maple limb from which her limp form hung suspended off the ground. Wild rose vines had been crushed around her bowed, bleeding head. An arrow shaft protruded from her side. Her nude, lifeless body twisted slowly in the lusty breeze.

Transfixed in horror the boys were incapable of response for several moments. Will forced himself to brace and pre-aim his rifle waiting for the next flash of light. When it came, it confirmed that it would be pointless to squeeze the trigger. Their mother was beyond pain. As they wept, they could do no more than whisper their love. Violent bolts of lightning flashed the scene on and off. Heartsick and devastated the boys turned away, but they knew that the image would remain with them for the rest of their lives.

In addition to his rifle and rucksack, Pim carried his benumbed little niece. Maurna had their provisions slung over her back in a bundled blanket. They had packed hurriedly; a sackful of dried corn, some dried beef, a few carrots, two loaves of heavy brown bread. For additional fire power, Pim had strapped Joseph's revolver to his belt opposite his sheathed skinning knife. A small hatchet was out of sight in his rucksack along with powder, slugs, and a canteen full of fresh water. All wore walking shoes and ponchos over the clothing they had been wearing for two days.

Pim led the way up the side of the ravine to the prairie plateau above the river. He had considered crossing the Cottonwood in front of their cabin in order to avoid the need to ford it near New Ulm, but had rejected the notion because the going on the other side would be slower and they would be more vulnerable to ambush. When they reached the plateau, they crossed the Cottonwood Trail into high prairie grass that would help conceal them as they paralleled the road toward New Ulm. Though basically flat the terrain was a rolling series of low rises and shallow swales that prevented them from viewing more than a few hundred yards ahead. Just below the crest of each rise Pim placed Ginny's hand in Maurna's and crept cautiously to look ahead. Moving slowly through the shoulder high grasses, their eyes searched for any movement or smoke. Fully aware of their vulnerability, Pim stopped them from time to time to simply listen. He fought down the panic prey must feel when surrounded by stalking predators.

Ginny had not spoken since they found her in the cellar. She responded to neither affection nor questions. Dear God, what did she see and hear, worried Maurna. Joseph had clearly devised her escape. "Dear Joseph," she prayed, "please welcome him into your Kingdom, Lord. His last act was the greatest love we can display." Maurna's mind struggled with the series of shocks that had overtaken them in such a brief period. She followed Pim, acknowledging his better knowledge of the terrain and his skill at movement through the countryside. When they were roughly two miles from their farm but still four miles from New Ulm, Pim settled them in a patch of heavy brush in the vast sea of high grass. After resting a moment, he told Maurna that he would scout ahead for a half mile or so and that they would risk no more travel until dark now that they were a safe distance from their farm. As he crept silently away, he reminded her to remain silent.

Maurna hugged Ginny to her breast, made soft soothing sounds in the child's ear, shut her eyes and tried to close out the image of Joseph on the ground. The soft warm breeze rustled the leaves of the bushes and the soft grasses. Most days the sounds would have been soothing.

In small groups the sated braves began straggling back to their command post, Little Crow's village. Small, unorganized bands had ravaged and plundered, attacking isolated settlements and farms, torturing and murdering settlers and destroying livestock and homes. The most concerted attack had been against New Ulm where 200 braves had nearly captured the town. They were finally driven off by the townspeople whose numbers had been tripled by refugees seeking safety and the timely arrival of volunteers from Mankato and Saint Peter.

Little Crow was adamant. He was the warriors' choice as spokesman and he intended to speak. The head soldiers, Cut Nose, Little Shakopee, and Gray Eagle assembled the Soldier's Lodge to forge strategies for the next few days. Except for the New Ulm attack, efforts had been scattered and disorganized. Blood lust had been satisfied during the two-day orgy, but it was time to band together in common effort.

Little Crow tried reasoning with his celebrating brothers. The only leverage they had, he told them, was to deal from strength while the whites reeled in defeat and panic. Arguing that they could not win an all-out, lengthy war, Little Crow challenged them to capture Fort Ridgely, then negotiate. Cut Nose and Gray Eagle were persuaded and told their warriors that Fort Ridgely must be overwhelmed or their uprising would be in jeopardy.

As battle preparations went forward, Little Crow visited among his people, toning down the more exuberant. His inspection of the prisoners assured him that, except for a few violations by young braves, most were being treated reasonably well. Big Eagle argued that they ought to be turned over to Lieutenant Sheehan at Fort Ridgely. He reasoned that the whites would fight harder to free their women and children, but Little Crow was determined to hold the hostages as bargaining chips.

Feasting and dancing pervaded the camp. Drums resounded. The euphoria of having struck a bloody blow and garnered long-awaited revenge fed on itself and inspired the desire for more. They boasted of their prowess as warriors as stolen provisions and liquor were passed about freely.

The prisoners looked on in horror and fear. Many had seen loved ones tortured or murdered. Knowing the capricious nature of their captors, they helplessly awaited their own fates. The revelry continued through the night. The beleaguered survivors in New Ulm heard and felt every drum beat until dawn as they feverishly rebuilt their defenses for the expected second attack. Further help from the east was nowhere near as yet.

To Maurna's great relief Pim soon returned from his scouting excursion. He whispered softly to her, "I didn't see a single light anywhere. It's as if all the lights in the world have been snuffed out. If not for the lightning flashes, I would have seen nothing at all."

The rain came in quick squalls, let up briefly, then came again. Maurna succeeded in keeping Ginny relatively dry, but was herself soaked from the waist down.

Pim reassured her. "This rain is a nuisance but maybe a blessing at the same time. The Indians may sit tight in shelters. We'd better eat a bit, Aunt Maurna, to keep up our strength. I know you've no appetite, but you have to force yourself. I intend for us to survive. I have debts that need to be paid." His intense tone frightened Maurna. "I mean it, Aunt Maurna, get some food in you and in Ginny, too. We've had nothing since breakfast at the Rivards. God knows when Ginny last ate. Come on now, if not for yourself, for Ginny."

Maurna reached into the bundled blanket and extracted a few carrots and a chunk of soggy bread. She tried to place pieces of bread in Ginny's mouth, but the silent child turned her head away.

"Don't worry about her. She needs food less than you do, Aunt Maurna. She's not used up much energy. But you have. Eat. She needs you strong. So do I. We need each other as never before. And some help from God, though He's not been very helpful to us this day."

Suddenly the child mumbled in her sleep, sat up and cried out, "Poteen, where's Poteen?"

Maurna squeezed her in her arms and spoke softly, "Poteen has gone on ahead, darlin'. He's helpin' to find the way for us. We'll catch up with him soon enough."

"Aunt Maurna, we must use the darkness to move closer to New Ulm. The wet grass and ground will muffle noise. We have to be absolutely silent. They're out there watchin' and listenin'. We need to be in sight of New Ulm by dawn. Then we can sleep for a while and look over the situation in daylight. For all we know, the Indians may have taken the town by now. I do know we have to get off this exposed prairie by daylight. Come on now, we have to be movin'."

Ginny awakened when he lifted her. She shook her head and squirmed to be put down. He looked at Maurna, then placed Ginny on her feet. She stepped off in the direction he had indicated. "Well I'll be durned." He smiled for the first time since the day before. "Hold on there, trooper, I'm the leader of this expedition." He quickly caught up with her. Maurna followed as her eyes filmed over with tears.

Just before dawn they positioned themselves on a ridge from where they could see a few flickering lights from New Ulm. Peering down on the Cottonwood ford, they could not see if it was occupied. Pim selected an area of heavy brush and high grasses where they fashioned crude beds. The rain had ceased, but it remained overcast and threatening. Water dripped from every surface. Pim took one last circle of their immediate area before the three lay down to try to sleep. The gray light of overcast dawn was their blanket as they huddled under their ponchos and retreated to their thoughts.

Pim came suddenly awake. Had he heard something? Alert, he did not move. The clouds had cleared. The angle of the bright sun indicated mid-morning. He looked over at his slumbering loved ones. I've got to keep them safe, he thought. Too much death already. As he quietly untangled himself, Maurna stirred. He touched her shoulder and gentled her awake. As she opened her eyes, he whispered, "Stay put, Aunt Maurna, and keep silent. I need to look around. I'll be right back."

Slithering through the high grass, Pim proceeded to a crest that gave him a clear view down to the ford. Before he saw them, he heard their voices. A gaggle of braves munched food and drank from jugs as they lounged on both sides of the river. There would be no crossing at the ford. They would have to wait for the Sioux to leave or work their way to the mouth of the river and the bridge to the village. He retreated to discuss the options with Maurna.

Maurna shook her head when she heard the information. "Pim, the decision must be yours. We will do whatever you choose and never doubt your judgment. Trust in God, Pim, He will guide us."

Pim thought that he could do with more of Maurna's blind faith. But she was correct in one thing. It was his decision to make. Time for you to step up, Peter Ignatius Murnane. Be the man your father was.

He began to concoct another option, the idea taking form as he spoke. "Aunt Maurna, there just may be one other way. Ben and I rode our flatboat up and down the Cottonwood many times. There's a sand bar about a quarter mile further down stream. It's shallow this time of year and the footing is solid gravel. We could cross there and be even closer to New Ulm. I know I can find it 'cause there's a huge maple tree right across the river and on this side there's a big rock with a rounded top. I'll sneak down that way and scout it. Eat, if you can. Stay still. I'll be back in an hour or so."

Pim was gone so long that Maurna imagined all sorts of tragic occurrences. She was grateful that Ginny slept the entire time. She heard a muffled sound. Her heart raced as she held her breath and placed a protective arm over Ginny. When the grasses parted and the tousled, rusty hair of her nephew appeared, she exhaled slowly and smiled her welcome.

Pim's enthusiasm rejuvenated Maurna's spirits. He spoke in low, excited tones. "Aunt Maurna, I think it will be the thing to do. I stayed well hidden but got close enough to see the maple and the rounded rock. The water looks about two feet deep. Easy to cross there. And no Sioux anywhere close to it. We'll work our way over after dark and get into position. Good cover on the other side, too, all the way to New Ulm. We'll cross over about an hour before dawn. Any Sioux around will most likely be still sleeping, and there'll be enough darkness left to make it all the way to the village. Nothing to do now but rest and stay hid and build up our strength. We're going to make it, ma'am. You can count on it."

She patted his hand and looked lovingly into his eyes. No words were needed. They covered themselves and awaited the blanket of darkness.

As the sun descended behind the trees, Pim reached across to Maurna and whispered. "I'll make one last scout before the light's gone, Aunt Maurna. Want to be sure the Sioux are still at the ford and won't be comin' behind us. Get everything packed and ready so's we can start right out when I get back. I'll just be a few minutes. Should be easy as a Sunday stroll in New Ulm." He smiled at her, patted Ginny's red-bonneted head and slipped away through the grass.

He worked his way back above the ford. The Sioux were still there, but he counted only four. He tried to ascertain from their activity what they might be planning to do. He did not see a fifth brave standing partially concealed on the far bank about fifty yards downriver. But the brave had seen him. Pim heard his shout to the others and spotted him as he moved to point up the slope at him. Damn, damn, damn, thought Pim. I could outrun them, but Maurna and Ginny can't. I've got to lead them away. He raced to his left away from Maurna and Ginny, got behind some brush, doubled back and sprinted for the shelter to alert Maurna. He burst upon her and frightened her speechless.

"Listen well and don't question," he rasped. "I've been spotted. I'll lead them off away from you. Stay hidden here. Cover yourself with grass. They don't know you're here. Saw only me. I'll be back for you after I lead them in the other direction. If I don't get back, work your way to the sand bar. Follow the plan. You can do it if you have to. I'll be back when I can, but don't wait too long for me. One hour before daybreak cross over and get to town. Bless you both!" And he was gone.

Pim hurried through the high grass and undergrowth down a slight draw back toward their farm. He approached the Cottonwood Trail above the ford where he parted branches to look down. Two painted braves, one mounted, were on the near side of the stream, sixty yards away. They were watching three other braves frantically climbing the steep slope toward where they had spotted Pim. The three were halfway to the crest that would bring them dangerously close to Maurna and Ginny.

Pim leapt out into the middle of the trail, took careful aim and fired at the mounted brave. As the man howled in pain and fell to the pathway, Pim sprinted across the trail, heading away from his kin. The climbing braves cut sideways off the slope and sped after him. Pim kept to the thickest cover. The territory he entered was the eastern end of his trap line. He eased down closer to the stream, reasoning they would expect him to stay in the brush near the crest. Being careful to keep his weapon and powder dry, he crawled into the water and bobbed across to the far bank. Quietly melting into the woods on the north side of the stream, he caught his breath, reloaded his rifle and watched.

In the fast fading light Pim counted five pursuers, not moving in their usual methodical manner but running headlong. He figured the combination of uncontrolled anger and whiskey had dulled their normal instincts.

War-whooping, they came abreast of his position and passed by. He watched them out of sight, then trotted up and away from the river, being careful to place his feet where they would leave no marks. He knew he would have only a few minutes to seek out a safe haven, for once they back-tracked they would have little difficulty detecting where he had crossed the river. Searching his memory as he ascended the far bank, he recalled a rocky ravine flanked by high banks, an area of thick bush, prairie grass and outcrops of rock. Its crisscrossing gorges and defiles would challenge even the best Indian trackers. Carefully hiding among rocks, he rested against a huge boulder, and watched in the direction of the river.

The Sioux emerged from the gray background, moving warily and fanning out. The light was failing and they'd soon have no option but to call off their pursuit until first light. The warriors gathered on a ridge fifty yards from Pim. Their voices carried, and Pim noted that their former frenzy had given way to calm discussion. He smelled smoke and saw fire glowing behind the ridge. If he remained concealed and silent, he was safe for the moment, but lying in safety in the ravine made him of no use to Maurna and Ginny. Much before dawn he would have to circle behind the Sioux. Maurna would not leave their refuge until a couple of hours before dawn and he intended to be there to lead them.

Pim was thirsty and scolded himself for not filling his canteen at the river. His stomach growled. His system was out of kilter. No wonder, he thought, considering what we've been through. He heard something off to his left. He listened but the sound was not repeated.

The braves would be around the fire resting, but one or two may be out prowling, watching, and listening. They would be patient as they were expert stalkers. The Sioux, such mysterious people. Like all people in many ways he had to admit. But different in one way at least. They were the murderers of his father. He prayed then for Joseph, and Maurna and Ginny, for their friends, and for himself. Heavy clouds concealed the moon. He dozed. Visions of Maurna and Ginny. He'd heard what people say the Sioux do to females. He shook himself. Best act like a man, Murnane, he chastised. That's what his father would tell him. He prayed to have the courage to be the man his father expected him to be. Out of nowhere came a thought. Pa, you're not dead are you? You're still talkin' to me, still teachin' me, still lookin' out for me. You're not dead at all, you're livin' in me.

When Pim had waited as long as he dared, he cautiously emerged. In his mind he had rehearsed the route and made what he thought was the best choice. As he moved ahead he heard a faint sound. Crouching quickly, he listened. The sound was not repeated, but he heard a muffled sneeze that told a tale. Animals sneeze like humans, he thought, but I've never heard one try to stifle a sneeze. That was a dead give away, my Indian friend. He circled north to avoid the danger.

It was taking more time than he had anticipated. When he sensed the river bend near their farm, he veered, but his foot found a badger hole and he wrenched his ankle as he fell. Barely suppressing a scream, he quickly unlaced the boot, saw that swelling had already started and hopped the few yards to immerse it in the stream.

Thinking he had only one recourse, he found a log with small branches and leaves at one end and used it to help him float with the current. He pushed into the water, rested his rifle across the floating limb and paddled quietly with his right hand. He listened and watched as he drifted and tried to ignore the faint light in the sky to the east heralding the break of another day.

Maurna and Ginny had barely moved while Pim had been gone. Maurna prayed for relief from the frightening task she faced. Sensing that her muscles had tightened, she clenched and unclenched her fists and stretched her biceps and legs. Since she had a fear of guns and doubted she could ever pull the trigger, she had refused Pim's offer of the pistol. Her only weapon was her scissors, sharp enough but could she wield them against a human being? She doubted it. But to save Ginny's life? She just didn't know and sincerely hoped she would never find out.

She tried to remember how to estimate the time in a night of overcast with no moon or stars to help. Do the birds begin to chirp and sing before daybreak? Do the crickets stop their chattering while it's still dark? Having heard the sounds a thousand times, she should know. She wasn't sure whether faint traces of dawn were already appearing. Better to be early than late. Dear Pim, we know you'd be here if you could be. She shot off a quick prayer for his safety and dismissed from her mind the gunfire she had heard. She needed her full concentration on her task and could wait no longer.

"Come on, little darlin', we must go to meet Pim. He's waitin' for us on the other side of the river." Ginny rose immediately to take her mother's hand. She still had not spoken except in her sleep, but seemed to be more aware. Maurna shouldered her bundled blanket and they crawled out of their grassy cocoon. Her leg muscles loosened as they moved along the ridge parallel to the river. Must keep my head, she thought. What had Pim said? About a quarter mile downstream. A large maple on the other side of the river and a round top boulder on this side. She tried to measure the distance as they walked. They moved slowly, wet branches slapping their faces, imagined sounds stalking them. Action lessened her fear. All her senses were focused. She would get her daughter through to safety. Fair enough to ask God to help, but she'd better do her part, too.

    She estimated where to begin their descent and reduced the degree of slope by angling downward. She tied the blanket around her neck to free up a hand to grasp at bushes and saplings while holding Ginny with the other. She rested from time to time by holding fast to a small tree or bush. The hard going consumed more time than she had estimated.

    Their clothing was shredded. Her hands were blistered and swollen and her hair spilled from her bonnet, distorting her vision. It seemed they had been descending for a long time when she heard the stream and felt the slope flatten at the bottom. The tree line across the water appeared darker than the foreground. She paused to get her bearings, searching the far side. Were they up or downstream of the maple? She listened for the gurgling water sound. It was coming from downstream. Would not a shallow place have rocks that make rapids? Would not rapids produce a gurgling sound? She strained to make out a large tree on the opposite shore. A maple? Perhaps. She looked behind them up the slope and spotted the rounded boulder. Thank you, Lord, for leading us.

    She approached the bank. A three foot drop to the water. She retied the blanket and stepped down to water level. She backed up to the bank and reached to help Ginny mount her from behind. When she felt her daughter's knees clasp her hips and tiny arms tighten around her neck, she stepped off the sand rim and into the water. With each step the water deepened, but didn't rise above her knees. She staggered across, nearly toppling at one point when Ginny unexpectedly shifted. With her last bit of reserve, she fell onto the north bank and managed to cushion Ginny's fall by half-turning to catch her. They lay like beached fish. At that moment all Maurna could think of was that they had crossed the river. The ordeal was almost over.

    She lay in a semi-stupor, completely drained, Ginny snuggled to her side. Exhausted and disoriented, she heard a voice coming from the tree line up the bank. It sounded a message she could not comprehend, and it was a laughing voice. How could anyone be laughing at a time like this? She searched the trees to locate who it was. The voice came again. "White people make much noise." Her eyes refocussed and the sight that greeted her brought her to near despair. Arms folded, clad only in a breech cloth, stood the tallest Indian she had ever seen. His eyes remained hidden in the faint light. Maurna heard him chuckling.

As he drifted noiselessly downstream, Pim became more concerned that he would not reach Maurna and Ginny in time. When he neared the ford, he steered toward the south bank. He did not know how he would climb the steep slope to the flats above, but he knew that he must. Light increased as he slithered up the bank, pulling himself from tree to bush to protruding rock. The inflamed ankle gave no support, only agony. His progress was maddeningly slow. Dismissing the pain, the fatigue, and his increasing desperation, he finally reached the level where he had fired at the Sioux horseman, crawled across the road and through the brush, and parted the grasses. Nothing but flattened grass beds. They had set off without him. God protect them, he prayed. I'll find them in New Ulm safe as can be. Probably at the Lundes already. I'll follow their trail down to the sand bar and cross. Just need to rest a few minutes.

Two drunken, laughing young braves appeared behind the first.

"We watch you come down slope," said the tall one. "You not make good Indian. Too noisy." His companions convulsed in laughter.

Ginny looked up at them, then away. Her blank stare returned. Maurna thought quickly of the scissors in her bundle, but knew they would be useless. In the dim light she could not make out their features, but felt their contempt and sensed their intentions. She stared defiantly at the one who was clearly dominant.

He strode down the bank, ripped off her bonnet, grabbed her loose hair with one hand and Ginny's hand with the other and dragged them up the bank. A brave dashed a few yards into the brush and quickly returned with a small torch that he thrust in Maurna's face.

"Oye Yi Yi," he mouthed. "She's an old one, but maybe not too old. But the little one is too little." The two laughed and danced around them.

"Where you go, noisy white lady? You go New Ulum? You one of German ladies? You no love Dacotah? Yi Yi, we show you Dakotah love."

They dragged them to the campfire site where she clearly saw their painted faces. She held Ginny, straightened her posture, and spoke with as much dignity as her condition permitted. "New Ulm, yes. Where we are goin'. German, no, we are not Germans. We have no hatred for the Dakotah or for anyone. We want only to be left alone."

One of the shorter braves came close and looked into her eyes. "You lie, I see you New Ulm." He spat out his words.

She was startled to be accused of lying. Of course it was possible he had seen her in New Ulm, and perhaps she had seen him. But his face was painted in streaks, his hair in disarray, his eyes reddened with whiskey. "I have been in New Ulm many times, but we do not live there. Live on farm south of Cottonwood. Not live in New Ulm. Not German."

The tall brave commented knowingly. "Lady not speak like German. German speak with ugh sound. White lady and little lady not go New Ulm. Go with us. Little Crow want lady and children prisoners to trade with whites. You go with us Little Crow village. Walk past New Ulm to Little Crow village."

"Please let us go, we can do you no harm. My daughter is ill, she needs doctor. Please, we cannot hurt you. We are weak. Let us go to our own people."

He was adamant. "Brave say go with us Little Crow village. Lady no talk of go other place. Go Little Crow village. Be prisoner hostage."

The others continued to leer and gesture crudely. Though subservient to the tall brave, their intent, if released from his control, was obvious. They continued to agitate. The tall warrior grasped Maurna and dragged her and Ginny closer to the fire. He offered them food and water. "Take for long walk to Little Crow village."

Maurna tried to feed Ginny a corn cake and some water, but the child clamped her mouth closed. Choking down a few bites, Maurna fortified herself for what lay ahead. Whatever it takes, she thought. Ginny must survive. As her nerves settled, her resolution overcame her fear.

The leader stomped the embers, mounted his pony and shot his arm out to the north and west. "Follow to Little Crow village. Long walk."

He led off at a leisurely pace. Maurna tied on her retrieved bonnet, clutched Ginny's hand and followed. The two braves walked behind them in single file. When they cleared the woods that framed the river, the smoldering ruins of New Ulm came into view. Black smoke hung low and thick in the windless air.

My God, Maurna thought to herself, could it be that we are the only whites left alive?

Chapter Eighteen

Response

A frantic special messenger was granted an immediate audience with Governor Alexander Ramsey and James Seymour. The two officials listened in horror to the sketchy report. Sioux on the rampage, Fort Ridgely and New Ulm under siege, hundreds of settlers slaughtered, the Agencies burned to the ground, and the entire Minnesota Valley filled with frightened citizens fleeing to the east for refuge. The tales were disjointed and many unconfirmed, but enough was known to generate mass hysteria. Recovering quickly, Ramsey asked several questions and extracted a few details. He dismissed the messenger, warning him not to add to the general panic by exaggerating the crisis. As the man exited, the Governor remembered to order him to rush his report to the Commander at Fort Snelling.

"Great balls of fire, Jim, what a mess and what an awful time for it to happen. Most of our able-bodied men off fighting the Rebs. This could set back our state fifty years. We'll never get settlers out here again unless we put down this rebellion quick and hard. Damn those red bastards to hell! We should have shipped 'em all out west years ago."

Jim Seymour kept his steady head. As always, he had a calming effect on the volatile Ramsey. "Big problems need massive solutions, Governor. We need immediate help from the federal government, from Iowa, from Wisconsin, from wherever we can. And fast! But let's get our local situation under control. You know who we have to call on, don't you?" He looked Ramsey square in the eye and nodded.

"Oh Mary, Mother of God, you mean Sibley, don't you? Sibley, always Sibley! He's the one who coddled those damn Indians for decades. He's a main cause of this mess, damn him." The Governor rose quickly from his chair and walked to a window looking downhill over the city of St. Paul. "We'd be much farther along building up this country if Sibley hadn't slowed down progress a dozen different ways."

Jim moved over next to Ramsey and said calmly, "Like him or not, he's the one to lead what forces we've got. The people believe in him, he's got military experience, and he knows those Indians. Can talk their language and think along with them. If anybody can bring order to all of this, he's the one. Can't let your personal feelings get in the way of the best solution we have available, Governor." Jim knew that he was right and knew that Ramsey would see the truth of it. Seymour waited for Ramsey to swallow that jealousy and pride and do the right thing.

Ramsey briefly pondered, then sprang to action. He shouted to his secretary in the hall. "Order up my carriage immediately. I've got to get across the river to Sibley's house in Mendota." He shrugged, reached in his desk drawer for his pistol, joined Seymour on the way out and shouted for the benefit of everyone within earshot, "We've got to get Henry Sibley, he's the man for this situation, no doubt about it!"

Jim Seymour smiled as he followed Ramsey out the main capitol entrance to the street and the arriving carriage. He knew his man Alex.

At the two-story stone house, Sarah Sibley ushered them into the ex-governor's study where Ramsey faced the man who had defeated him in his first bid for the governorship in 1858. Sibley, seated by the window, rose to offer the two men vigorous handshakes and a welcoming smile.

"Henry, a calamity is upon us. The damnable Sioux have broken out." Ramsey burst out the news.

"What? Where, how many?"

"All of them, sounds like. Reports are sketchy. Settlers killed, attack on Redwood Agency," lathered Ramsey. "Seems to be general from the Upper Agency all up and down the valley. We need you, Sibley. You're the one they know and respect. You know how best to stop them." He fell back into a chair, out of breath.

Sibley re-seated himself by the window, looked out across the river toward Fort Snelling, thought for a moment, and began to speak. "Sounds bad, least as you describe it, Governor." He looked directly at Ramsey. "Hard not to know what caused it though, Alex. We should have felt it coming. There's been plenty sign. It's been waiting for a spark to set it off. You knew that or should have expected it. I should have, too." He let his words sink in for a moment, looked out the window again and shifted gears. "But the blaming can wait. How to stop them before it escalates. Must be Little Crow, I'd guess. He's lost power among the young braves, but this could be his chance to get it back. They know most of our soldiers are out of the territory. God, what a time for all this."

"There's been lots of folks already killed." Ramsey had caught his breath. "You've got to take charge of our forces, Henry. I'll draw up the official appointment putting you in full charge. You can't say no, too much riding on it."

Sibley was genuinely reluctant to take on the burden but knew Ramsey was correct. Nobody else had his status among Indians. Good God, he thought to himself, I'm too old and tired for this. But there's no choice. I've got to do it or die trying—nice thought that. He walked over to the two men, lifted his heavily lidded eyes, and nodded. "Reluctantly I accept, Governor Ramsey." He shifted his gaze to Jim Seymour, knowing he would be the one to put their plan in motion. "But before the papers are drawn up, alert the troops at Fort Snelling and notify the federal government of our predicament. Get more troops, arms and ammunition here as soon as possible. Don't rest until you've found whatever's available. If Fort Ridgely can stand, we'll be able to contain them. Believe me, gentlemen, if we don't stop them early, Fort Snelling and Saint Paul could go under."

Governor Ramsey edged toward the door. "The people of the State of Minnesota will be forever in your debt, Henry. You have already eased my mind. We'll be on our way. Every moment counts." The two men departed running. Sibley heard Ramsey's hurried goodbye to his wife at the front entry.

The ex-governor turned back to the window, his face creased, his eyes tired. Oh yes, he thought, your concern is commendable, Ramsey, but you and I both know that duplicity in dealings with the Indians spawned this rebellion. The redmen are in the way of greedy people. Watch them run now when trouble comes and put all the blame on the "savages." But that kind of thinking won't help now. The Indians have to be stopped and punished. Lots of innocents in their path.

He called through the open door to Sarah. "Come in, sweet lady. I need your good counsel."

She appeared wearing a worried expression, went into his arms, rested her head on his chest and looked up into his lead-gray eyes.

"You heard most of it, I presume. You know that I have no choice. I'll have to get packed and get to Fort Snelling."

Her eyes filled with easy flowing tears as she shook her head sadly. "Always you, isn't it, Henry? Always you to mend the fences that others keep tearing down. Will it ever be over for you? How much can they take from one man?"

He held her tightly for a moment, then said, "It's a tribute they pay me, dear, and an expression of faith in what we stand for. Trouble is, I find it hard to condemn the Sioux. We've been pushing on them for more than thirty years. I can understand their feelings and thinking, but of course I can't condone their actions. Dear God, what have they started out there? How many will suffer before it's over?" He shook his head as together they went to start packing.

Fort Ridgely served as both symbol and reality. To the white settlers, it represented protection and a deterrent against the restive Sioux. To the Indians, it represented the white man's government, its failed obligations, and oppression of the Dakotah people.

Should the fort fall, the entire Minnesota River Valley from Yellow Medicine Agency all the way to Fort Snelling would be laid open.

Little Crow and his war chiefs organized their disconnected bands of marauding brothers to unite for a concerted attack on the vulnerable bastion. Over 450 well-armed braves filed to the unwalled cluster of log buildings, surrounded the compound, and began a sustained attack.

The soldiers' strategic deployment of their cannon and their creative manner of constantly moving the pieces to different fields of fire kept the Sioux confused, frustrated, and unable to concentrate their forces to capture the big guns. Both sides fought ferociously, and the Sioux nearly overran the bluecoats. But in the final analysis the fort held because the artillery dominated.

When the battle was over, Fort Ridgely soldiers remained locked in their stronghold unable as yet to become active pursuers of the rebellious Indians. But their fort remained as both reality and symbol. Little Crow knew that its presence doomed the cause of his people. From the evening of August 22, after the failed second attack, Chief Little Crow's strategy became one of conciliation. His people did not yet realize the only hope left for the Sioux lay in his ability to cut their losses by trading prisoners for favorable terms of surrender.

Chapter Nineteen

Travois and Travail

It had to be a nightmare. The sudden shocking series of events that had engulfed Maurna and her family couldn't possibly have happened. Joseph murdered, Pim in desperate flight, Ginny and herself herded along and paraded in full daylight past the New Ulm refuge they had been trying to reach. As she clung tightly to her daughter's hand, she saw the barricades and the sentries and realized that the Indians had not occupied the town but that it had been under attack. What about Belle and Abigail and Ansgar? And Rose and her boys and old Pa, what's become of them? And the Rivards with the new baby and Carole near helpless?

Their captors deliberately paraded them single file, slowly, provocatively, just beyond rifle range of guards at the barricades. The tall warrior rode haughtily in front of Ginny and her mother; his two laughing subalterns shuffled close behind.

Ginny remained mute. Maurna feared that the child's mind had simply stopped functioning. "Oh, Dear Jesus, let her remember none of this." Ginny trudged along, her red-bonneted head bowed. Maurna felt totally powerless, but had learned one truth about herself. She now knew that she would fight and, yes, even kill, to save Ginny. She resolved that whatever she had to do. . . .

Though her spirits were deeply deflated, she managed to retain some dignity. She remembered Rose's comment that one should never show fear to an Indian, that they can smell fear. Rose had told her of instances at Redwood Agency where she had been threatened and challenged but had countered the intimidations by standing up bravely in the face of the perpetrator. They will see no fear in my eyes, she vowed to herself.

The smoldering outskirts of New Ulm were soon behind them. Their procession turned north toward the Minnesota River and the road toward Redwood. Maurna saw small groups of painted, well-armed braves and laughing, chattering women off to the sides dragging sacks of plunder and loading them into wagons.

Smoke hung heavily in the still, humid air as they entered the tiny German settlement of Milford. Most of the buildings were either burning or reduced to charred rubble. She began to see bodies. Violently mutilated, flayed, scalped, lying as pitiful bundles caked with dried blood, mouths and eyes open, flies and maggots swarming. Maurna turned Ginny's eyes to the front. Her own revulsion was controlled by supreme force of will and her resolve to show no emotion. She could feel the eyes of her captors studying her reaction to the carnage. Only once did her eyes betray her when they veered to a pair of corpses lying entangled in a bloody embrace. She estimated that she had seen more than two dozen dead white men, women, and children by the time they had passed out of Milford.

A mile further on, the horseman stopped and beckoned Maurna to come abreast of him. He quickly reached down, grasped Ginny and pulled her up beside him. Maurna held on to the child's hand and refused to let go. The brave let the child down, grinned at Maurna and said, "Little One ride. Legs too short, steps too small, grow tired. She ride, go faster. No harm little one."

Maurna relented only because she suspected that Ginny was nearing exhaustion, but she kept hold of the tiny hand and walked along at the horseman's pace. Maurna closed out both fatigue and fear. The saving numbness that gripped Ginny descended upon her and she welcomed it.

After another mile the leader stopped again. He pointed to an abandoned Indian travois tipped over beside the road and gave instructions in Sioux. The two walking braves stood the travois upright, brought it behind the horse and attached it. The horseman handed down Ginny to Maurna and pointed at the conveyance. She hesitated, then understood, and gratefully reclined with Ginny on the precarious travois. They proceeded at such an increased pace that the unmounted braves were forced to trot to keep up. As the little party came opposite Fort Ridgely, muted musketry, cannon and distant war whoops became discernible. The two trailing braves ran forward to the leader, conferred with him, and at his nod whooped shrilly and ran off toward the river. On their way to join their brethren in the assault on the fort, they disappeared into the underbrush. Maurna felt a wave of relief.

How many miles had they travelled? He had said that Little Crow wanted hostages. Dead hostages would be of no value! They mean to keep us alive, she reasoned, and grabbed at that bit of hope.

The battle sounds faded as they approached the Redwood Agency. What they had seen at Milford had been preview. Bloating corpses were scattered around the grounds, many with protruding arrows, lances, or pitchforks. The Indians paid them no mind, seemingly impervious to the nauseating stench. Crows fluttered amidst the decomposition. Throughout the entire compound, Maurna saw not one Indian corpse. A bit further on, near the traders' stores that had been picked clean, Indians stood about drinking and gorging themselves.

When they had moved on several miles, Maurna heard ahead of them the unmistakable buzz of a large gathering. They were nearing the village of Little Crow, where lodges and tepees had been erected over several acres. Litter was everywhere. Broken wood crates and barrels, torn and discarded clothing, bottles, jugs, rucksacks, paper, torn feather pillows, garbage, and feces—human and animal. Scores of fierce dogs fought over bones and chunks of carelessly discarded meat. Since most of the braves were either at Fort Ridgely or on independent forays, females predominated. A few older warriors were stationed around the perimeter, but there was little concern about prisoners escaping. Where could unarmed women and children go?

As the horse and travois entered the village, curious women and children formed a tight gauntlet. Hags taunted and screeched, grabbing at Maurna's shredded gown, spitting at her, hissing, and shaking their fists in her face. The horseman cursed the hecklers and struck out at them with his fists, but hardly discouraged them. Farther up the line the ranks closed tighter and the horseman was compelled to either stop or force his way through. He stopped, but did not dismount. Despite his shouted threats, the tormentors pressed.

Out of the mob a commanding voice roared. The cackling and screeching stopped. Through a small opening, grudgingly formed, a paint-streaked brave strode. Sweat-covered and naked but for a breechcloth, the warrior stopped, folded his sinewy arms and waited for complete silence. He walked the few steps to the travois, gesticulated fiercely, and glared at the occupants. Then the frown changed to a grin as he reached past Maurna to grab the child by the arm. "Ginny, my little lady."

Maurna reacted by beating on the reaching arm but stopped when she recognized the voice. Ginny looked at the painted face, smiled into his eyes and said, "White Spider."

Chapter Twenty

"We Did It Ourselves"

Pim's greatest fear came true. When it was clear that Maurna and Ginny had not reached the safety of the village, he blamed himself. The Lundes tried to ease his burden. After hearing his account, they told him he had made the best decision under the circumstances and his actions had been courageous and selfless. He remained inconsolable.

His lament continued, "I traced the route they followed to the ford, saw heel prints in the narrow strip of sand and the marks of moccasined feet. There was a cold camp fire. I followed the signs leading in the direction of the village and then veered off west to merge with the main trail. A little farther on, I was ordered to halt and raise my hands. Two pickets forced me into New Ulm. They said absolutely no one was allowed outside the perimeter. I had no choice."

"You did all anyone could ask, Pim," commiserated Ansgar.

"And losing your beloved father. Land sakes," added Belle. "And Will and Rob came in before dawn after burying their mother and grandfather on the ridge."

Ansgar told Pim about the attack on New Ulm. "The townspeople and volunteers from St. Peter barely held off the attackers. We're afraid another attempt will be made."

Pim listened, shook his head in disbelief, and left to continue his inquiries on the slim chance that someone had seen Maurna and Ginny.

After repeated queries of the guards, one recalled seeing a small party soon after dawn consisting of a mounted warrior leading a white woman and a red-bonneted little girl. They had been headed toward Milford, he said, adding that the child looked to be about five or six years of age.

"We Did It Ourselves"

Prisoners. In the hands of the filthy Sioux. First, my father, now them. Pim felt rage, then sadness and fear, and finally, gut-ripping guilt. Why did I leave them? My father or Ben would have saved them.

He sought the head of the militia and begged him to organize a rescue of the prisoners. When the man refused, Pim accused him of cowardice and had to be restrained.

When New Ulm was founded nearly seven years before, the German settlers considered organized religion stifling and oppressive. They vowed to become prosperous farmers and businessmen on the strength of their own efforts. God's help was neither needed nor wanted. "God didn't do it, we did it ourselves," was their boast in the early years of success. Only recently had religion been permitted entry, a concession still deeply resented by adamant members of the original core group.

More than two-thirds of the 1500 people currently in New Ulm were settlers seeking safety. Only 200 of the 450 adult males possessed workable rifles. Hatchets, axes, scythes, pitchforks, clubs, and sharpened rake and shovel handles armed the others.

Commander of the defense preparations was Colonel Charles Flandrau whose volunteer group had arrived from near Saint Peter barely in time to help save the town. Flandrau ordered women and children into buildings and homes within a compressed four square block enclosure. Breastworks of fencing, furniture, mattresses, wagons, crates, and barrels were erected. Under the leadership of the few trained soldiers in the complement, men were formed into organized companies. Those not on guard frantically cleaned and repaired weapons and distributed ammunition. Throughout the daylight hours, booming cannon were heard from the direction of Fort Ridgely, and it was clear that New Ulm's fate depended on holding the fort. The occupants of New Ulm shuddered at each distant cannonade as they awaited their turn. No serious thought was given to flight to the east. In the open, the Indians would cut them down like a herd of ponderous buffalo.

Charred ruins on the fringe of town constituted a hazard that the attacking Sioux could utilize as cover. Colonel Flandreau ordered that all buildings outside the barricades be burned to the ground. New Ulm homeowners were forced to witness the destruction of their dwellings. Several women including Belle Lunde protested, but finally conceded the need.

The second full scale attack began at noon on August 23. Pickets fired their weapons in warning as they fell back before the advancing Sioux. Six hundred screaming braves surrounded the slopes to the south and west while small parties circled to the east along the Mankato road. The main force pinpointed its attack at the southwest barricade, rushing furiously with war whoops sounding from 150 throats. Colonel Flandrau ordered one hundred men to meet the braves in the open. The bold tactic broke the Indian's momentum, causing them to hesitate, then fall back. As the exposed defenders in turn retreated, the regrouped Sioux came after them. The New Ulmers stopped, knelt and delivered a volley that was augmented by their comrades at the breastworks who now had the Sioux within range. The Indians suffered severe casualties as their initial attack was thwarted.

Smaller war parties rushed from the north and the west, probing for a weak point. All the while the Indians fired long range into the compound from elevations around the town. The attackers continued the pressure until nearly 5:00 P.M., their efforts becoming less and less enthusiastic. Little Crow soon felt his early optimism begin to fade. He raced back and forth giving encouragement but his braves were losing heart. Disgusted with the failure of his soldier chiefs to inspire their men, he angrily drove his totem into the earth, looked longingly at the fort that had been a town, shook his head and rode off.

As the shadows lengthened, the Indians began pulling back. They retired to three separate camps and built enormous bonfires, assuaging their frustrations with roasted beeves, whiskey, carousing and dancing. Drums thundered all-night reminders to the huddled townspeople that they remained surrounded. Little sleep accrued to members of either faction. Fearing a renewed attack the next day, a few refugees tried to slip out of New Ulm by creeping through the bullrushes along the Minnesota River. Protracted screams carried a clear message back to town. No further escapes were attempted.

Just before dawn on the twenty-fourth, the three Indian camps conjoined. The embattled New Ulmers braced for another assault, but the Sioux had decided to abandon the siege. The Indians formed a procession that began to move slowly to the north and west on the road to Redwood. The caravan stretched nearly four miles and included braves, women and children, stolen cattle and horses, and wagons filled with booty scavenged from the outer buildings of the village. Turning their backs on New Ulm signalled the end of the Sioux dream of sweeping south and east to drive the whites from the Valley.

Unsure whether the exodus was a ruse, Flandreau and the relieved garrison watched the dust-generating procession fade into the distance. The Colonel posted extra pickets in the direction of their departure then quickly organized the weary populace. Gathering them in the street before the Dakota Hotel, he announced his decision to evacuate. Putting down a few half-hearted objections, he reminded them they were dangerously low on

"We Did It Ourselves"

provisions and ammunition. He ordered them to load up whatever was portable into wagons immediately.

Pim gravitated to the site of the Lunde home where Ansgar, Belle, and Abigail stared forlornly at the charred remains. At Ansgar's request, Will, Rob, and Pim assisted in searching through the ruins for what was salvageable. Surviving the flames were several trunks of clothing, a few pots and pans and most of Ansgar's tools, blackened, but repairable. Belle and Abigail's sporadic sobs punctuated the still air as their tears soaked their pathetic belongings. They worked all day and into the night.

At first light Colonel Flandreau solemnly rode past 153 wagons arranged in procession. When he reached the front of the column, he signalled the start with a vigorous thrust of his fist. Heavy with their burdens of women, children, goods, and fifty-four wounded, the wagons eased into motion. Flandreau placed armed riders out front, at the flanks, and to the rear. Pim, who had volunteered as a rear guardsman, took one last look westward to where his aunt and cousin were either in agony or dead. As he breathed a prayer, he fought back tears, set his jaw firmly, and turned back to the trail.

The Battle of New Ulm had seen the destruction of nearly all of its homes, but most of its gallant citizens had survived. The heroic defense had been bolstered by Colonel Flandreau and his volunteers, and by the influx of refugees who had added to their numbers, but the New Ulm townspeople themselves had been resourceful and intrepid in the face of a vengeful enemy. Many of them graciously thanked the Almighty for their fortunate deliverance and acknowledged His assistance. A core group, however, boasted loudly to all, "We did it ourselves!"

Chapter Twenty-One

Captivity

The prisoners were not thrown into one large pen but were divided into small groups and distributed in lodges and tepees. Each group was watched closely by self-appointed elderly women guards whose eyes appeared hopeful that someone would be foolish enough to try to escape. Jabbing them with pointed sticks, they relished the pain they inflicted and the helplessness of the white women. The captives were fed in sufficient amounts, but the food was mainly rancid stews and stale corn cakes. A pail of tepid water was provided for drinking but there was none for washing either themselves or their clothing. Earthen pottery chamber pots were emptied once daily by the contemptuous old women. Each captive was allowed a two to three minute walk around her tepee twice per day, but never after dark.

White Spider escorted Maurna's group to a lodge near his own. Kindly and solicitous, he managed to extract occasional responses from Ginny. On the first evening she asked him to please take her and her mother home. White Spider told her they would go home in a few more days.

Two women shared quarters with Maurna and Ginny. Elderly Emma Walton mumbled mindlessly, occasionally laughing outright. Thirty year old Patricia Jensen had been separated from her husband and four children and had no idea what had happened to them. Maurna was convinced that Emma Walton's mind was gone when she began speaking in quick bursts that made little sense, mostly about Ohio where their farm had been prosperous and they had been happy. She apparently sought peace in being transported back to that pleasant period in her life.

Captivity

Maurna focused on Ginny and her needs, subjugating her own fears and discomforts in her concern for her daughter. She became a protective lioness, standing up to their sadistic tormentors, taking no abuse from them, and keeping her dignity to the degree possible under the conditions. The Indian women seemed to begrudgingly respect her defiant, feisty attitude. Maurna assumed their respect and deference were attributable to warnings they had received from White Spider.

Their blizzard guest visited each evening after dark. White Spider spoke mostly to Ginny and occasionally to Maurna but ignored Emma and Patricia. On his second visit, he warned Maurna to be alert, that there were some bad Indians in the village, especially when drinking. He slipped her a hunting knife with a four inch blade that she quickly concealed in the folds of her blanket. "I tell braves not to harm little girl or her mother or White Spider punish them. When they drink, they maybe forget White Spider's warning."

In the evening of their third night of captivity, White Spider told them that "Little Crow say to move camp north to Yellow Medicine at dawn. I come then to help you."

After eating the barely digestible paste, they attempted to fall asleep immersed in the unrelenting stench of their unwashed bodies, clothing, and blankets. Drums had been beating since sundown and continued through the night. Perhaps, Maurna thought, they are a signal to those along the trail that Little Crow's camp is about to move. Despite the drums she was blessed with sleep. She dreamed of Ireland and their last days there, of Harper's Ferry and Ginny's birth. Friends with smiling faces paraded before her. The Campbells, Pa, Rose, and her boys, the Lundes, the Rivards, and Joseph, and Ben. Then she saw crows circling above all of them. She shouted at them to watch out for the predatory birds, but they laughed and paid her no mind. She shuddered and came suddenly awake.

Was that a shuffling sound by the tepee entrance? Was that a brief streak of light from the camp's fires? Absolute silence and darkness afforded her no answers. Fighting panic, Maurna snuggled closer to Ginny and stealthily drew the knife. Barely breathing, all her senses alert, she detected heavy breathing. But that could be Emma or Patricia. Was that a movement of air or was it her imagination? Trembling, heart pounding, she gripped the knife handle as their lifeline. With her eyes locked open, she remained under the strain of uncertainty and fear for more than an hour until the breaking dawn gradually began to reveal the interior of the tepee.

Thank God, no brave in sight. But Emma's blanket was thrown back. Patricia stirred awake, scratching at the busy lice, and immediately noticed Emma's empty space. Patricia's eyes met Maurna's. Maurna shrugged and gently awakened Ginny.

A short time later the watchers came to get them. They signalled Patricia and Maurna to gather their belongings and follow them. Maurna carefully concealed the knife in her bundle before the three dragged themselves blinking into the early light. White Spider appeared, smiled at Ginny, and led them to the center of the camp. There a sight greeted them that caused Maurna to shield Ginny's eyes and force back rising nausea.

Strung to a post, hands tied behind her, hung Emma Walton. Her head was bent sideways, her chin rested on her bodice. Beneath her jawline ran a bloody slash that opened her throat from ear to ear. Over caked blood covering her gown front like a thick scab, her staring eyes seemed to be observing the sight with little concern.

White Spider explained the Sioux logic. "Lady try escape. When she caught, she say she go Ohio. Braves told to kill any who try escape. You not try escape with Ginny."

The procession was quickly formed and began moving north and west, paralleling the Minnesota River. Dakotah men, women, and children, cattle, horses, dogs, and wagons and the ragged, filthy, dispirited prisoners trudged along, churning dust back through the ranks. With no sense of pursuit and no hurry to reach their destination, the leaders set a leisurely pace. Indian villages along the trail folded up and joined the morose caravan. The Sioux showed none of the exuberance that Maurna recalled immediately after their capture. Heads were down, conversing was minimal. The Sioux had not lost a battle, but the movement west was undeniably a retreat.

Little Crow still harbored hopes, but he desperately needed allies. His Mndewakantons had begun and sustained the uprising to this point. If the Sissetons, Wahpetons, and Wapakutes would organize their support, the Sioux might still drive the Whites from the Valley. And if the Chippewa nation and the Winnebagoes would join them on the war path, they might be able to expel them from the state.

The western tribes knew Little Crow, and he hoped to use his familiarity to convince them. He would argue that all Sioux were committed and would be driven off to the plains if they failed to negotiate favorable terms. As the Little Crow train neared Yellow Medicine, the Chief rehearsed the words he would use to influence his western brethren. United they could act against all the abuses their people had suffered. United they could repay the Whites for their broken promises. United was, in fact, the very meaning of the word Dakotah. So unite they must, or all would be lost forever.

The new camp was established beyond the recently burned Upper Agency at Yellow Medicine. White Spider saw to the erection of a small tepee next to his own lodge where Patricia, Maurna, and Ginny were settled in, retaining the same old guards who had plagued them at Little Crow's village.

Life for the prisoners included a few minor changes. Because they were farther north and less likely to attempt escape, the women captives were permitted more freedom. They were allowed to leave the tepee whenever they chose but were restricted to a small perimeter. To their revulsion they were forced to use the putrid common latrine, but were at last allowed to soak their clothing and wash their faces and hands in the stream.

Patricia mentioned one other difference. "They are arguing among themselves, Maurna, have you noticed? They seem uncertain."

"Yes, I agree, but I don't know whether it's good or bad for us."

At the stream, Patricia encountered a half-breed prisoner who told her the men disagreed about whether the Sissetons and Wahpetons should join in the war and whether the captives should be released to the whites or retained as pawns. The Mndewakanton were adamant about retaining the prisoners. Speaker for the western tribes, Little Paul, was determined that the prisoners be released and stated that the western Sioux were reluctant to go on the war path. Little Paul shouted, "Little Crow started the trouble. Let him and his Mndewakantons finish it!"

Ginny's spirits were lifted by White Spider's nightly visits. He seemed to represent a measure of certainty in her confused new world. His stories fascinated and distracted and his affection was genuine. He enjoyed being with his "little lady," and never failed to inquire about their treatment. Maurna was grateful to him for so many reasons and simply could not visualize him "on the warpath," looting, torturing or killing. His was not a violent nature. She never thought that she'd thank God for a blizzard, but the one that had blown them their friend and savior, White Spider, had been a genuine gift.

Chapter Twenty-Two

Convergence

The morning after Governor Ramsey's visit, Henry Sibley took command and rushed his 800 man contingent in a forced march toward the troubles. Precious time was expended in negotiating 120 miles of big woods country bringing his troop to the village of Saint Peter. An advance party of sixty men was sent to reinforce Fort Ridgely.

Sibley was concerned his men lacked combat experience. He had no cavalry for scouting, and the Sioux were masters of the ambush tactic. The people under immediate threat in the Mankato-New Ulm area became highly critical of Sibley's plodding, deliberate pace. But he knew the Sioux and would not be rushed.

Word of troops on the march spread before them. This welcome news reached Mankato, where five men from the Flandreau retreat party from New Ulm whose family members had been taken captive, volunteered to join the Ridgely relief party. Pim Murnane joined the five who intercepted the advance party north of Mankato. The Captain in charge denied their request to enlist, but the determined men simply fell in behind the marching troop and followed them to the fort. From that point on they were accepted as members of the company.

Colonel Sibley's main force, bolstered by the members of the Minnesota Third Regiment, increased to 1300 by the end of August when they finally reached Fort Ridgely. Major J. R. Brown, former Indian Agent, moved out with 150 men to probe the area west to Redwood Agency and Birch Coulee for hostile Sioux and possible survivors. Pim and his five fellow volunteers joined one of the squads.

The bodies of the Captain Marsh patrol were discovered first. They had been ambushed at the Redwood Ferry and had been lying in the blistering heat and rain for nearly two weeks. The elements and scavengers had done grisly work and the stench in the breezeless air was overpowering. Pim fled behind a nearby bush and retched. His embarrassment was brief when he noted that many soldiers had reacted in the same manner. The slain were quickly identified, shrouded in blankets and stacked in wagons for transport to Fort Ridgely and a military burial service.

Major Brown split his force to work upstream on both sides of the river. They found corpses with protruding arrows and lances, knife and gunshot wounds, heads smashed by tomahawks, and limbs and heads dismembered by hatchets. Many were flayed and scalped and a few disemboweled. The soldiers attempted to identify each victim, but in most cases they managed only a sketchy description before burial. From Redwood Ferry through the Agency grounds on the west side of the river and through Beaver Creek and Birch Coulee on the east side the silent troopers performed their grisly duty.

As he approached each victim Pim feared it was his beloved aunt or little Ginny. His throat constricted and he gagged when he spotted a red bonnet near a mutilated form. He felt momentarily guilty when he realized the slain child was unknown to him and rejoiced.

When the sun set that day in Hell, the men were branded with sights and smells they would carry forever. They had buried eighty-five white men, women, and children during the day. Men whose wives and loved ones remained captives of the Sioux were particularly anguished.

Near Birch Coulee, Major Brown decided to camp in the open with his reunited total force of 150 men. The troopers circled the wagons and tied the horses to the vehicles ahead to tighten the ring. Ravines surrounded their campsite on three sides. To the north of their bivouac, heavy woods offered a more protected position, but the open site was selected.

Gray Eagle and Cut Nose, Little Crow's war chiefs, returned with 300 braves to seek any loot overlooked during their withdrawal. Early on, they spotted the soldiers of the burial detail, but remained concealed hoping for a chance to pounce. They were likely pleased when they saw Major Brown select the unprotected campsite.

At twilight the braves silently crept into the ravines and woods to encircle the soldiers' camp and await a pre-arranged signal. One loud thump on a war drum triggered 300 fingers. A devastating crossfire raked the vulnerable encampment. Half a dozen soldiers were killed in the first volley. The startled men sought cover where there was none. The more enterprising found protection behind fallen horses. Others tipped over wagons or shot their own horses to provide a breastwork of animal flesh. A soldier next to Pim was hit in the throat in the first volley, gushed blood through his mouth and nose and died as he fell. Shocked, Pim dove behind a fallen horse and feverishly dug into the grassy sod. The soldiers began to return fire, but due to their concealed position, the Sioux suffered few casualties and kept the pressure on the grounded men.

Shattered and frayed nerves from the thunderous din began to tell on the defenders. Major Brown asked Lieutenant Sheehan to find his way through the Indian lines to bring word to Sibley. Just before dawn the courageous Lieutenant maneuvered past the attackers and, though spotted and pursued, managed to avoid capture and reach Fort Ridgely. Colonel Sibley immediately dispatched a rescue force.

Anticipating Sibley's response, the Indians pinned down the reinforcements several miles short of their objective. The small Sioux band shrewdly bluffed the relief group into overestimating their number and held up a force of 200 soldiers for several critical hours while the main attack at Birch Coulee continued. When Sibley sent more men to force a breakthrough, the Sioux delaying force withdrew to rejoin their main body which then melted away into the hills.

As Sibley's rescue troop came up to the camp, they saw no movement, only overturned wagons and rotting horseflesh. Eerie silence prevailed. As they peered over the rude breastworks, they made out the beleaguered soldiers burrowed into the turf. Many survivors rose from shallow pits cursing their rescuers for taking so long to arrive. Pim said nothing. He was simply grateful to be alive. They all somberly returned to Fort Ridgely.

Little Crow rejoiced at news of the victory at Birch Coulee but was troubled by the growing dissension among the tribes. Not only were the Sissetons, Wahpetons, and Wapakutes opposed, but his Mndewakanton were beginning to divide. His dream of uniting the Dakotah Nation was fading in the face of Sibley's army marching up the valley.

Fancying the impression of benovelent concern it conveyed, Governor Ramsey used the term "neighbor" whenever he addressed members of his constituency. He had been making personal visits to thousands of refugees sheltered in Mankato, Saint Peter, and Saint Anthony Falls, and the huge gathering housed in the German Athenaeum in Saint Paul. More than 3,000 of the desperate had crowded into Saint Paul, 450 at the Athenaeum alone.

With Jim Seymour at his side, the Governor made his rounds, stopping to visit with virtually every family group, shaking hands, patting the heads of children, and speaking consoling words. To those who complained of the slow response to their needs, Ramsey placed the blame on the federal government. To those who praised the relief efforts, he smiled humbly and accepted the accolades. To those who expressed their intention to return to their Valley or Big Woods homes, he promised generous support. To those who declared their intention to leave Minnesota, he explained the many advantages in staying.

"All the reasons for choosing Minnesota in the first place are still valid, and new advantages will now exist. You can be assured the Dakotah tribes will be either destroyed or deported. They will never be allowed to set foot in Minnesota again. We tried to change them into God-fearing Christians and they thanked us by killing, torturing, and looting. Ungrateful heathens! They have proved to be unteachable, incorrigible, and unmanageable. Now their land will be available to decent settlers whose hard work will bring prosperity. All that and no Indians to fear ever again. I guarantee it. Stay, neighbors, and be part of the boom that will come. You'll never regret it!"

Jim Seymour listened to Ramsey's pitch over and over, each time delivered with fervor and sincerity. No man could possibly sound that sincere if he didn't believe it himself. Jim knew that Ramsey deplored the rampaging and killing by the Sioux and felt real sympathy for the victims. But he also knew that Ramsey was innately shrewd and perfectly capable of exploiting the situation by ensuring the Indians would bear the total blame and be severely punished. Retribution would, of course, include forfeiture of all their treaty rights and the loss of their reservation lands. A way to make those lands available to pioneers as he had always wished was handed to Ramsey. Without having to forcibly take the acreage from the Sioux, he now had the solution. Jim shook his head, smiled to himself. Alex, my friend, your luck holds. The credit for the land bonanza will accrue to your administration. Just try not to look so pleased, governor!

Chapter Twenty-Three

Little Boy Lost

As Colonel Flandrau's wagon train began its evacuation of New Ulm, Belle Lunde commented to Ansgar that she found it ironic that Tony, Ox, and Ben were in a war zone, little dreaming that their people at home were in more danger than their soldier sons.

But, in fact, the young Minnesotans were far from safe. The Minnesota First Regiment was a small cog in McClellan's Army of the Potomac that had marched and fought its way to a position just east of a small creek called Antietam near the small Maryland hamlet of Sharpsburg. General Lee had crossed his forces into Maryland, marched past the town of Frederick, and passed west over the Catoctin range. He split his forces to confuse the pursuing Union Army, but when a copy of Confederate orders fell into his hands, McClellan became privy to Lee's plans. The information led to several small Union victories that forced Lee to consolidate his divided army into a defensive position at Sharpsburg. Both generals expected their maneuverings to climax in a major confrontation. The ground at Sharpsburg was of Lee's choosing. His pride would not permit him to go back to Virginia without a victory.

Neither army appeared disposed to disengage. Anticipation was high on both sides of Antietam creek. It was a foregone conclusion that the armies would clash at first light on September 17th. Pickets for both were probing and reporting enemy dispositions and concentrations. Corps were being positioned, strategies forged. The night was vacuum still.

Each soldier dealt with his own anxiety. The worst trial was enduring the uncertainty. Some wrote hurried letters and secured them in shirt pockets. Should a man be killed, the burial detail would see to the mailing. Most tried but only a few realized sleep.

Pudge Henderson, who had rejoined the regiment at Frederick, spoke to no one. He had requested and been granted front line duty. Sensing that he wanted privacy, his friends left him alone.

Tony suffered from stomach cramps. He blamed it on bad water from one of the hill streams. Ox told him it was more likely the food. "Neither one," Shakey commented. "It's nerves, pure and simple. Tomorrow will be hot in more ways than one," he predicted.

Sarge agreed. "We'll have at 'em tomorrow, that's sure. Might's well get it over. Like in a fist fight, you can jab and dance around each other for a while, but sooner or later, you got to close and throw some heavy punches. Boys, I'm thinkin' the dancin' is over."

Shakey was curious. "Who's gonna cross the creek, Sarge, us or the Rebs? Not much of a stream but it'll still take some doing to get over."

Sarge pondered a moment, then ventured, "Well, hard to know, but Lee's over there in a pretty good spot with the woods and the town and he's got the road back to Virginny open behind him if we whip him. If he tries goin' north again, we'll just harass him. If he comes out of there to charge over at us, he's got the stream to cross, and he'll expose his men. Doubt he'll do that. We may sit here lookin' at each other for a month afore old McClellan moves at him. Could be a wait but somehow I'm thinkin' it'll be tomorrow. We whipped the Rebs pretty good in them hills behind us. Maybe McClellan's got his nerve up. If I had to bet, I'd put my money on us crossin' over to get at them, Shakey."

"Get some sleep, you grand strategists. We'll be needin' it tomorrow," groused Ben.

Sarge immediately countered. "Look who's talkin' sleep. The one that keeps us awake most nights. You sound like my little wife, Murnane, always naggin'. You'll never sleep less'n you close your own yap first, Mr. Murnane. Huh? Huh?"

Sarge had been correct in his guess that the Union forces would cross over the Antietam. General Joseph Hooker's First Corps had forded the stream a few miles north of McClellan's headquarters in the pre-dawn darkness. With artillery fire laid out ahead, his entire corps moved at 6:00 A.M. against the Confederate left along the road to Hagerstown.

The bedlam of the engagement and the enveloping smoke dispelled any doubts in the minds of the Minnesota boys. Sarge nodded knowingly. "Told you lads. Some of our boys sure 'nuff got across that stinkin' little crick.

There's holy hell to pay over yonder. Never heard nothin' like this in Ol' Mexico, no sir." He had to shout to be heard though they were nearly a mile from the action. "Sounds like the Rebs ain't fixin' to go on back to Virginny jest yet."

"Somebody said it was First Corps went over and started in at the Reb left. That's old Joe Hooker headin' that bunch," commented Shakey.

"He knows how to fight from what I've heard," responded Ben.

"He better," Tony intoned, "'cause we'll be over there bailing out his boat if it starts to sink. Listen to that racket. My God, worst yet."

Sarge laughed at Ben. "Better quit suckin' on that coffee, Mr. Insane Murnane. Get in the thick of a fight you don't want to be lookin' around for a place to pee, huh? huh?"

"Whole thing scared the pee out of me already, Sarge," said Tony.

"Old Thor the Thunder God. Could use a few of your thunder bolts today, Mr. Lunde."

They waited and chattered and suddenly were up and moving. Part of Sumner's Second Corps, with a New York and a Massachusetts Regiment, they crossed over and marched to the west through a patch of timber and then a field of stubble that merged into corn stalks.

The clouds of choking smoke blocked visibility beyond ten yards. The noise came in waves, crashing, percussing, blasting. Whining minié balls, cutting canister, screaming, raging voices. At their eye level, they saw shredded corn stalks. At their feet appeared bodies, twisted grotesquely, eyes blank, a few still twitching. Blue and gray clad bodies lay in small discriminating groupings at the edge of the field and then corpses in windrows as if cut down by an efficient, heartless reaper. The slaughter was profane. They spread rank to avoid stepping on comrades and foes and hurried on, though their legs were receiving urgent messages from their brains to run. Run! Get the hell away. Not a man didn't ask himself what in God's name he was doing there. Not a man didn't come close to obeying his instinct to sprint away.

They cleared the corn and climbed a fence, then crossed a road and left obliqued directly into a flaming volley that cut down the front ranks. They dropped to their knees to return the fire, got up and went forward, seeing glimpses of gray-clads in front of them. Ghosts they were, not men. Total confusion. What are our orders? Where's the officers? They forged ahead, found themselves on the far right flank, then felt artillery rounds coming into them from out farther right. They kept on into a woods, walked into another volley, and surged forward. Men fell. Horrible howls came from the left.

Ox was between Tony and Ben with Shakey and Sarge farther left, stepping forward loading, firing. More bellowing passed from left to right, the meaning not clear. Then it was. Fall back, the left is folding. Quick glances showed the Massachusetts lads firing and retreating in the face of a Reb counter attack. The Bay State boys fired, walked forward, then back, then began to panic and run. The Minnesotans fired another blast, then began to back pedal. They saw the Rebs coming, heard their wild yells. "They're coming, too many, fall back." The First Regiment gave more ground, didn't know how much. They fired and fell back some more. Smoke thickened. Men became disoriented. Worst fear of all was to be cut off. "Where are the Rebs? Where are our own?"

They felt relief coming in behind them, stopped, knelt again, fired into the gray gloom. They were back nearly to the place Hooker had begun before dawn, near a farm house east of the Hagerstown Pike. They were herded into the semblance of a line, flopped on the ground, drank pails of water, rubbed smoke out of their inflamed eyes. But they'd never rub out the scenes those eyes had witnessed. They felt their bodies to be sure there were no holes. They stared at the sky they could see again, the sun dimly speaking late morning. Drained, shattered. The battle was beyond any action they had ever experienced or could have imagined. They'd been in it for nearly two hours. Seemed like two days to some, two minutes to others, and eternity for too many.

No talking. Each man attempted to recover in his own way. They wondered whether they had done well or poorly and were thankful to be alive. Did all our friends make it through all right? That's when Pudge noticed Ben was not there. He told Tony and Ox and Shakey, and they started looking for their friend.

Later Ben would remember only a blinding flash, a quick, hot pain, then nothing. The ball had struck at a shallow angle just above his left cheek bone and gouged a furrow past his left ear into his hairline. Coated with bits of his flesh and blood, the projectile had whined on harmlessly but left in its wake an individual suddenly bereft of purpose, will, and reason. It had not even dislodged his kepi, but had painted the side of the cap with gore. Ben had sunk to his knees, remained for a moment bowed as if at prayer. His brain was concussed, his senses distorted. Released from the disciplines of reason and training, his mind rejected and denied what he had seen and experienced. His young, strong body was no longer controlled by an intellect that was conditioned to duty, honor, and loyalty. Its basic instinct to flee from the chaos, the bedlam, and the threat to life took over.

His legs propelled him northward away from the smoke and din along the road to Hagerstown. The slashing wound leaked blood, but the flow was abating as it coagulated. His senses continued to function but sent confused signals. The battle sounds behind him faded as he rotely marched on, impervious to his surroundings. He passed by small groups of soldiers who were too exhausted to be curious that he was heading north. Unchallenged, he trudged mechanically with no reasoned destination.

A mile north he turned sharply east and ambled across fields and pasture toward sun-splattered hills. His pace became constant, slow but rhythmic. His perspective shrank, peripheral vision narrowed, and he moved as if through a tight tunnel. Crossing a shallow stream, he hardly broke stride and didn't feel the cool soaking up to his knees. He was unaware of the rocky underfooting or of the grasping reeds as he ascended the far bank. He turned his ankle on a protruding root but limped on, not acknowledging the pain or the alteration it caused in the rhythm of his march.

He stumbled onto a narrow footpath and followed its winding course. The faint trail began ascending into the low mountains. He stopped briefly to rest but instantly fell asleep in the meadow grass beside the trail.

When he awoke, shadows had begun to lengthen and would soon disappear. Breathing was more labored, though he had no sense of approaching fatigue. His mind was functioning but was not focussed on the present.

He was a small child again in Ireland near Drimoleague, lost in the windswept hills. The topography was confusing, one hill indistinguishable from another. He was afraid his father and older brothers would be angry, his mother worried. He quietly sobbed. Then he remembered the tales he had been told of night creatures, and he glanced fearfully around him. Striding on, his rate decreased with his diminishing strength. Upon reaching the crest, he began to descend the far side, still searching for the cottage of his youth. As darkness fell he found himself in a valley of farm fields. He crossed the flat terrain heading toward another range of hills a few miles farther on.

On the flat valley floor he passed near several lighted farms, but avoided the beckoning pathways. The two-story, shadowed houses did not resemble the shape of the stone cottage he sought, the peat-heated hut that was home. He knew that his grandmother would be rocking out front, watching for him to appear out of the gloom. His brothers would be off looking for him. His sister, Maurna, and his mother would be bustling about doing distracting chores.

Slowly the wanderer became conscious of his throbbing wound. The numbness was receding, permitting the onset of pain. He gently touched his blood-caked temple where the flow had ceased, but a rough ridge of raw flesh felt tender to the touch. Leg muscles sent urgent messages to his brain. He stopped, looked up, and moaned pitifully. Reaching down into his physical reserves, he started off again and soon sensed a changing strain in his legs. He was descending the second range of hills when the path played out in a confusing field of large rocks and heavy brush. In a grove of pine where the underbrush thinned, he staggered on from tree to tree until he found himself on an outcrop of rock. He peered over the edge and saw a streak of moonlight reflected off the twisting ribbon of a rushing waterway. The stream beckoned and became his destination.

He sought a way down the cliff face. Holding tightly to stems of bushes and rocky protrusions, he let himself down slowly. He had managed about two thirds of the distance to the level of the stream bed when a rock gave way beneath his hand. For a second he held with the other hand, but as his grip failed he began to slide. Reaching desperately for purchase on the rocky face as his face-down momentum increased, he tumbled over a ledge and fell awkwardly to the rocks below.

He felt a jolt of pain in his leg and breath expelling from his lungs caused him to gasp for air. As his lungs refilled he concentrated on reaching the stream a few yards away. Head throbbing, he crawled over the rocks until his face was over the lapping waters. Immersing his head, he luxuriated in the soothing flow and drank through swollen lips. He dunked his head like a puddling duck and raised it only when breath was required. He drank more draughts, then began to investigate his moon-lighted surroundings.

Senses were sufficiently alert to let him know he was nearing total collapse. As any wounded animal will, the drained soldier began to seek concealment. He slithered toward low bushes, but lost consciousness before reaching refuge. His last thoughts were that he would rest for a while, then look for the cottage again in the morning. His mother would be frantic but he simply had to sleep. An owl sounded a lonely call.

Buddy Bauer, a stocky, square-shouldered young man with stringy blond hair topped by a leather cap, finished his chores as dawn broke. He was anxious to get to his breakfast so he could hurry off to check his trap and snare lines beyond the south ridge. His sister, Ilsa, was laying out his sausage and eggs and bread when he entered the kitchen.

Smiling delightedly as he attacked the food, she teased, "Buddy, is your trap line where you're headed?" His given name was Herman but everyone called him Bud or Buddy.

"Yup. You coming along as far as the glade?"

"Not today. You remember I'm going into town with Mama and Poppa. Mama will be choosing from some new yard goods that should be in from Baltimore."

Willowy Ilsa's braided, blond hair formed a golden crown framing a heart-shaped face. Ivory skin and deep set, sparkling, hazel eyes promised development into classic beauty.

As he gulped the remains of his breakfast she added, "We won't be leaving until after noon dinner."

"Ask Pa to check to see if those new traps are at Swanson's store. One is broke and somebody stole two others I had down by the cottonwoods."

"Who'd do such a thing?"

"Don't know, but I'd like to catch 'em."

A rare frown appeared. "For a fifteen-year-old, you're getting mighty belligerent, aren't you?" She laughed, but meant her warning. "Better be sure they're not bigger than you before you get too feisty." She was a worrier and especially concerned herself about her impulsive brother. "Dear Lord, watch over Buddy," she thought. "Anything happen to him, Mama would be devastated."

Ilsa instinctively knew her mother favored her brother, but she knew that she was loved, too. Besides, her father more than compensated by favoring her. She and Buddy were mutually loving and respectful.

He gulped the last pieces as he rose. Grabbing his cap, gloves, and rifle, he sailed out the door shouting as he went that he'd be back for dinner. He was gone up the path at a half run.

Her amused eyes followed him until he disappeared along the rocky trail, then she called out to her mother who was ironing in the shed off the kitchen. "Mama, the food's going to get cold. Where's Pa? Down at the barn, I suppose. I'll fetch him up."

She danced lightly toward the barn, humming a silly tune she'd heard at the last festival in Frederick. Her perspiring father was backing a loaded wheelbarrow out of the barn. As his short, stocky frame bent to balance the load, she marveled at his bulging, muscular forearms marking him as one of the strongest men in the valley. Augustus Bauer, Gus to his friends, reigned as the undefeated local arm wrestler. He'd made many a dollar wagering with strangers who invariably underestimated his strength. Just over five-feet-five, his stature had fooled men trying to bully him. Though amiable and slow to anger, his response was quick and decisive when aroused.

"Pa, your breakfast is long ready and getting cold." Ilsa kissed him quickly on the back of his neck, then stepped around in front of him.

"Ilsa, darling, it's dangerous to kiss a man who's laboring under a burden. He's liable to drop it on his foot, or worse, on hers." Laughing he set down the barrow, reached for her, and gave her a bear hug, lifting her lithe frame completely off the ground.

"Oh, Pa, you're gonna crush me."

They walked arm in arm back toward the kitchen and the beckoning aromas.

Lucille watched them come, noting that Ilsa was nearly as tall as her father. My side of the family, she thought, thinking of her tall brothers and uncles. Lucille had met and married Gus Bauer in 1838 after he discovered her in the east central part of Pennsylvania. She had loved him instantly and that love had grown over their twenty-four years together.

As Gus and Ilsa entered, Lucille began serving up the eggs and sausage. "Just in time. Hope there's enough for you there, husband. If not I can be putting on more." She wiped her hands on her apron and sat with her hand curled around a cup of coffee, eyes squinting into the brightness out the east window.

"Enough for a threshing crew here, wife. Where's Bud? Is he off to those traps again?"

"Left a bit ago," said Ilsa. "Gulped his food. You'd think those rabbits and mink would run off if he didn't get right to 'em first thing. By the way, he wants you to see if the new traps are in at Swanson's. He had a couple stolen."

"He did? Wonder who would do such as that," posed Lucille.

"Probably some folks from the other side of the ridge though it could have been anybody, I guess. You don't s'pose caught animals could have just drug 'em away, do you?" asked Gus.

"Ilsa, you coming to town with us later or are you going to stay out here and daydream and write some more of your love poems?"

"Mama, I guess my authoring can be put on hold for a little while. Getting the right material for my new dress seems more important at the moment. That festival's not too far off, you know. Besides, I don't want to be worrying Mr. Longfellow or Mr. Whittier about being replaced just yet." Ilsa finished her breakfast, rose and sauntered over to the south window.

Gus began to speak again, "We'll be leaving just after dinner, so . . . "

He was cut off by Ilsa's alarmed shout. "Pa, Mama, here comes Buddy running full out with a wild look. What's wrong?"

She dashed through the door to meet him. Gus and Lucille were right behind her as they met hard-breathing Buddy in the yard. He pointed back along the path. "Pa, there's a bad hurt soldier down by the crick. His head's bleedin' somethin' awful. He's alive, but barely, I think. We gotta help 'im! Hurry!"

Gus was already sprinting to hitch up the wagon and shouted over his shoulder, "Get some bandages and rags, and Buddy get my shotgun. Now hurry."

They traversed the half-mile as fast as the wagon could be negotiated along the rocky lane that usually accommodated only foot traffic. Buddy ran ahead, his tousled blond hair bobbing as a beacon. He was bending over the soldier when they arrived. Lucille quickly examined him and helped Gus and Buddy gently roll him on his back. A swollen, searing slash ran from his cheek bone into the auburn hair that was blood-soaked and matted into the wound. The crusted, dirty scab hardly yielded to Lucille's careful washing with a cloth she had dipped into the creek.

Ilsa gently whispered encouragement into the soldier's unhearing ear as Lucille checked his pulse. She pronounced it faint, but steady, and squeezed cold drops of water from the cloth onto his forehead to try to bring him to consciousness.

"Gus, Buddy, lift him onto the wagon. Then Buddy, you ride in to get Doc Butler. Don't come back 'til you get him. Even if this boy's not hurt as bad as it looks, he'll need some stitching to close that wound. Ilsa run ahead and start heating some water. Gus and I will bring him along in the wagon. Where you wandering to, girl?"

Ilsa spotted something off under the cliff face near the creek. Walking the few yards, she bent down and retrieved a tattered, bloodied blue kepi. She looked up at the cliff. "This is his cap, Mama. You don't suppose he fell from up there, do you, and then maybe crawled to where Buddy found him? Mussed gravel here where something was dragged across."

"'Spect he'll tell us that later. Bring his cap and get to running for the house. Move, honey. Minutes count sometimes."

Ilsa ran off after Buddy. Lucille and Gus gently lifted the young man and settled him on the straw in the wagon bed. Lucille climbed in and rested the soldier's head on her lap. Gus was ready at the reins.

"Go easy now, dear. We don't know how bad hurt he is, and the jostling may harm him."

"As easy as I can, darlin', but it's a rough trail even slow and easy."

They didn't speak of it, but were both having similar thoughts. If their eldest son, Kurt, were to find himself in this young man's circumstances, they could only hope and pray that some kind folk would help him as they were doing for this stranger. Kurt had joined the Maryland Fourth Regiment and been in three major battles. They hadn't a letter from him since April.

Doc Butler came down the stairs and went directly to the kitchen table where Gus and Lucille rose to meet him. Ilsa quietly filled a cup of coffee for him. Buddy stood by the window.

The doctor spooned sugar into his cup, cleared his throat, and spoke decisively. "He's bad hurt, Lucille. A concussion, maybe a skull fracture, and his left femur is broken. I'll need help, Gus, to set that bone right. He's deep unconscious. Nature's way, but I can't let him stay that way too long. The wounds are less than a day old. Heard about a big battle south and west of here by the Virginny border. Probably where he wandered from. Come a long way, though, if he did."

He sipped his coffee, blew on it and set it down. "We'll go right back up there 'n set that leg. Doubt even that pain will wake him. Then we'll let him sleep into tomorrow if he will. You can all make as much noise as you like. He won't hear you. If he should wake before morning, Lucille, give him water in small sips but nothing else, no matter how hungry he is. You don't need to sit up with him. If he wakes, he'll moan so loud in pain, the devil will hear him in Hades. I'll just finish this good coffee, and we'll get at it. You come, too, Buddy. Need your strength."

"I've cleaned and stitched the head wound. Shouldn't leave much of a scar. Don't try to clean it better, once I'm gone. Come on, gents, let's get the bone set. Don't worry now he seems to be a right strong young fella."

Ben had been carried to Kurt's former room. Ilsa threw the curtains open to illuminate the task. With the men straining for leverage, the leg bone was set as the patient moaned and sweat broke out on his forehead and upper lip. Doc Butler affixed a heavy splint, firmly held in place by heavy cloth wrappings. As they exited the room one by one, Ilsa pulled the curtains shut, paused to look at the shadowed face now in repose. She said a brief prayer, turned, and softly closed the door.

Chapter Twenty-Four

"Miles of White Soldiers"

While notes were exchanged between Little Crow and Sibley, the latter continued to move his force of 2,000 men directly at the Sioux. Indian scouts reported back to Little Crow and his soldier chiefs that "miles and miles of white soldiers" were coming.

The captives' lives became more tense. Braves hassled and threatened them, convinced that the prisoners were causing the division among the Sioux. Actual acts of violence against the captives were rare, but the constant fear took its toll.

Maurna kept the knife hidden but handy. Patricia Jensen had only a stick she had sharpened. They agreed to a system of alternating sleep times so that one would be alert. White Spider's visits continued, but Maurna could see that he was troubled by the Sioux disagreements. She talked with him to try to draw him out. "What will they do with the women and children, White Spider?"

"Don't know. Some want let go, some want keep for hostage. A few want to . . . " Realizing the impact of his words, he didn't finish the statement.

"Surely brave men don't make war on women and children."

"That true. Some forget when they have fear themselves. Don't know what they might do. Sibley and white soldiers come. Fight or go prairie."

"Have you enough braves to fight them?"

"Enough if all Sioux fight. Not enough if many not fight."

"How much longer, White Spider?"

"Soon, fight or go prairie. White Spider watch over you. Not worry."

"We only worry when White Spider is not here."

"Big battle soon. White Spider be gone then."

But when the day of the battle came, White Spider was not gone. The braves gathered in the pre-dawn. Frenzied activity made it clear that something was imminent, and within twenty minutes, every young brave in the camp had departed. A few older warriors remained. Without warning he threw back the flap of the lodge and went directly to Ginny. Maurna was shocked almost to the point of bringing the knife to bear. "Get Little Lady things," White Spider said in a hushed voice. "We go other camp. Other camp want save prisoners. Hide you there. When braves come back, you be in other camp. Hurry. We go now."

Throwing what little they possessed in a bundle, Maurna took Ginny's hand and Patricia followed. White Spider held Ginny's other hand as they ran to the other camp and into a pre-arranged lodge. The three were put into a deep pit in the floor and covered completely with straw. White Spider spoke. "Little Lady and mother and other lady stay hid. Braves fight battle. If win, they be back happy, get drunk. Bad! If lose, they be back angry. Bad! Stay hid. Friend of White Spider watch over you. I go fight. Then come back. Stay hid." And he was gone.

The odor was frightful, gagging. Loud angry voices. Horses galloping by. Heavy dust. Lice. Maurna could feel them crawling and dreaded their infecting Ginny. She hid her fears from her silent, withdrawn daughter. The heat in the nearly airless hole was stifling. Retaining sanity became the goal.

They lay foodless and waterless through the remainder of the day and into dusk, then darkness. Suddenly a guttural voice sounded from above. "Ladies do good. Stay still. White Spider come soon."

Whose voice? Any voice was welcome. Patricia started to respond but was hushed immediately. "Ladies not speak." They waited for several hours.

When Ginny sobbed, Maurna patted her head. "White Spider will be back soon, Ginny." But what if he didn't come? What if he had been killed in the battle, or wounded, and could not come? Who was the other brave? Oh, Dear Lord, let White Spider come.

A while later, a voice out of the darkness above, down through the filthy straw, out of the gloom, in a whisper. "Little Lady all right?"

White Spider, dear man, thank God. He pulled up the straw by the handful, lifting Ginny out of the pit. Maurna was so cramped from the awkward position she could hardly come erect. A strong arm reached down to help her, then reached down again for Patricia.

Maurna could have hugged him. Blankets were spread for them around the perimeter of the pit, and he guided them to their beds.

"White Spider be back in morning. Sioux lose battle. Little Crow leave. Go prairie. Sibley come. White Spider sleep outside lodge. Watch over you. Go with Little Crow at dawn. Ladies sleep now."

They closed their eyes, but sleep was not possible for Maurna. She stared at the lodge cover and prayed for deliverance. After weeks of filth and fear, almost any resolution would be welcome. She didn't know if she had dropped off, but first light began to show and activity increased around them. Low talk, the smell of smoke and the odor of food. Light increased. The thrust-in head of a brave. White Spider!

"Ladies in peace camp, not war camp. Little Crow braves want kill prisoners. Little Crow give speech. Say no. Too many killed already. Let go free. Braves argue. Little Crow say no, captives go free. I leave now with Little Crow. Others watch out for you. White Spider say goodbye to Little Lady." He approached Ginny, patted her hair and smiled. "Little Lady grow fine woman. White Spider hope Little Lady be happy." He turned to Maurna and smiled. He reached out his hand for her to touch.

She did, and solemnly said, "White Spider, we owe you our lives. Bless you. Take care of yourself. We'll be grateful forever."

He nodded and smiled, patted Ginny again, nodded to Patricia and was gone.

Maurna wept uncontrollably. It was impossible to hold in her emotions any longer.

Two more days of uncertainty tormented the prisoners. With Little Crow and his followers gone to the prairie, the leadership of the Sioux devolved to Little Paul. Half-breeds were used as messengers to exchange proposed terms with Colonel Sibley whose command had established bivouac near the Indian camp. On the twenty-sixth of September, as per Sibley's demand, the Sioux prepared their area for his arrival and displayed white flags throughout their camp. Holding brightly painted lances, beads, feathers and other ornaments, they arranged themselves in rows of welcome. Sibley let them wait for more than an hour.

Martial music sounded from the White Soldiers' Camp and under its resounding waves the Colonel led his troop to the Sioux camp. He had his men encircle the Indians to display his power and dominance, knowing that such a show would defuse any Sioux militants harboring hostile ideas. Then he rode triumphantly through the parting crowd to its center where he stopped and waited with his aides. He paused, then nodded his head. Drums rolled as officers brought forward those men of his troop who had loved ones among the captives. The anxious men stood at attention looking hopefully down the center of the double row of Indians. Colonel Sibley nodded to the other end of the long line.

An officer started the women forward in single file. Some clutched children as they began their slow procession. Many patted and smoothed their hair to tidy their appearance. Filthy, ragged, pale, and exhausted, their eyes sought solace and understanding. The frantic men in front braced themselves and searched the faces. The first few women reached the mouth of the gauntlet, then stepped to the side to allow room for those coming up behind. A soldier leaned forward, tentative, and asked, "Is that you, Sarah?" Then another, "My God, it's Millie." The released captives spread out sideways in full view with heads and eyes cast down. Their men rushed to embrace them. Simultaneously pitiful and glorious. The joy of reunion mixed with the realization of the captives' agony and degradation was overpowering. Tough, crusted troopers bled tears. A Lieutenant aide leaned over in his saddle and was heard to say to the Commander, "All you have done in your life, all the honors you have received, cannot match this magnificent achievement." Henry Sibley nodded proudly.

Pim had pushed up close to the front. Praying silently, he watched the bedraggled procession approach. When he saw Maurna, he wasn't absolutely sure the emaciated woman was his aunt until he saw Ginny whom he recognized immediately. He rushed to them, his arms open, tears filling his eyes, his heart pounding, joyfully exclaiming, "Ginny, Maurna." The three enveloped one another and stood enwrapped and swaying. Soft moans eased forth as burdens were released. They clung desperately, not wanting to let go, still not sure the ordeal was finally ended.

"Oh, dear brave Pim, we love you so," breathed Maurna.

"I should never have left you alone, Aunt Maurna; I should have stayed with you. Can you ever forgive me?"

"Forgive you?" She was incredulous but looked into his eyes lovingly. "Pim, my dear, dear Pim. What you did took great courage. You had no other choice. We owe you our lives."

Ginny reached up to him again, and Pim went to his knees to hug her to his chest.

Some of the released women and children had no kin to greet them, but others were welcomed with heart-wrenching emotion. Reunions were joyful, but constrained. Fear and suffering had been constant for such an extended period that the prisoners could hardly be expected to leap in exhilaration and celebration. Exuberance could wait. Release from anxiety and debasement was sufficient for the moment. They instinctively searched for means to remedy their frightful appearance.

The released captives were escorted to Sibley's camp where considerate preparations had been made. The Commander had anticipated their needs. Ready and waiting were delousing facilities and barrels of hot water and luxurious soap in several enormous tents to ensure privacy. They bathed and washed their stringy hair and soiled clothing. Most bathed again, soaking in the soothing waters, attempting to regain their self-respect. Dignity was reborn as they brushed their hair and re-dressed in boiled dresses and undergarments. The Colonel had been remiss in only one department. There weren't nearly enough hand mirrors. But the scrubbed ladies and their shiny children began to emerge from the tents to be greeted with kettles of beans, potatoes, vegetables, soup, roast venison, beef and gravy, bread, butter, milk, tea, coffee, jam, and fruits and puddings. They took their time and luxuriated in the abundance.

Once hunger was relieved, their eyes softened, their heads began to rise, and their minds began to accept the fact that their ordeal was over, and that somehow, they had survived.

The former captives were then led to waiting wagons where they were assigned seats, fourteen per vehicle. A company of mounted soldiers surrounded the train that would carry 252 women and children on the long return trip to Mankato. The train followed the Lac Qui Parle route that most of them had traveled west as prisoners. To the abused women and children captives, the Minnesota Valley unrolled before them for a second time in less than a month. The return trip was under considerably less stress and discomfort but was no less solemn.

No crowds lined their route. No cheering throngs. No elaborate welcomes or sounding bands. Just the disinterested river at their side, the nonjudgmental trees bowing in the fall breezes, the disputed soil rolling out beneath the wheels. They traversed the land that had been the setting for an uneasy co-existence, then a confrontation of conflicting cultures. The passing of the white prisoners' train seemed to be the symbolic claiming of the land.

The pace was slow, deliberate, nearly without human sound. Conversations were rare and subdued. The creaking of harness, the clopping of hooves, the squeaking of wooden wheels became the lugubrious background music to what had been a tragic opera. The devastation, the rending, the destruction, the violence were essentially over. The shed blood was slowly soaking into the absorbent soil and draining into the rivulets and streams that fed into the Minnesota River. The red taint would thus be carried off east to the Mississippi never to be seen in the valley again.

Maurna, Ginny, and Pim had another warm reunion when the wagon train of released prisoners stopped to eat and rest in New Ulm on their way to Mankato. Belle and Ansgar were part of a group of forty men and five of their wives who had returned to the village to start the enormous task of rebuilding their homes. All the men were armed with rifles. Several were posted around the village at all times to be alert for renegade Sioux who had not turned themselves in to Sibley.

When Belle spotted Maurna, Ginny, and Pim in the wagon, she let out a whoop of joy that brought Ansgar running. They hugged and wept, and Belle offered news of the Rivards and Cossettes and Will and Rob Koukkari. Abigail was in Mankato at the Cossettes, the Rivards were just about ready to return to their farm, and Will and Rob were bunking on cots in Cossette's livery stable. Belle suggested that the Cossettes could make room for Maurna and Ginny while Pim might join Will and Rob at the livery.

Maurna had learned of the deaths of Rose and her father from Pim at Camp Release. She asked about others from their area.

Belle had received a letter from Tony, written on September 16, the night before an anticipated battle near a small town in Maryland. They had since heard that the battle had taken place and there had been heavy casualties. Ansgar tried to downplay their concern, but Maurna instantly shared Belle's fears. Belle later told Ansgar she had deliberately dominated with her chattering because she knew that Maurna was not ready to discuss their experience as Indian captives. "Maybe someday she will speak of it, Ansgar, but not now, not yet."

In Mankato the Cossettes were indeed very welcoming. Maurna and Ginny moved into their crowded home, and Pim joined Will and Rob at the livery. Every available space in Mankato was in use to provide for refugees, though some were beginning to either move on to Saint Paul or back to their abandoned homesites. Pauline Cossette was as considerate as had been Belle Lunde, and the young women of the house quickly took their cue from her. None broached the subject of their captivity. Their attitude made it clear that if Maurna opened the subject, it would be discussed; if she did not so choose, it would rest.

Maurna slept and bathed and ate, and then slept and bathed some more. Ginny, at first withdrawn and spiritless, began to slowly recover. By the third day Maurna knew that she could put off a difficult task no longer. She thought it through carefully and composed in her mind before she took up her pen. She chose her words to insure that the message would reach Ben with appropriate sensitivity. She agonized over reliving the period she was describing, but managed to tell Ben of the death of their brother, Joseph, his burial on the hill and the miraculous saving of Ginny's life. She described Pim's heroic behavior, their capture and eventual release. She finished by relating the deaths of Rose and Pa Kotelnik and the hundreds of others who had perished.

Before posting the letter, Maurna approached Will and Rob. "Have you written to your brother, Ox, to inform him of your mother and grandfather?"

Their eyes dropped and they shook their heads. Will commented, "I thought of doing it but just didn't have the words." Maurna gently encouraged them by suggesting that Ox should hear the news from his family, not second hand from others. Rob asked her to help them compose a note. She said she would, but urged them to try their own version first. A few hours later, the two young men brought her their letter. After reading it, Maurna dried her eyes and told them, "'Tis from your hearts as only you could express it. I'd not profane it by changin' a single word." They posted the two letters at the same time.

Dear brother Ox,

    We hope you are in good health. We have terrible bad news to pass on to you. Our mother and Grandpa were killed by bad Sioux. They were caught outside, and we couldn't save them. We were in the house and safe because Grandpa warned us. He went off to save mother, but they were both caught and murdered. Hundreds of people were killed. The Sioux are now all prisoners and will be punished.

    We will bury mother on the hill behind the Murnane house, her favorite place. Grandpa we will bury near the new house that he built.

    We miss them both very much. We miss you, too. Stay safe and hurry home.

    Love,
        Will and Rob

Chapter Twenty-Five

Red Stain Eradicated

From Saint Paul, Colonel Sibley received a priority shipment of custom-designed leg chains to shackle those Sioux found guilty by a hastily-formed military court. Hearings commenced during the last days of September.

The Sioux who had not fled with Little Crow numbered over 2,000. It was not necessary for Sibley's force to hunt down most of them for they had resigned themselves to waiting near the camp. It was the Indians' impression, partly self-conceived and partly based on rumors generated by whites, that they would be dealt with humanely and justly. They expressed faith in the judgment of their "brother," H. H. Sibley, and believed that only those who had killed white civilians would be severely punished. Others who had fought "soldier against soldier" expected to be treated as prisoners of war. They acknowledged the justice of penalties for those who had stolen white men's goods, but it was inconceivable to them that the penalty for all Sioux, guilty or innocent, would be exile and deportation.

Most warriors surrendered rather than flee to the plains to suffer the harshness of winter without provisions. The court heard individual cases through the first week in November. The trials included accusations of guilt, defendant pleadings, testimony of witnesses, and swift declarations of guilt or innocence. All accounts of white witnesses were accepted at face value. Incarceration was immediate; those adjudged guilty were shackled and placed in a fenced-in, guarded compound. In all, the cases of 425 accused braves were heard individually; 321 were judged guilty; eighteen received sentences of life imprisonment; 303 were sentenced to death by hanging.

Colonel Sibley signed the order to carry out the executions. He intended to hang them as soon as he received confirmation from General Pope, Commander of Western Armies. He was anxious to complete the task so he and his force could escort the non-guilty Sioux to confinement near Fort Snelling.

Sibley received a message by courier from General Pope, informing him that neither he nor General Pope possessed the authority to carry out executions. Though executions could be officially delegated, the President alone could trigger the mechanism down through the chain of command. Lincoln demurred, insisting that all documentation of court trials and recommendations for sentencing be sent on to the White House. Executions had to await his confirming signature in each case. Sibley had no choice but to comply.

Two separate wagon trains began the long trip east. Comprised of 1400 elderly and women and children, the longer of the two would pass on to Pike Island near Fort Snelling. The advance shorter train carried the 303 judged guilty. They were destined for a prison camp outside Mankato named Camp Lincoln. The heavily-guarded, slow-moving trains passed by the burned Yellow Medicine Agency, through the deserted Sioux villages, the destroyed Redwood Agency, the charred village of Milford, and on into New Ulm. Vengeful citizens hurled invective and stones at the Indians as they passed.

Still swollen beyond its pre-uprising number, Mankato's population came out to greet the approaching Sioux trains. Many shouted, jeered, and threw rocks until the soldier guards disciplined the most unruly. Pim, the Koukkari boys, and the Rivard and Cossette men were among the Mankato throng. The young men approved the meting out of justice to the murderers of their loved ones. Making distinctions between guilty and innocent Indians was not their task, but they stood as part of the white mob sentiment stamping guilty on every Sioux forehead. Maurna, Ginny, and the Rivard and Cossette women stayed home while the two trains of Indians passed through.

The 303 all male Sioux who had been declared guilty by the prairie court were escorted to Camp Lincoln. The inmates were afforded two-man tents, blankets, firewood, food, and water. Guards were posted around the enclave to prevent escape by the leg-shackled braves and to keep irate whites away. The fate of the young male core of the Santee Sioux tribes awaited the final judgment and disposition of President Abraham Lincoln.

The 1400 innocent Sioux women, children, and elderly continued on past Mankato up the shores of the Minnesota River toward Fort Snelling. Snow began to fall as they entered Saint Peter, where crowds jeered and spat but allowed them to pass. At Henderson, however, the waiting mob went out of control. Women led the onslaught. Climbing upon several wagons, they smashed and slashed Indian heads with iron skillets and knives. The frenzied attack caught the soldier guards by surprise. By the time order was restored, a score of serious injuries had been inflicted. A crazed Henderson woman snatched a baby from a young Sioux mother's arms, hurled it against a wagon wheel, and stomped on it's head with her boot. She was restrained by soldiers, but the harm had been done. The infant died in its mother's arms an hour later along the trail.

Snowfall increased as the train moved on. The glorious Minnesota Valley receded behind the exiles. When they reached the crest of a hill just west of Fort Snelling, they were allowed to descend from the wagons and spread out to relieve themselves and stretch. Young Indian mothers kept close watch on their active children while the elderly men and women gathered in small groups to gaze back up the valley they would likely never see again. Silently they mourned the 303 convicted braves, the core of their tribe. The old ones' faces were expressionless, exuding an aura of profound sadness and resignation.

At the guards' command the prisoners shuffled back to the wagons and reboarded. Prairie grasses had dulled to a feeble beige. Wild flowers had paled and wilted. Fallen leaves had become slaves to the chilling wind. The Sioux felt on their backs the last faint warmth of the dying day as the accumulating snow gradually covered the valley under a pure white blanket.

Chapter Twenty-Six

Eternal Valley View

Maurna was opposed to Pim's proposal. Since the Uprising, Pim had asserted a new independence. He listened to his aunt's appeals, remained polite and calm, but set his jaw and said, "Aunt Maurna, try to understand. We can't delay any longer. Will and Rob feel just as strong on it as I do. We'll be careful and be back in two days."

She agreed that the trip was necessary, and in the face of Pim's determination, ceased her protests and made several requests. "Besides the main suggestions I've made, whatever can be salvaged of our clothin' and pots, pans, and dishes. Same with blankets, sheets, pillows, candles, whatever is usable. I want you to bring my rocking chair, even if it's broken. And the shawl, very precious to me. And my journals under my bed. But promise me that you'll take no risks. Stay close to Will and Rob. Don't forget that the Rivards will be just a few miles away if you need help. Pim, remember now that Ginny and I need you." She was worried there would be roving bands of Indians. They had heard isolated reports, mostly unconfirmed, of Indian sightings and sporadic raids.

The three young men left at dawn in a rented wagon, each with a rifle, ammunition and food. Three fresh-made pine coffins covered with shrouds bounced in the wagon bed. Most farms they passed enroute remained deserted, no livestock in sight. The only activity they observed were a few flatboats and one packet on the river loaded with waving soldiers. The Captain blew the whistle for their benefit and they waved back. A few miles short of New Ulm they angled onto a faint trail that was a shortcut to the Cottonwood Trail. Passing by the Rivard's turn off, they saw wisps of smoke from the chimney in the distance. Anxious to get to the task they took the turn in to the Murnane farm.

The wagon rode slowly into the approach and passed the picked bones of Johanna and Poteen. They did not comment but looked straight ahead until they pulled up at the porch.

"I'll just take a quick look inside," Pim said solemnly.

Rifle cocked, he strode onto the porch, entered the open door, disappeared for a few minutes, then came back out. "The Indians have been here, but it's near as we left it. Go do what you have to do. Get back when you can. I won't be goin' anywhere."

Will nodded, drove the wagon to the path at the base of the hill and pulled up. The two jumped off, opened the rear gate, and maneuvered one of the pine boxes onto the ground. They leapt back on the buck seat and headed off for home.

Pim re-entered the house and looked around. He noted Maurna's rocker lying on its side, one curved rung split, a brace broken and the seat cover sliced diagonally. He picked up the cracked whiskey jug and carefully replaced it above the window. Gently folding the shawl, he set it by the front door. He looked around both bedrooms, then bent down to refit the splintered trap door into its slot, tears forming in his eyes as he recalled the sight of Ginny as he had found her.

In the main room, blankets, dishes, pots and pans, and clothing were scattered about. He sat down and sadly surveyed the room. Each item reminded him of a person or an incident. It pained him to see their home violated, but he knew that their real loss was in human terms; his father, the man who had led them all here to fulfill a dream. *Pa, you tried so hard. God rest your soul. And Rob and Will's mother. Such a good person.* He remembered all the ways she had welcomed them and eased their start. *God rest you, too.* He thanked God for protecting Maurna and Ginny and asked Him to help them overcome any lasting effects of their imprisonment. Sighing heavily, he picked up his rifle and went out the door.

On the porch lay Poteen's food dish upside down. He walked over and turned it up, then continued off the porch in the direction of the river. Standing on the bank he noticed the flatboat, half way up the bank, two of the boards punched out of the deck. "They didn't miss much," he mumbled as he turned back toward the house.

He went to the shed where he rummaged around until he found a spade and a pickaxe that he placed along with his rifle in the pine box. Grasping the rope handle at one end, he dragged the coffin up the hill. The ground was dry and hard making the task fairly easy, but he had begun to perspire by the time he had managed it to the top. He rested a moment before he dragged it over to Joseph's temporary grave. Being extremely careful where he placed the shovel and leaving plenty of room on all sides, he began to dig. His jaw was locked firm, his eyes burned.

He did not unwrap the dirt encrusted form he exhumed, but wound fresh sheeting and a blanket over the old. Surprised at its light weight and rigidity, he very tenderly lifted his father's body into the rectangular box and replaced the lid. After dragging the coffin over to the northwest corner of the clearing, he straightened up to look out at the view of the Valley. Stepping two paces to the left and slightly downslope, he drove his knife into the turf to mark the place, and went back to retrieve the spade. Husbanding the dirt and carefully preserving the top sod, he dug two graves, the second just slightly shorter than the first. The two excavations veered toward the west and just slightly north, the best angle for a full view of the Minnesota River Valley. Pim then shuffled over to the coffin and dragged it to the side of the longer grave. Resting briefly, he looked once more at the view, sighed and proceeded over past the oak tree onto a rocky ledge. He selected carefully, then dislodged two flat rocks that he dragged to the grave sites. Placing one marker at the head of each grave, he studied the effect for a moment before walking over to the path and down the hill.

Re-entering the cabin, he began to choose salvageable items and carry them out onto the porch. The shawl, the rocking chair, two trunks of clothing, dishes, pots and pans, bedding, Maurna's journals, a bundle of letters from Irish relatives and from Harper's Ferry, and other items that Maurna and Ginny had requested. He had nearly covered the porch when he stumbled over Poteen's food dish. He looked at it sheepishly, grabbed a torn curtain, went out the door and across the yard to the road by the ravine. Laying the cloth on the ground, he scooped Poteen's bones into the shroud, bundled them and carried them up the hill. He dug a shallow grave, placed the bundle into it, refilled the hole with soil, and patted it down. The covered spot was just at the foot of the longer of the two graves.

Will and Rob returned mid-afternoon swinging the wagon to the foot of the uphill path. Pim watched them lift Rose's coffin off the back of the rig, then silently carry it up the hill. The Koukkari boys brought the box to rest beside the shorter grave. They stooped to place their mother in the ground, then helped Pim lower his father. They took off their caps and stood silently for several moments.

In a hesitant voice that grew stronger as he spoke, Pim intoned, "Dear God, we do not have a preacher or a priest here to say the words, but we'll try. We bury today our parents that we loved very much. They were both very good persons. Aunt Maurna suggested to bury my father here 'cause she said it was his favorite place. She also said that Mrs. Koukkari had first discovered this spot when she lived over here and that she loved it, too. Will and Rob decided to bury their mother here, too. Aunt Maurna said that my father and Mrs. Koukkari were good friends and would be pleased to be buried here where they can spend eternity lookin' out at their beloved valley together. Please welcome them, Dear Lord. They were good and faithful servants. Amen. Oh just one more thing. Poteen's at the feet of his master, where he liked to be. He was a good and faithful one, too, Lord. Amen."

They filled in the graves and resodded the site silently. A final prayer was said before they descended the hill.

When they reached the porch, Rob told Pim they had buried Pa Kotelnik "deep and permanent" on the ravine where they'd found his body.

"I'll see to it that the names are carved into those stones up there," promised Pim.

When they began to load the wagon, Pim noticed it was empty. He looked at Will for an explanation.

"We left all of our belongings at the house, Pim. Boarded it up good and will be coming back out permanent right after Christmas. We don't think the Sioux will be a problem, and even if they come around, we'll be ready for 'em. We felt that Ma and Grandpa would want us here. They worked awful hard to build us a home. Our minds are made up. It was Ma's dream to build this place into a real good farm, and we aim to carry out that dream. No place else for us, after all."

Rob pitched in, "'Sides, Grandpa won't be left all alone out here."

Pim nodded in understanding. He'd been thinking along the same lines. "My father's dream, too. I'll most likely do the same, just don't yet know for sure how soon. Got to see to Maurna and Ginny first. My aunt won't come back out here, says there's too many memories. She's set on Saint Paul. Says there's lots more advantages there for her and Ginny, too. She's probably right. Just don't know for sure yet what's right for me. It'll work its way out soon enough. I'd be proud to keep on bein' your neighbor, and I want you to know that the business deal that your mother and my father made still stands. My word on it."

They nodded. "Who's making supper?," Rob asked. "We got to eat and then get a good sleep and get on back to Mankato early tomorrow."

Chapter Twenty-Seven

Beads That Bind

According to Doctor Butler, Ben's healing was progressing well. The ripped flesh across his temple had become slightly infected and required frequent disinfecting and cleansing. Finally satisfied, the doctor had removed the gut stitches and pronounced it clean and healing beautifully. He told Lucille, "There'll be a scar, but it'll become barely noticeable."

The shattered leg was another matter. The break was severe and was resplinted in an unyielding cast immobilizing it completely. It would need time.

At Ben's urging, Doctor Butler notified the Captain of the Frederick Militia, who relayed the information about Ben's condition and location to the Sanitary Commission in Washington. Officials there passed on the data through the Army of the Potomac chain of command to the Minnesota First Regiment. By October 1, Ox, Tony, and the others were aware of Ben's survival and anticipated return to the regiment. Ben wrote a short note telling them he'd be released by Doctor Butler and sent on for final treatment at Union Hospital in Georgetown, where they could come see him when they could arrange a pass. He'd let them know when he got to D.C.

By October 10, Ben was ambulatory on crutches. He was confined to the house at first, but was soon taking jaunts around the yard. His headaches became less severe each day. The care given him by the Bauers amazed him. He suspected their attention was associated with their own missing son, but also out of genuine growing affection. Their conviviality as a family warmed him, and he felt not only gratitude but real love.

The main burden of his care fell to Lucille who clucked over him, changed his bedding, helped him wash and shave, applied disinfectant, changed bandages and carried a tray with his meals. Ilsa helped her mother to the degree that she was permitted, but was never "improperly" in his room without Lucille present. Ilsa was also dismissed when there was a nursing requirement constituting anything intimate or personal.

Lucille, Ilsa and occasionally Buddy and Gus spent time with Ben in restful conversation that served to help all of them get to know one another. Mother and daughter learned of Ben's life story, his Irish origins, the family's sojourn in Harper's Ferry, and the Minnesota adventure. The subject that Ben would not discuss was the war and, in particular, the battle at Sharpsburg and his subsequent walk through the night. The only comment he made was about the sudden flash of white light and that he remembered nothing until he awakened in their upstairs room. Any reference to the battle brought a frown and silence. The Bauers determined he was troubled and unsure about the subject himself.

Ben also learned a great deal about the Bauers. Lucille had been a young woman living on a farm north of Hagerstown when she met Gus. "We'll be married twenty-five years next April. Our eldest son, Kurt, is twenty-three and a second son who would be near your age, Ben, died in his second year. Ilsa was born in 1847, Buddy a year later. I have Dutch origins mixed with French. Gus was born in Austria. His family came to America in 1815, and soon thereafter his father and four of his older brothers founded a brewery in Baltimore. The business still prospers and Gus trades cured hams to his brothers for all the beer he can drink."

An officer in the Frederick Militia accompanied the doctor on one of his calls to inform Ben his status and location were known to his regiment. The news of Ben had reached headquarters in time to prevent them from sending a missing in action notification to his family in Minnesota. He also passed Ben a note forwarded from members of the Minnesota First Regiment. The note was brief but significant to Ben. They were relieved to know that he was alive and getting well and were looking forward to his return. The note was signed with more than twenty names, including Captain Messick. Old Sarge had added a postscript (probably written by Ox or Tony) that said, "Hurry back, Murnane, I miss you. I need somebody to pick on."

Because Doc Butler insisted that Ben get as much sun as possible, Gus set out a bench on the sunny side of the house. Ilsa joined him more often than the others "in front of God and everybody else," where she was safely within the bounds of propriety.

Ben learned of Ilsa's poetry writing and gradually much more about the pretty young woman with a healthy curiosity and an eagerness to learn. Ilsa explained. "We have a library of more than fifty books, mostly geography, history, and literature, including Shakespeare. You're welcome to use any of them."

Ben told Ilsa about his friend William Shakespeare Cosgrove and some of Shakey's antics and attempts at humor. Though he persisted in avoiding the subject of war and the battles that he'd been in, he talked readily about his friends in the regiment. His fondness for them and his eagerness to rejoin them was evident and secretly disheartening for Ilsa. She was dreading the thought of his departure, but was careful to disguise her feelings.

Buddy was more taciturn and withdrawn. Ben was a little uncomfortable with him, being occasionally confused by Buddy's mood swings. The young Bauer was quite protective of his sister. Ben observed that Ilsa was well aware of her brother's near-obsession and extremely annoyed by it.

Though it was awkward, Ben felt compelled to broach a subject with Gus. "I want to offer some payment for the cost of my keep. The food, the medicines, the bandages, and the doctor's fees are adding up. I intend to pay what's fair as soon as my army pay catches up with me."

Gus calmly described to Ben that he had been taught and fully subscribed to the idea that situations like this were "opportunities, not burdens." He then told Ben about their son, Kurt, and his current status as prisoner of war in Richmond. "When we heard that he was missing, we prayed that a family somewhere would find him and help him. Not another word will I hear on the subject of payment, young man. The only compensation we want or need is a healthy young soldier named Ben."

A few weeks later Ilsa persuaded her mother to let her accompany Buddy as far as the glade, and bring Ben along on his crutches to wait with her while Buddy went on to check his trap line. Lucille was at first reluctant but knew in her heart that Ben could be trusted with Ilsa.

Ben managed the uneven lane using only one crutch for the first time. Since the doctor had permitted him to set his own pace, Ben fully intended to be at a point within a week or so where a cane would be sufficient. Even though it was early November, the day was sunny and warm and the air crisp and clean. Ben knew the glade was where they had found him and was naturally very curious about the place, having heard the Bauers describe it as their special haven. As a family, they had enjoyed the site for picnics and the beauty and solitude it provided.

As they approached, the little creek gurgled a welcome. The clearing near the north bank was carpeted with soft grass where the sunlight penetrated. The three of them meandered over by the cliff face that Ben had been unable to negotiate that fateful night. Buddy pointed out to Ben where he had found him on the rocks below.

When Buddy went on to his trap lines, Ilsa led Ben to her favorite perch, a low, smooth rock that had been dumped there eons ago by a long extinct glacier or movement of the earth's crust. Ilsa knew that Ben's time with them was nearly over. She sensed that he felt guilty for having been out of the war while his friends carried the burden. This hateful war, she thought. Why do these nice young men have to endure that horror? This one, Ben, has no violence in him. He could never hurt anyone. He's sensitive, almost fragile and has so much innocent faith in people. And he's so full of love.

Ben looked over at her and smiled. Goodness, she thought, has he read my thoughts? She began to blush and loosened the shawl from around her neck hoping that perhaps her flushing cheeks would be less noticeable.

"I've been noticing that unusual necklace of yours, Ilsa," Ben said. "I've never seen one like it. It's stained hardwood, isn't it?"

Relieved to have his eyes distracted from her burning face, she took off her bonnet and released her golden hair. She pulled the wood piece over her head and carefully resettled her hair behind her thin shoulders. "It's more than a necklace, Ben. It's a rosary, made for me special by my Uncle Alvin, mother's brother up in Pennsylvania. All the pieces are maple, oak or walnut. He made it in his spare time, making sure that the beads were sizes and shapes signifying the different prayers of the rosary." She handed it to Ben and continued. "It took him more than a year to cut the pieces and do the carving. He's a wonder worker with wood. He even makes clocks and sailing ships."

"It's beautiful."

"By feeling the different bead shapes I can say the decades in the dark," she chuckled. "See the different shadings of color and the smoothing and polishing?"

Ben turned it in his hand. "Even the crucifix is carved. The body of Jesus, the crown of thorns, and tiny red dots where the nails went in."

"That's bull hide thong he strung the beads on, Ben. Uncle says that's the strongest there is. No man alive has the strength to break that thong he says. Soaked it in brine, then dried it, and soaked it some more. Maybe my father could break it, no one else. Notice how the Our Father beads are little squares and the Hail Mary's are ovals. Pretty clever, eh?"

Ben was truly intrigued. "It's a work of art, Ilsa. How he made the holes through each bead without splittin' the wood I can't imagine. I've worked some with wood, but it beats me. How'd he do that?"

She shook her head. "You'll have to ask him, Ben. He's got every wood tool known to man and some nobody's ever seen. Makes them himself. He told me that every tool ever made was invented by somebody who was frustrated at not being able to do something or other."

He continued to turn it over in his hands. As she watched him, an idea formed in her mind that she acted upon immediately. "When you leave us, Ben, I want you to have it, as a reminder . . . of the Bauers."

The slight hesitation did not escape Ben. Her eyes were upon him in such an innocent and loving manner that he had to turn away. "I could not possibly accept it, Ilsa. It was given to you by your uncle who obviously loves you very dearly. It's yours and it will please me to think of you wearin' it and usin' it. Besides, I'll need no object to remind me of the Bauers and all they have done for me. I've received the love of your family and been nursed back to health. Even more importantly, I've been reminded that there is goodness in this ugly world."

Her eyes were moist with deep feeling. "Ben, God sends us a lot of tests along the way to help us develop our true character. My father says that life is like western Maryland, full of peaks and valleys, rain and sun, good harvests and bad. Joy and pain come to each of us, but it's what we make of them that counts. I know that you believe the same way that I . . . that we do about those things, Ben. I can feel your goodness when I'm near you. I so believe in you and in the good you'll do . . . Oh, you're laughing at me."

She had been speaking so earnestly and sincerely that his smile had begun to form. "In the name of all that's holy, I'm not laughin' at you, Ilsa. It's just that you have a way of spreadin' joy in everything you do or say. You're so full of hope, you embarrass anyone who isn't. I would never laugh at you."

She smiled and nodded. Both knew instinctively that enough had been said. Just then a flock of pintails whistled low, then elevated and headed for the marsh past the ravine. Ben watched them disappear.

"I suppose that means the same here as it does in Minnesota," he commented, glad for the distraction. "The ducks are restless and flockin' up. What they're sayin', Ilsa, is it's almost time to be movin' on. They always seem to know when it's time."

Buddy reappeared and displayed two snared rabbits. As the three walked back to the house, Ben's thoughts took him back with his friends. In the peace of the past few weeks, he had to force himself to remember that not far from where they were now sauntering, young soldiers on both sides were being blown into eternity. Ilsa's father, Gus, said that life is peaks and valleys. The men fighting this war have been in a deep, dark valley for some time now. Will they ever reach another peak? And if they do, how many will survive to enjoy the view?

When they got back to the yard, they were greeted by Lucille waving a letter in her hand. "Ben, a letter from your people in Minnesota. Been forwarded by your regiment."

Ben recognized Maurna's script and ambled over to the bench to read the news from home.

Chapter Twenty-Eight

Dakotah Disposal

Throughout the months of October and November, the main topic among Minnesotans was punishment of the Indians. General sentiment was nearly unanimous that the guilty be severely dealt with, including execution for all savages who had taken up arms. Righteous wrath had great appeal and built on itself with vehemence and furor, fueled by newspaper editors who competed to write the most incendiary editorials.

After satisfying himself that the cases had been examined carefully, President Lincoln sent documentation to Sibley authorizing the execution of thirty-nine of the condemned 303 Indians. Father Abraham's criteria for approving execution was murder of civilians and/or rape of white women. Lincoln's message ordered the hangings to occur on Friday, December 19, at Mankato. A later communique postponed the event until December 26 and reduced the number of condemned to thirty-eight.

When news of Lincoln's order was made public, many Minnesotans objected and maligned the President. Most protesters merely made noise, but in Mankato more than 200 men took up arms and marched toward the prison camp where the guilty Indians awaited their fates. Sibley had anticipated such a response, however, and had sufficient troops available to dampen the fiery wicks of the lynch mob.

On the day after Thanksgiving (the day celebrated as such by most people, though it was not an official feast until 1863), Maurna, Ginny, and Pim had loaded their belongings into a wagon for the trip to Saint Paul. Will and Rob

Koukkari departed Mankato the same day to re-establish themselves at their home. The two of them and Pim agreed to meet again in Mankato for the public hangings of the Sioux. Pim informed Maurna that even though he would have to forego spending Christmas in Saint Paul, for his father's sake he intended to witness the hangings in Mankato on December 26. Will and Rob would be there for their mother and grandfather. Though she disagreed with the young men's purpose, Maurna held her tongue. Tragedy causes different responses in different people, she reasoned.

Maurna had exchanged letters with Angus and Iris Campbell regarding her decision to quit the Valley for better opportunities in Saint Paul. Acting on her request, the Campbells found her a modest rental home not far from the Campbell's store and only a few blocks from the Cathedral School. They told her that she was automatically hired with work projects available for her capable hands as soon as she arrived.

Pim helped them get settled in their small Saint Paul house. A day was spent registering Ginny with the Sisters of St. Joseph for their Cathedral School and in establishing themselves as new citizens. Maurna was excited about the change. Though she carried deep sadness in her heart for the loss of Joseph and Rose, she reasoned that the pain would be easier to bear far from the acute memories.

Chapter Twenty-Nine

Georgetown

"This release form contains the preliminary information I will ask you, but I must also verify it verbally. Name, rank, and military unit, please," said the young lady.

"Benedict Casey Murnane, Ma'am. Private, Minnesota First Regiment, Second Corps, Army of The Potomac."

"Age and place of birth?"

"Twenty-two, born in County Cork, Ireland, January 2, 1840."

"Wounded at Sharpsburg according to the information we've been given. What was the nature of the wound?" she asked.

"Crease in the head from a minié ball or cannister. Concussion, and a broken leg."

"A Doctor Butler of Frederick, Maryland, treated you and then released you to us. His detailed report of that treatment is being sent. You are assigned here until we release you for further military duty or declare you unfit."

"Yes, ma'am."

"Please report now to the supply room down the hall. They will assign you a cot in the ward and issue hospital garb. We will appreciate your compliance with all of our rules and regulations, which are listed on a sheet of paper they will give you. Welcome, Private Murnane, we will do our best for you." She smiled fleetingly and dismissed him.

Ben had caught a ride on an army supply wagon out of Frederick after taking his leave from the Bauers and receiving a release form signed by Doctor Butler and Captain Manelli of the militia. The driver let him off at a small hospital in Georgetown that specialized in rehabilitating recovering soldiers who had received their primary treatment at more comprehensive hospitals. Operated exclusively by volunteer women of Georgetown, the hospital had formerly been the aging Union Hotel. It contained a small surgery and an infirmary equipped to treat lacerations, diseases and other disorders. Three wards provided forty-eight patient cots. A small kitchen, dining room, and a supply center completed the facility. One of the establishment's assets was a wooded yard area where the men could exercise.

The head administrator was a handsome, elegant widow, Mrs. Julia Howard, who had marshalled a bevy of patriotic Georgetown women to serve as volunteers. The U.S. Sanitary commission had stamped its approval on the operation and provided advice and supplies. Civilian doctors gave of their time that could be spared from their regular practices. Mrs. Howard's niece, Ellen Lowry, the young woman who had registered Ben, was her able and dedicated assistant and resided with Mrs. Howard at her stately Georgetown home a few blocks from the hospital.

The routine for the patients consisted of rest, wholesome food, medication as required, and exercise. A small but well stocked library was available to the men, as was a table and chairs set up with pens and stationery for letter writing. Time was a burden for the soldiers. Visitors consisted mainly of their healthy soldier comrades on pass. Liquor was not allowed on the premises. Most of the rehabilitants were anxious to complete their recovery programs even if it meant return to the war zone. Like Ben, they were eager to get back to their comrades and felt guilty for not being there to share their fates. To a man, however, they were high in their praise of the treatment they were afforded at Union Hospital and departed the facility with pleasant recollections of the kindly, warm Julia Howard and of the diffident, but comely Ellen Lowry.

Ben had written home soon after his arrival. When it became known that he was from Minnesota, several patients asked about the Indian troubles. He dashed off a short note to Ox and Tony to inform them of his transfer to Georgetown and to ask them to come to see him if they could. He heard nothing from them until December 8, when a short note arrived.

Dear Ben:
    We hear you are getting well. We tried to get a pass to get in to see you, but no passes being given out. We think it means that we'll be crossing the Rappahannock to try to take Fredricksburg soon. Big fight likely. Burnside is itchy to prove himself.
    Hope you get back with us soon. You've been resting long enough, the Sarge says. Bad news to give you. Our friend, Pudge Henderson, was killed out on patrol.
    Sorry about your brother, Joseph. Lots of us lost loved ones and friends in Minnesota.
                    Your friends,
                      Ox, Tony, Shakey, and Sarge

The September 17 Battle of Antietam had spawned more than the usual number of experts, who argued endlessly whether it had been simply a bloody standoff or a marginal Northern victory.

Those same experts agreed with President Lincoln that the Army of the Potomac had lost a great opportunity when it had not pursued the retreating Southerners. After the September battle, the Union juggernaut had malingered. For weeks Lincoln had attempted to inspire McClellan to press Lee into a war-shortening, show-down engagement. Finally in early November, the frustrated Commander-in-Chief removed McClellan and replaced him with the plodding corps commander, General Ambrose Burnside, who did not want the role but pledged to do his best. Though deficient in strategic insight he was determined not to be guilty of inaction. He would strike at Lee and bloody his forces no matter what the consequences or the casualties.

General Burnside moved his 100,000 man force to Falmouth just across the Rappahannock River from Fredricksburg. On December 11, Union forces crossed the river, occupied Fredricksburg and confronted the Rebels entrenched on Marye's Heights above the town. On the thirteenth, Burnside ordered regiment after regiment to try to dislodge the gray soldiers shielded behind a high stone wall on the slope. His ill-conceived offensive cost the Yankees 12,700 casualties.

On December 14, all Washington was buzzing. The casualties were criminal. The wounded were arriving by the boatloads up the Potomac and overland on wagons. The Fourteenth Street Bridge sagged under the load of broken bodies and shattered lives.

The Christmas season and a new year were fast approaching. The only groups with any cause for either joy or celebration were the Abolitionists and the Negro slaves who were poised to loudly proclaim their triumph when the Emancipation Proclamation conditions became official on January 1, 1863. New Year is traditionally a time of hope and renewal, but both were in very short supply in Washington and throughout the Nation.

Maurna's Journal
Christmas 1862

It began with such promise, but such a woeful year was 1862. We shall never again be what we were, full of hope and promise, rich in friends and neighbors, free to grow and thrive. How changed are our lives.

Ben far off in a seemingly endless war that was to have ended in just a few months. Ever escalating, and devastating lives throughout the land. Why must he go back to the war? Has he not faced enough? May God protect him, and Ox and Tony and the others.

Our loss of Joseph is beyond consolation. First Timothy, now Joseph. Our two pillars! Can our house stand without them? We were five who left Ireland, six when God sent Virginia, only four now alive. Timothy's and Joseph's strong wills and goodness remain part of us, but their absence is so painful. Pim has inherited their strength of character and is trying to assume their roles. His courage and quick thinking saved Ginny's life and mine. Even with that, he is determined to join Sibley's expedition to pursue the renegade Sioux this spring. He says that he feels obligated because of the murder of his father. I will attempt to dissuade him.

Ginny is nearly herself again. The elasticity of youth has aided her in recovering from our dreadful captivity. I shall need more time, but am making progress. God sent us both the anaesthetic of shock and denial that sustained us through the horror and gloom of those forty days and nights. More than 200 women and children survived the ordeal, and can never forget it. Without the courage and love of White Spider and other kindly Sioux, many more would have perished. I have met few individuals as basically good and caring as White Spider. God sent him to us; may He spare him to go on doing good wherever he roams.

For Ginny and me, the decision is final. We will make our future in Saint Paul. The advantages for Ginny are obvious; schooling, friends, activities, books, culture. For me, the opportunity to work doing what I love and making a fair living with prospects for building those efforts into a good life. The Campbells are God-sent. The loneliness of the farm was barely endurable with the companionship of Joseph and the sisterly love of dear, dear Rose. With those dear souls gone, I could not bear to live out there.

Ginny, Pim, and I were hospitably treated by the Cossettes while in Mankato. We are in their debt not only for the shelter and food but for the repair of our sagging spirits. So understanding and loving. The people of the Valley who have become our friends are among the finest on earth.

Tomorrow, the day after Christ's birth, the town of Mankato will be permanently stained with the public hangings of the convicted Sioux. The penalty seems to be more revenge than justice. What can be accomplished by more killing? I detest the whole affair. Ginny and I will be two of the few who will not be in attendance. I shudder to think of the gruesome scene.

The other Sioux prisoners will be imprisoned until spring, then deported. We are effectively ridding ourselves of them. They lose their lands, their possessions, their annuities, and in truth their very freedom. What else have they? Justice is mine, sayeth the Lord. God save the poor souls!

Let 1863 bring Ben back to us whole and safe and keep Pim from harm with Sibley next spring. And may it bring peace to our nation, so rent and torn. And may that peace, when it comes, be a more just peace than the one we now enjoy in Minnesota.

Chapter Thirty

Hawks Unfettered

Christmas Day in Mankato was not the traditionally joyful celebration of the birth of the Christ Child. The focus was on death, not birth; on endings, not a beginning. The usually tranquil community was bulging with thousands of Minnesotans, many who travelled hundreds of miles to witness the largest mass execution in the eighty-six-year history of the United States of America.

Rented at a premium rate were rooms in hotels, boarding houses and private homes, floor space in businesses, barns, sheds, and any form of shelter. General stores, shops, and public buildings were kept open to accommodate the free-spending holiday visitors. Because martial law had been declared, taverns were closed but liquor was available and consumed in great quantities.

Church services were well attended but it was suspected by the cynical that some of the worshipers sought the full hour or so of heated interior as much as they did the religious comfort.

The celebratory mood grew throughout the day, and its clamor almost drowned out the low, incessant death chants emanating from the throats of the 303 convicted Sioux, including the thirty-eight condemned to the gallows. The guard soldiers kept the overzealous spectators from jeering, cursing, or even viewing the unfortunates, though hundreds made the attempt.

As the sun set on Christmas Day in snow-encrusted Mankato, the followers of the Child born that day drifted off to bed, though their excitement and anticipation would prevent many from deriving the benefits of a refreshing rest. Achieving sleep was made difficult by one other factor. The doomed thirty-eight chanted their death canticles steadily from Christmas sunset to dawn on the twenty-sixth.

A few among those thirty-eight warriors actually slept for part of their last night, but when awakened joined their compatriots to utilize their last three hours painting their bodies, attaching beads, feathers, and shells to their clothing, smoking begged cigars and pipes and permitting Reverend Stephen Riggs and Father Augustine Ravoux to circulate among them. During the previous four days, all but Cut Nose and one other of the condemned had been baptized, twenty-four by Father Ravoux. Knowing their dread fate was imminent, the doomed warriors continued their soul-rending, mournful chant that helped drown out the growing clamor of the gathering avengers.

When the condemned men's preparations for their rude and final leave-taking were completed, the guards led them single file from the camp along a corridor framed by troops being pressed by the eager, virulent crowd. With hands bound behind them and feet shackled so they could manage only a pathetic, undignified shuffle, the prisoners held their heads erect to display their personal and tribal pride and their unyielding conviction that they had been cruelly provoked into their criminal behavior.

Pim Murnane and Will and Rob Koukkari studied the inscrutable faces as they passed. Pim wondered whether the murderer of his father was amongst the group. Will and Rob could not prevent revisiting the hideous scene of their crucified mother and their mutilated grandfather.

As the thirty-eight convicted warriors approached the town square, their eyes were assaulted by their first stark view of the ten foot high platform, supporting a scaffold from which dangled thirty-eight coarse rope nooses. For the first time since leaving their prison camp, the eyes of many looked downward. After a brief pause they were steered to the platform steps, assisted in their awkward climb, paraded around the rim, and finally positioned, each beside a noose. They stood nearly shoulder to shoulder on trap-door panels, one for each row, held horizontal by straining hemp. Profane, degrading remarks cast at them from the mob impressed them not in the least and only seemed to brace them for the pending ordeal.

Shivering in the mid-morning cold, soldiers ringed the gallows framework at ground level to restrain any aggressive spectators. The thirty-eight braves stood erect and impervious to the cold as their eyes devoured the vivid Minnesota sky, their final earthly view. Pim's eyes followed the direction of their gaze and noted that a high-soaring hawk drifting freely in the gentle breeze was the focus of their attention.

Suddenly, a crisp command. Nooses were guided over feathers and headdresses and tightened around throbbing necks. Blindfolds were fixed in place over unblinking, lively eyes. A pause. A startling, unearthly war whoop shattered the calm. Cut Nose had screamed his final defiance. The crowd stirred and waited while the soldier attendants made certain that the feet of the Indians were positioned properly over the panels. As the soldiers stepped away, the regimental commander nodded. A brief delay, then a short series of drum rolls. The master rope that controlled the trap-doors was slashed and the condemned braves fell.

The scaffolding strained to support the gross weight, but held. The slackless ropes vibrated under the strain but efficiently performed their function. The audience hushed for a heartbeat, then a thunderous roar burst the brittle air. An approving, delirious cheer rose in volume into waves of lusty bellows sent forth by more than 5,000 soldiers and civilians. The thunderous noise drowned out the gurgling gasps of thirty-eight swelling and hemorrhaging tongues and throats. The sight of the braves' faces contorted in agony became the mob's visual reward. Moccasined feet dangled, kicking toes strained to reach the cherished, disputed soil just three feet down but an eternity away. After several minutes the twisting, writhing torsos became still, as spirits were unfettered from scorn and bondage and other earthly concerns.

Cheering and primordial screaming continued for more than thirty minutes. The crowd gradually split into more intimate groupings where congratulations were exchanged and satisfactions shared. His emotions roiling and in disarray, Pim struggled to sort out his feelings. His mind and heart waged the age-old battle seeking balance between justice and mercy. Though he approved of the executions, he was revolted by the agonies of the hanged and appalled by the response of most of the people. He silently wondered how they could feel so elated and exhilarated in the face of such cruel suffering.

The soldiers remained in position around the platform until another command ordered the assigned men to step forward, draw a knife, and cut the rope suspending "their" Indian. When the bodies fell the final three feet, nooses and blindfolds were removed from silent throats and no-longer-caring eyes. The corpses were thrown aboard three wagons that were driven through applauding spectators toward a pre-dug site at the edge of Mankato.

Pim and the Koukkaris detached themselves from the mob and spoke not a word as they trudged toward the Cossette livery. Suddenly remembering, Pim turned to look up for the soaring hawk, but it apparently had been pushed beyond the west horizon by the rising wind from the east.

Because the soil was deeply frozen, a more penetrable sandy river bank had become the most feasible grave site. A long shallow ditch became the burial plot for the uncoffined Dakotah braves. The spectators who had followed the soldier-guarded wagons cheered once more, then turned back to rejoin their fellow celebrators in the jubilant, festive town. There would be music and dancing and carousing until the wee hours. The people had come from far and near to witness and be party to the mass punishment that was the final act of the Great Sioux Uprising of 1862.

- Gettysburg

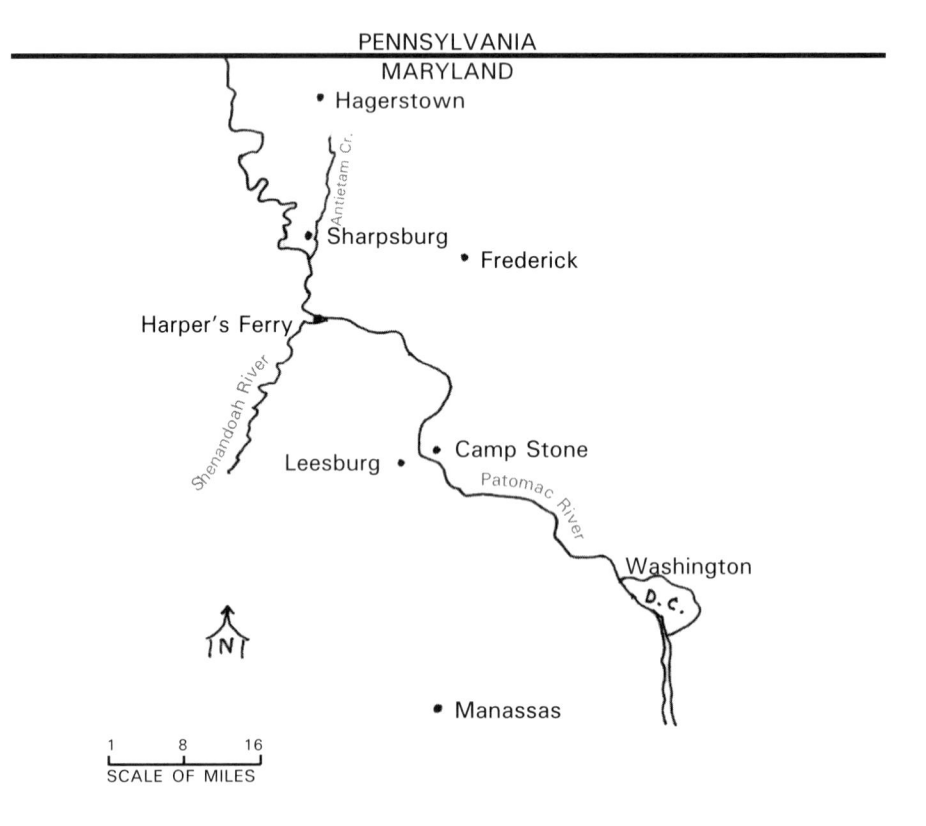

PENNSYLVANIA
────────────────────────────
MARYLAND
- Hagerstown

Antietam Cr.

- Sharpsburg
- Frederick

Harper's Ferry

Shenandoah River

Leesburg • Camp Stone

Patomac River

Washington
D.C.

↑N

1 8 16
SCALE OF MILES

- Manassas

PART III

Home

January 1863 to April 1864

> . . . *at the brief command of Lee,*
> *Moved out that matchless infantry,*
> *With Pickett leading grandly down,*
> *To rush against the soaring crown*
> *Of those dread heights of destiny.*
> **Will Henry Thompson**

> . . . *But if you saw which no eyes can see,*
> *The inward beauty of her lively sprite,*
> *Garnisht with heavenly gifts of high degree,*
> *Much more then would ye wonder at the sight.* . . .
> **Edmund Spenser**

Chapter Thirty-One

The Gray Ghost

Though still limping slightly, and in less than ideal physical condition due to his long inactivity, Ben Murnane was able to persuade the hospital authorities that he was sufficiently recovered to rejoin his regiment. When he thanked her for the excellent care he had received, Julia Howard told him he had been an exemplary patient and one of the most polite young men she had encountered. He even extracted a smile from Ellen Lowry who said as he left that they would pray for his safety.

Ben arrived in the Union camp along with a sleet storm just in time to spend a dreary, cold January 18 with his friends. He was welcomed heartily but teased about his long "vacation" in Maryland and Washington, teasing that seemed to Ben less enthusiastic than normal. He soon learned why. Though the Minnesotans had not been involved directly in the wasteful assault against the heights at Fredricksburg, they shared the defeat and the infectious deadening of morale. Ben was amazed at the difference in the spirit of his friends from what it had been at Sharpsburg. "Until you showed up, Ben, not much good has happened to us for quite a while," said Ox. "Welcome back, my friend."

Gathering around a campfire his friends quickly brought him up to date. The saddest item was, of course, that Pudge Henderson had been killed while on patrol in early December. The loss of Pudge depressed them and they were reluctant to describe how it had happened. His death was the first among their close group and was painful to talk about.

Several passing references to a Gray Ghost were made, but the subject was passed over so fast that Ben didn't get a chance to ask them about it.

Tony and Ox mentioned news from home about the Sioux Uprising. Belle Lunde had written Tony that their new home was rebuilt, as was most of New Ulm. The Koukkari boys, the Rivards, and most other families were resettled. The Sioux reservation lands were being grabbed by land speculators, and Governor Ramsey and others were busy trying to downplay the impact of the Indian rampage. Most of the regiment soldiers felt President Lincoln had been too lenient, reducing the number of hangings from over 300 to just thirty-eight. Good God, they'd massacred more than 500 whites, hadn't they? What was the man thinking? Of course their attitudes about the Sioux affair were formed from the viewpoints of their relatives and friends who had written understandably one-sided accounts. Exaggerations, biases, conflicting and false reports, inaccuracies, prejudices, and politician's shadings all mixed together. Fair assessments and truth were hard to come by.

Ben finally got his chance to ask. "What's this great mystery you keep mentionin' about some Gray Ghost?"

Ox responded, "That's right, Ben, you were gone during all that crazy business, weren't you? Well, it's awful hard to explain something you don't understand yourself. So many versions you can't get a real handle hold on it. But the New York boys sure do believe it. Nothing more lately though, not since Fredricksburg. Seems to be done with. Least ways we hope so. Maybe somebody shot that gray ghost."

"Every New Yorker's still looking over his shoulder, you can bet. We all were for a while," Tony contributed.

Ox went on. "'Course nobody can pin a tail on it. But after Antietam we followed the Rebs down south, keeping 'tween them and Washington. They settled in across the Rappahannock around Fredricksburg with us across from them near Falmouth. We stared across the river at each other on into November. It became a real boring time with awful weather, freezing, then thawing, sleeting, mud thicker than porridge. That's when the killings started."

"Killings you say," Ben inserted. "Who got killed?"

Ox spoke again. "Soldiers, one after another. Three of 'em, all New Yorkers. Each one found alone with his head stove in. Two of the three was done in when they was standing perimeter guard. The third one was off in a grove of trees near Falmouth. All alone like the other two. Head smashed in, a rock most likely. Strangest thing of all though was that they were all stripped down to their underwear. Seems like the Reb was trying to humiliate 'em as well as kill 'em, Ben."

Shakey added, "And their pants was found near their bodies hanging from a tree limb. Weirdest thing I ever heard."

Ben shook his head disgustedly, "Did we know any of these New Yorkers?"

"None of us knew any of them. Not by name at least. We'd probably seen them around but didn't know them. Lieutenant Messick, he said he knew the last one got killed. Man from the Bowery called Haney. The Captain said it was the strangest business he'd ever seen. They doubled the guards after they found Haney. Should have had two all along with that ghost sneaking around," said Tony.

"I know I sure feel better with another man around when I'm standing guard out there." Shakey added. "That gray ghost slips in and out without a sound. We were all running nervous and jumpy. For all we know that ghost may be wearing a blue uniform, way he gets so close to his victims. If he's wearing gray, he's as quiet as an Indian and disappears like smoke. Some claim they saw him, and others thought they might have, but no Reb was ever taken on our side of the river. Far as we know, he's still out there waiting to pounce again. Hasn't been another killing though since just before the big battle at Fredricksburg six weeks ago."

Tony concluded, "Some soldiers even figured it might not have been a Reb at all, but a civilian doing the killings. Not likely. Some mysteries just never do get solved, but that ghost sure did get our attention. Who knows, he might have drowned going back across the river."

Ben then introduced the subject that troubled him and one he knew his friends would have difficulty discussing. He hesitated a little, then asked. "Tell me about old Pudge. Doesn't seem possible he's gone. Good human being. Liked him a lot. How'd he die, Ox?"

Ox knew the question was coming. He'd even rehearsed a little in his mind how he'd tell Ben about it. He'd thought of an indirect way to tell him the hardest part, but before he got to that, he had to tell the first part right. He cleared his throat, looked straight at Ben, and began. "Pudge died a man, Ben. You'd have been proud. All of us were. We miss him. We wrote a letter to his family telling them how he died. We wrote up a rough copy, then the company clerk was kind enough to make a clean ink copy in good hand writing to send on to the Hendersons. I kept our copy. Got it in my rucksack. You can read it. But before you do, I got to tell you, you wouldn't have known the new Pudge. You remember, Ben, he came back to the regiment just before Antietam, just in time to get his first real fighting action. What a time to pick for your first one, huh? Well, Ben, after that battle, he just wasn't the same person we'd known since Fort Snelling. Sudden like. He got quiet and brooding. Sort of heavy headed and deep thinking. That old giggling and joshing? Couldn't hardly get him to talk, let alone laugh. Just stared ahead, hard-eyed. You wouldn't have known him. Guess Antietam and the killing got to him."

Tony elaborated. "'Member how he used to just be led any which way, always agreeable, and humble as anything? Nicest, easiest person I ever knew. I wondered if anything could get him riled. Timid, he was. Liked everybody. Well all at once he was downcast, solemn like. Not the same cheerful soul. Hard to figure out. We saw some real ugly things at Antietam and it must have got to him deep inside. Noticed the change in him soon as we got down river here. Never saw anybody change so much so fast."

Shakey nodded in agreement and said, "Ben, you were the one he really favored. You befriended him before any of us did, and watched out for him. You taught us all to respect him instead of belittling and teasing him like everybody was doing. After a while we were all watching out for him and came to 'preciate him, thanks to you, Ben. When he heard you were missing at Sharpsburg, he was the first to volunteer for the burial detail, so's he could get back out there to look for you. We all know how hard that was to do. He shamed us all into volunteering. We searched through those bloody bodies for over six hours the day after the battle. Identifying those that we could, but all the time looking for Ben Murnane, both hoping and dreading we'd find you. Lots of death on display in front of us, all over, and some dying going on inside us, too. Nobody who walked that field of slaughter could ever be the same again. And nobody was more affected than Pudge. In his mind, his friend Ben was out there someplace. We had to drag him away, or he'd be out there yet looking for you. He was wet-eyed for days afterward, Ben, thinking you was dead and gone for good."

Ben barely controlled the emotion rising up on him. They all shuffled their feet and looked everywhere but at each other. The moment stretched, then Ben broke the gloom and stillness.

"I'll read that letter now, Ox," he said softly.

Relieved to have something to do, Ox led Ben to his tent, dug out the letter, then left him alone to read it privately.

> Dear Mr. and Mrs. Henderson and family:
>
> We delayed sending this letter to you about your son and our friend, Parker, until now to be sure that official notification of his death had reached you.
>
> We want you to know how much he meant to us and how he died of which you can be truly proud. We were there, so what we tell you is the God's truth.
>
> On December 6 last, Parker, Tony Lunde, Ox Koukkari, and nine other soldiers were sent on a patrol across the Rappahannock River north of Fredricksburg, Virginia. Lieutenant Messick was in command. We proceeded up a creek bottom that led into a rocky ravine with high cliffs on either side. We started into the valley but were surprised by a Reb patrol in ambush. They took us under fire, so we holed up in some big rocks. The situation had us pinned down where we would become exposed in the daylight from the sides above. The lieutenant rightly judged we would have to retreat or be surrounded, but we couldn't all

go at once or the Rebs would be on us from the front. He ordered Sergeant Hughes to lead eight men back to the boat immediately and cross back over the river in 20 minutes whether the rest of us got back or not. That left the lieutenant, Ox Koukkari, and Parker to hold back the Rebs. We could hold them because they had to expose themselves over 50 yards of clearing in front of our perch.

After about ten minutes, the lieutenant ordered Parker and Ox to dash back to the river to catch the boat. He intended to hold them off by himself, but asked for their rifles so he'd have more firepower. Ox handed over his rifle but your son stepped back, pointed his at the lieutenant and said, "I'll kill you where you stand, sir, if you don't go with Ox. Those men need you to get them back across. I can hold the enemy here. This is one time in my life when I'm giving the orders." His eyes said he meant it. The lieutenant argued, but Parker put the barrel to his chest, and said, "the first duty of an officer is to take care of his men. Now do your job, sir. Move on out."

The lieutenant pushed Ox toward the trail. Parker was already firing back at the Rebs, keeping them busy. Just before he left, the lieutenant called out to your son, "Soldier, good luck," then snapped a smart salute at Parker.

Some of us owe our lives or at least our freedom to your son. It was the bravest act we ever witnessed. Later the Confederate officer sent official word of Parker's death along with the compliments of their squad in a note that said: "Regretfully, we killed a brave American today. He refused to surrender. The Minnesota First Regiment should be justifiably proud of their soldier, Parker Henderson. Our compliments."

Lieutenant Messick has recommended a medal for Parker. One he truly deserves. Please know of our love and respect for your son. We will ever cherish his friendship. We hope this note describing his actions brings you comfort. Greater love hath no man . . . .

        Parker's friends,
        Ox Koukkari, Tony Lunde,
        Shakey Cosgrove, Sarge McMahon and
        Ben Murnane (missing)

Maurna's Journal
April, 1863

Pim left us yesterday to return to the farm. Our home seems bereft. He has become more like his father every day, strong-willed, decisive, conscientious, but impulsive, and not quite at peace with himself. I weep when I think of how fast he's been forced to mature.

He is moving in with Will and Rob at the Koukkari place. Together the three will prepare the land of both farms, seed the crops, and work them. I'm relieved that he will not be alone. Our former home will remain boarded up until such time as Pim decides to move back.

Both Pim and Will are determined to join the Sibley Expedition in June. While the two are gone, young Rob will reside with the Rivards. He will continue working the farm fields with some help from Clem Lachance. Pim and Will anticipate returning in time for the harvest. Of course the timing will depend on the success of Sibley's campaign to punish the Sioux and drive them farther to the west. I can't imagine that the Indians remain a serious threat, but public fervor is such that the campaign against them has universal approval. Until they are forced beyond the Missouri River, people will not feel at ease.

According to newspaper accounts and hearsay, the more than 1200 elderly and women and children held as prisoners on Pike Island fared very poorly during the winter months. The island provided little shelter from the winds and cold. Their rations were less than adequate. More than 150 have died since their confinement began. Plans call for their deportation as soon as the river ice is gone. The intention is to carry them south on the Mississippi to where the Missouri River intersects, then up the Missouri to desolate lands in Dakota. God help the poor souls!

Ginny is doing well in school. She loves the Sisters of Saint Joseph, dedicated women who hold out very high standards and expectations. Saint Paul is fortunate to have them.

Governor Ramsey and civic and business leaders are tireless in their determination to build up the area. We have more than 12,000 in Saint Paul now and the communities of Saint Anthony Falls and little Minneapolis are growing fast. The former Sioux reservation lands are selling briskly. It's truly exciting to be a part of the evolution of an area. Saint Paul will be my home for my remaining days and Ginny's, at least until she reaches an age to make her own decisions. As for Pim and Ben, it remains to be seen.

Despite the loss of dear Joseph and Rose and other friends, God has been good to us. My precious daughter, my younger brother and my nephew, my gratifying work, our wonderful friends, and my adopted city, Saint Paul, are my life now.

Chapter Thirty-Two

Violation

Ilsa Bauer had always thought of the glade as her own special place. Oh, she happily shared it with her family members, but they were unaware that she considered them only guests. It had become her sanctuary. She often thought of it as a cathedral with open vaults to the sky and beyond. To her the blend of its essences was nature's incense, and the surround of its beauty was the manifestation of the existence of her Creator. The glade never failed to calm her and bring her a feeling of tranquility and the assurance of God's love. Those feelings were strongest at this time of year, in budding springtime, the season of poets.

Buddy left her there to hurry across the creek through the dense woods and up and over the high ridge. She caught a distant glimpse of his tousled hair as he had crested the crown and started down the far side. Checking his lines would take him about an hour.

With the intention of finishing stanzas put off too long, she brought her writing tablet and hoped that the inspiration of the setting would generate salubrious thoughts and words. She tucked her legs under herself, settling on the low, flat rock by the edge of the woods that would soon be bathed in bright, warm sunlight. Her gaze briefly followed the lazy, fluffy clouds as they drifted eastward, unhurried, heralding spring. She closed her eyes, allowing her senses to function freely and her mind to wander.

Her first thoughts were of her brother. In January, the Bauers had received the first official notification that Kurt was indeed a prisoner in a Richmond camp. The authorities offered some hope that a prisoner exchange with the Confederates could possibly free him by mid-summer. More months of uncertainty. They all prayed for good news.

Ilsa prayed for the other soldier in her life, too. "Please keep Ben safe," she said a thousand times a day. She shuddered when she thought of him in danger. She knew Ben thought of her only as a friend, dismissing her as too young for the kind of thoughts she entertained about him. In fact, she concurred in his judgment of the situation. I am too young for him now, she thought. Six years difference is a lot at this age. But in a short while, those years will shrink and melt away and the difference will be meaningless. She smiled to herself. If it is to be, Dear Lord . . . She let the thought hang, savoring it, believing it was destined.

As most young women do, she thought a great deal about that mysterious condition called love. Was this what was meant by being in love? It had happened to her so swiftly. From the moment she had first seen Ben, he seemed so right to her. She had been drawn to him and felt so comfortable and relaxed with him. When he looked at her, the blood rushed so fast that she thought surely he would see her face flush. Her secret was safe and she would keep it until the time was right.

She suspected that her mother was vaguely aware. Hard to fool another woman, she laughed to herself. Mother's not let on, and won't of course, but suspects and is a little bit worried about it. A mother's protective instincts. She knew that Lucille was very fond of Ben and highly approved of his good character, fine manners, and upbringing. It's not Ben she's worried about, Ilsa chuckled, it's me. She probably remembers how she felt about my father. Girls can be obsessed with love and can have their hearts broken. If I were to marry Ben, I'd probably go way off to Minnesota to live. So far away, and with the Indians still rampaging from what we hear. Oh, silly Ilsa, you really are getting ahead of yourself. Already married and off to the west. Goodness, you'll be having babies if you don't slow down your thinking. At the thought, though she was alone, she blushed, but then smiled to herself, savoring the fantasy.

The sunshine had reached her and felt warm on her face. She shed the shawl, placing it beside her on the rock. She removed her bonnet, letting her hair settle over her shoulders. The sun would be good for it, give it luster. Mustn't get too much sun on her face though. Brings the freckles. She inhaled deep draughts of perfumed air, listened to the chattering birds and watched them as they flitted about picking up moss and twigs to build fresh spring nests. All creatures want a warm, safe place of their own, she thought. She again watched the drifting clouds and imagined them floating over Ben, too. She was totally relaxed, warm, at peace, brimming with hope and dreams.

Violation

Ilsa heard him before she saw him, but only briefly. The suddenness of his crashing entry into the serenity of the setting startled her. He was lean, with wild, red, flowing hair and full beard. Heavy features. Astride a buff-colored stallion. In Yankee blue. Filthy, mud-splattered boots and trousers. Red-rimmed eyes. He very nearly rode past without noticing her, but stopped to water his horse at the creek. Ilsa was frightened, felt vulnerable, tried to remain absolutely still, held her breath, and prayed.

But a pair of combative squirrels erupted noisily behind her. The soldier turned to the sound, not seeing her for a moment, but then a smile began to form as he led his mount toward her. "Well now, Jake," he chortled. "Look at what we got us here." He said to Ilsa, "Pretty girl, you weren't gonna let old Jake ride by without even sayin' hello were you?"

Buddy Bauer finished with his last snare, tied the rabbit to his belt next to the other two, reset the snare, and started back along the uphill trail. Mighty slim pickin's, he thought. He had taken a few minutes longer than usual, looking over a cold camp fire where someone had recently spent the night. He had seen more and more sign of folks crossing through the wooded ravines and switchbacks. Oh well, unless they're the ones who stole my traps, not my worry, not being on Bauer land, he reasoned. He hurried on, short-cutting up a steep bank then onto his usual trail. The sun warmed his back as he bent north to the crest of the last ridge. Just at the top was a clearing where he invariably stopped briefly to look out over the valley hardwoods and the creek that marked the boundary of the Bauer property. It looked so neat and orderly from this distance. Crops in rows in season, patches of fallow, a spot of woods, then some pasture, cows grazing. Bare, turned earth at this time of year though, just a few weeks until planting time. Won't have much time for trapping once that starts. Sunup to sundown in the fields. Hard work but a good feeling time for a farmer.

He was too far away to hear him, but his eyes picked up the rider galloping hard through the woods beyond the creek, heading east. The buff animal and rider flashed in and out of view among wooded patches. On Bauer land, Buddy thought. A blue coat soldier, his bright red hair and beard vivid in the sunlight, his hat thrown back on his neck and tied under his chin. Buddy hollered as loud as he could, but the man paid him no mind, if he heard him at all, and passed out of view. Buddy didn't like it. He'd tell his father.

He threw the sack over his back and worked his way down the shaded north side of the ridge. Ilsa probably got tired of waiting and went on home, he thought. Never can tell about those writers though, he chuckled to himself, they get lost in their reveries. Gonna have to read a few of those poems one of these days, if she'll let me. He reached the valley floor and stepped carefully on submerged rocks to cross the creek. Stepping up the far bank, he turned upstream toward the glade.

    The sight of Ilsa's shawl tossed carelessly on the bank instantly alarmed him. He hurried around the slight bend and saw his sister reclined by the low, flat rock. At first she appeared to be in repose. But as he approached, he saw the awkward twist of her torso. His heart jumped and fear enveloped him as he raced toward her.

Chapter Thirty-Three

Unfinished Poem

Letter from Maurna
May 2, 1863

Dear Brother Ben,
 It was so good to hear you have recovered from your dreadful wounds. The healing is welcome, but I regret that it has permitted you to return to the fighting. I hoped that you had served enough to be released. The news we receive about your regiment is so unreliable we find it difficult to separate the truth from speculation. We've heard of battles near Fredricksburg again, but don't really know of your unit's involvement. Please be careful, Ben, and greet dear Ox and Tony and urge them to be careful, too. We were sorry to hear of the death of your friend, Henderson. Our hearts go out to his family, and we have included him in our prayers.
 Pim is going on the Sibley Expedition that will leave in a few weeks time. My persuasive powers failed. Please include his safe return in your prayers, Ben. Ginny and I need both of you home. We are so reduced without the two of you.
 We recently witnessed a heart-wrenching scene that haunts me. Twelve hundred Indians, elderly men, women, and children, were jammed into steamboats at Pike Island to be transported out of the state. They were shipped like livestock to desolate, treeless prairie land to be dumped there to survive if they are able. Their faces told the story of a confused, deposed people. They looked at us with neither fear nor hatred. Ben, I swear they looked right through us. After all, these souls were judged *not guilty* by our prairie courts. These were the non-participants. Oh, I know many deaths

and violent acts occurred, some to people we dearly loved, but the acts weren't performed by the innocents on those boats.

Many in the mob of spectators behaved shamefully and crudely, shouting and hurling fruit, vegetables, and stones at the forlorn creatures. For their hate-filled efforts, the vengeful received no satisfaction, for the Sioux ignored them and patiently endured. Their self-control was edifying. I was struck particularly by a young man perhaps ten years of age who stepped in front of his two little sisters to protect them from the flying objects. I couldn't be sure, but I believe he was the same young man that Joseph caught taking one of our chickens. He stood dignified and courageous in the face of the crowd and showed not contempt but pity for the abusive antics. That young man was not defeated, Ben. The best of his people and their heritage courses through his veins. I saw in him a young White Spider who will carry on through whatever travails lie ahead. I wept when they started down the river and out of their beautiful homeland.

Experts are labeling the troubles as a conflict of cultures, saying that the two could not co-exist, that one or the other had to give way. But the Indians may have adapted over time if they had been treated justly and had seen more in our "civilized" way that seemed worthy of adoption. We have hardly been good models for them to wish to emulate. God help them in their quest for a place to call their own.

Ginny and I have found our place, Ben. We feel part of the energy of an emerging, evolving area that will be fruitful and rewarding for thousands of people. It's been a tortuous route from Cork to here, with jolts along the way, but Saint Paul feels home to us.

God keep you safe, dear Brother. Know that you are truly cherished, and the three of us pray constantly for your safety and early return.

Our best love,
Maurna, Ginny, Pim

Ben put away her letter and rejoined his comrades.

"Lee's goin' north again," announced Sarge. "'spect we'll be headin' him off. Get your gear packed."

"That man won't let it rest," Shakey responded. "Always pushing."

"Sooner beats later, Shakey. Sooner gets going home closer," said Ox as he began assembling his pack.

Sarge cuffed Ben and teased, "Come on, Irish, we got to keep 'tween the Rebs and Washington."

By June 26, the Minnesota First Regiment was encamped several miles south and west of Frederick. Ben had calculated their route with more interest than his comrades. They were approaching an area that would be only a quick jaunt to the home of the Bauers. He was anxious to visit them and thank them again for all they had done for him.

Unfinished Poem

Ox and Tony requested pass time to accompany Ben. Captain Messick reasoned it would be safer with three than for Ben to travel alone. The first sergeant quickly noted, however, that Private Koukkari was listed for mess duty in the A.M., Private Koukkari's request was denied, but Private Lunde's was granted. That evening Ben and Tony cleaned their uniforms and shined their boots. Tony retired but Ben stayed up to pen a quick letter.

Dear Maurna, Pim, and Ginny,
 I trust that all of you are healthy and settled in Saint Paul. It is good to know you are recovering well from your terrible time with the Sioux. Apparently the Indians did more harm than we at first heard. Tony, Ox, and I can hardly believe that it was so bloody and widespread. It's hard to imagine New Ulm nearly destroyed. The loss of our brother and Pim's father is difficult to accept though it is comforting to think of Joseph on his cherished hill with the good company of dear Rose Koukkari. May they forever rest in peace.
 Pim, my good friend, please take the advice of a war veteran, though of only a few battles. When you go out to Dakota with Sibley, trust in your comrades and in your officers and don't try to be a hero. War is not glory-filled as your uncle once believed. It's ugly and miserable. Go, if you must. I understand your feelings, but take care of yourself, and don't do more than the situation calls for.
 We have endured another change in command. First, Burnside replaced McClellan, then Joseph Hooker took over just before the spring renewal of fighting. The Rebs gave us another thrashing at Chancellorsville. Most say that the fault was Hooker's for hesitating when he needed to act. It seems that the Confederates have better generals than we do. They seem to be a step ahead of us. Our soldiers are just as skilled as theirs and equally determined, but we get outmaneuvered. Word is though that the Rebs lost their General Jackson, the one they call "Stonewall." His absence will hurt them for sure. Rumors about another attack. Some say that Hooker may be relieved. The troops want McClellan again, but the President has lost all patience with him. Meanwhile, the killing goes on. All my friends except Parker Henderson are healthy and whole. My wounds are still bothersome but don't compromise my activity.
 We have a new Colonel to replace Colonel Sully. William Colvill of Red Wing is the new Regimental Commander. Our group knows him well since, you may remember, we were all originally in his Red Wing Company.
 Ox and Tony urge me to greet all of you and to tell you that they can't wait to get home. We are all very tired of army life. Remember how eager we were when we left? That doesn't mean that we are any less eager to win. The North must win. The Nation cannot be divided. The South must come back where it belongs.

All of us want to get back to our families and friends. Except for poor Parker, so far our prayers are working. Let's hope he's our only casualty and that this wasteful struggle soon ends.

Love to each of you,
Ben

After a dusty walk of just under an hour and a half, Ben and Tony reached the fence marking the boundary of the Bauer farm. Looking for signs of activity, they approached from the side where the main barn stood. Ben saw Buddy loading a hay rack and hollered out. Buddy turned, saw them, shouted toward the interior of the barn and ran quickly to the corner of a shed for a rifle leaning against the wall. Raising it he aimed at Ben and Tony.

Ben doffed his kepi and shouted in alarm, "Buddy, Buddy, it's me, Ben. Ben Murnane."

Buddy stopped in midstride as Gus Bauer hurried out of the barn to come up beside Buddy. He, too, held a rifle. Gus squinted and yelled over to them, "Is that you, Ben? Come on in, come in. Sorry for the unfriendly greeting. You're welcome as can be." Gus uncocked his rifle and advanced to meet them. Buddy stayed where he was.

"Mr. Bauer, this is my friend from Minnesota, Tony Lunde."

"Pleased to meet you, sir. Heard a lot of great things about your family from Ben here," Tony enthused.

"Good to meet you, too, son." Gus turned to the recalcitrant Buddy. "Buddy, get over here and meet Ben's friend and greet Ben."

Buddy shuffled over. "Lo, Ben," he mumbled, then shook Tony's hand and turned toward the house walking slowly and dejectedly.

Gus said, "Come on up to the house. Lucille will be pleased to see you, Ben." He turned to lead them, but Lucille swept onto the porch.

"Ben, dear Ben, so good of you to take the time to come see us. What brings you out our way?" She embraced him, then burst into tears she could not contain. She wailed painfully. Gus patted her shoulder to calm her.

Ben and Tony felt uncomfortable and Ben was puzzled by their peculiar response to him.

Gus led the two young soldiers over by the barn as Lucille headed back for the house, her body shuddering with sobs.

"Ben, you and Tony. The Yankee uniforms. Not your fault. You had no way of knowing. We've had a terrible tragedy in the family, Ben. Happened three months ago, late March." Gus stopped, choking on his words.

Ben asked, "Not your son, Kurt. Sorry to hear . . . "

"Not Kurt, Ben," interrupted Gus. "He's coming home. Will be exchanged. It was Ilsa."

"Oh my Good God, Gus, what? What happened to Ilsa?"

Tony spoke quickly. "I'll be going back now, Ben, not my place to be here. Meet you back at camp later. Privilege to meet you, Mr. Bauer. Terribly sorry for your troubles, sir." He spun and strode away, not waiting for a response. Ben started to shout after him, but realized Tony had done the proper thing under the circumstances. "I'll be there. Tell the sergeant," he shouted at his retreating friend. Tony signalled with his arm that he had heard.

Gus led Ben into the kitchen where Lucille sat softly weeping. Gus went over to her and rested his hand gently on her shoulder. Ben waited for them to speak. Gus put his arm around Lucille, then gently led her toward the door and motioned to Ben to follow. They walked the lane toward the glade. The path with its beautiful trees and flowers reminded Ben of Ilsa's comments about each variety, her appreciation of their beauty, her artist's eye for detail. The flora had been the subject of several of her poems. They walked the full distance silently, Ben a few steps behind, remembering the times he had spent with Ilsa. Dear God, he asked silently, what has happened?

The beautiful glade opened up to them, where Ben had been found, the idyllic spot where he had spent joy-filled, peaceful hours with the Bauers and with Ilsa. They turned the few steps to the flat rock near the tree line. Fresh flowers lay in front of it on a slight rise where fresh sod grew. At the base were two rows of roses. The Bauers stepped before it. Ben moved next to Lucille and looked down. Chiseled into the stone were the words:

ILSA MARIE BAUER
OCTOBER 26, 1847 - MARCH 24, 1863
SHE SLEEPS WITH THE ANGELS

They stood with heads bowed. Ben silently prayed for the repose of her immortal soul. Tears streamed from his eyes. He put his arm around Lucille's shoulder as much to gain comfort as to give it.

"Her Uncle Alvin chiseled the letters in the stone, Ben," Lucille whispered.

He had to speak, though his words seemed inadequate. His voice cracked as he spoke in a low, reverent tone. "I have met no person in my life as pure as that dear girl. Knowing her was a privilege I will treasure for the rest of my days. She was so kind and good to me. Please, Mr. and Mrs. Bauer, accept my heartfelt condolences and know that my grief cannot reach the level of yours, but that it is very deep." He turned away and wept silently.

He heard a soft, barely audible, "Thank you, dear Ben. She loved you so much and talked of you often. She said that you would someday do great things. She believed in you. You were a joy to her. Thank you, dear Ben."

When they returned, Gus led Ben along the grove behind the barn. He told Ben how Buddy had found her that morning. She lived for two days but was never conscious. Gus then pursed his lips and recounted what Buddy had seen before he found her. The Yankee soldier galloping away as fast as he could fly. The red hair and beard. Buddy had tried later to follow the trail, was gone for two days asking people along that route east if they had seen such a man. After the funeral Buddy left again to continue the search and still goes off from time to time.

Gus sighed deeply. "He hasn't recovered, Ben. I doubt any of us will, until that red-haired bag of garbage is caught and dealt with."

Chapter Thirty-Four

Brewing Storm

They registered the usual complaints of soldiers on the move. Lousy food, sore feet, unfathomable orders, and monotony. The submerged anxiety always present when a battle seemed imminent had hold of them, except Ben Murnane who was preoccupied with anger.

Tony spoke to Ben's despondency, evident since his return from the Bauer farm. "Come on, Ben, spit it out. Let's throw it around among friends here. Might make the whole ugly thing easier for you to deal with."

At first Ben resented the brusqueness of Tony's suggestion, but when he read his friend's facial expression and eyes, he saw only concern and good intentions. "Tony, you met the Bauers and likely sensed the kind of people they are. Salt of the earth. And she was the best of them." He hesitated, but then went on feeling their eyes on him. "What kind of animal would do that to someone as gentle and innocent as her? What kind of goddamn predatory beast?"

"World's full of that kind, Ben. That's no answer to your question, but a god-awful fact all the same," commiserated Shakey.

Ben added angrily, "Never get caught either. Sneakin', slitherin' bastards like him."

"Justice comes late sometimes, Ben, but it comes," Ox offered.

"The bastard has to live with himself. That's misery he can't get away from," said Tony.

Ben was inconsolable. "Her father told me what was done to her. Raped. Used, then tossed away. Broke her neck so she couldn't identify him later. What a goddamned coward."

"Good as she was, Ben, she's in heaven sure. And safe from the likes of the one who did that to her," consoled Shakey.

"What gave him the right to send her there? And the real question, how come God let him do what he did? Answer me that one, somebody." Ben's anger was not dissipating.

"Nobody here qualified to try to answer that question. But every man here has asked it at one time or other, and not for the last time you can bet," drawled Sarge. "The preachers say we can't never understand God's plan. Well, they're sure right about that. I sure as hell can't understand most of it."

"Well at least we got you to talk on it, Ben," said Tony. "Sound of things, we're gonna need all the anger we can find pretty soon. Save some of it for the Rebs, Ben. Something is shaping up. Feels like it did just before Antietam. Ol' Lee is shifting around out there. And here we sit with a new general in charge again. Hope to hell this one knows what he's doing."

Shakey said quickly, "I heard a New Yorker officer saying that the cavalry's out front bumping into Rebs every few hours or so. Nobody knows exactly where the main bunch of 'em is at or how many they got. But then those horse soldiers sit on their arses so much their brains end up resting on their saddles."

"Much as I hate getting shot at, I'd sure rather be fightin' than diggin'," said Sarge. "These damn breastworks by the creek here have got my hands blistered bad. Rather get on with meetin' the Rebs than bein' made into a mole."

"Sarge, you ain't been a private long enough yet to toughen up your hands. You sergeants work your mouths more than your hands," laughed Ox.

"You know, Koo Koo Ri, when you grow up big enough, I may have to take you down a peg or two, huh? huh?" Sarge feigned a haymaker at Ox.

"Seriously, anybody know anything about Meade?," asked Shakey. "He any good or just another Hooker or a Burnsider?"

"Nobody seems to know much about Meade. Some say he's been pretty good as a corps commander," said Ben.

"That don't mean nothin'. Soon's they get the big job, they change fast. Turn into either idiots or maniacs. One's as bad as the other," commented Sarge.

"I'm hitting the blankets," yawned Tony, "though in this heat a blanket sounds kind of stupid. Ben, you all right or you need me to rile you again?"

"I'm fine, Mr. Lunde. But I'll be lookin' at every blue coat with long red hair, I can tell you that. Just thinkin' that the bastard might be around us someplace puts my teeth on edge. Hate to be in the same army with the miserable coward. Ilsa's brother Buddy is out lookin' for him. Sure hope he can take care of himself, bein' only fifteen. I'll tell you, I'd hate to be that skunk if her father meets him."

Just then a corporal from the Forty-second New York came up, laughing and shaking his head. "You Minnesota boys hear what happened to your colonel?" The corporal's laugh was merriment, not ridicule.

"Who? Colonel Colvill, you mean? What happened to him?" asked Shakey.

"I ain't lying to you. General Hancock or General Gibbon, one of the two, they put him under arrest."

Several of them shouted. "What the hell for?"

"God's truth. Just heard it from Lieutenant Street. Seems the colonel disobeyed an express order this morning, and they called him in and gave him what for."

"What'd he do? Tell us if you know." demanded Ox.

"From what I understand, he marched you First Regiment boys over a bridge 'stead of through the creek like he was supposed to. Shoulda gone straight on through the water, they told him."

"Well, I'll be double damned," said Tony. "You mean to tell me they arrested him for that? For just keeping our feet dry? Good God, they must not have much to do up there at headquarters. I can't believe it."

"You sure?" asked Ox. "If you're joshing us, you'll catch it later."

"Only reporting what the lieutenant said. Said it was ridiculous. But then he got serious and said that ol' Hancock is one tough soldier. Nobody fools with him. I'll be moving on. Don't think the arrest is serious. No court martial or nothing like that."

They laughed about it, but it made them uneasy. They thought highly of Colonel Colvill. Later they learned from others that Captain Messick was put temporarily in charge. They liked him, too, but wanted Colvill to lead them if they went up against the Confederates.

One by one they drifted off to bunk down. Sarge commented as he left that his bed was going to be hard, but at least he wouldn't have to sleep in the brig. The fires were left to burn down. After the long day's march, the blue soldiers were bone tired. Soon all but the guards and pickets were asleep. The sky was clear, stars winking, the slight breeze warm, the air heavy with humidity. The crickets were unusually garrulous, a sign to some of the old-timers that a big storm was brewing.

The First Minnesota was still bivouacked at Pike Creek but by mid-morning the air was charged with rumor and fragments of news. Dispatch riders were coming and going. It had begun somewhere just north. The word Gettysburg was spoken, then oft repeated. Some little college town. They could feel the pull of it, knew the signs, and checked their gear. Headquarters was a turmoil of activity. Officers rushed to staff meetings, quickly called, then dashed off to their commands. The air was humid, already stifling, and electrically charged. Gettysburg. A strange sounding place. Just a little crossroads. It had to be some place, might as well be Gettysburg.

Captain Messick relayed Colonel Colvill's orders. With action pending, General Gibbon released the colonel from his arrest charge. They were to form up and join regiments from Pennsylvania, New York, Massachusetts, and Maine, to march up the Taneytown Road and directly into Gettysburg passing just east of two hills called the Roundtops. As they stood to order, an officer with four aides galloped by. Word passed that it was General Hancock sent ahead to scout the situation and report back to General Meade. Not just rumors anymore. Hot fighting had already started. Better be getting up that road. First and Eleventh Corps are up there all by themselves.

They moved out briskly. After just minutes, they were in Pennsylvania. Then inexplicably they were halted and ordered off the road to wait in a grass-filled ditch as the Third Corps under General Daniel Sickles marched by.

They rested and ate while the Third Corps cleared, then fell in behind them to eat their dust along the Taneytown Road. No doubt now about what they were hearing up there. Cannon and musket mixed. Heavy fighting. "First and Eleventh must be in trouble. What's the hold up? The Third Corps front echelon must be close by now."

Second Corps was again ordered off the road. Thousands of voices spun random comments. "Looks like we'll be camping here, boys. Get some fires going. Need some coffee. There'll be fighting plenty tomorrow. Sounds big and still growing. Not just a skirmish. Town of Gettysburg. Some men from Pennsylvania hadn't heard of it. Why would they want to fight over a place like that? Get some vittles in you, boys, might not be much time for eating tomorrow. Stoke up the old furnace with plenty of fuel. Then get some sleep. Man that's fresh, fights better, survives better. Get to sleep, boys, no singing tonight. We'll save our songs for tomorrow night. They'll be victory songs for sure."

At dawn, they were set to march the last three miles. Battle sounds erupted up ahead. Shakey said, "Maybe the Rebs are digging in. Wish they'd find their way back to Old Virginny."

They dawdled and marched, dawdled and marched, and passed by the east side of the Roundtops just before noon. Formed up down by Rock Creek. A long, low ridge was stacked with Union troops and artillery looking west to where the Rebs must be. Second Corps was on line up on the ridge, a few regiments behind them to give quick support where needed. First Minnesota was assigned a 200-yard swath by a cemetery at the north end.

The firing intensified about 4:00 P.M.. Smoke billowed above the elevation. Most of it seemed to come from the left of their position, but the ridge shut off their view. They watched the frantic activity as companies and regiments were shifted. About 4:30 when the bedlam was even more intense, the Minnesotans saw several regiments double-timing toward the Roundtops. Officers screamed for more men.

As they marched back and forth in columns of four just below the crest of the ridge, scattered mutterings could be heard. "Looks like trouble on our left, boys. All hell's breaking loose. When they gonna call us? Can't even see over the damn ridge. Take us over the top, Colonel. Going crazy with the waiting. Let's get at 'em. Let us at least see what the hell is happening over there. Damn it, Colonel, turn us loose!"

A mounted officer charged at the Minnesota formation, pulled up the panting beast and screamed, "What unit is this, Colonel?" Colonel Colvill responded, "Minnesota First Regiment, sir."

General Hancock pointed back over his shoulder at a Rebel force 400 yards away converging down the opposite incline. "See those Confederate banners, Colonel? Take them!"

"Yes sir." To his columns he bellowed, "First Minnesota . . . forward . . . charge!" They sprinted instantly over the ridge and down slope in columns of four, then spread into a forty-to-fifty-man front. Adrenaline and fear provided the fuel. Legs pumped. Eyes opened wide and unblinking. No time to think, follow the lead. Forward he'd said, forward it was. Bayonets fixed, straight at them, almost there, here they come. Take those banners.

And the mostly Alabamians were coming right at them, just as determined, banners flying, yelling insanely, blood in their eyes, and the open Union ridge in their sights. A breakthrough could win the day. Split the Blue line and widen the breech! Their officers screamed them on, sensing the prize was theirs. They would have it or die trying.

The Minnesotans had the advantage of freshness. Their adversaries had been in the fight for two hours and were near exhaustion. The Alabamians had the numbers on their side and momentum from earlier successes. It became a matter of total effort, unyielding determination, denial of even the thought of defeat. Individual wills blended into collective resolve. Rebel and Yankee soldiers instinctively knew that the moment was critical. Desperation drove both forces to a thunderous collision at the dried up bed of little Plum Run.

Rebel artillery raked the descending Minnesotans and ripped their ranks. Men had fallen, but the others hadn't faltered or slowed. When the front lines slammed together, bayonets flashed, slashed, and gouged. Those behind ran over their fallen comrades. The impact was monumental. In the failing light and the blinding smoke, the foes became impossibly entangled. The Alabamians were stopped cold, then recoiled, collected themselves and came on again. Another wild tangle, unearthly din and clamor, choking smoke, muffled blasts from weapons at close quarters. Bayonet thrusts, swinging rifle butts, fists as clubs, muscle to muscle, nostril to nostril, yelling, screaming. The Rebs half-encircled the small, packed force of surviving Minnesotans. Close quarters from three sides. Brain matter splattered, blood spurted and splashed out of and onto the struggling men and the ground. Each man against one other and then another and still another.

Ben was in the process of thrusting his bayonet at a Reb in front of him when he was struck a heavy blow across his chest, neck, and jaw that expelled air from his lungs. He was flung back and down. He landed face up, but wedged between two large boulders, thinking he was dead, unable to move, fighting for air, wheezing and woozy. He twice tried to raise himself, then saw a shadowed, hulking figure above him with bayonet poised to thrust down into his defenseless chest. His eyes met and locked with those of the enemy soldier. The Rebel started the death thrust, then held back at the last instant. He hesitated, mumbled something unintelligible, and began to move away. As the Reb turned, he was hit, lifted off the ground and tumbled awkwardly at Ben's feet. His shocked eyes met Ben's, then rolled up behind closing lids. His legs twitched several times, and then he was still.

The collision at Plum Run had lasted no more than ten minutes. Dead and wounded lay by the hundreds, Rebels and Yankees mixed together, side by side, over and under one another, sharing the same fate. The fallen were as brothers again. Reinforcements finally came in behind the Minnesotans and drove the Butternuts back from the creek bed toward their own lines. The Confederate breakthrough had been stopped, then turned. The breech in the Union line on Cemetery Ridge had been patched. The Minnesota First Regiment had plugged the gap. They had not taken the Confederate banners as ordered, but neither had they lost their own.

General Hancock sat on his exhausted animal back on the ridge watching the thunderous conflagration as he waved reinforcements forward. He looked over the scene and noted the Confederates moving back and away. He nodded toward the torn but still waving Minnesota regimental flag, threw a snappy salute down the incline, then reversed his mount and cantered off to look over the rest of his regiments. The sun set, the afterglow barely visible through the smoke and haze shrouding the battlefield. In the wake of the ear-shattering bedlam had come a somber silence broken only by the moans of the wounded and the dying.

Blood slowly drained from men who had moments before been vital, confident, exhilarated young warriors. The fluids soaked into the soil that had been so hotly disputed. Dusk muted the stark scene.

Ben gathered his strength to force himself out of the wedge between the boulders. The young Confederate who had spared his life lay on his side. Ben crawled to him and saw spurts of blood ejaculating from a wound on the shattered upper arm. Ripping out his kerchief, he tied it tightly above the flow and wedged a bayonet in the knot for leverage to hold it in place. Examining further, he rolled the soldier onto his back. A rip in the shirt revealed an entry wound in the upper chest, the bleeding a lazy leak already beginning to coagulate. He pressed the shirt tail over it to stop the flow. He could hear the agonized moaning all around him, men begging for help, screaming for water. He tore off his shirt, bundled it and placed it under the soldier's head. On a sudden impulse, he removed the rebel soldier's shirt and trousers and threw them into the rocks. To the unhearing young man he whispered, "I will be back."

Ben viewed the shadowed scene. Bodies everywhere, slashed, eviscerated, already stiffening into grotesque unnatural attitudes. Corpses stared, mouths locked open in interrupted screams. He was overpowered by the earthy odor of blood, the scorching fumes of smoke and the stench of feces from relaxed sphincters. The near-darkness stole all color from the scene.

Focussing on the wounded, Ben fashioned tourniquets, spoke encouraging phrases, and searched for friends. Some of the fallen he recognized, men with whom he had shared guard duty or mess or competed with in contests. Most were incapable of recognizing him. A few pitifully tried crawling up the incline. The medics worked silently, moving from form to form, dismissing the dead and concentrating on those whose lives were salvageable.

Torches and lanterns were added to better illuminate the work of the comforters. But they also lighted the field of spilled, broken bodies stretching from the far bank of Plum Run. The flickering light created an otherworldly condition, a nightmare landscape only Dante could describe.

Ben watched soldiers carry some of the less seriously wounded up the incline toward field hospitals by Rock Creek. His own balance was precarious and his head ached fiercely. He touched the right side of his jaw and discovered a lump the size of a hen's egg. Blood oozed from his ear. He began to panic, then saw silhouetted against the flame of a torch the familiar figure of the redoubtable Ox. Searching among the bodies, Ox appeared desperate.

Ben yelled and rushed toward his friend. Hearing the voice, Ox turned, his face contorted, wrenched, but he held out his arms to receive Ben. He held him a moment, mumbled "Old Ben," then pushed him away. "Shakey's killed, Ben," he whispered hoarsely, "and I can't find Tony. You all right?" Ben nodded and Ox turned away.

They searched together through the littered field, looked up close at death-darkened faces, and into pain-filled visages. With a rising feeling of dread, they sought their friend. Ben knew the worst when he heard an agonized moan from Ox. He went quickly to where Ox was bent over a twisted form near the bank of the creek.

Ox rose slowly. In a tender voice he breathed, "He's gone, Ben. Tony's gone. Tony and Shakey both gone." Then came the sudden, violent rage. "God damn this filthy war. God damn the bloody sons of bitches who keep it going."

The anger dissolved as he slid back into the torment of grief. Both wept silently. "I failed him, Ben. I failed Tony. How am I going to tell his ma, Ben? How am I going to tell Mrs. Lunde?"

Ox bent to Tony, touched his eyelids closed to cover the final stare, reverently lifted the body into his huge arms and started the long, slow journey up the slope. Head bowed, his steps were heavy. He cradled Tony like a baby, taking his friend home as he often had done. Ox didn't look back. He reached the crest, then slowly passed from view behind Cemetery Ridge.

Tear-clouded eyes hindered Ben as he turned back to the area by the boulders. Picking his way between bodies lying like discarded logs, he relocated the wounded rebel soldier. He felt for the pulse, checked the tourniquet, released it, and probed the chest wound that had coagulated and crusted over. A quick inspection found no other wounds. He waited a few moments, then reapplied the tourniquet less tightly than before. Satisfied, he lifted the man and staggered up the incline. Struggling to keep upright, he stopped twice to put down the burden and check whether the jarring had triggered more bleeding. His strength was waning as he finally reached the summit. Setting the rebel soldier down once more, he straightened up and looked out over the area below the ridge.

The panorama was irregularly illuminated by bonfires and posted torches. The flickering flames revealed a scene staged by an overzealous director, or the devil himself. At the bottom of the east slope, row upon row of mostly blue-clad corpses were arranged precisely, as if for inspection. The lamp light seemed to cause them to move, to ripple as waves, to undulate in a rhythm only they could sense.

Beyond the slaughtered, enormous tents were the focal points. The prevailing theme was chaos. The characters were bustling doctors, nurses, and orderlies in a frenetic dance for life. Laden stretchers everywhere. Men being carried, supported, led to treatments. Hundreds of wounded soldiers lying, sitting, leaning and standing in long lines leading to the infirmary and surgery tents. The breadth of the scene incorporated acres. All actors on that vast stage were in pain: the victims, suffering and twisted in body and mind; the medical staff, on unbroken duty for more than thirty hours, exhausted and frustrated as they ranted at the shortages of space, equipment, supplies, and time. Despite herculean efforts, the medics could not possibly cope. They were forced to make immediate medical decisions that if wrong meant needless loss of limbs or a lifetime of disfigurement. Delay meant death.

Ben had managed his unconscious former foe to the end of the shortest line he could find. When they moved closer, the stench enveloped him. Sweet but revolting, it settled and clung as a stifling mist. Ben noticed a huge wagon beside the tent. Every few moments a bloody object was tossed into it's high-sided cargo box. His mind was slow to realize that he was seeing amputated limbs thrown, still dripping, into the wagon bed. Few words were spoken except by the doctors screaming for sharpened knives, more bandages, and "for God's sake, try to clean those damned instruments."

Ben was finally to the front and into the tent where the Reb was torn from him and quickly thrown onto a long, blood-soaked table. A medic examined the arm and the chest, made a quick decision, rejected the case and had the untreated body carried out the other end of the tent.

Mouthing protests that went unacknowledged, Ben followed to where a table served as a work bench for three blood-splattered surgeons. The young Rebel's arm was sloshed with water before a doctor dug into the chest wound with his bloody hand, ripped the flesh apart, reached in with a forceps, raised his eyes to heaven and probed. After a moment, he gripped hard, and yanked a jagged chunk of metal from the cavity. He looked at it disgustedly, then threw it over his shoulder into a pile of other discarded pieces. He poured water into the open wound, slapped the flesh together, drew thread through the skin flaps with quick thrusts and tied a knot. An orderly was called to remove the patient. The doctor took a quick breath as the next soldier slid down the slickened table in front of him.

Ben followed the orderly to where he laid the rebel soldier, just a few yards beyond the tent. Placed on a blanket, he was one of a lineup of forty or fifty men in similar condition. Ben asked the orderly what kind of cases they were. "These 'uns will be looked at again in the morning and if they is still alive they'll get another look." Ben looked down at the young Confederate. He could help him no more 'til morning.

He staggered back to Cemetery Ridge, asked a lieutenant where the Minnesota Regiment was located and was told that they would answer muster south of the stone fence where he pointed a few yards away.

Ben shuffled along the ridge in a daze. The enormity of all that had transpired had not penetrated his befuddled, fatigued mind. He didn't consciously reject the images, but simply let them drift as in a dream. Even grief required energy, and his resources were completely drained. Seeing a small group of soldiers, he flopped down with his back against a low earthen breastwork, not sure which unit he had joined and not really caring. Stupefied, staring, waiting, he hoped that nothing would require him to respond or think or feel.

Sarge McMahon found him there. "Murnane, you made it. Hell of a fight. Hornet's nest down there. Worse'n Antietam. We stopped 'em cold though, we did. Took a lot of casualties. Colonel Colvill got hit pretty bad. First sergeant's dead. Can't believe old Shakey and Tony are out of it. We'll see those Reb bastards again tomorrow you can bet. We'll muster in a few minutes. Get ready, boy."

Ben's eyes went in and out of focus. The form in front of him was a huge buffalo. With a massive hump. A big, mangy buffalo. The image came and went. Ox sat down beside him. Looked to be in the same mental state as Ben. But he was there. That helped. Oh, Sweet Jesus, how that helped, thought Ben. His mind began to clear and the shocking, ugly scenes began to replay. Thrusting them away, he found it easy to let his mind drift again.

Shortly after, Sarge McMahon addressed the small group of Minnesotans. "Ten-shun, the Captain will speak with us, gentlemen."

Captain Messick spoke solemnly, "Colonel Colvill was wounded, but will recover. He asked me to take over the First." He paused, then went on, "General Hancock has placed the Second Corps south of the stone fence a few hundred yards north of here. We'll march there after muster. We'll be in line between the Fifteenth New York and the Seventy-First Pennsylvania. An excellent defensive position. If the Rebs come at us tomorrow, they'll catch real hell. We'll call the muster now. 'Stead of calling all names, we'll ask you each to speak your name. The corporal will check them off as we hear them. From the right now, speak your name and company."

The spoken names were checked off. It was not the way muster was usually taken, but was, under the circumstances, a most humane method. If all 262 names of those who raced down the slope to Plum Creek had been read, only forty-seven would have been there to answer.

Chapter Thirty-Five

Pines, Lakes, and Cold Winters

"I'll hear your reports, gentlemen," said lean, haggard General Meade. "Then together we'll decide whether to hold this position or fall back to Pike Creek."

General Hancock, a favorite of Meade's, spoke quickly and decisively. "All due respect, sir, our current position is very favorable and has been dearly paid for with gallant lives. We hold the high ground. Let's keep it."

Others concurred. "Lee won't be able to resist trying to knock us off this perch, General Meade, and he'll get punished bad if he tries. Let him come. We'll eat him alive," commented General Sedgwick. "Stay, General, we've a position any commander relishes," was General Warren's assessment.

"All right, Gentlemen, include your recommendations in your report. We'll stay where we are and live with the consequences. Now report."

General Governeur Warren spoke to the fierce early afternoon battles on and around two hills at the end of the ridge. "Hood's and McLaw's men attacked with superior strength along a line from the Round Tops to the Emmitsburg Road. They forced their way in despite heavy casualties, but they were finally prevented from turning our left and occupying the two hills. If they had won the hill positions, our entire line would have been exposed and forced to abandon the high position."

General Hancock was next to report. He began by officially berating General Sickles for having advanced his corps to a position forward of the ridge line which not only endangered his own men but the integrity of the whole Union defense. Hancock was adamant in his criticism. He went on to say that partly due to that "glory-motivated" act, the Union forces were fortunate indeed to have survived the all-out effort of The Alabamians. He stated that the breech in the line was now repaired.

General Meade asked Hancock if he was aware that General Sickles had been hit and required amputation of his leg.

"Yes, sir. I'd heard that and I'm sorry for him. But it doesn't alter the fact that his poor judgment caused many of his men to lose more than a leg. They lost their lives. But more importantly he made our entire line vulnerable. Unforgiveable."

Other officers made their reports, reviewing the major thrusts of the day's activities and an assessment of their current postures. Each man reinforced the decision to hold Cemetery Ridge at all costs.

General Meade reminded them that he required their reports to be expanded in detail in written form by dawn. He added that he expected General Lee to attack their center the next day with all the force he could muster. "If I know his mind, he will hit our center hard. He tried our right and left today. His pride will dictate a frontal assault tomorrow to the death. He doesn't want to go back South a second time having failed in the North. Expect it, gentlemen, and be ready. Get back out there now and ascertain what you have left to fight with. Then get them placed where they'll do the most good tomorrow." He paused for effect, then said pleasantly, "Anything further that we should discuss? I know how exhausted you and your men must be and how much you still need to do, but I want you to advise me in any way that might help."

General Warren inserted, "I will need reinforcements and replacements for the Twentieth Maine, sir. They held that hill with some of the bravest, toughest fighting I have ever personally witnessed. Colonel Chamberlain and his men were magnificent. Kept our left from being turned. Held Hood off and hurt him bad, sir. Those Maine boys took heavy casualties but kept our line from being flanked."

"Thank you, General Warren, you'll get your replacements. What about you, General Hancock. Is your corps at fighting level strength?"

"Judging from those units already reported, sir, we're about eighty percent strength overall, except for First Minnesota Regiment. They were decimated. Bravest performance by a unit I ever witnessed. I had to throw them in at the last minute to patch the hole created by General Sickles' retreat. Our lines were broken, and the Wilcox Brigade was coming with nothing in their way. If they had reached the ridge, sir, they would have split us, and we might all be half way back to Washington by now. Minnesota saved the line or we'd been cracked. Can't say enough about them, General. If we can't win with men such as them, we better fold our tents and run down the flag. I got their muster report just before this meeting. Two hundred sixty-two men charged down that hill, General. Never hesitated. Rushed right at a superior force. They stopped the Rebs cold with bayonets, rifle butts, and their bare hands. Held 'em off 'til we got them reinforced. Of the 262, sir, only forty-seven were able to report for muster back on the ridge. Over eighty percent casualties. I will be formally recommending them for a unit citation when I get the time."

General Warren interjected, "I will recommend the Maine unit for a citation, too, Sir. And, General, I witnessed the action General Hancock described. He in no way exaggerated what those Minnesota boys did."

General Meade listened thoughtfully, then commented, "Interesting. Maine and Minnesota. Pine trees and lakes and cold winters must breed tough, resolute men."

Chapter Thirty-Six

Day Three

At sunrise on July 3, 1863, Confederate forces were spread in a semi-circle along Seminary Ridge, through the village and around the north base of the hills that framed Gettysburg. The Confederate Army was stretched and extended; the Union force was compact and concentrated.

From near the cemetery southward and slightly downslope to the west, ran a three-foot high stone fence. The wall paralleled the ridge for a few hundred yards, right-angled west to bypass a grove of trees, then turned ninety degrees south again to continue under and along the ridge line. All through the night, the Union infantry had converged to post themselves in defensive positions behind the stone wall in a line south with batteries of artillery behind them. The Yankees were confident that their position was impregnable.

Over on Seminary Ridge, General Robert E. Lee was seeing things differently. His armies had nearly broken the Union line on several occasions during the past two days and, but for delays, a few faulty judgments, and some bad luck, he believed they would have prevailed. With the arrival of General Pickett's brigade of 5,000 men and the return of his cavalry commander, J.E.B. Stuart, Lee was at last at full strength. The Yankees would be dislodged from Cemetery Ridge by the best soldiers in the world. Never beaten. There could be no other outcome.

The rising sun struck the Minnesotans awake. Many of the Regiment's survivors had minor wounds, but if they could crawl and handle a musket they

Day Three

were on line. They were stiff and sore, their muscles extended beyond normal during the bitter struggle at Plum Creek. Nobody had to remind them that the Confederate Army was in front of them. Not much was said. Friends had been lost, men they mourned by their silence. Sensing their feelings, Sarge used a subdued tone to ask them to count off. With the return of Company F, the total came to 128. The odd-numbered men were sent to breakfast first, a procedure that separated Ox and Ben. Ox patted Ben's arm and stepped away.

Ben raised himself to peer over the barricade at the enemy a mile and a half away in trees just being touched by the rays of the new day. Most were concealed on Seminary Ridge and, like the Union troops, waited and wondered what the fresh new day would bring. Many of them and us may have just seen our last dawn, Ben thought. Funny thing, he should hate them. They had taken his friends away in bloody rage. He thought of crazy Shakey, a beloved nut, and of laughing, vibrant Tony, and then of kindly Mrs. Lunde. He remembered his first lonely days in Minnesota and the hospitality of the Lundes. But Mrs. Lunde wouldn't be angry. She'd just be terribly sad. Ben didn't feel anger either, just irreversible loss. He lifted his eyes and thought of Ilsa who was as much a casualty of this war as Tony, Shakey, or Pudge. What beautiful people have been taken away.

Ox came back, sat down beside Ben and spoke. "I saw to their bodies, Ben. Both Tony and Shakey will be buried here in that cemetery a little way up north of here. I made sure their identifications were right and tagged on tight. They'll bury them as soon as all the fighting is over. 'Course that's only if we keep the Rebs from overrunning us here. Officers think they'll come on up here after us. I hope so. Blow 'em to hell if they come. Better be getting some food, Ben."

Ben nodded and in a crouch started away. Ox stopped him. "Better get that cut and bump on your jaw looked after, Ben. Could get to paining you bad."

Ben nodded and set off. Foregoing breakfast, he headed for the surgery tent where he had last seen the young Reb. He walked down the line of wounded that now had many gaps. He found the young man, staring out of dilated, pain-filled eyes, breathing in shallow gasps. Ben sat down close to him and looked into the strong, hard face. Blond matted hair, prominent forehead, sallow complexion. The Rebel gave no sign, but Ben was certain that he knew someone was there. Edging close to his ear, Ben spoke in a whisper. "Reb, even if you can talk, don't. Just listen. If you can hear me, just nod your head."

No movement or sign that he had been heard. But Ben noticed a slight change in the rhythm of the man's breathing. "I know you hear me, soldier. I'll talk even if you don't want to hear. I'm the soldier whose life you spared.

Remember? I was down between the boulders helpless. You didn't finish me off when you could have. You got a ball in your chest and a ripped upper arm. I stopped your bleedin' and dragged you here. Do you remember any of it?"

Ben thought he saw the eyes blink and went on. "The doctors saw to you last night. I don't know how bad hurt you are, but I want you to know, I'll stick by you. Some'll go hard on you if they find out you're a Reb. Stay quiet so you don't give yourself away. I took your uniform off and threw it away. Nobody knows you're not Union. You lost your voice 'cause of shock. Do you understand? I'll see to it you get medical treated the way any soldier deserves. We expect another battle today. I have to get back to my unit. If the Rebs break through, they'll find you here and take care of you. If we knock 'em back, I'll see that you're treated right. You have my word on it." He placed his hand on the healthy shoulder and added, "Good luck, soldier."

He took a last look into the half-lidded, deep gray eyes, which slowly moved to meet his. It was enough for Ben. He hurried back to his position next to Ox behind the low pit near the center of Cemetery Ridge.

After a bit, Ben became sorry he had skipped breakfast. As the day wore on, his hunger pangs increased. When he thought about it, he recalled that he hadn't eaten since noon the day before. He scrounged a few hardtack biscuits that he threw into a tin cup full of water. He was hoping that a soaking with an assist from the heat of the sun would soften them so they would not be a risk to his molars, never mind his stomach. But they proved to be as repellent as a turtle's carapace. He finally placed them on a rock and hammered them into pieces with his rifle butt. The chunks softened slightly in his mouth before he swallowed and left the rest of the job to his gastric juices. At least there was something in his stomach.

Ox and Sarge napped on and off or mumbled inanities. Sporadic artillery fire and skirmishing had been heard since first light. The firing was intense at times, but by mid-morning died down to just an occasional musket or two.

They peeked over the barricade from time to time, but except for scattered shots by both army's pickets, all was serene. Hardly any movement was seen on Seminary Ridge, only enough to insure that the Confederates were still there. General Hancock rode back and forth checking his regiments' positions and offering encouragement. He stopped in front of their ragged pocket of men and asked Sarge if the ripped banner was that of the First Minnesota. When Sarge responded in the affirmative, the General shook his head sadly and said, "Those were good men who plugged that hole in the line yesterday. Had to be done. What a job they did. First Minnesota Regiment, our shattered thunderbolt," and he rode off.

Day Three

While they leaned back against the dugout wall, the hot mid-morning sun beat down. The short bills of their kepis were pulled down for a little shade. Having worked it over and over in his mind, Ben decided to risk talking with Ox about the Reb soldier.

"Ox," he began, "I know how you're feelin' right now. The friends we lost yesterday will pain for a long, long time. I'm hurtin' just like you. But even knowin' your feelin's, I want to tell you what happened and what I've done." Ox showed no sign of either acceptance or rejection.

Ben described what had happened down near Plum Creek, how the Rebel soldier hadn't really saved his life but had let him keep it, and then been wounded in the chest and arm. He then told Ox how he helped the wounded of the regiment first, then brought the Reb to the field hospital.

Ox wasn't wearing a look of approval. "Ben, that Reb and his damn Alabamians killed Tony and Shakey and a hell of a lot of our Minnesota boys. How the hell can you help the bastard? What the hell you thinking?"

"Ox, that was my gut feelin', too. But there's somethin' about him. I can't hate him, Ox. He's just like you and me. Don't forget we killed a lot of his friends, too. The killin's what's bad not the one's doin' it. The Rebs are fightin' same as us. Most don't even know why. Just 'cause we're here, and it's what's expected of us to do. I've tried, Ox, but I can't hate him or any of the others. Oh, I hate. But I don't even know for sure where to aim it. Whoever the bastards are that caused all this, they're the ones I hate. Not the soldiers. Fightin' and killin' just 'cause we're tryin' to save our own hides and our friends."

Ox was not convinced, but didn't say anything more.

"Ox, I'm goin' to help that soldier. I owe him my life. He's hurt bad and has no friends around him. If people knew him for a Reb, no tellin' what they'd do to him. Must be scared as hell. And, Ox, I was a good friend of Shakey and Tony, too. Knowin' them as I did, I have to believe they'd approve of my thinkin'. They didn't hate anybody. Rebs and us are more alike than different. Not my job to try to bring the two sides together, but I'm goin' to try with this one man. Feel obliged. Want you to try to understand, that's all."

"Ben, some sense to what you say, but still and all they're the enemy. They'll kill us without blinking. In fact, we'll be killing each other some more before the day is out. It's our job to kill 'em."

"Ox, you're right. We've got no choice but to go on killin', and I'll be firin' as fast as I can load, but that's got nothin' to do with helpin' one human bein' who's in real need. And one I owe. Ox, if you'd have had a Reb all helpless the way he had me down in those rocks, you'd have done the same as he did. You couldn't have killed him. I know you. Doesn't that tell you somethin' about that boy."

Ox looked over at Ben then and said, "Maybe, Ben, I just don't know."

Ben knew Ox wasn't convinced. The loss of Shakey and Tony was too fresh. But he also knew that Ox would ponder his words and plow his way through to the conclusion that suited his standards of justice. Ben thought he already knew what that conclusion would be.

At precisely 1:00 P.M. the Rebel artillery barked the end of the hiatus. More than 140 Rebel cannon fired in salvo from right to left, then blasted at will, concentrating on the central target of the small grove of trees where the stone wall formed the angle. The volume mounted as the gunners fell into a rhythm.

The effect on Cemetery Ridge was chaotic, but not where the Southerners intended. Their targets, the Blue infantry, were reasonably safe and protected behind the stone wall and the improvised earthworks. The Rebel shells struck behind the dug-in troops, up the slope to the crest and over on the far side. A few artillery units were hit directly as were reserve and rear echelon personnel. When General Meade's headquarters absorbed several direct shell blasts, the Commander quickly moved with his staff to safer quarters in the rear.

The Minnesotans looked on in awe when they heard the iron winging over and the shells hit the slope behind them. Huge craters opened and Yankee caissons and horses were ripped to pieces. The men behind the breastworks burrowed deeper into the soft earth and tucked up as tight as they could. The earth shook as chunks of rock were hurled high in the air and showered down erratically. Ear-splitting, panic-generating. After twenty minutes it seemed to them that bedlam had become the norm. After a full hour of ceaseless thunder, dust, smoke, and chaos, they watched in disbelief the indomitable General Hancock ride slowly by their position several times, appearing to give the impression that the shelling was nothing but a small annoyance. The bombardment raged on into the second hour without respite.

Suddenly out of the smoke on their right, a team-pulled limber came racing between them and the ridge line. When it came abreast, a Rebel shell hit flush and exploded the rig in a shower of dirt and smoke. Sarge was up and running as were several others. Ben and Ox were half way to the blast crater when another shell hit in virtually the same place. They saw a Yankee lifted in the air like a scarecrow in a high wind. One of the horses had broken free, the other tried to get up to follow, but it had no hind legs. The shattered soldier's severed left arm lay a few feet from his body, the stump pumping blood in spurts. Ox rushed for him but was thrust aside by Sarge McMahon who screamed, "Outta the way!"

Day Three

Sarge ripped off his shirt, rolled it lengthwise and lighted the end of it, holding it so the flame would rise up on the cloth. He held the blazing bundle against the prone man's bloody stump. The body recoiled and body fluids crackled as the intense heat seared. The pumping artery and veins melted, curled up, and sealed themselves. The burned-flesh odor drowned out the other smells of blood and smoke. The ragged end of the arm was charred black and the blood had stopped spilling, but the nerves continued to respond as the man's body bucked and jerked.

McMahon stomped out the burning shirt, cursed, picked up the severed, still-dripping arm and swung it in an arc, sending it flying over the ridge. He went to his knees and retched. Litter bearers were quickly there, lifting the comatose soldier and rushing him back up and over the crest. The victim's head rolled, eyes closed, teeth clenched tight, his ghostly white face frozen in agony.

It had all happened in a few seconds. Ox and Ben were in a daze. They had been subjected to so many shocks their systems could hardly register more. With Sarge, they staggered back to the barrier, oblivious to the noise and smoke and chaos. The three were soon as they had been, waiting mindlessly in their shallow trench.

The ear-splitting, smoke-generating Rebel bombardment continued unabated. At approximately 2:30 P.M., the entire Union alignment of artillery began a counter bombardment. They felt the blasts of heat from the exploding black powder. The inferno persisted, then suddenly the Union big guns went silent again. The Rebel cannonade intensified for several moments, but inexplicably it, too, ceased. After the constant, shattering din for nearly two solid hours, the quiet was at first even more threatening and sinister. More than 5,000 blue clad soldiers in Meade's center held their breaths. They began to uncoil and peek over the barricade to the west. Smoke and dust hung low and thick, obscuring Seminary Ridge, but slowly began to dissipate. After a few more moments the Yankees had an uncluttered view across the valley and each slowly let out his breath, saying either aloud or to himself, "Here they come!"

The butternut-clad infantry slowly emerged from the woods and paused to dress their line as they looked across the distance of open, unsheltered terrain they would have to cross to reach that stone wall. Regiments from Tennessee, Alabama, Mississippi and Virginia awaited the "march" order that quickly came. "Forward . . . Guide center . . . March!" And off they stepped, concentrating on that small cluster of trees. They were forty-two regiments spread a half-mile wide with over 12,000 fighting infantry. They believed in their officers and their own invincibility and, by God, they believed they would take yonder ridge.

Sarge, Ox, and Ben watched the long line of Gray form up, then spread. They appeared so organized, controlled, matter-of-fact, confident. Under the mid-afternoon sun their ranks were resplendent as they marched resolutely at an even pace, their muskets shouldered with affixed bayonets spearing the air with short jabs in time to their steps. Diamonds of reflected sunlight winked off the cold steel as on they came and their point of attack became immediately evident.

Sarge McMahon could barely contain himself, "What a sight! Never, never seen anything like it. Not even close. God Almighty, how many of 'em do you think, Koukkari?"

"Looks to me thirty regiments or more, Sarge. They got a long way to come though. And nothing to protect them on the way." Ox's resolve matched what he saw in those coming at him.

After a three or four minute march, the Confederate brigades on their right began to oblique inward to fill a gap between themselves and the next regiment. Just then, the Union artillery began its barrage. The roar from behind them and from near the cemetery and the Roundtops shook the area. And the bite was even worse than the roar. Great gaps appeared in the rebel line where the shells cut through, but the Southerners didn't falter or even break stride, merely closed ranks and continued their steady march. The artillery was insistent and the effect was devastating and continuous. Regimental and company flags fell but were picked up immediately and carried on. They reached about the half way point of their march in a low swath and halted. Yankee artillery continued to rip into them, but the Gray closed ranks and dressed their line as if on a drill field.

Someone down the line at the wall hollered, "God, they're dressin' their line. Can't believe it."

The Rebel line began to move again with the same pace as before. The oblique angle of the regiments on their right were causing the full force to funnel at the tree target behind the stone wall where every gray-clad soldier had his eyes fixed. Despite obscene casualties, on they came.

Yelling and hollering reverberated among the entrenched Yankees, generated by men who had experienced the Fredricksburg fiasco. "Remember Fredricksburg. They laughed at us as we died. Remember Fredricksburg!"

The big guns on the Roundtops now had the Confederate marchers in enfilade. Shells were fired straight down their flank and even if the aim was high, Rebs were hit somewhere along the line. The Gray right was shattered. On their left, if possible, it was even worse. The more than twenty cannon near the cemetery had a perfect angle on the Confederate left. A few Confederates broke under hellish fire and sprinted back toward their lines, but the others marched on relentlessly, stubbornly.

The Union gunners switched to canister to wreak even more devastation at closer range and sliced the Rebel lines like scythes through ripe barley. The Confederate confluence had narrowed to a 150 yard-wide bludgeon crudely aimed at the low wall only 200 yards directly up the incline. Their concentration, however, made the Blue cannoneers job easier. At that instant, half a thousand Ohio troops folded down from the north and squeezed the Gray left inward. A corresponding group of Vermonters effected the same hinging action from the south onto the Gray right. The pinched Rebels were herded into a three-sided killing pen, a trough leading up the slope into a solid sheet of winging iron. It became a funnel of fury, a vortex of vengeance for previous humiliations, for Bull Run, for Fredricksburg, for Chancellorsville.

Ox, Ben, and Sarge fired at the concentration of Rebs in front of them as fast as they could load. The charge had degenerated into a slaughter, but the bloodied Confederates forged up the incline. A wild collective Rebel yell inspired those in front to thrust forward with a desperate surge that, despite the gruesome carnage, carried a few to the wall and over, flags flying.

Hearing a tumultuous roar on their right, Captain Messick led a small group of Minnesotans who were leaving their positions to scramble north to attack the bunched Confederates and those who had breached the line. First Sarge, then Ox and Ben bolted toward the conflagration fifty yards north. Screaming to add their voices to the bedlam, they raced with bayonets fixed into a brawl that was man to man and totally disordered. Ben lost touch with the others as he closed with a flailing Rebel. He fired into the soldier's chest, then swung the weapon at another. He was savaged off his feet by a pulverizing blow to his left side, fell forward heavily and saw only stomping boots as his vision dimmed slowly into darkness.

It was all over in another few minutes. The Rebels who had braved the wall were either taken prisoner, wounded, or killed. The remaining Gray force raced down the hill, stepping over their slain and wounded comrades, and turned to dodge canister and musket fire as they fled. Pickett's Charge, as it became known, had been repulsed, but barely. The back of General Lee's army had been broken. He had asked too much. He would regroup the survivors and fight on for many more bloody months, but there remained for them only a stubborn stagger down the far side of the mountain.

Chapter Thirty-Seven

The Reb

At dawn Ben was gently shaken awake. He had vague recollections of being carried from near the stone wall to the hospital tent. While applying fresh bandages, the doctor described the injury and gave his preliminary prognosis. "A minié ball pierced your left shoulder area in an upward path and shattered two ribs and the collar bone as it passed through. Muscle and ligament damage is severe, but we believe full recovery is possible over time. No use of the left arm or upper left side for several weeks, soldier. Your constant companions for some time will be a sling and heavy chest bandages. In a day or so you'll be transferred to Providence Hospital in Washington, soon as wagon space becomes available. I will recommend that your soldiering days be over. Return to full strength on your left side is a long time off."

The pain came in sharp jolts but was in the main a deep, dull ache. When he shifted position even slightly, however, the rib area sent sharp messages. Throughout the tent, activity prevailed, backgrounded by the ministrations of medics and an occasional moan from a wounded soldier. Most of the injured endured silently, realizing that others were worse off.

Ben worried about Ox, Sarge, and the others. He saw that it was a bright, sunny morning and heard no musketry or artillery. The last he remembered, the Rebs had broken through. We must have thrown them back off the ridge, he reasoned, and they haven't tried again this morning. At least not yet. Don't know how they could have, given the men they lost coming up that hill yesterday. God, we ripped their ranks to pieces. But how they kept coming. He wondered at what drives men to hurl themselves eagerly into a death trap.

His eyes picked up two hulks approaching his cot. Ox and Sarge. They made it. The grins on their faces served to reduce his pain. They stood on either side of him and began their onslaught of words.

Ox said, "Ben, you're pale as skim milk. We talked with the doc. Says you'll be laying around for awhile getting paid for resting. Free room and board and all."

"I was sleepin', too, 'til this Koo Koo Ree come woke me up," inserted Sarge.

"You told us that soldiers ain't 'sposed to sleep past dawn, Sarge," chuckled Ox.

Sarge's eyes twinkled, "But I was dreamin', you idiot. You took me away from somethin' beautiful. When I can be dreamin' of her, why would I want to be talkin' to a dumb farmer like you, huh, huh?" He shifted to Ben. "How're you boy? You got hit hard they tell me, but you'll live. Them Rebs broke over the wall, remember? Just a few of 'em. We killed most of 'em, threw the other ones back or took 'em prisoner. Then they run, remember? Huh, Huh?" He laughed again. "You know, Murnane, every time we get in a fight, you get yourself shot. You like hospitals, boy? You been on your back half the time you been in the army. Don't know why. Not many female nurses, and the ones they got are mostly old and ugly. Why you not know how to duck, boy? Huh, Huh?"

Ben laughed too, even though it hurt. "Sarge, you're crazier than a Minnesota loon, you know that? I've been wantin' to say that to you ever since Fort Snelling." Ben had noticed Sarge's bandaged hand. "You must've forgot to duck, yourself. Looks like it wasn't quite fatal."

"You may be right, boy, 'bout bein' crazy I mean. 'Course the only reason you're sayin' it now is 'cause I can't hit a man already down. But I'll get you later, Murnane, I'll make you pay. You know that, don't you? Anyways, I lost me three fingers on my left hand. Only got the thumb and the little one left. Two's better than none though, right?"

Ox told Ben that the regiment had taken fifty-five more casualties yesterday, about half of them fatal, and that Captain Messick had been killed during the breakthrough at the wall. He said the word was out that the regiment was to be disbanded and mustered out around August first. "Not official yet, but likely."

McMahon smiled and said, "I got mustered out yesterday. They don't need an old buzzard with only one wing. Not much use to 'em. 'Tween you and me though, boys, I can still whip any three farm boy recruits one-handed. You know that, don't you? Huh. Huh?"

"I believe you, Sarge." Ox said. "No doubt in my mind about that."

"Only one real regret I got, boys. My poor l'il wife'll suffer somethin' awful, me only havin' one hand left to fondle her with."

Ox went along with him. "I'm sure she'll still welcome you, Sarge, even though you'll only be able to do half as much as you used to."

Sarge thought about that for a few seconds, then countered, "Not true, Ox, not true. I'll do just as much as I ever did, but take twice as long doin' it. Even more fun that way. Huh, Huh?" He roared and they joined him.

"How bad the Doc say yours is, Ben?," Ox asked.

"Said the ball went through the upper chest, tore some muscles in there, then busted a few bones and went on out. Least it didn't have to get dug out of there with a knife. Then he said they wouldn't do much more for me here. They'll shoot me into Providence Hospital. Leave tomorrow or next day. I'll be sleepin' outside tonight under the trees. My luck, it'll probably rain. They need the cots in here for worse cases than mine. Kind of feel guilty already, still usin' this one."

"Could have been worse, my friend. But then it didn't have to happen at all either. You ran at that breakthrough like a maniac, Ben. You were swinging that rifle like a lumberman with an axe," commented Ox.

"Seems like I remember you were right there next to me, Koukkari. What're you talkin' about? And old Sarge here was out ahead of both of us, eh Sarge? Huh, Huh?" Ben laughed so hard it hurt.

Ox spoke again. "I'll be getting on back to what's left of the First. We're still on line up there, wondering if they're crazy enough to come at us again. Hope not for their sake and ours. Been enough killing on both sides. Just look at our bunch. Tony and Shakey and Pudge gone, you two banged up. Casualties must total a big number after these past two, three days. Sure has for Minnesota anyways. Nobody I've talked to has ever seen the like."

Ben jumped in at a time he considered opportune. "Ox, you said it yourself. Been enough killin' on both sides. I hate to ask you for a big favor, but I've got no choice. You and Sarge gotta help me keep my word."

He described to Sarge the episode down by Plum Creek and told them the Reb was alone and helpless. He concluded by saying, "I'm the only one he can count on. You two gotta help me see to him. He's probably scared to death waitin'."

"You mean right now?" asked Sarge.

"Right now."

"Ben," said the solemn Ox, "I'll help you, but remember that I'm doing it for you, not him. I know over all you're right in what you're doing, but it's still hard for me to do, understand?"

"I understand and I 'preciate it even more knowin'."

Sarge provided the clincher. "Soldiers do what they're told to do. Can't fault that boy for doin' his duty, just the same way we was doin' ours. Come on, Ox, let's get this Irish mule here up on his feet."

The Reb

The two giants half carried Ben from the tent and the short distance to where Ben had last seen the young soldier. Spotting the Reb lying under the tree, Ben approached and let himself down beside him. Sarge told Ben, "We'll go see if we can find out about this soldier's condition and disposition. We'll be back in a few minutes to help you back to the hospital tent."

Ben sat as still as possible. The Reb did not acknowledge him. A small sheet of paper stuck out of the waist of over-sized gray orderly trousers he had been furnished. Ben leaned close and read the scrawled message on the paper. "Name and regiment unknown. Amnesiac."

"I said I'd be back." Ben spoke very low, up close. "Got delayed yesterday. You feelin' better?" No response. Ben went on, "I'll talk. Just like before, you listen. My name's Ben. Ben Murnane. From Minnesota. I'll be sleepin' outside tonight. Two tents over. My two friends are tryin' to find out what they'll be doin' with you. Just remember what I told you before. You're not alone."

Sarge came to see Ben later that evening to tell him what they had found out about the soldier. The Doctor told Sarge that he knew the boy was a Southerner, but it didn't matter. He was pledged to save lives and ease pain. He'd said they had decided not to amputate the arm, but still weren't sure if it would be necessary later. The patient would be sent to a hospital in Washington.

Sarge guaranteed to find a way to get Ben and the Reb assigned to the same wagon train going into D.C. "I know the first sergeant of Headquarters Company, and he'll see to it." Sarge promised.

After Ben thanked him for everything he had done, Sarge began saying goodbye. Having gained permission to head back to Minnesota and receive his official discharge at Fort Snelling, Sarge had quickly arranged a ride to Hanover where he'd catch the train to LaCrosse, Wisconsin, and then upriver to Taylors Falls. "Ben, in four short days, I'll have a cold beer in one hand, my little wife in the other, a little girl on each knee, and I'll be sittin' back lookin' at that gorgeous view over the Saint Croix River. Luckiest man on the face of the globe, I am."

Ben forced down a rising lump in his throat. "Sarge," he said, "We all owe you. You taught us to be soldiers and hopefully to be men. Lots of teasin', but you mean a lot to all of us, and always will. When I get back, you'll get some company up at your place. Count on it. And you'll be forever welcome wherever I put down."

"I know that, Ben. You Minnesota farm boys did the U.S. Army proud and yourselves, too. Best bunch I ever served with. We lost some fine boys,

Ben. Hurts deep. But they went out men, they did. Tony, Shakey, Pudge, miss 'em, I do, and I'll never forget 'em long as I live. You take care of yourself, too. I'll look forward to your visit. Bring the old Ox along. We'll have a time. Old Sarge'll be too old for any more wars, Ben. This is it for me. God, let's get the damn thing over, 'fore we lose more good boys. Be seein' you, Ben. Keep your head down." And he was gone.

Lee's army began evacuation in heavy rain during the evening of July Fourth. He carried some of his wounded, but left behind thousands of others who were deemed unable to travel. Union medical personnel tried to service all of the casualties but fell far short of the need due to limited equipment, facilities, supplies, and professional staff. Civilians from Gettysburg and neighboring villages pitched in to help where they could, but the enormity of the task was overwhelming.

Many of the dead were hastily buried where they had fallen across the vast field between Cemetery and Seminary Ridges and around the Roundtops. Some of the fallen were buried under simple markers in the Gettysburg Cemetery. Dead horses and mules by the thousands were dragged into trenches and hastily covered to erase the horrendous stench made worse by broiling heat and intermittent rains. Broken cannon, limbers and caissons, smashed wagons, discarded weapons, ammunition, rucksacks, canteens, and torn and bloody parts of uniforms and boots littered the area. Splintered trees and shrubs, decimated crops and orchards, huge craters in the earth from detonations, and defoliated landscape had transformed the Eden-like area into the terrain of Hades.

Forty wagons with ten wounded per vehicle were loaded and set to make transit from Gettysburg's crude field hospitals to Providence in Washington. Other trains of injured were going to Harrisburg, Philadelphia, and Baltimore. Their cots were needed for the men whose injuries required further treatment before they could be transported. The injured filled tents, sheds, homes, and barns opened to them by local residents.

Ox came to see Ben off. He looked forlorn with his five close comrades all separated from him in one way or other. And had other disquieting news. He and the other few surviving Minnesotans were rumored to be part of a special unit assigned to go to New York City to help put down a budding disturbance. Mobs were roving the city, burning, looting, and murdering. Most of the victims were Negroes. Ox commented that the duty completed a circle. "Now we're fighting Northerners. What'll come next? They say most of 'em are Irishers. Hope none of 'em are your relatives, Ben." Ben shook his head and then solemnly shook his friend's hand.

"Ox, you take care of yourself. You're the only healthy one left. Don't be a damn hero. Most of the heroes I knew are dead. When you get done in New York, try to get down to see me. We'll crack open a beer keg and do some howlin'. Been too long with heavy stuff and sorrow and all. If I don't see you in D.C., I'll find you back in Minnesota soon's I can get there."

"You take care, too, Irish. Don't fall in love or do anything foolish without old Ox to look out for you. We got a lot of years as neighbors ahead of us, don't ever doubt that." He stepped in front of the Reb soldier next to Ben on the wagon. "Want you to know, soldier, that a friend of Ben's is a friend of mine. Good luck to you, too." He shook his hand, turned to Ben, nodded, and strode away.

The wagon train of injured soldiers moved out on the Taneytown Road, heading south. Some were missing limbs. Most were pale, forlorn and exhausted. Seemingly unable to slake an eternal thirst, they guzzled water constantly. Eyes were dull, lifeless, downcast. Ben assumed that the retreating Confederates must look the same or worse. The days of Gettysburg had left few unmarked.

The doctor had furnished Ben's Rebel friend with a denim shirt to complete his civilian attire. He still wore the printed note explaining his status. The doctor told Ben the young man's name was Tom Fuller. He had extracted the name by telling the soldier he needed it for his records.

The wagon train came to a halt several times to allow those who were ambulatory to stretch and relieve themselves. They munched cold vittles on the move, washed down with luke-warm coffee. Some couldn't keep it down and retched where they lay, triggering vomiting by others. The stench was barely relieved by the breeze and the movement of the rig. They stopped again at twilight near an isolated copse and were told that the wagons wouldn't move again until dawn. Those who could manage were invited to spread a blanket under the trees and stretch out. Half the men wandered off to seek privacy. The spaces they vacated in the wagons afforded more room for those who could not walk. A few men assembled around small fires for coffee and whispered conversations, but most were asleep almost instantly. Silence, motionlessness, and darkness were welcome medicines.

Ben and Fuller found a dry bed of bent grasses under a sprawling oak. They settled on their blankets, each trying to find a comfortable position. In whispers they began to converse.

"Ah don' want y'all to think me not grateful, Murnane. Believe me, Ah am. Wasn't fer you, Ah'd be a prisoner, sure as hell, or dead from bleedin'."

"Fuller, weren't for you, I'd be sure dead. Don't think I'll forget that. You don't owe me any thanks. It's me that's owin'."

"Guess thet evens things then, Yank. Bein' prisoner is bad as bein' dead, way Ah hear."

"Tell me where you're from, Tom. All I know is, when you looked down on me with that bayonet ready, I was dead meat. What made you stop and turn away? What were you thinkin'?"

"Yank, y'all honest believe that was thinkin'? Nobody warn't thinkin' in thet fight. Just survivin', if'n they was lucky. Ah looked down at y'all helpless, an' Ah 'member thinkin' that it warn't a fair fight, boy squeezed down like thet, all puppy dog-eyed. Jus' didn' seem right to stick a man defenseless like thet. Enemy or no, y'all was helpless. War'n' fair thet's all."

"Took a good man to see it that way, Tom Fuller. Most wouldn't have. Sure glad it was you, not someone else. I'd be gone sure."

"Maybe, maybe not. Jus' the way it hits a man at the time."

"You're from Alabama, accordin' to the doctor. What do your folks do? Did you live in a town or in the country? I'm awful curious, I guess, sorry."

"Ah ain't niver met a body from Minnesota afore either. Colder'n hell they tell me. And Indians cuttin' up white folks and mixin' right in with 'em. Thet true?"

"Woah, hold on there, Fuller. You and Alabama first. Get to Minnesota later."

"Not much to tell. Name Fuller was give me by my maw. Well, she's not mah maw really, but Ah call her Maw. She tells me Ah was left in a basket on her porch by mah real folks. Note was pinned on my blanket that said somethin' 'bout that they had twelve little ones already and couldn't feed 'nother. Please take him and raise him. Maw found out later thet mah real folks had been around town a couple days 'afore they dumped me. They'd asked around to find out if'n there was a married pair without no kids or with only one or two. When someone give 'em Maw's name, they took a chance and left me, then skedaddled down the road. Never did find out who they was. Jes kep' on goin'."

Tom's arm was paining him. He tried several positions before reaching a satisfactory level of comfort, then continued.

"Mah maw's husband, Ah won't call him mah paw, didn't want to keep me. She fought him hard, finally won out. He refused to let her give me his name though, and swore to have nothin' to do with me. Wish now he'd of kep' his word on thet. Maw, she give me her pre-marriage name of Fuller. Her husband's named Purcell. Ah like Fuller better anyway, don' you? Anyways, she called me by her dead paw's first name, Thomas. Name become Tom Fuller, but she always called me her Moses after that Bible feller left in the rushes. Most folks around our country call me "Mose." Ah don' mind 'em callin' me thet, 'cept some of 'em claim its a nigger's name and they kind of spit it out sometimes. Ah don' like thet."

"So you never knew your own parents. Don't even know your nationality, do you? Must make you ponder sometimes."

Tom laughed. "'Member now, Ben, Ah'd have been the thirteenth child in thet family. Might have been some hungry days. Far as nationality goes, Ah'm 'Merican, thet's enough. Right now Ah'm Confederate, as long as it lasts. Ah'm alive and reasonable healthy, least if'n they can save this here arm at the hospital. Don't want to go on home with one arm off. He'll try to kill me sure."

"Who? Who'll try to kill you?"

"Purcell, thet's who. Ah tole him when Ah lef' for the Ahmy, if'n he as much as touched Maw while Ah was gone, Ah'd come on back and kill him cold. Got some friends watchin' him. He knows Ah'll find out if'n he hurts her again. And he knows what Ah'll do. Won't be no holdin' back no bayonet over his chest, no siree."

Tom rolled over and stared up at the black sky. "When Ah was a babe 'til about age fifteen, he beat Maw and me least three times a week just outa meanness. He'd get drinkin', get ornery, and hit out at us, claimin' we was the ones holdin' him back from success and all. We was costin' him hard money with no return. He'd been workin' a pore claim for over twenty years and barely keepin' alive. He never had him no nigger. When Ah got seven, eight years old, he made me his nigger and Maw stayed his house nigger. Worked us, beat us, fed us 'nuff to keep us workin'. She didn't dare tell nobody. He'd of killed her sure. Ah was too little to help her 'til Ah growed and filled out some. One day soon after mah fifteenth basket day . . . " He laughed aloud. "Maw called mah birthday mah basket day 'cause she didn't know mah real birthday. Well, anyhow, he hit me a lick out by the wood pile like he'd done lots of times 'afore. All a sudden, Ah picked up the axe, wacked him across the haid with the handle end and laid him out cold. Surprised mahself. When he woke up, he come at me again in the barn. We fought bare hands, and Ah whipped him bloody. Damn near kilt him. Maw pulled me off or Ah might of. Told him he ever touch Maw or me again Ah'd use the other end of the axe next time. Meant it, too. An' he knowed Ah meant it."

"Will you be goin' back there?"

"Yup, have ta. For Maw's sake. She's not real kin but as close as Ah got. She stood by me, treated me good, loved me like a son. Ah gotta see she's took care of, 'fore Ah look to mah own way. Owe her, it's thet simple. Got a big debt to pay, an' it'll get paid."

Ben's admiration was evident in his response. "My older brother always said that a man's main job is to take care of his own. Sounds like you think the same way."

One more night on the road and another half day brought them to Providence Hospital. Since Gettysburg had put a strain on medical services, they waited two days before the beleaguered doctors got to their cases. The hospital facilities and staff were serving three times their normal load. The stifling heat, hungry flies, nauseating stench, frenetic pace, and overall gloom took its toll on patients and medical folks alike. Ben's shoulder and upper chest were checked. The prognosis was for near complete return to normal functioning, but it would take considerable time. Ben told the doctor and nurses that Fuller had lost his ability to speak. They weren't fooled, but didn't bother to question his claim, too busy to worry about trivialities. They didn't fuss long over Fuller. They cleaned and stitched his chest wound. The shattered arm was savable, but they doubted it would ever attain full strength or function. Tom said that he'd prove them wrong.

Chapter Thirty-Eight

Providence

Though it was called Providence Hospital, it was by no means a typical medical facility. Just south of the partially domed Capitol, every available shelter was converted. Tents and new wood shelters were added to keep up with the increasing need. Little disconnected medical empires sprang up, staffed by regular army physicians, local doctors, and women from the area donating their time and energy. The U.S. Sanitary Commission was in charge, but little central administration was exerted. Subsequent to major engagements, and especially after Gettysburg, lanterns and torches burned through the night as the squeaky ambulances rolled through the streets around the clock, disgorging the casualties. Citizens of Washington had a first hand view of the scourges of war. They stood at their windows and on their porches and witnessed the parade of damaged men.

Tom Fuller and Ben were assigned to a thirty-cot shed. Tom's wounds were severe, but he never complained or expressed self-pity. "Once something happens," he philosophized, "you know it was meant to be." According to the doctors, any movement would delay the recovery process and possibly cause permanent damage. His immobility kept him immersed in the stifling air and depressing atmosphere.

There were days when Tom withdrew, staring at the unpainted ceiling engrossed in his private thoughts. Ben learned to sense the Alabamian's moods and adjust to the moment. At least three times daily he came to Tom's cot and sometimes just sat silently when his conversation was not welcomed.

The remaining days of July passed slowly. By early August, the pressure of Gettysburg casualties eased and the bedlam decreased. Ben began to take slow, easy strolls around the capitol area. Though he felt it more nuisance than aid, the doctors insisted that he use a cane, saying that he needed it for his balance, but maybe even more for his own protection. The area outside the hospital compound was a rough part of town with hooligans looking to prey on soldiers walking alone. Ben knew that he was pushing too fast, but he pestered the doctors for a decision regarding his status. His return to the Regiment was doubtful. Dr. Carpenter said it would be a staff decision, but, if left up to him, he would declare him unfit for duty. An idea occurred to Ben. "I was hospitalized at Union in Georgetown last fall and wonder if I could be reassigned there for rehabilitation."

Dr. Carpenter replied, "I know Mrs. Howard and will inquire. It will depend of course on availability of space at Union, but it would provide an additional cot here at Providence."

Ben was elated. His stay at Union had been very pleasant, and there were grounds for walking and building his strength which he knew would hurry his recovery. If I can be transferred I'll find a way to get Tom over there, too, he plotted. Every day for a week he watched for Dr. Carpenter as he arrived for his duty shift. Finally the smiling doctor greeted him with the news that the shift to Union would come on August 16. He added that Mrs. Howard remembered Ben and would be pleased to welcome him again.

Ben had written to Maurna and told her about Tony, Shakey, and Sarge and the devastation of the First Regiment at Gettysburg. He also sent off a note to his uncle and aunt in Harper's Ferry. There was nothing left to do but be patient and wait.

Soon after his transfer to Georgetown's Union Hospital, Ben was favored by two pair of welcome visitors. Bernard and Mary Russell appeared unannounced at the hospital reception desk and were quickly brought to Ben who was exercising on the grounds. The sight of them, being led by Ellen Lowry, filled his heart with a flow of love. Mary dismissed his praise by saying that she had "some shopping to do in Washington anyway." They stayed with him for the better part of the day, updating him on their latest news of Maurna, Ginny, and Pim.

Mary was disappointed with the hospital facility, the general condition of the equipment and the limited care he was receiving. She urged him to seek permission to rehabilitate at their farm. He was grateful for the offer, but doubted whether the army would permit such an arrangement. He did promise he would visit when the doctors gave their approval. After Bernard and Mary departed to meet the late afternoon train, he felt considerably cheered and reinvigorated.

Wearing a silly grin, ever-welcome Ox appeared two days later in the company of Jason Hartman, a recently appointed Second Lieutenant. They told Ben the First Minnesota had just been assigned temporary duty in New York City to be on hand to help quell any renewal of the ugly race riots that had occurred in July. They were to report to Governor's Island and would encamp in Brooklyn Heights. Lieutenant Hartman, himself recovered from wounds sustained at Gettysburg, was ecstatic about the opportunity for the regiment.

"Murnane," he enthused, "too bad you can't come with us. This duty will be a real picnic for our boys. Kind of a reward. General Hancock was so favorable towards us and our Gettysburg performance that he recommended us. Real chance for our troops to see the big city. Doubt there'll be any more trouble up there. They squashed those thugs pretty hard in July. More precautionary than anything else. Sure hate to have you miss the fun."

Ox laughed. "Lieutenant, Ben here wouldn't do us much good up there anyways. Most of those rioters were Irishers you know. Ben here's about as Irish as you get. He might join the opposition."

The Lieutenant laughed along with them. "Doubt he's the kind of Irish those men were." He pointed at his rather recently earned officer pasteboards. "You see how desperate the First Minnesota has become, Murnane? They're down to people like me for officer material. They made me a lieutenant which is bad enough, but Koukkari here being made a corporal, that's really hard to believe."

"Cream rises, Lieutenant, simple law of nature," cajoled Ox. "Just wish Sarge was still here to show it to."

"Did our old friend, Sarge, get home all right, Ox, have you heard?"

"Heard that he did, Ben. Tough old buzzard. He's a better man than most even with only one hand. Whatever happened to that Reb you was looking out for, Ben? He make it all right?"

"He's still here recoverin' over at Providence. He'll make it though. Just take some time. Fine man."

"Murnane," interrupted the Lieutenant, "I talked with a doctor about you and several other Minnesota boys over at Providence. They haven't made up their minds yet. Said they'll know more in a few weeks. Won't be rushed, he said, now that the pace has slowed a little bit. He did say though that if it was up to him, he'd have you declared unfit for further service. Said your upper body won't be ready for a long time and by that time maybe the damn war'll be over."

"Still a chance though you think, Lieutenant? I'm doin' all I can to hurry it along."

"No harm in that, Ben, whatever they decide. Just get healthy and leave the decision up to them."

"Yes sir. All of you take care of yourselves up there in New York. Hate to miss that little adventure. Lieutenant, want you to watch over our little farm boy, Koukkari. Those bright lights of New York attract poor innocent country lads, you know. Those big city girls'll have him out at the end of his chain."

"How about all these nurses fluttering around you, Murnane? Poor little hurt Irish boy. My! My!"

"We'll be moving on, Murnane." the lieutenant said. "Take good care of yourself. See you back in Minnesota, if not sooner."

Ben waved them away, then remembered. "Ox, hold on just a minute. Wanted you to know, I had some time on my hands and wrote letters to Mr. and Mrs. Lunde, to Shakey's mother, and Pudge's parents. Stop by on your way back through now, old friend."

Ox clapped him affectionately on his good shoulder, "Good of you to write like that, Ben. I'm sure it's appreciated. I wrote the Lundes and Mrs. Cosgrove, too. Miss those three something awful, Ben. Guess we always will."

"Take care of yourself, Ox. Can't afford to lose you, too."

"You won't, Ben. You won't."

Letter from Mary and Bernard

Dear Maurna, Pim, Ginny,

Bernard asked that I do the writing. Of course he's standing over me telling me what to say.

We've been to see Ben in Washington at Union Hospital. We're pleased to tell you he is doing fine. His wounds are healing well, and his spirits seem high enough. He's thin and looks tired, but good food and rest will cure both in time. He asked us to greet all of you when we write. He is not sure yet how long he will be kept at the hospital. The doctors are telling him that it will be at least two more months, but Ben says it won't be that long. Until he is released, he can't talk of when he will be coming back to Minnesota. He said to tell you that he will write you again when he knows for sure.

He has a friend who was a Confederate soldier who is healing in another hospital. Ben didn't tell us the circumstances of how they became friends, just said they met at Gettysburg. His name is Tom Fuller, a farm lad from Alabama. Ben is trying to get him transferred to Union Hospital.

Bernard and I are fine. We had a good harvest and the furniture business is brisk. We don't have as many soldiers going through as we did the first two years of the war. Some Union men are in camp nearby. They don't bother us, and we pay them little mind.

Bernard and I hope your grief over Joseph is easing. We know it is difficult for you, and we pray for him every night. We pray for all of you. You've been through so much. We're glad you are now in the city. It must feel safer there. We have read little of the Indian War in Minnesota. The newspapers here talk of nothing but the North-South War. We hope the Indians are subdued and cannot kill others.

You have our love and best wishes and our open invitation to come to Harper's Ferry for a long visit.

Love,
Bernard and Mary

Chapter Thirty-Nine

Bonding

Mrs. Julia Howard was a tall, willowy widow with black hair framing a bony face dominated by a high forehead. Alert, constantly moving gray eyes missed little but conveyed warmth and high intelligence. Care lines terminated near well-shaped lips. Her long, thin nose seemed to superintend the other features. A graceful, long neck gave her the appearance of great height and exaggerated an erect posture.

She had volunteered her services before Bull Run and was the senior matron at Union Hospital, where she assumed command of the distribution of supplies. In addition, she scheduled and managed the non-medical personnel and the volunteer women from Georgetown. She had learned to anticipate the doctors' needs and was relentless in her demands for cleanliness and order. The Sanitary Commission was well aware of Mrs. Howard who plagued them constantly with supply demands for "her boys."

No one could remember a day when she was not present at the facility. Her response to those who suggested that she occasionally take a rest day was "pain takes no holidays." She was tireless, and ever-gentle and warm with the soldier patients, who learned that in her, they had a champion. Efficient, able, and cooperative with the doctors and nurses on duty, she was tyrannical with inefficient clerks, aides, and especially with bureaucrats. Her late husband left her well off and ensconced in an elegant, three-story home near Rock Creek on N Street.

Julia's niece, Ellen, also a widow, was as tall as her aunt, lithe and graceful. She moved with an effortless glide, head held high, but with deep green eyes cast down. Worn in an upswept, severe style, her chestnut hair featured cleverly loosened wisps and tendrils, serving to partially cover a high forehead. Her slightly flushed cheeks required no pinching. Her features were classic, but true beauty was just missed because the eyes and demeanor lacked that spark that kindles and illuminates. Where Julia was involved, demanding, emotional, and energized, Ellen was mechanical, proficient, and controlled. Julia cared deeply and it showed. Ellen cared, too, but her concern seemed impersonal and leashed. The men appreciated both ladies and didn't waste much time on analysis.

As did all the patients, Ben came to know and love Julia. She knew them by name and related to each personally. When the doctors and nurses made their rounds, Julia went with them from cot to cot, listening to the exchange between healers and patients so she could know what supplies would be required. As the doctor moved on, Julia often lingered to offer a final encouraging comment.

Responding to urging from Ben, Julia Howard used her influence to arrange for the transfer of Tom Fuller to Union. Both expressed their gratitude and promised to be model patients.

A week later, Ben was seated at the end of Tom's cot when Julia stopped by to ask Tom if he needed her to help write that letter home he'd been postponing. He had admitted to her that he hadn't written to his mother since before Gettysburg.

"Tom, your mother has a right to hear from you. Now you get busy thinking out what you want to say. You're too nice a young man to neglect her."

"Yes'm, Ah've been thinkin' on it. Maybe tomorrow."

"I heard that yesterday, Tom. Now you get to it."

"Yes'm."

"How you doin', Murnane? You taking those walks regularly? Build up those muscles. Good looking man like you will need lots of strength and endurance to get away from the ladies." She was up and away but admonished over her shoulder, "Tomorrow, Fuller, I'll be back tomorrow to check on that letter."

Tom chuckled. "Nice lady."

"Isn't she though? Always a cheerful word. Don't know where she gets all the energy. Man, does she hate those politicians. Not so nice when she's talkin' 'bout them, Tom."

"That alone shows her good sense."

"And the sharpies that make money off the war. Does she tie into them. Wants Congress to do somethin' to stop those parasites. Fat chance for them to do anythin' about it."

Tom's jaw was set firmly. "Heard a lot of my friends in the Fourth Alabama call it 'a rich man's war and a poor man's fight.' We got that kind of buzzard down South, too."

"The Lord made a lot of that kind, Tom. No matter how much money they've got, they're still lookin' for more. Now Mrs. Howard, they say she got left rich by her husband a few years back, but she's not greedy. Bein' rich is no crime. It's how you come by the money and what you do with it makes the difference. She spends her own money buyin' some of the supplies for the hospital. Furnishes all the writin' materials for letter writin', I know that."

"That pretty one over there is her niece. Not overly friendly, but sure does work hard."

"Name's Ellen, Tom. Kind of shy and stand-offish. But good-hearted and works like a trooper. Don't see many that young workin' in the wards. Mrs. Howard says Ellen's a widow for over two years now. She doesn't seem old enough to hardly be married, let alone widowed. Must have married awful young. Don't know whether her husband was killed in the war or what. From Kentucky, both of 'em. Pretty ladies as I've ever seen. You and I ought to visit Kentucky some day, Tom, if they look like Ellen down there."

Ben had indeed noticed Ellen, her comely appearance and mysterious manner. He spoke with her on several occasions but she had simply commented politely and moved on. As unobtrusively as possible, Ben watched her, enjoying the sight of her gliding about the halls and wards, head held proudly, concentrating on her work. The kind of a woman a man feels he wants to protect, vulnerable looking. Her eyes had met his a few times, but she looked away quickly. She knows that I've noticed her, he had thought to himself, and she doesn't seem to 'preciate bein' noticed. Well, I sure won't press it.

Since they felt one of them should be on duty at all times, Julia and Ellen seldom had lunch at the same time. Whenever he could, Ben maneuvered a place for Tom and himself at the table where the women chose to eat. He enjoyed being with both of them, finding them a welcome relief from strictly male talk. Though Ellen spoke sparingly and never of herself, he was able to converse with her on general topics. On the other hand, Julia was loquacious and opinionated, possessed a sparkling wit and spiced her comments especially when inveigling politicians. Because her deceased husband had suffered many setbacks and betrayals at their hands, she was unforgiving of the breed. President Lincoln was the only public servant who drew praise from Julia, but she was wary even of him. "Too good to be true for a politician," she often said. "He'll either prove to have been a clever fraud or be destroyed by those who can't abide an honest man."

Ben and Tom had abundant opportunities to talk and discover more about one another. Their affinity was natural, unforced, a pleasure for both. As mutual trust and respect became well established, Ben felt comfortable in inquiring about a topic that intrigued him. "What do most of you Southerners think about the war, Tom? You as confused about why you're fightin' as we are? Most of you think pretty much alike?"

"Wouldn't say that, Ben. As many reasons as they is soldiers, probably. Lot of us joined up 'cause somebody told us there was a fight goin' on. I never thought much about why. Some of the officers argue about it. Ah've listened to 'em. Some say it's to keep our niggers, but that's crazy, most of us not havin' any to keep. Others say it's about what they call state's rights, some political thing. Ah always thought it was people ought to have rights, not states."

"Tom, you told me you're not educated, but that sure didn't keep you from bein' smart, did it?"

"Don't know about smart. Just listen better'n most, Ah do. Maw always says that you learn a lot more with your mouth shut than when it's flappin'. Those educated fellas get fixed on a high-soundin' idea, then they end up defendin' it. Ah 'member one officer, from Mobile he was, he said we just didn't want nobody in Washington tellin' us how to live. That's why our ancestors come over here, he said. Claimed that was why he was fightin'." Tom laughed. "Always seems silly to me to hear grown men end up arguin' and fightin' about why we was fightin'."

"Same with our soldiers. Some say we're fightin' to stamp out slavery, but most of us from my state never saw a Negro 'til we got to Washington. We make it sound like we wouldn't ever treat people like you Southerners do, but truth is, we've been known to treat the Indians awful bad. So bad in fact they rose up in a bloody war about it. Seems we can see the other fellow clearer than we can ourselves sometimes."

"Lot of truth in that. They say Lincoln talks of preservin' the Union. That political talk, Ben, or you think that's what he really means?"

"I believe him 'cause he said it right from the start. He feels awful strong about it. United we stand, divided we fall, he says. Old England sits over there watchin'. I know about those folks and their appetite. Some think they're still wantin' a piece of this country. The more states we've got banded together makes us overall stronger as a nation. Least ways, that's my main reason for fightin'. Bein' united is important. To be truthful though, the first reason for joinin' up for me was to get away from havin' to decide what I was goin' to do with my life. Kind of a handy way to avoid all that and people influencin' me what I should do. Liked the idea of adventure, too. And the glory of it. That sure was a fooler, though. Glory is a lot more scarce than misery in this damn war."

"That's the God's truth. One other thing Ah've noticed since Ah've been in the north that Ah cain't quite figure, though Ah ain't seen enough yet to make up mah mind on it. That's the women folk. Seems like our Southern ladies are stronger on the war than women up here. Some of the loudest talkers about killin' Yankees was our ladies. Haven't seen that many Northern ladies, but the ones Ah've heard talk mostly seem against the fightin', more the way you'd expect females to be. Maybe now with all the casualties our women are toned down some."

"Tom, you really tryin' to understand women? Maybe you aren't so smart after all."

Ben noted that Ellen Lowry was in the habit of taking a brief walk after her lunch on days that weather permitted. Probably to get a break from the persistent odors and tepid air of the wards, he guessed. He plotted to occasionally cross her path as he began his own exercise excursions. Unable to gracefully ignore the coincidental encounters, Ellen tolerated his company. These brief get togethers gradually served to bring about a level of comfort between the two. Though no outward sign was ever displayed, Ben felt certain that the patrician young woman was not offended by his forwardness. In fact, he convinced himself that his company gradually became anticipated and even welcomed. He was drawn to her and found that thoughts of her were becoming increasingly prevalent. He attempted no deep self-analysis but simply relaxed and permitted his instincts to guide him.

By mid-September, Ben felt himself healed and nearly as good as new. His left side had not regained it's former strength, but the pain had diminished. Feeling the burden of inactivity and purposelessness, he spoke to Julia Howard. "Mrs. Howard, I need to make myself useful and earn my keep. I'm pretty handy with tools and such, and some things sure do need repair around here. Mind if I try my hand at some of them?"

"Why Ben, how thoughtful. But I don't want you overdoing, you hear? I'll write up a list of things that need fixing, but you only do what you're ready for. Fair enough?"

In late September, the doctors officially declared Ben unfit for return to duty. With mixed feelings he received his official separation, dated October 14, 1863. He longed for his remaining friends in the regiment and felt a twinge of guilt for not being there to do his part, but also privately rejoiced that his soldiering days were over.

To celebrate Ben's mustering out, Julia Howard invited Ben and Tom to her home for dinner. The lady of the house was an accomplished hostess who enjoyed entertaining, though her social activities had been severely reduced since her involvement at Union Hospital. She carried the burden of the conversation because her table companions deferred to her cosmopolitan aura and conversational skills. Ben and Tom contributed little more than brief responses to her questions or polite comments about her anecdotes. Ellen nodded from time to time to encourage her aunt.

"There is talk of an official dedication planned for the cemetery at Gettysburg," Julia stated. "President Lincoln is favorable and has consented to say a few words. I'll say this, he's the first politician I ever saw who is capable of saying just a few words. Talk is that Lincoln sees the event as an opportunity to pay tribute to the men who died there from both sides. He's an amazing man. All the time he's fighting the Confederacy with all the North can bring to bear, he's trying to bring the two sides together again. He reasons that honoring the dead of both armies will help the uniting down the road. Critics call him a bumpkin and a fool. I say he's a shrewd and visionary man."

Ben responded. "Tom and I both lost good friends at Gettysburg. I think it's a good idea to honor them. What about you, Tom?"

"Seems like," replied Tom thoughtfully. "Might seem too soon for some though. For me, the sooner, the better. Wait too long, folk tend to move on and forget. Us that was there'll never forget, Ah know that."

Tom excused himself shortly after the discussion, saying he had some things to do back at the ward. He thanked Mrs. Howard, said goodnight to Ellen, and told Ben he'd see him back at the hospital.

Ben realized Tom was getting out of the way so that he could have private time with Ellen. Always one step ahead, thought Ben, smiling to himself. The evening was windless and balmy, prompting Julia to suggest they have their coffee in the back yard. They sauntered to a gazebo where they relaxed on wicker chairs.

They were barely settled when Ellen blurted quickly, "Please excuse me Aunt Julia and Ben. I'm feeling a trifle indisposed. Nothing serious, overly tired perhaps. Look forward to seeing you here on Sunday, Ben. We'll take a walk then, if you like."

Julia and Ben sat uncomfortably for several minutes. She seemed to be making up her mind about something. When she spoke it was in a low, modulated voice. "Ben, I'm a woman of some perception. And I'm more aware than usual where Ellen is concerned. I want you to bear with me because I've decided to try to explain some things that I'm sure you've been curious about but too polite to ask. Very like you though, not to have probed. I've grown quite fond of you and Tom."

"The feelin's are mutual, you can be sure of that."

"Thank you, Ben, I have felt that to be true. But I want to talk with you regarding Ellen. You've noticed, of course, how timid she is. Diffident, withdrawn. My heart breaks for her." She paused and looked out past the lantern light into the darkness.

Matching her tone, Ben said softly, "Timid, yes. Withdrawn much of the time. Every so often she seems to break free of whatever holds her, but then slides back. Seems to be deep thinkin' most of the time. Unhappy."

"She's got a right, Ben. Terrible things happened to her, none that she brought on herself. Tragedy without warning, stark, and final." Julia paused again, dabbed at her eyes with a kerchief. "She's been staying with me for over two years. Sometimes I wonder whether she'll ever recover. Needs to make friends, get out, do things young people do. She's only twenty-three, but acts like someone twice that age. The hospital work is both a blessing and a curse. The work demands her concentration, so it helps her to forget her troubles, but it also takes up all her time and energies. I worry about her. I know a cure can't be forced. She's fragile. It's got to come from inside her, Ben, or it won't be permanent healing."

Ben waited for Julia to continue, but sensed that she wanted some response. "I've talked with you about my sister, Maurna, up in Minnesota. Strong and wise woman. She says that time is a great healer. She's known tragedy and carried on. Her husband died soon after their child was born. Terrible loss. She lives for her daughter, Virginia, and for the rest of the family, I guess. When trouble comes, she says that life has its vicissitudes. Then she just picks up and goes on."

Julia thought for a moment about what Ben had said. "I'm sure she knew deep pain, Ben, but, at least she has her daughter. Ellen lost everyone. I want you to know her story so you can better understand and maybe help her. You must promise to never tell her I told you. I want your word on that."

"You have it."

"I know I can trust you, and also I sense that you and Ellen . . . , well, I do have eyes to see, my young friend. I also know that you're a kind young man, Mr. Murnane. You're nearer her age and have insights long lost to an old fossil like me. You can perhaps give me advice on how to help her. Will you do that, Ben?"

"I'll try."

"Ellen as you know is my niece, my brother's daughter. We are from the hill country of east Kentucky. I ran away from home when still young, got in some mischief, and after a long, winding trail ended up an old widow, as you see me. I never went back to Kentucky, but kept in touch by mail. Fortune smiled on me more than I deserved when I met the man who became my dear husband. We had a great life, did a lot of interesting things, but, to our regret, I never birthed a child. My brother and his wife were blessed eight times, Ellen being the youngest. At seventeen, she married a neighboring farm boy. Jim and Ellen settled on a modest little place. A couple of real love birds, they soon had a son and daughter one year apart. I never got a chance to see the tykes, but I understand they were cute as puppies. Their farm was prospering and everything was beautiful until one fateful day, Ben."

Her voice faltered momentarily but she recovered and continued. "The four of them were going in to town, the two little ones snug in the wagon box in back. It had been raining. They started around a curve on the mountain road when a big rig came wheeling too fast from the other direction, forcing them to the outside. They skidded over the edge and down a steep drop to the rocks below. Ellen crawled to each of them. Jim and the little boy were stone dead. The baby girl was barely alive. She climbed that steep slope carrying her daughter and started for town. She wasn't even aware that she had a broken ankle and lacerations from head to foot. Some folks came along and rushed her into town. Kindly townspeople went out to bring in the bodies of Jim and their son. The daughter, Carrie was her name, lived the night but died before dawn the next day. Ellen buried all three together."

Julia looked away for a moment, fixed her eyes on Ben's and in a more controlled voice finished her narrative. "My brother and his family tried to help her, but she just didn't respond. He wrote me to ask whether Ellen could stay with me for a while, hoping that getting her away from where it all happened might hasten her recovery. Having this big house to myself, I told him that I'd sure give it a try. But in a little more than two years, there's not been much improvement that I can see. She's so deep hurt. She's welcome here as long as she wants, but maybe it keeps her from having to make decisions about her future. I'm not much help or at least not the kind she seems to need." She was softly weeping and looking dejectedly at her hands.

"Good Lord, Mrs. Howard, some people get more than their share of sadness thrown at 'em."

"Never got a handle on who was in that other wagon. They kept right on going, though they must have known what they had caused. Later the sheriff asked her to describe the other rig and what had happened, but she wouldn't talk of it."

"That kind seem to always get away clean," Ben spat out angrily. He then spoke in a controlled voice again. "No wonder she's so quiet and vulnerable. She probably can't shake the pain for seein' it in nightmares. Does she have religious faith, Mrs. Howard? Sometimes that helps bring some comfort."

"What she had, she lost, or threw away. Our people were religious. My brother still is, I think. He and his wife brought her up to religious thinking. She's never mentioned it though."

Julia arose then and stood at the gazebo railing peering off into the darkness. "You know, Ben, when you see a night as pretty and peaceful as this one, you feel the old inclinations to give God credit for it. But then you think about what he lets happen to people like Ellen and to those beautiful boys in this ugly war. It gets hard to reconcile it all. Need to get some sleep. You, too, I suspect."

He walked her to the house, thanked her, and made his way back to his narrow cot at the hospital.

Since he no longer was classified as an army patient, Ben relinquished his cot to a soldier and gladly accepted modest private quarters in a windowless closet near the hospital's main entrance. A cot, a chair, and a small foot locker furnished the room.

Ellen flooded Ben's thoughts. He had to restrain his impulses, lest he become a pest. Though she had become increasingly comfortable with him, his instincts advised to move slowly. She's like a young doe, he thought, ever wary and at the slightest disturbance ready to spring away into concealment and safety in the underbrush of her own introspection.

Meanwhile he devoured the Washington newspapers that were filled with news and editorial comment about the progress of the war. In the West, a Union hero had emerged. Ulysses S. Grant, the conqueror of Vicksburg, was named by the Commander-in-Chief to head the newly created Military Division of the Mississippi. The Confederates won a bloody encounter that forced the Blue army to retreat to Chattanooga where they were placed under siege. The Gray soldiers looked down on them figuratively and literally from nearby Missionary Ridge and Lookout Mountain.

Grant took over at Chattanooga. A great climactic battle was in the works. The War in the West would be won or lost near the Tennessee-Georgia line.

When Ben discussed the impending battle with Tom, he learned some quick geography from one who knew. "Ah live not too far from Chattanooga, Ben, just a few miles west and south out on the Tennessee River. Hilly country all around there, lots of ravines and low mountains and high ridges. Hell of a place to be fightin'. Lots of small streams and woods and heavy brush. Be a struggle to move anybody out of there if they wanted to stay."

"I know there's some Minnesota regiments out there. Sure hope it gets over with soon or my young nephew'll be enlistin' if I know him. Damn,

Tom, you don't 'spose Alabamians and Minnesotans are goin' to hit head on out there, too, do you?"

"Could happen, Ben, could happen. Those boys are fightin' on 'Bama and Georgia turf. They'll be ornrier than surprised hornets. Wouldn't want to bet on the outcome, Ben. Should be interestin'. Glad we're here readin' 'bout it, 'stead of in the middle of it."

"Ben and Ah sure do owe you for these wonderful dinners, Mrs. Howard, best Ah've ever et."

"That's sure," affirmed Ben.

"Oh, good gracious. All that you two have done at the hospital and for no pay at all, just room and board, such as it is. Don't be silly. We're happy for the good company, aren't we Ellen?" soothed Julia to lure her into the conversation.

"Both of you are true gentlemen and excellent company," Ellen said. Her demeanor seemed to Ben less guarded than previously. He hoped it wasn't just temporary, because he wanted to speak with her and had made up his mind that tonight he would present his case.

He heard himself talking. "We'll be leavin' early for the cemetery dedication on Wednesday. Should be back sometime late Thursday or early Friday. Lookin' forward to it. I've only seen the President once, and he was goin' by so fast I only got a quick glimpse."

"Ah ain't nivver seen mah president." said Tom, smiling.

"Well, perhaps all Americans will have the same one again soon, Tom. No offense meant but that'll be best for the country I think, don't you?" asked Julia.

"Ah hope Ah'm smart enough not to question the good judgment of a nice lady who feeds me great dinners, Mrs. Howard."

Julia didn't miss the ruse. "Tom Fuller, you're better at avoiding an answer than a politician. And you do it without offending. Mighty clever, young man."

Tom bowed his head slightly and grinned. "Just bein' a true Southern gentleman, Ma'am."

She howled in delight, then added, "By the way, Mr. Fuller, I need some of that shrewdness of yours to help me solve a bookkeeping problem. If you'd be so kind, I'd ask you to accompany me to my business office. It's some figures that are perplexing me, and I know how good you are with numbers."

Another slight bow and a sly smile. "Lead on, dear madame. Ah am of course delighted to be of service."

The obvious design of the two absconders was to leave Ellen and Ben alone. Knowing they were victims of a conspiracy, they were nevertheless appreciative of the opportunity to talk privately. Ben smiled at Ellen and was hopeful that her earlier mood had persisted. Her return smile seemed to say so. He had both anticipated and dreaded this moment.

"Ellen, I would like to talk with you about somethin' that is extremely important to me. I know you are aware of my feelin's for you. They're too strong to hide. I've been dreamin' that you are of somewhat the same mind regardin' me. I want to know you better, share your thoughts, and hear of your hopes and dreams. If you have any interest in me, please let me ask Mrs. Howard if I may call on you formally. May I do that, Ellen?"

Tears formed in her lovely, deep green eyes. She dabbed them, looked away for a moment, then spoke softly. "You must know that I'm fond of you, Ben. I admire your gentleness, compassion, and good humor. All are very evident and unquestionably genuine. What you need to understand is that your qualifications are not the issue. I am the one with shortcomings. I know my present state of mind, Ben. I must first of all prove to myself that I am sufficiently ready for someone such as you. Ben, I was once full and complete, but I don't know whether the container can ever hold a full measure again."

He waited, heart pounding, then relieved her. "Oh, dear Ellen, what you say about yourself is undoubtedly true to you. You feel deep pain, but I'm convinced it can be eased. I honestly believe, also, that I can be the one to help heal it permanently, if you'll let me try. We both know that only love can cure someone who hurts. I don't mean to sound forward by using the word love, but it's what I feel. I am only suggesting that we find out the truth together. I would jump off the Chain Bridge before I'd harm you in any way. I won't press the issue, but would like to explore it with you at whatever pace you set. Will you give it a chance?"

"Ben, your words are sweet and wise. I could ask no more than you have so gallantly suggested. But I cannot let you be hurt. As I said, my doubt is not with you. You deserve someone who is ready for your beautiful offer. Not someone who is unsure and unable to give you fair return. I am not ready to explore it fairly and openly. You would enter into it with genuine hope. I'm not even capable of returning that in equal measure. I need more time before I can consider that kind of commitment."

"Ellen, selflessness is a rare human quality. But I am strong, and patient. And I'm a battler, Lady. I fight hard for what I believe to be of value. I respect your truthfulness, but, I promise you, I'll not go out of your life unless you send me. I will wait until you are ready, no matter how long it takes. I know in my heart that it is right for us, and will be well worth the wait."

"Ben, you don't know what you are proposing. You have your own life, decisions to be made that will determine your future. You can't be burdened by uncertainty. I cannot predict how much time I will need. When the time comes, I shall know, but it may not ever come and that is not fair to you." She was sobbing softly, her eyes closed. He went to her and gently touched her hand. She opened her eyes and said plaintively, "Please, Ben." He withdrew, sat across from her again and waited.

Gathering herself, she looked at him and said, "Ben, it really comes down to this. Right now, at this time, I am incapable of taking the risk. Not any risk that you might have shortcomings. I fear that not at all, but, as I live now, my life is nearly risk free. There are few ways that I can be hurt. I have no one except my aunt and family members in Kentucky who I can lose. Since they are all linked to me already, with them I have no choice. However, in bringing another love into my life, I would add one more beautiful person and that addition would make me that much more vulnerable. Please understand my dilemma, Ben."

"I do understand you, Ellen. I watched my sister Maurna go through the agony of three still births and the loss of her husband. She suffered and still does. But she also knew love. Deep, abiding love that sustains her to this day and always will. And she has warm, beautiful memories. With love comes risk, undeniably, but without love, life's lonely, and can never be lived to the full. Without love what does one really have?"

"Invulnerability, Ben, that's what one has, and as I feel now, it is more critical than love. Oh, I know the sweetness of love, its joy and memories. And I hope to know it again, but only when I can give to it what it deserves."

The finality of her argument defeated him. He yearned to bring joy and peace and renewed vitality to someone he knew had every right to it. And, somehow, he knew that he was the one to lead her back.

"Ellen, I must go. Tom and I have miles to go. I had intended to come back on Thursday, but I'm thinkin' now that I may go on back to Minnesota. You say you need time. If that is right for you, then it is right for me, for us. You shall have whatever time you need. But, I want you in my life, Ellen. I want you with me every day. I leave it in your hands. If and when you are ready, write and tell me. One word from you, and I'll be here. I promise you I will not pressure you or contact you in any way. If a year should pass without a message, I will consider your decision as made. Promise me though, that if during that year you decide that your answer is no, you will let me know. I love you very dearly, that is without question. If that love cannot be returned, I will be terribly disappointed, but will understand and always wish you great happiness and freedom from your burden."

He went to her. She rose to meet him, tears in her eyes and wrenching pain in her heart. He held her tenderly for a moment, then whispered in her ear, "I love you. I want you to be my wife. One year, sweet Ellen. Listen to your heart. That's where love resides." He gazed into her tear-filled eyes, and smiled. He slowly turned and walked toward Julia's office.

"Mrs. Howard," he said as she and Tom looked up at him, "I'll be sayin' goodbye to you and for more than just a couple of days. After the ceremony at Gettysburg, I'll be goin' on to Minnesota. I can't thank you enough for all that you have meant to Tom and me, all your kindnesses and friendship. I'll see your fair Washington again someday and call on you when I do. I'd also like the privilege of writin' you from time to time. Please know how fond I'll always be of you."

Both Julia and Tom stood frozen through his farewell. Questions were emblazoned in their eyes, but they remained unasked. She graciously accepted his and Tom's gratitude and asked them to be sure to write. Ben knew she would get answers to her unasked questions from Ellen and Julia knew that, too. Tom was not quite sure whether he'd get any answers from anybody. The parting was tearful on Julia's part. The two former warriors left for their last sleep at Union Hospital before they began their return trip to Gettysburg.

Chapter Forty

Gettysburg Revisited

With packed rucksacks containing a change of clothes, shoes, and a pistol each for protection, Tom and Ben decided to save shoe leather. They caught the dawn train to Baltimore and with others bound for Gettysburg switched to a ponderous, stop-at-every village local train that passed through Hanover. They walked the fifteen miles to Gettysburg. Just before reaching the village, they observed small pockets of men camped out on the east face of Culp's Hill. They filed away the information for later reference.

Amazed by the crowds descending on the little college town, they learned that hotels were at double occupancy, homes were letting rooms, barn space was rented, and all sheds and shelters within several miles were reserved.

The home of Pennsylvania College and the Lutheran Seminary had become world famous. For the past four months and a few weeks, press reports had made people aware of the town's existence, and its hotels, shops, liveries, restaurants, and especially the taverns and saloons, had done a year's business. The current crowds stomped the boardwalks, trampled the grass and took battlefield tours guided by fee-charging locals who were dead-sure experts on every phase of the recent three-day battle. Truth to tell, most of the "experts" had been burrowed deep in their cellars from the first cannon's roar on July 1, through the retreat of the Confederates on the Fourth of July.

Tom remarked, "These folks seem a trifle too festive for the dedication of a cemetery. They're gettin' liquored-up pretty good, too. Frolickin' now, but it might get some ugly in a few hours, Ben."

Tom and Ben had intended to walk together along Cemetery Ridge to the site of their first meeting, but because of the crowds already streaming that way, they decided to postpone their visit until the early morning hours, when most of the celebrators would still be abed.

Ben and Tom enjoyed a few glasses of beer and, after waiting in line for over an hour, a good meal. They saw no one they recognized, but did josh with a few claiming to be veterans of the Battle of Gettysburg. They walked past the gates of the Cemetery where the ceremony was scheduled to take place the next day, and followed a winding path along a ridge line toward Culp's Hill.

In the fading light, they stepped carefully to steer away from the many sharp dropoffs into rock-filled gorges and defiles. Soon they became more confident of their footing and learned that if they stayed faithfully to the pathway there was little to fear. When they arrived at the east side of Culp's Hill, they found fully a third of the space already occupied. Most of the claimed spaces were toward the bottom of the slope where they could see a few sophisticated tents erected on the flats. Finding a satisfactory tree-sheltered shelf near the top, they spread their gear.

The evening was clear and balmy. Everyone hoped the weather would hold through the ceremony. Men were clustered around small fires where card and dice games generated excited shouting, complaining, cheering, and a few scuffles. Harmonicas and an accordion livened the atmosphere.

Ben and Tom cupped their hands behind their heads, gazed at the stars, and privately recalled their previous sojourn in Gettysburg only five months ago. Despite the noise and activity around them, in a very short while both were asleep and hardly stirred until the sun hit their eyes.

As he built a small fire at dawn, Tom said, "Ben, my friend, Ah sure don't want to carry that sack with me all day, but Ah don' think that leaving it here is very smart either. They'll be a bother to carry but maybe worth having for seats during those god-awful speeches we'll be hearing later on."

Ben chuckled and off they went in search of a cafe. Tom suggested that they "really load up" because the parade was scheduled to start at 10:00 A.M. and after that they'd likely find it difficult to find a place to eat.

After a heavy breakfast and several cups of coffee, the one-time enemies headed for the cemetery, passed along its western edge and moved out along Cemetery Ridge. They walked silently up to the angle of the stone fence and the small cluster of trees that had been the focal point of "Pickett's Charge," as it was now being called. As the Rebel and the Yankee gazed out over the tranquil, murky scene, Ben remembered that Tom had been in the hospital on July third when the Confederates made their gallant, suicidal assault across that valley.

He pointed to the west and reverently said, "Your troops came out of those woods way over on that far ridge, Tom. More than 12,000 infantry spread out a half mile wide. It couldn't be done, but they almost did it. Not only couldn't be done, shouldn't have been tried. They were magnificent and pitiable at the same time. It was a slaughter, just like us at Fredricksburg. When they got in close up here, we had 'em from three sides. Stupid, stupid waste. It's got to end, Tom."

"It probably won't be long now, Ben. Soon won't be enough men left to fight. It's over for you and me, that's for sure."

They moved along the ridge to the point where Ben estimated the Minnesotans had started their fateful charge. The two stood quiet, looking to the west down the near slope to Plum Run and up the far incline to the Emmitsburg Road. Their minds were recreating that smoke-shrouded twilight scene, hearing again the crashing sounds and the screams.

"We come from up over that way," said Tom as he pointed just a bit south of due west. "The Captain, he told us that there was a break in your line, and we was to charge through it clear up to where we're standin'. It looked wide open when we started off down that slope over yonder. It did look wide open, Ben."

"It was open, Tom. Later we were told that our General Sickles got himself and his corps too far out front, got cut off, and created a hole in the line. We had come up that day about noon time, short two companies and held in reserve over here. Ever been in reserve, Tom? We could hear all the wild fightin' and the boomin' of cannon and see the smoke risin', but didn't know what the hell was happenin'. Just before dark, we were marchin' behind us here with the Colonel in the lead, when General Hancock rides up, grabs Colonel Colvill, points at you Alabamians runnin' down that hillside screamin', and he told Colvill to take your flags. We got a quick order to double trot right at you, which we did. I remember all of a sudden feelin' Rebs on three sides. But we stayed! And then got relieved just in time to throw you back."

"We had you in numbers, Ben. We had this ridge up here in our hands almost. Might have made a big difference if we'd have gotten up here. All I know is we were plumb wore out from runnin', and then butted smack into Minnesota. Awful fightin' down there, Ben."

They walked the route of the Minnesota charge down to the dry creek bed. They stood where Ox had found Tony Lunde. Ben looked down and shook his head, said a silent prayer and rejoined Tom. Without a word, they moved to the left where a few large boulders were clustered. They relived the same scene, but from different vantage points of memory. They lingered a moment, then Ben put his arm around Tom's shoulder as they walked back towards the crest.

For a moment they looked to their right at the innocent appearing Roundtops, then east as Ben recalled the eerie scene before him that night when he had looked over into the chaos of the litter bearers, the surgery tents and the rows of Union dead.

They proceeded down the east side and across the swale to Rock Creek which was still littered and trampled down from the thousands of boots, hooves and wagon wheels that had mashed the grasses flat. They stood at the tree grove where Ben had first talked with his friend, then wound their way back to the village cemetery.

Tom and Ben separated to seek the grave markers of friends. The stones marking the resting places of William S. Cosgrove and Thor Anthony Lunde were simple gray rectangles. Head bowed, Ben stood over his two friends for several minutes. He could see their bright faces, hear their laughter, feel their love. He felt guilty to be alive, and bereft. At last he nodded to each grave, and pulled himself away to wait at the gate for his new friend.

For a village the size of Gettysburg, it was an overwhelming crowd. Many more had arrived that morning, and later estimates placed the crowd at 15,000. How many of the spectators were soldiers and ex-soldiers was never recorded. How many of them had been engaged in the three day battle was never even guessed.

A parade wound slowly to the cemetery. An hour was expended in making final preparations, seating officials and guests on the platform, and managing the masses of people into a milling semi-circle before the dais. Local politicians spoke briefly, but collectively devoured another hour. Fortunately the temperature was mild, the sun peeking in and out through fleecy, rolling clouds, and the wind was soft.

The main speaker was eloquent. Edward Everett had culled material from the recollections of Generals Meade and Hancock and other Union officers. He spoke clearly in a stentorian voice. The theme was professionally addressed and delivered. He paid a dignified two hour tribute to the men who had fought and died during the three critical days.

During the Everett address, the top hat of President Lincoln bobbed and tilted as the ungainly man shifted uncomfortably. His long legs appeared to be difficult to control and awkward to place. The organizers requested that he confine himself to making just "a few appropriate remarks."

When his turn to speak finally came, the Commander-in-Chief rose, put on his glasses, and towered over the lectern at the front of the platform. His high, squeaky voice intoned only ten sentences, albeit each one was complex in the extreme. He spoke for just under three minutes. The audience, that had survived over three hours of harangue, gave little response when he finished. The ceremony was soon over, the color guards marched off, and President Lincoln was escorted to the train. The next day's newspapers either ignored his brief address or provided professional disapproval.

The crowd did not exit the cemetery en masse. Some churned off to taverns, others went on battlefield tours, still others departed for home. A few sought family names on tombstones.

Tom and Ben had no clear objective. They followed the mass of people heading into the village. In preparation for their intended departure for Harper's Ferry, the two ate a full dinner, then started up the street that would lead them out along Cemetery Ridge. They hadn't walked fifty feet when they found themselves in the center of a maelstrom.

Several well-imbibed ruffians had sparked a fight that instantly involved a dozen men. A few well-aimed fists and feet connected, and the brawl soon spread to others. A lean and ugly man with a completely shaved pate stood out with his ferocity. He wielded his bulging rucksack as an extension of his arm and whacked an adversary across the head and neck with such force that the sack flew open, spilling its contents in several directions. Since the victim of the blow to the head took umbrage and immediately retaliated, the skin-headed man did not seek to immediately regather his spilled items, but was forced to defend himself.

Among the objects strewn from the sack, one caught Ben's eye, causing his nerves to leap. He began to shake violently. Quickly snatching the item, he shoved it into his pocket, and looked around at the ongoing brawl. The only person who saw his quick theft was Tom who met Ben's eyes in a quizzical stare. Ben leaned against the corner of a shop and tried to collect himself. The brawl continued for a few more minutes, then ended with the usual result of torn and bloodied clothing, smashed lips and noses, and missing or cracked teeth. Ben's eyes never left the man whose sack had revealed its contents. Two of the skin-head's friends helped him pick up the objects and stuff them back inside his sack. The three were so unsteady from drink and distracted by the fight that no inventory was attempted. They staggered off toward the Bigelow Tavern.

Ben and Tom crossed the street and stood opposite the tavern where Ben kept a watch on the front door. He grated the words, barely controlling his voice. "Tom, there can be no doubt. There is not another rosary exactly like this in the whole world. It's Ilsa's, made by her uncle. I told you about her. Remember? The young girl who was raped and murdered near her farm. He stole the rosary from her after he killed her. And Tom, her brother saw a rider with red hair. That's why his head's shaved, Tom. He's makin' sure that if somebody saw him that day . . ."

"Simmer down, Ben, simmer down," interrupted Tom. "Can't do anything about it 'til you get yourself under control. And even then Ah don't know what y'all can do."

"The hell I can't. I can't let him get away. Gus Bauer and Buddy would never forgive me. He's got to be punished, Tom. I'll get the sheriff to arrest him."

Tom shook Ben hard. "Keep your voice down, Ben. Cool down and think. What the hell you think the sheriff can do? What proof you got to give him?"

Ben interrupted. "The rosary, that's what. We can prove without a doubt it was hers. Her uncle only made one, for God's sake! No doubt at all."

"Ben, even if it's hers, don't prove nothin'. He could have got hold of it a lot of different ways. He'll just say he bought it or won it in a card game, or anything he wants to say. You can prove it was her rosary, but that doesn't prove he killed her, now does it? He'll just laugh at y'all, and the sheriff won't have a thing to charge him with."

"Well then, the red hair. You can bet he's got red hair. It's obvious that's why he shaved it off, Tom."

"Ben, how many red-haired men y'all think there are in the Yankee Army? That's not proof either. Come on now, be sensible."

Ben's emotions began to ebb. Tom's logic made good sense, but he still knew that he had to find a way. "Tom, my friend, this is not your problem. It's mine to do. You can come along or wait down the road for me 'til it's over, but I'm goin' to find a way to deal with this killer. I'm goin' over to that tavern and sit in there to keep an eye on him, and I'm goin' to figure a plan. That sweet girl's killer is goin' to answer for what he did. That's a damn promise."

Ben began crossing the street. Tom shook his head and ran a few steps to catch up with him so they could enter the tavern together.

"Ben, the only thing y'all can do if you're bent on takin' him on is to run a bluff. You've got to figure a way to get him to admit the rosary was hers and that he killed her. How you're gonna do that is beyond me. Why he'd admit it or how to get him to, Ah just can't figure out, but it's the only way Ah can think to try." Tom's low tone insured he could not be overheard. They chose a small table near the entrance of the half-filled tavern. With the ceremony over and the day waning, most of the crowd had already moved out of Gettysburg. The man with the shaved head was seated with three men at a table near the wall. They heard his friends call him Jake. Except when the four raised their voices in exclamations or oaths, Ben and Tom could distinguish few of their words. There had been references of scorn and ridicule of that "ape" Lincoln. Jake and his pals were drinking beer steadily and feeling feisty, but did not appear to be drunk. The man called Jake continuously stroked his skinned head, which Ben sensed was an indicator that the condition was fairly recent.

Thanks to Tom, Ben's brain was in control again. He responded to the idea about a bluff. "Those people with him would make it damn near impossible, Tom, you're right. I'll have to get him alone somehow, wait for the right time. They won't stay with him forever."

They conversed in low tones to make sure that their interest in the foursome went unnoticed. Jake dominated the gathering, pounding the table and forcing comments on the young woman replenishing their drinks, trying to fondle her several times. The barmaid was not amused, and the burly proprietor finally made a visit to the table, shut off Jake in mid-sentence, and put a stop to his behavior.

Ben utilized the time in fashioning a plan to get Jake alone, and deciding what to do when he confronted the murderer. The term murderer caused his first slight doubt. Might the man possibly be innocent? Could it all be only coincidence? How to be absolutely sure? He thought and plotted until he came to a simple conclusion. When I get him alone, I'll hold a pistol on him and accuse him. How he reacts to the accusation will tell the truth. Confronted suddenly, he won't have time to concoct a response or hide his feelings. He'll give himself away for sure. He'll show his guilt or innocence by what he does or says first thing. If he's innocent, I'll find out from him where he got the rosary and try to trace it back to the guilty one. If he rushes me, I'll shoot him and take my chances with the sheriff after.

Ben confided his plan to Tom who thought that it had possibilities, but too much depended on Ben's being able to judge the response. "Y'all an expert on readin' minds, Ben?"

"No, not an expert, but a man like him's no expert at hidin' his feelin's either. 'Specially when he won't have time to think it over."

The four men shoved back from the table. Jake bought a jug of whiskey and said a few conciliatory words to the glaring proprietor. Toting the jug, he followed his friends out the door. Tom and Ben tossed back the contents of their mugs and followed. The sun was near setting as Jake and his group stood talking at the corner. Two of the four slapped Jake on the back and walked off down a side street while Jake and his pal trudged in the direction of the cemetery. With the exception of a few staggering drunks, the streets were deserted.

Following at a discreet distance, Tom and Ben saw the two turn onto the street leading toward Culp's Hill. They recalled that the path branched off and included switchbacks that could confuse one unfamiliar with the area, but the various routes all eventually brought one to the east slope. They chose a path at random.

When Tom and Ben emerged from the woods and looked down the slope, Jake and his friend were settling in about two-thirds of the way down the incline. Ben and Tom found a spot among a stand of birch roughly thirty yards above Jake.

Ben verbalized his evolving plan. "Even if the other man should leave, I can't take on Jake here with so many others so close around. I'll have to wait 'til he goes off someplace. When he does, Tom, I want you to stay here to keep an eye on his friend. Can't have him walkin' in on me from behind when I'm facin' Jake down. Good Lord, Tom, the man has to have a bladder like a camel. All that beer and now the whiskey. You'd think he'd get a call sometime soon."

"Won't do you no good, even if he does. Won't go very far off to take care of thet problem. The way they're inhalin' that liquor down there, their tanks must be pretty full by now."

The rising, nearly full moon revealed the two men competitively guzzling until Jake's pal finally surrendered and rolled into his blankets. The victor finished off the contents, flung the jug away, lay quiet for a while, then began to snore. Ben was too charged to even consider sleeping. For over an hour his mind worked over alternatives and tactics. He was concentrating so thoroughly that the sounds he heard did not register for a moment.

Jake staggered to his feet and kicked his companion in the middle of the back. Showing no concern for those sleeping around him, he shouted at the inert form at his feet, "Up, Sam. Too early to sleep. More whiskey. We need more whiskey." His pal didn't move. Disgusted, Jake kicked him again and lurched off up the hill toward the path. A few moments after Jake passed by, Ben rose and spoke in a whisper. "Tom, stay here and watch that other one. I'll be back before you know it."

Tom watched Ben feel for the rosary in his left pocket and the loaded pistol in his belt, then asked, "Sure that thing's loaded, Ben?"

On his way up the hill to find the path, Ben didn't bother to answer.

Slightly wobbly on his feet, Jake travelled slowly and cautiously. Ben had no trouble keeping his target in sight along the lane lighted by streaks of moonlight filtering through the branches. He stayed far enough behind to remain undetected, but close enough to reach Jake in a few quick strides when he chose to. He waited for an open area with abundant space for maneuvering and sufficient light to see. When he saw Jake step into a small clearing, he quickened his pace to reduce the distance, reached his left hand for the rosary and held the pistol in his right.

He shouted clearly and sharply, "Jake!"

His quarry spun around, balled his fists, assumed a pugnacious stance, squinted into the partial gloom, and demanded, "Who the hell wants Jake?"

Ben held up the rosary in the moonlight, close enough that Jake could not fail to recognize it. "The owner of this, Jake, that's who wants you. Her brother saw you ride off. You're goin' to pay for what you did to her, Jake."

Jake looked hard at the rosary, saw the pistol, then tried to read Ben's eyes in the dim light. He ran his hand over his bald pate, stalling to try to come to grips with the situation. Then he chose his strategy. "You ain't gonna shoot, sonny. You don't even stand like a shooter. You ain't man enough to kill ol' Jake." He smiled and came at Ben in a rush.

Ben hesitated, then it was too late. Jake swatted the pistol out of his hand and bent back the wrist that was holding the rosary. Pain rushed up Ben's weak left side as the rosary was ripped from his hand. Jake's fist blasted the side of Ben's head, dropping him to his knees.

Shaved pate glistening with sweat and shining in the moonlight, he swayed unsteadily but triumphantly over Ben whose head spun as he tried to regather himself. Jake began to laugh and taunt. "This here is Jake's necklace. Nobody else's. Just ol' Jake's. Pretty l'il girl give it to ol' Jake. Pretty necklace. Pretty girl. Nobody steals Jake's pretty necklace from him, nobody."

He reached the rosary up over his head to fit it on himself as a necklace. When Jake's hands were occupied above his head, Ben struck. Focussed on the unprotected belly, he lunged out with all the force of his coiled legs, straightening and locking them for full leverage. He buried his healthy shoulder into the solar plexus with such impact that Jake staggered back, lost his balance, and with a startled bellow toppled backwards over the edge of the gorge. Jake's raging roar was cut off abruptly. Fallen forward on his stomach, Ben heard a sharp crack, a gurgling sound, then silence.

Stumbling to the brink of the dropoff, he searched below. In the distorted light he wasn't sure that his eyes saw true. "Good God," he mouthed and ran down the path several yards to where the bank provided a less steep descent. To prevent falling, he grasped the base of saplings growing horizontally out of the bank. He skidded the last few feet to the bottom, struggled to his feet and rushed over to where Jake had fallen.

Jake's form was suspended off the ground. The crucifix had wedged in the forked branches at the base of a sapling and the bullhide thong had held as Jake's neck took the sudden jolt. Head flopped to the side, eyes bulged, face frozen in rage and surprise, Jake was turning ever so lazily, hanging by the loop of the rosary.

Ben nearly retched and his hands began to shake. After a moment he steadied, stepped over to the pendulous cadaver and wrapped his arms around its thighs. Lifting the body, he tried to create slack to free the head from the noose of beads and thong. Again and again he raised the corpse, seeking release from their repulsive embrace. Finally the head slipped out of the loop, but the sudden release caused Jake and Ben to fall heavily in an obscene coupling. Horrified, Ben disentangled himself and scrambled away. He shifted his eyes from the distorted angle of the broken neck to look up the steep slope. Reflecting the moonlight, the polished beads of the rosary hung still and benign. Created as a work of art and designed to perform a passive, simple function, the rosary was a mute object conveying total disinterest in the scene below.

Chapter Forty-One

Sleep Well, Sweet Ilsa

Tom Fuller was a very independent young man. Ever since his rebellion against his cruel stepfather, he was determined not to accept orders from anyone except legally constituted authority. Tom was bright, but, even more critical for his survival in the conditions he had faced, he was shrewd and kept his own counsel. When Ben had described the plan, Tom was already concocting his own role. When Ben left to follow after Jake, Tom waited a few moments, then followed. He was determined that nothing tragic would happen to his friend.

He spaced himself to avoid detection and hid about twenty yards from where Ben called out to Jake. Tom's pistol was drawn and cocked throughout the confrontation in the moonlit clearing. He started a few steps toward them as Jake stood gloating over the fallen Ben, but quickly drew back when fortunes were reversed by Ben's desperate lunge. Tom remained hidden above and witnessed Ben's waltz with the corpse and climb up to free the rosary.

Tom hurried back to their bed rolls. After checking to see that Jake's companion was yet asleep, he crawled into his blankets, intending to be calm and controlled when Ben returned. Estimating three hours until dawn, he stared at the silvery sentinel moon, thought about what had transpired, and threw a salute to the heavens.

Tom's mind replayed the event. What a weird ending. Killed by a rosary. If he hadn't stolen what he probably thought was a necklace, he'd never been caught. Ben had been lucky up there on the path. Could have got killed instead of Jake.

Tom heard Ben slide into his bedroll. He waited for Ben to speak. When nothing came, he broke the silence by whispering, "Jake's friend never moved, Ben, he's been dead asleep." Turning to look over at the troubled Minnesotan in the dim moonlight, he could see that he was staring, jaws clamped tight, breathing quickly, shallowly. Tom wondered if his friend would ever be the same again.

"Job got done, Tom. Jake paid for what he did. It's over."

Even though he was emotionally drained, Tom was able to drift off into light slumber, or at least that zone between awareness and stupor. When he shuddered back into full consciousness, he noted immediately that the eastern sky was beginning to show faint indication of daybreak. He shifted his eyes to Ben who was in the exact position as before with the same transfixed stare. Tom decided it was time. Nothing to be gained by waiting. He whispered softly, "Best be movin' on, Ben."

Ben forced his eyes to his companion, slowly brought him into focus, then nodded. Noiselessly the two rolled up their gear, wound their way up the incline and found the path toward Cemetery Ridge. As the sky brightened behind them, they trudged past the copse of trees where Pickett's men had cracked the Union line on July third. The moonlight illuminated the slope and beyond to the darker area of Seminary Ridge in the distance. They paused for a moment, then walked along Cemetery Ridge and down the slope where the Minnesota boys had charged into death and glory. They didn't stop until they reached the rocks by the dry bed of Plum Run. Ben said, "You know, Tom, this'll be the first time I cross this creek bed. I didn't make it over the last time."

As they passed over to the far bank, Tom retorted, "Guarantee you, Ben, things ain't been the same fer me since Ah crossed it. Maybe crossin' back will change mah luck again."

Tom threw his arm across Ben's shoulder as they wound through the ravaged wheat field towards Emmitsburg Road. The sun had now risen behind them and seemed to be lighting the way home.

They hitched a ride to Frederick and walked the remainder of the distance to the Bauer farm. Tom had been told about Ben's relationship with the Bauers and was impressed with the respect Ben displayed for them. He knew the visit meant a great deal to the Minnesotan, but that his feelings were mixed.

Ben would be forever grateful to them and genuinely wanted to be with them. On the other hand, he knew that these next few hours with the Bauers might well be their last together. Ben felt the pangs before they even arrived.

As they approached, he recalled his visit with Tony in June when he was shocked to learn of Ilsa's death. He relived those mournful feelings as they neared the house.

The barking dogs sounded the alarm and brought Lucille onto the porch. When she recognized Ben, she waved excitedly, shouted back into the house, and ran out to meet him. "Ben, so good to see you. What brings you our way? Where's your uniform?" She hugged him, then looked at him closely, "Are you all right, Ben?"

He smiled at her. "Feel great, Mrs. Bauer. You and the others?" As he asked, he saw Gus striding to join them.

"We're all healthy as can be."

"Haloo, Ben," welcomed Gus, grabbing Ben's hand and shaking it firmly. "You hungry, young man, or should I say young men?" He laughed and turned to Tom.

Ben introduced them and said, "Tom has something in common with you, Bauers. He saved my life, too."

"Pleased to meet both y'all. Mah friend, Ben, exaggerates all the time, don' min' him."

The Bauers noticed Tom's accent, but graciously ignored it. They chattered as they walked toward the house.

"Where you two boys coming from and where you headed?" asked Gus.

Lucille laughed. "Answering those two questions would keep a woman talking for an hour or more."

Chuckling, Ben replied, "We've been to Gettysburg for a couple of days. Heard the President give a speech and dedicate the cemetery. Tom and I both lost some friends in that battle. Very nice ceremony they had for the ones killed, but not good enough for what they did. So many dead and maimed."

"War's so ugly, Ben. Our Kurt is back with us, but he'll be a long time getting over that prison. Treated awful. No offense meant to you, Tom, 'cause I've heard the prisons on both sides are bad, real bad," said Lucille.

Tom's nod spoke agreement.

"I'll be getting another chicken for these two handsome galluts, Mother. Be right back in," said Gus, moving to the door.

Ben guessed that Gus was going out for more than chickens, more likely to find Buddy and prepare him for the two of us bein' here.

"Sit you down at the table there, you two. Want some ice cold buttermilk? Coffee? What's your pleasure, gents?" asked Lucille.

"If the coffee's made, I'll have some," replied Ben.

"Ah jus' love that buttamilk," enthused Tom. "Missed it for these coupla years Ah've been sojerin'."

Gus, Buddy, and Kurt came filing in. Buddy appeared as morose as he had in June. Kurt looked haggard. Ben brought the Bauers up to date and both Ben and Tom described the ceremony at the cemetery dedication and answered a few questions about the battle itself. Ben related the episode about Tom sparing his life, and Tom described what Ben had done for him ever since. Lucille commented that Northerners and Southerners ought to all treat one another that way.

Buddy and Kurt had hardly spoken. After dinner Ben forced himself to broach the subject he knew would bring them pain. He reached in his sack and pulled out the rosary. Lucille began to sob. Gus told Ben to go ahead with what he had to say. Ben gently placed the rosary in Lucille's hand and began his account.

He described discovering the man who had caused Ilsa's death, how the rosary had fallen at his feet, the shaved head, and the confrontation on the pathway near Culp's Hill. He told them that an attempt was made to turn the man in to the sheriff, but that in trying to avoid arrest, he had been killed. Ben assured them that there could be no doubt that the guilty man had been found and punished.

Without comment, Buddy rose and walked out the door towards the barn. Kurt hesitated, then excused himself and followed his brother. Lucille remained silent. Gus said that it was good to know that justice had been served. Feeling the discomfort, Ben mentioned he and Tom had to be on their way. But first, he wanted Lucille and Gus to accompany him to the glade. They nodded and rose from the table. Ben asked them to give him just a few moments, and he'd meet them out by the lane. At their nod, he strode out the door toward the barn.

Kurt was nowhere in sight. Buddy was cleaning harness. Approaching Ilsa's stern-faced brother somewhat apprehensively, but feeling that it had to be done, Ben attempted to pierce the shield of pain and bitterness.

"It's taken care of, Buddy, it was without any doubt the right man."

Buddy looked up and soul-searched him. "You sure then? You absolutely sure, Ben?"

"I was there, and I saw him die. I'm sure, Buddy." Ben's eyes held steady, locked with Buddy's. Silence built. Buddy seemed to be deciding, then he did. He nodded to Ben, then looked down to his work as before.

Ben stood a moment longer before walking toward the barn door. Buddy's voice stopped him as he exited. "It helps, Ben, but it doesn't bring her back."

Ben responded as kindly as he could, "No it doesn't, Buddy, but I believe she sleeps more peacefully now. I hope we all will. I truly hope and pray so." He stepped off to meet the others for the walk up the lane to the glade.

As the four of them began the sad trek, Buddy loped up and joined them. Ben broke the silence. "Tom and I will go on to Harper's Ferry to my uncle's place. You remember me tellin' you 'bout the Russells, him bein' a farmer and furniture maker? His name is Bernard, his wife's Mary. You ever get to Harper's, please look them up. They'd welcome you. They know how grateful I am to you."

"We may just do that, Ben," said Gus. "Be proud to meet them. We might even get news about your doings in Minnesota from them. They'll know, won't they?"

"I guess they will at that. Might seem peculiar to you but when we leave here, I plan to try to find the route I took when I stumbled over from Antietam. See if any of it looks familiar. It led me to a family I'll be grateful to for as long as I live." The five of them stood at the foot of Ilsa's grave. Gus and Ben were on either side of Lucille, who reached inside her shawl and pulled out the rosary. She turned to Ben and said, "We want you to have this, Ben. Ilsa told me that she tried to give it to you once, and I know she would want you to have it to help you in trying times ahead."

Ben protested, "It's your family's, it's . . . "

"Ben," Lucille interrupted quickly. "She would want you to have it as a remembrance of her. We have other things of hers. Please us and please her by accepting the rosary and treasuring it. The simple love that it represents is the most precious gift in the world." She placed the rosary in his hands, embraced him warmly, and walked a few paces to wait for the others.

Ben's eyes met Buddy's. Buddy nodded and the faintest of smiles communicated his approval. He shook Ben's hand, walked over and stood beside his mother.

Gus grabbed Tom with one hand and Ben with the other. He looked at Ben and said, "You have given us more than you have received, Ben. You're part of our lives and always will be. Now get on with you. You've got miles to travel. Take care of him, Tom, and of yourself, and good meeting you, too." He walked to his wife and son.

Ben and Tom stood with their heads bowed over the grave of Ilsa. Ben made the sign of the cross, then turned to the Bauers and waved. He and Tom walked along the creek toward the steep slope that had nearly been his undoing that September night in 1862. They disappeared briefly on the curving trail to the top. As they emerged at the crest, they turned back and saw the Bauers waving them on their way.

Chapter Forty-Two

Paths Retraced

Ben recognized nothing as they wound their way through the rocks, trees, and brush of the Catoctin Range and down the western side to the valley below. He came to realize how dazed he must have been that night and marveled at the distance he had travelled in his delirium. They pounded up the eastern side of South Mountain, and soon found themselves at the crest looking out over rolling terrain that had as a background a multi-hued pastel sunset just thinly veiled by wispy clouds. Sore feet, weary legs, protesting old wounds, and a sharp drop in temperature combined to persuade them to seek a sheltering canopy of poplar where they built a generous fire and flopped.

Boiled coffee tempered the chill. Dry leaves cushioned their bedrolls. Tom lit his recently acquired pipe as they settled back to gaze at the emerging stars. The setting inspired conversation.

"What in hell are you smokin' in that thing, Tom? Horse manure?"

"Bad enough smell, y'all ought to taste it."

"Why you smoke it then if it's so bad?"

"Ah had to search real hard to find somethin' to keep me from bein' perfect. Settled on smokin'."

"You're crazy as a loon, Fuller."

They talked of the Bauers. Tom mentioned the troubled Kurt and hoped that time would help him recover. "Ah confess that Ah feared being a prisoner even more'n being killed. What Ah'd heard of prisons was that they beat a man down to a groveling animal. If captured, Ah'd have escaped or died trying. There's never gonna be a cage for me. Purcell back home was mah warden when Ah was little, but he was the last one."

Ben gazed up at the clouds passing the rising moon and decided to approach a subject he had been thinking about for some time. "Tom, my friend, we'll be sayin' goodbye before we know it. A few more days and you'll head back to Alabama. I'll be goin' on my way, though I'm not certain sure just when yet. But whenever it is, Minnesota is my destination. I don't know whether I'll be a farmer, or on the railroad, or a carpenter, or what, but I saw enough of Minnesota to know it's the place for me. Sure the winters get cold, and the area's isolated from the rest of the country, and it's still sort of primitive, but, Tom, you should see the people flockin' in. By the thousands. You can't fool that many folks, Tom. My brother Joseph always said that the people comin' west are the doers and the builders who want freedom to think new ways. They're comin' for the opportunities, Tom. And the beauty of the country. I haven't the gift of words to describe it. Except for a few months in dead winter, the climate is near perfect. And you should see the lakes. Deep blue, clear, and full of fish. Tom, I'm tellin' you, it's close to paradise. Now after all that buildup, I want to put somethin' to you straight." He paused to read Tom for any reaction.

Tom rose, stretched, stirred the fire, and lay back down. "Ah'm listenin', Yank. Say your piece."

Ben continued. "I want you to promise me somethin', Tom. Once you get the situation with your mother straightened out, you'll give Minnesota a thought for your own future. Now, Tom, before you say anything, let me finish."

Tom chuckled, "Let you finish? Sounds to me like you're wound up for a while. I got no place to go, Murnane. Fire away."

Ben was unruffled and determined. "From your own account, Tom, there's not much for you in Alabama. No property, no real job, not many prospects by your own describin' of it. The North is goin' to win the war, Tom, like it or not. The Confederacy will get worn down and after the war for quite a few years it'll be poor prospects down there. The side that doesn't win always has a hard time. Come on up where there's opportunities and space to move. You'll be welcome in Minnesota. I'm askin' you, Tom, think hard on it. No need to answer now. In fact, you don't ever have to answer you don't want to, but think on it. Think on it all the way to Alabama and when you get there, think on it some more. You come west, we'll go at it together and make it work. I've found myself a damn good friend, and I don't want to lose him. Think on it, Tom, think on it long and hard."

Tom lay there for a few moments without responding. Ben waited, then looked over at Tom and said, "Well?"

Tom chuckled, looked over at Ben and replied, "Quiet, Murnane, Ah'm thinkin' on it."

"You Rebel," Ben exploded. "Don't say much but always the last word."

With a dawn start, Tom and Ben wound their way down the west face of South Mountain. The sky was laden with a fast-moving gray cloud bank that brought with it a quick drop in temperature. They had awakened shivering in their bedrolls and quickly built a fire to warm themselves and boil coffee. Refreshed by the caffeine and brisk air, they walked a rapid pace with very little conversation. Both were preoccupied with private thoughts.

Tom was pleased and flattered by Ben's invitation of the previous evening. Truth was, he had been tossing the idea around in his own mind for a couple of months but had never opened the subject. He could not discuss such a prospect until he returned to Alabama to assess the situation with his "mother." But his growing affinity with Ben was real. He put no stock in the destiny theory. The fact that he had spared Ben's life or that Ben had reciprocated was not the primary source of his feeling. It was simply that they hit it off, thought alike, shared attitudes and values, enjoyed each other's company and trusted one another. A good friend. He'd never really had a close friend. Lots of pals both at home and in the Fourth Alabama, but never one he would classify a friend. Friend was a word Tom used sparingly. He didn't offer his friendship easily, nor would he give it lightly.

Minnesota. Seemed almost a foreign land. Ben's description was appealing, but would it strike him the same way? Would a "southron" be welcome there or feel comfortable? He knew for sure he was a Southerner, whatever that meant, but it was all he knew to be. On the other hand, most Minnesotans, according to Ben, were new to the area themselves. They weren't entrenched families like in the South. They had to be open and tolerant of new people because so many of them were new themselves. He'd have to think about it, but he didn't have a closed mind. He was young enough, he thought, to maybe give it a look. If it wasn't right, he could always go back to Alabama. He'd think about it some more.

As they drew closer to the Hagerstown Road north of Sharpsburg, Ben's anxiety heightened. That battle had been so vicious that his flesh tingled. He remembered nothing after the ball creased his temple, but he could never forget the ugliness of the battle prior to his wound.

They were silent, both remembering, trying to locate landmarks as they approached. In a few more steps they were opposite the Miller family farm near where Union General Hooker had launched the first attack. A few yards along they came to the cornfield on the left where nearly as many North and South boys died as there were stalks growing when the battle started. A fresh set of stalks, recently harvested, stood as silent honor guard now. On the west side a familiar patch of woods caught their eyes. They stopped to look around. Remnants of the battle remained, broken wagons and caissons and limbers, a few rusting artillery pieces, rifle butts amputated from their barrels, shoes and boots, damaged and decaying rucksacks, scarred trees.

"I don't recognize much except those woods. But, hell, it was so smoky and noisy I don't wonder. Wasn't lookin' at the scenery that day," said Ben.

Ben was amazed that he was so emotional after more than a year. They walked on. They who had seen it felt death still hanging. They saw the badly damaged Dunker Church on the right, then the road veering east, a narrow lane that was burrowed a few feet down like a wide furrow. Tom told Ben that it was the infamous "sunken" road that he heard survivors talk about after the battle. And very few survivors there had been. They took the jog and went on in to Sharpsburg village and out the other end.

They trod the pike heading for Harper's Ferry. Off to their left was Burnside Bridge but they didn't take the time to view it. They had seen enough of Sharpsburg for a lifetime. Tom told Ben the road they were on was the one General A.P. Hill had used to bring up his corps late in the day, just in time to save the Confederates from disaster.

Ben's only comment was that maybe even for the South it might have been better if Hill hadn't saved the day. "The damn war might have ended then for both sides. We'd both have our friends still with us if it had," he said. Tom didn't respond.

They strode the eight miles to Harper's Ferry at a leisurely pace along the banks of the Potomac flowing almost due south in that stretch into it's meeting with the Shenandoah River coming up out of Virginia.

Not wanting to disturb his uncle and aunt late in the evening, Ben suggested they spend another night in their bedrolls in a sheltered area south of Harper's. They built a fire and talked about the future. Ben finally told Tom about his proposal to Ellen. "Her acceptance will be in doubt for some time, but I intend to force it from my mind as much as I can in the meanwhile. If I let myself, I'd think of nothing else."

Tom agreed. "Ah hope it works out for both of y'all, and Ah do believe that both parties are well worth waiting for."

Mary Russell saw the two young men turn in off the main road, but didn't recognize Ben until he lifted his cap. She rushed out to meet him, arms open wide, and tears gushing. She hugged him warmly, looked into his grinning face, then stepped back a pace retaining hold of his hands. "Oh, Ben, you look so good. Lean though, too lean, but we'll take care of that."

"And you, you're gettin' younger 'stead of older, Aunt Mary. 'Cept for that short visit in Georgetown, last time we were together was when I came in '62. Early spring it was, remember?" It hurt to recall the time, remembering that Tony and Pudge had been with him on that occasion.

Mary turned to Tom with a welcoming smile as she was introduced. "You're very welcome, Tom. You're a good man or this nephew of mine wouldn't be calling you friend."

"Thank you, ma'am. Mah pleasure to meet y'all."

"Come on in. I've got a fresh-baked cake. Must have known somebody important was coming. Bernard's in the shop. Soon's I get you gentlemen to the table with a hot cup of coffee, I'll fetch him." She led them directly into the kitchen and poured out four cups of steaming coffee. "We've got a recent letter from Maurna, Ben. You can get caught up with her news. Always writes an interesting letter, that lady." She rushed out the back door and said, "Be right back."

Bernard beamed as he brushed off clinging wood chips and followed Mary into the room. "Ben, you're lookin' better, happy to say. Sit still, no need to get up." They shook hands warmly. Ben introduced Tom, and they settled down to enjoy each other and the quickly served, generous wedges of angel food cake.

"You good folks sure seem to stay healthy," commented Ben. "The war's been goin' back and forth past here for three years now. You get bothered much?"

"We're a little off the main roads here as you know, Ben," Bernard replied. "We've been spared the trampin' by of soldiers. The town of Harper's itself though has seen plenty. Seems like it's been the funnelin' point for both sides. Yankees own the town right now. Troops stationed there and on the heights around it."

"You got a Yankee and a Rebel under your roof right now, Uncle Bernard," laughed Ben.

Mary sighed deeply. "You two might be a sign for the future."

While Mary stayed behind to start preparing dinner, Bernard showed Tom his acres. They wound their way to Bernard's workshop where Tom was impressed with the pieces of furniture in progress. Bernard replied that he must be getting old because he couldn't keep up with the requests anymore. Ben told Bernard that he had a piece of woodworking art in his rucksack that he would show him later.

They went in to a roast pork dinner topped with tart apple pie. Tom convincingly described it as "the best Ah ever et." They stopped just short of gluttony and adjourned to the parlor for coffee.

Bernard mentioned Maurna's recent letter. "You can read it whenever you like, Ben. She's sure worried about you. Fears losin' another brother. I still can't believe Joseph is gone. A brutal loss. Just gettin' on his feet. Sure admired that man the way he grabbed hold. He was a dreamer, that Joseph. He'd of carried it out, too. Must be hard for Pim."

Mary added, "Such a good, good man. And trying so hard for the family. We're so sorry about dear Joseph. And then, what Maurna and Ginny went through."

Ben nodded saying, "Joseph was the rare combination of both dreamer and doer. Pim'll carry on for him. Awful the way Maurna and him found Joseph up on that hill. No warnin'. Don't know Pim'll keep farmin'. 'Spect he will but I'm not sure."

Mary said, "Maurna says she's not worried so much about Ginny and the time they spent as prisoners anymore. Ginny seems to have put it behind her. Those nightmares can go on and on sometimes. Must have been awful for them. Heavens sakes!"

Ben said, "If I know my sister, Aunt Mary, it'll only make her stronger. Lot of iron in that soft-lookin', gentle lady. Ginny's goin' to be just like her. They'll both recover fine."

"And what'll you be doing with your young life, Ben?" asked Mary. "Just curious, not prying you understand."

"Aunt Mary, I'll need some time with that one. Been thinkin' 'bout nothin' but the war for so long, I haven't had much time to think about what's ahead. Had some time at the hospital, but we were pretty busy there, too, weren't we, Tom?"

Tom nodded thoughtfully. "Never endin' stream of hurt soldiers comin' in. When you see war from a hospital, it shore ain't pretty. Politicians should be forced to see 'em."

"Doubt anything would wake up the likes of them, Tom. Sounds like you've got the same kind of fools down your way as there are in Washington," opined Bernard.

"Ah believe the good lawd did a fair job of distributin' jackasses pretty even all over, Mr. Russell. Ah know Ah've met mah share and not the last one either."

Tom stayed at the Russell farm through Thanksgiving. Tom told Mary she'd better shoo him out pretty soon or she'd have to call out the militia to drive him off. She said she got great enjoyment out of fixing for them and seeing them take such pleasure in it.

The night before Tom was to leave, after they'd said good night to Bernard and Mary, Ben and Tom talked most of the night. Tom said, "Ah'll go on home by heading through the Shenandoah Valley, then cut over to Knoxville, then Chattanooga, and down home to the farm, a little ways west of Huntsville, not far from the Tennessee River. A letter addressed to me at Monrovia, Alabama, will reach me."

"I'll give you my sister Maurna's address in Saint Paul," Ben responded.

After an enormous breakfast and with his rucksack bulging with as much food as Mary could stuff in, Tom thanked the Russells and bade them farewell. Ben walked down the road a few miles with him, finally stopping at a crossroads. Tom's road headed directly south to the far away horizon.

"Ah'll be on down the road then. Lots of steps to take." He put down his sack and embraced Ben, hard but quickly. "Take good care of mah friend, Ben. Not the last we'll see of one another. Y'all would make good money on that bet."

"I won't let it be, Tom. Your friendship is too valuable. Hope your ma's fine, Tom. Take good care of her. And Tom."

Tom held up his hand. "Murnane," he chuckled, "Ah give you mah word, Ah'm thinkin' about it." With that he picked up his sack, turned and started down the road, turning back several times to wave.

Ben stayed in the middle of the crossroads to watch him out of sight, then looked at the roads going in several directions. Seems appropriate, he thought to himself, lots of directions to choose from, how the hell does one know the right one?

Chapter Forty-Three

"Uncle" Talk

Ben trudged back toward the farm, but sensing a need to be alone, turned away toward Harper's Ferry. He loved Bernard and Mary, but suddenly realized that his gloom was caused by a basic need for contemporaries, friends with the same frames of reference, fellow travelers who had experienced the same rainbows and storms, calm waters and cataracts, smooth and rocky paths. He felt bereft, adrift, without direction. And why not, he thought. I've lost irreplaceable friends and been separated from Ox and the men of the regiment. Now I'm out of touch with Tom and Ellen. He remembered Joseph used to say that except for family and a few friends, life was nothing more than an empty bag. He thought he finally understood what his big brother meant.

Walking the streets, seeking some kind of distraction, he found himself irresistibly drawn by the surrounding hills. Choosing at random, he crossed over to follow the trail that led to Maryland Heights. His mind flitted from subject to subject like a slowly spinning roulette wheel skipping from slot to slot.

Reaching the summit he was afforded a long view in all directions. To the south where Tom was finding his way home and two great armies continued to rip precious lives from one another's ranks. To the east where lay the Capital, the burdened Abraham Lincoln, and Ellen with her private war. To the north where the Bauers mourned and where Tony and Shakey were wrenched from life and ended up in "hallowed ground." To the west where the bewildered Sioux were exiled and the Russells and Murnanes and friends and opportunities awaited him.

After surveying the horizons, he looked in his heart for truthful answers. How to get at them was the real mystery. He knew that he needed to ask the age old questions of the young. Where do I go from here? What do I do with my life?

For him, the war was over. He knew he was not the same person who had left Minnesota in the spring of '61. So much had happened to broaden his simple view of matters large and small. He had survived the fighting. Blessing or curse? Twenty-three years of age. Not a boy anymore. Time to choose a direction and get on with it. Can't use the war as a refuge from decision any longer.

Maurna's word, vicissitudes. Already enough of those for a lifetime. She often speaks of Timothy's simple formula, what he had called the big three, your God, your family, and your work. He'd said many times that if one stayed on good terms with those three, all the rest would fall into place.

Ben looked down to where his brother-in-law was buried in the Harper's Ferry cemetery. He began to speak to him in his mind. "All right, Tim, let's look at your formula. See how I measure up. Startin' with God, who makes only two simple demands of us. Love Him above all others and love our fellow man as ourselves. Not so simple to love my fellow man when it includes the likes of Jake and the traders who cheated the Indians and the animal who drove Ellen's husband and children off a cliff and all the profiteers of the damnable war.

"Family. How am I in terms of my family? Good brother to Maurna? Good uncle to Pim and Ginny? Not lately. And how about my work? I've been a warrior and not a very good one and now a feeble relic. Furniture maker, carpenter, farmer? Candidate for the priesthood? I have no real mission. Just ideas floatin' around in my head.

"Since my own father was taken when I was young, Joseph and Bernard and you, Tim, have been my fathers. Fine models, but two of you are gone. I have only Bernard for counsel and advice. He's a very wise man, loves his work, his wife, and his God and is on good terms with all three. I'll seek the good advice of your brother and his worthy mate. Thank you for your good counsel and for listenin', old friend."

The supper dishes were washed and put away. Mary joined them at the kitchen table where Bernard was reading the newspaper and Ben was composing a letter to Maurna. Mary was at her needlepoint, but her mind was on Ben, who seemed introspective, withdrawn, troubled. She suspected that he may want to talk, but didn't want to burden them with his problems. He should know they would welcome the chance to help. She hesitated, didn't want to appear meddlesome.

"Ben, would you like more tea or pie?"

"No, thank you, Aunt Mary. I've been eatin' too much and gettin' a bit soft."

"Oh pshaw," she said, "you're finally getting to look healthy again."

Bernard looked up. "A touch of tea sounds good." He rose to get the steaming kettle, filled her cup and his own and settled back to his reading.

She tried again. "Tom must be halfway home by now, Ben. Sure liked that young man."

Ben looked up and spoke, "Long way for him to go. One thing's sure. He'll get there. Aunt Mary, even with not much schoolin', he's one of the brightest I've met. I put it in his head about maybe comin' to Minnesota. He's thinkin' about it. If he decides to come, he'll write me there in care of Maurna."

She saw her opportunity. "Hard for young ones to know what they want to do. I remember being that age. Choices to be made."

Bernard didn't look up from his paper and said, "Turned out fine for you, didn't it?"

"You old scudder, you look to be reading and never miss a word."

Bernard smiled and kept on reading.

"One thing's sure, Ben. You seem to have had enough of army life. No thought to being a soldier anymore?"

"None. Enough for a lifetime. Hope to never have to put on a uniform again. One thing about the army, though. You just do what you're told, no decisions to make. Somebody with more rank made 'em for you."

"No good way for a man with a mind for thinking, like yours is, Ben," she said.

"Don't know 'bout that, Aunt Mary, but I do know I've got some decidin' to do. Can't be a permanent guest here. Have to be movin' on."

"Ben, you know you're welcome long as you want to stay. No burden to us at all. Lots of room here, more'n we need or even use." She laughed, "'sides it gives me someone to talk with, only other one here just reads the paper and doesn't hardly say anything."

Bernard's eyes showed over the lowered newspaper. "Now, Mary, you know you trained me over these years to be a listener. Just shows what a good teacher you've been." But the paper stayed in his lap. She had drawn her husband into the discussion.

"You hear that, Ben, you've a ready listener if you want to do some talkin'." There it was, she finally had the door open if he wanted to walk through.

"You two are very kind and wise, and live peaceful, happy lives. What you've got is what I'm lookin' to find, a simple life with some usefulness to it. Don't have any great talents or big dreams. But things have turned over and around on me 'cause of this war and what happened in Minnesota. It's still all spinnin' around."

Bernard filled the opening. "Don't make a big decision 'til the spinnin' stops, Ben. Easier to hit your target once it holds still."

"I wasn't sure before the war came along. Just started sortin' things. Back then the choices were to be among the priesthood that you know I'd been considerin' and farmin', that I took to some, but wasn't at long enough to know, and then the furniture makin'."

"How can you know about the priesthood 'til you give it a try?" asked Bernard.

"Can't really, I suppose. I have a lot of respect for them and what they try to do. Tell the truth, I've always thought that I'm not good enough."

"Oh pshaw, Ben Murnane, your as good as any of them. Better I suspect," countered Mary.

Ben laughed. "Aunt Mary, you're sure good for a fellow's estimate of himself. But you don't know what a great sinner you're sharin' tea with."

Bernard laughed along. "Ben you're still too young to be an expert sinner. Sinnin's like wood workin', you don't learn all the different ways to do it 'til you experiment. Your best sinnin' days are still ahead of you."

"Satan's main helper talkin' to you, Ben," chuckled Mary.

"Look who's talkin', Ben. No man alive's got the imagination of a woman for sinnin' or anythin' else for that matter."

Ben enjoyed their banter as he contemplated the best way to proceed with a request he wanted to make. He felt the stage was set, so he opened the subject.

"Aunt Mary and Uncle Bernard, you're both so good to talk things over with. You're not quite so close as parents would be, yet you care and your wisdom is valuable. Lettin' me bounce my thoughts off you gets 'em out to be looked at. I'm real uncertain 'bout lots of things. If I make a judgment 'fore I'm ready, I'll kind of be stuck with it. What I think I need right now is some sortin' time. Even just goin' back to Minnesota right now would get people influencin' me right off. I wouldn't want to hurt Maurna or my friends by ignorin' their advice. I'm thinkin' that if you could tolerate me, I'd stay a bit longer while I sort and have your help. I'd help you in the shop, you bein' so busy Uncle Bernard. Work off my room and board that way. Not 'cause you request it, but so's I would feel better about my stayin'. What do you think?"

After Mary and Bernard retired, Ben returned to his letter to Maurna. After making his decision to stay for a while, he had something conclusive to write. He labored over the wording, finished, and read it to himself.

"Uncle" Talk

Dear Maurna, Ginny, and Pim,

I hope that all of you are in good health and settled in your home in Saint Paul. It is comforting to see you there in my mind. I am fine. My wounds are well healed, and the doctors told me that I will have no permanent weaknesses or scars. I was lucky.

I have been with Uncle Bernard and Aunt Mary since before Thanksgiving. My friend, Tom Fuller, the Confederate soldier I told you about in a previous letter, has gone home to Alabama. He became a close friend during the months since Gettysburg and may decide later to come to Minnesota to look it over for his own future. Tom and Minnesota would be good for each other. He went with me to the dedication at Gettysburg. The President spoke. It was a good tribute to the men who fought and died there, both blue and gray. I visited the gravesites of Tony Lunde and William Cosgrove. Tony's parents and Abigail must be very sad.

I will try to explain my plans for the next few months. I am anxious to see all of you, but will not be coming to Minnesota for a while yet. Bernard and Mary discussed this with me, but please don't blame them for the decision I have made. I need some time to think out my future. If I come back now before I weigh the options, I am afraid that I will make a hurried decision. So I will stay here a couple of months, work and talk with Uncle Bernard and Aunt Mary and try to sort things out. I will then come back more ready to settle in. Please try to understand.

One condition I attach to my plan, though. If you need me there, I will come immediately. Your needs are more important than my wants. Be honest with me if you need me to come. Please understand my poor attempt to explain. I will be there no later than mid-April. I will be with Bernard and Mary at Christmas. All of us wish each of you a blessed Christmas and may the year 1864 bring us all peace and a clear path to follow.

My best love to all of you,
Ben

A few weeks later, Mary handed a letter to Ben and said, "From Maurna, Ben. Sure hope it's good news."

"Could use some, Aunt Mary." He tore open the envelope and began to read.

Dear Ben,

Your letter of December 15 was received. It was good to hear from you, dear brother. Ginny read it so many times it is nearly in tatters. Your trip to the Gettysburg dedication must have been heart-wrenching. They are saying now that President Lincoln's talk there was better than they first had thought. I must read it sometime.

None of us is very pleased with you, Ben. (Just joking). Of course, we understand your decision after all that has happened to you. We regret the delay but knowing you will be here soon is all that really matters. By all means think things through. I know the feeling well. When our ordeal as prisoners was over, I had a period of time in Mankato when I had the opportunity to think before any decisions were required. I was so confused, so devastated, with Joseph and Rose gone and you so far away. It was a blessing that I did not need to make a quick decision.

And, oh Ben, the decision when finally made was the right one, at least for Ginny and me. The Campbells have been so good to us. God put them on that steamboat way back in '60, I know He did. I've a good paying position with lots of work. Pim has decided to take up the farm again this spring. He'll live in our house. Will, Rob, and the Rivards will be near by. He'll likely be at the farm when you return. The three of us will want to go out to see him then. And visit the gravesites, Rose's boys, the Rivards, and Lundes. Pim won't try to talk you into farming with him, Ben, he'll leave that up to you. But he would welcome you if that's your decision.

And now, dear Ben, I come to the part I dread talking about, but I must. I have thought it through very carefully, both the pluses and the minuses, and my mind is clear. I want you to have the undertaker disinter Timothy's body and have it sent home with you when you come. I know it will be difficult for you, but it's so important to me, Ben. Please try to make sure that Bernard and Mary understand my purpose. I know they have cared for his burial site lovingly. But to me it is more than symbolic, it is right to bring him here. Please understand. I will write Bernard and Mary directly to tell them what I want and why. You need not mention this to them.

What I am doing it for, Ben, is this. When the five of us left Ireland more than six years ago, we had to leave behind our home, probably forever. Our roots were in the air, not touching soil, just hanging down loose, searching for a place to take hold and grow solid. I've found that place, Ben. Even though there are only three of the original five alive, we have finally found a place for those roots to grasp and burrow deeper as the years pass. My daughter, my nephew, and my brothers all in bountiful Minnesota. I want Timothy to complete his journey home too, Ben, where he will be near me until I am laid down beside him. All of us home, Ben. It will not be complete until we are finally all here together.

Stay healthy, Ben. Yes, I understand your delay to think through your future. Please understand my desire to have Timothy come home.

Best love from all of us,
Maurna

"Uncle" Talk

Ben finished the letter, set it aside and said, "No bad news at least. You can read it after a bit, but before you do I have to say, Uncle Bernard, you and Aunt Mary are the two most contented people I've ever known. Wish I knew your secret."

Bernard smiled, looked fondly at Ben for a moment, then replied, "Nice of you to think so, Ben, but it wasn't always so. Yours truly had years of doubt and troubles, too. In fact, most of 'em when I was about the age you are now. You just didn't know me then."

"Can't imagine you or Aunt Mary doubtin'. You two have more faith than anybody I ever knew, exceptin' Maurna, of course."

"Don't forget Timothy," inserted Mary. "He had more'n the rest of us combined. Faith is a gift of God, Ben, but you have to work at it or you can lose it."

Ben pondered a moment, then plunged ahead. "Want to talk with you about that. My faith's been slippin' last year or so. God doesn't seem quite so real, or maybe what I mean is, He doesn't seem to be in control of things. He sure lets a lot of bad things happen."

Bernard chuckled, "God just isn't measurin' up to your standards for Him, right, Ben?"

Ben looked at him and grinned. "Put it that way, it does sound a little pompous, doesn't it?"

"Not pompous Ben," he said. "You're just confused. But God's still doin' his job, never fear. Just not always the way we want. He's kind of independent. But I don't mean to make light of it. Spill it out and we'll look at it."

"My thinkin' probably will sound foolish to you, but here goes. I've lost three close friends in this war, saw hundreds of men from both North and South slaughtered, and a wonderful family torn wide open by a cowardly murder. Had my brother and friends killed by Indians, my sister and little niece suffer as prisoners for over a month. I've heard of politicians and business vultures gettin' famous and wealthy from the war. I've listened to priests and preachers explain it all away by sayin' it's just God's mysterious plan and we should quietly accept it. Somehow it just doesn't wash clean the way it once did. I'm not lookin' for pity or sympathy, just justice."

"Justice, Ben?" Bernard mused for a moment. "Oh, we'll get justice some day. Yessir, each one of us. We may be wishin' then we'd never heard of justice. We may not be quite so clean ourselves. But, that aside. Why you want to blame God? He isn't responsible for it, evil men are."

Ben was vehement. "He watches it all happen, doesn't He? All powerful, He could stop it."

Bernard scolded, "Sure, He could stop it, but what would we have then? He gave us free will, remember? We'd be the first to complain if He hadn't. He knew that all men wouldn't make good choices, that some folks would do evil acts and some innocent people would get hurt. With freedom comes responsibility. We've got laws to deal with evildoers, but we sit back and don't stop them from doin' it again and again. Our fault, not God's."

"You tellin' me we should wait for man's justice then, Uncle Bernard? Not much of that around that I've seen. Let me try to explain what I'm feelin'. Out on the prairie, there are coyotes that most folks treat with scorn. Well, I've watched those independent rascals and learned to admire them. They take what they need and don't apologize for doin' it. Shrewd, alert, tough, mean as they have to be, they say here I am. If you leave me be, I won't bother you. But, if you get in my way, then be prepared for the battle of your life."

Both waited for a moment, then Mary responded, "Coyote does what it does by instinct, Ben, not by reason or a sense of right and wrong. Two things you've got that it hasn't. It's your duty to use both of 'em, Ben."

Ben continued as if he hadn't heard. "Then there's rabbits. Timid, scared, apologizin' for their existence. Hide in a hole all day, sneak out at night, lookin' around for all the ones wantin' to make a meal out of them. Sure, the rabbits survive and have forever, but only because they send out so many little ones that some of 'em live because of the numbers of 'em. But what are the odds for any one rabbit? In constant fear of the strong. I've had a lot of rabbit bred into me and trainin' to be humble and turn the other cheek. Lately I've seen the strong exploitin' and connivin'. I don't want to be like them, but I don't intend to be prey for them either."

Mary nodded, showing she understood, but then spoke firmly. "Ben, you've got some anger to get out, need to get rid of it. Doesn't harm your enemies at all, just eats away at you."

"You think those greedy people get the best of it, Ben?," asked Bernard. "You think their lives are easy? Nobody escapes, Ben. Everybody struggles and everybody'll face God's judgment."

Ben wasn't convinced. "You really believe there's a just God? Could it be wishful thinkin' maybe? Some say that the wealthy and powerful invented God to give the rest of us somethin' to keep us from rebellin'."

Bernard was getting a little exasperated. "Ben, do you think it's possible that this whole complicated world just happened by accident? Even those scientists say that you can't make somethin' out of nothin'. Then they turn around and say all this universe just happened. Contradict themselves, don't they? Oh, yes, Ben, there's a just God all right."

"Uncle" Talk

Though only a small article in the *Washington Post*, it had caught Ben's eye. In fact, it leapt off the page, causing him to call out.

"Aunt Mary, my regiment is being mustered out of the army on February fifth. They're to be sent home early. There'll be a celebration dinner and then the veterans will be free to leave. Ox is goin' home. Isn't that great?"

"Lord above, I thought the war was over when I heard you. That is good news though. They've surely been in service a long time and served well." Mary was trying to read over his shoulder.

He read from the article. "The renowned Minnesota First Regiment, as they call it here in the paper. Yes, Aunt Mary, the original men enlisted in May of 1861. Their three years will be completed in May this year. The men will be sent home and officially be free on May first. They'll spend their last few months at Fort Snelling."

"Ben, you'd ought to go down to Washington for that celebration. See your friend Ox, and the others. You earned the right same as them. You'll have a grand time."

"Aunt Mary, I'm goin' to do it."

"Your clothes will be washed and pressed, and a fine lunch ready to take along right after breakfast. Now you get on into Harper's and get yourself a ticket for the morning train. Leaves at 8:00 A.M. on the dot. Now get yourself goin', nephew."

Ben detrained at Union Station in Washington the next afternoon. The newspaper article had indicated that the Regiment was temporarily housed at the Soldiers' Rest, a quick walk from the depot. As he strode the short distance, Ben reviewed in his mind the early days when Ox, Tony, and he had gone off to Fort Snelling where they met Sarge, Shakey and Pudge.

He found Ox and was warmly welcomed and invited to the evening testimonial banquet to be held at the National Hotel ballroom. They spent the remainder of the afternoon reminiscing.

"Ben, we got mustered out of federal service at a ceremony this morning, and we'll board the train for Minnesota tomorrow. We'll complete our three-year enlistment under Minnesota state service. Two hundred twenty Minnesota recruit replacements will continue the Minnesota First Regiment duty in the Second Corps of the Army of the Potomac," explained Ox.

As Mary had foretold, the banquet was a grand affair. Guests included Vice President Hannibal Hamlin, Ignatius Donnelly, representing Governor Ramsey, and Secretary of War Edwin Stanton. Each of them gave complimentary speeches praising the regiment for its long and distinguished service and reviewed its major engagements. Secretary Stanton read excerpts from a congratulatory note sent by Second Corps Commander General Hancock, concluding with a reference to the famous charge down the slope at Gettysburg. "No more gallant deed is anywhere recorded in history." The highlight of the evening was the appearance of Colonel William Colvill, so hobbled by severe wounds at Gettysburg that he had to be carried into the hall. The men cheered him lustily and brought tears to his eyes. The Vice President conveyed the gratitude of President Lincoln and "a grateful nation" and wished them "Godspeed." The Chaplain concluded the evening with a solemn prayer for the Regiment's dead and for the speedy recovery of its wounded.

Ben spent the night with his former comrades and was there to see them off the next day. "Ox, I want you to look up Maurna and Ginny when you get to Saint Paul. And greet your brothers and all our friends in New Ulm and along the Cottonwood."

"I'll do that, Ben, and I'll see you soon back in paradise."

They shook hands and Ox leapt aboard the already moving train. Ben waved them off and smiled when he heard their happy voices break into homeward-going song.

He was left alone with a difficult temptation. Though he had deliberately submerged the thought, he could not prevent its re-emergence. This close to Ellen, the urge to see her was palpable. But he had promised her a full year without any contact and a mere three months had passed. He sat on a park bench and considered his alternatives. He could position himself to see the Union Hospital grounds, stay out of sight, and hope to get a glimpse of her. He could carefully avoid being seen by Ellen but lie in wait for Julia, hoping she might convey Ellen's feelings. He could approach Ellen directly and force a decision. Whether he based his decision on honor or fear of rejection he wasn't sure, but in the end he dejectedly waited for the return train to Harper's Ferry. He arrived at 8:00 P.M., with mixed feelings, joy for his comrades with the First Minnesota, and depression regarding his own unsettled affairs. He showed only the first face to Bernard and Mary.

Ox and his regiment confreres rode the rails all the way to LaCrosse. Special arrangements had been made to accommodate the heroes from that point on. The entire complement of 325 veterans were issued two buffalo robes and assigned a space on team-pulled sleighs that used the frozen Mississippi River as a highway to Fort Snelling. Eight men per sleigh, they formed a lengthy train that made the trek up the winter-encased Mississippi Valley. Word of their arrival preceded them. They were feted in Winona, Red Wing, and Hastings by adoring citizens. During their layover at Red Wing, Ox made a special effort to seek out Mrs. Cosgrove with whom he spent a few

"Uncle" Talk

minutes, consoling her on the loss of her son and describing his resting place in the field of honor at Gettysburg. She planned to visit the site as soon as the war was over.

It seemed as if the entire population of Saint Paul was at the dock when the sleigh caravan made the final westward turn from Dayton Bluff. The men were welcomed with sobbing, cheering and loud band music. They disembarked and mingled with the crowd who braved zero degree temperatures. Governor Ramsey and Mayor Stewart made complimentary speeches at a banquet at the Athenaeum, and the Commander of Fort Snelling welcomed them back into state service. Maurna and Ginny sought out Ox and greeted him happily and warmly. The men were later transported to Fort Snelling where each received an automatic thirty-day furlough. Three day passes were generously awarded during their remaining ten-week tour of duty.

Chapter Forty-Four

Even Coyotes Go Home

Bernard finished a pine chest of drawers and handed it off to Ben for sanding. Working silently, Ben's thoughts turned to Ellen. "Dear God, help her find the capacity and courage to take on the joys and risks of life again. She knows it's impossible to have one without the other." She's going about this in the right way, he admitted. If she agrees to blend our lives, she wants to be unencumbered.

Thinking of Ellen as his wife, Ben turned to his uncle and said, "I envy you your peace of mind. Aunt Mary and you are where I want to get. But I don't know if I've got your qualities, Uncle."

"Here now, don't be makin' a saint out of me. I struggle every day. If life were easy, more people would be good at it, Ben. Each person has to find his own way. No two ever face the same problems and situations. When I was near your age, I saw conditions for the Irish get awful bad, and I let myself get angry and disillusioned. Got so bad I knew I couldn't stay there or I'd do somethin' drastic. Full of bitterness and lost hopes, I ran away to America. Got even more belligerent and hateful and full of myself. And then God sent me a treasure I didn't deserve."

He paused and smiled at the remembrance, "I met your Aunt Mary. The sun was shinin' again and the storms blew away and the whole world looked different. To win her, I had to be worthy of her. I threw off the anger and negative thinkin' and found my real self somewhere under the pile. Wasn't easy to get shook of bad habits. But Mary was the difference for me, Ben. Get yourself linked up with goodness and it'll bring out your own."

"She was your inspiration, Uncle Bernard, but the change had to come from inside you."

"True, Ben, and it's difficult to find it and drag it out in the open. Might be there's a Mary out there for you."

After that exchange, Ben remembered something and said, "Be back in just a minute." He ran to the house, was back in a hurry and stood waiting until Bernard looked up from his work.

"Told you I'd show you a piece of woodworkin' that was given to me by those Bauer folks up by Frederick. You remember, I told you and Aunt Mary 'bout 'em, the ones who nursed me back to health after I got wounded at Antietam."

"Yes, I recall."

"Want you to meet those fine people, Uncle," Ben said as he handed him the rosary.

Bernard took it in his hands, then reached in his shirt pocket for his spectacles to examine it. He fondled it, studying the beads, the tiny wood discs, the knots in the bull hide thong, and the intricately carved crucifix. He held it up in the light and turned it slowly, catching the various shades. He looked at Ben and slowly shook his head.

"Ben, what a wonder this is." He examined it further, moved his fingers over and along the surfaces and laid it out on his workbench. "I'll have to meet the one who created this, Ben. I thought I knew somethin' 'bout workin' wood. Who did this? What skills and patience the man has. This is a priceless piece."

"Man named Laval, Alvin Laval, brother of Mrs. Bauer. Made it for his niece name of Ilsa. Sorry to say, she died. Her mother wanted me to have the rosary to remember them by."

"Don't know how you could ever forget the Bauers, rosary or not. But, Ben, this man has skills, tools, and techniques the rest of us don't even know about. Tell you somethin' else I see here. This man has a deep faith that's carved right into the wood. Come on, Ben, we've got to show this to Mary and enjoy watchin' her eyes brighten up at the sight of it."

Ben had arranged with the Saint Paul Packet Company to send him a telegram when the Mississippi River was free of ice for boat travel up to Saint Paul. When word was received, he passed it to the undertaker to proceed with the disinterment of his Uncle Timothy's remains. He purchased his train ticket to LaCrosse and saw the casket safely on board.

At the depot the following day, last words were difficult.

"Greet Maurna, Pim and Ginny for us, Ben. Perhaps some day we'll visit your Minnesota. And remind each of them how welcome we will make them if they visit us. You and Pim are the closest we ever had to a son of our own." Mary gave him a fierce hug and turned away.

"I love you dearly, Aunt Mary."

Bernard had his arm around Ben's shoulder. "Remember now, my young coyote, you've got some of all the Murnanes and Russells in you and the heritage it represents. You'll do fine. The war bruised you, Ben, but you've got so much in your favor. Hope I didn't wear you out with all the preachin' and advice givin', but then you asked for it, didn't you? Just one main thing to remember. The world will knock you down time and again, happens to everybody. But the secret to it all is to struggle back up again, Ben. Get up one more time than you get knocked down. . . ."

The trip was replete with the sights, aromas, and sounds of blooming spring. The country he passed through was alive with activity. Farmers in the fields, towns and villages vital with commerce. He rode through states that had not received the direct scars of battle, but whose women had suffered their men's absence. Many were still waiting and praying for their return. The war had to end soon and when it did, the joy would spread, the nation would be reunited, and the boom would start.

Everyone knew that the impetus would be west. It could already be felt, inexorably, inevitably west. Chicago was the great hub of a wheel of growth and Saint Paul would be the next westward focal point. And then on to the nearly endless prairie, the majestic mountains and the Pacific. Millions of acres and immeasurable natural resources. The reborn national unity would be the springboard for the building of a great nation. Ben felt excited to be part of it. But what part? Maurna had written that a Saint Paul man named James Hill foretold of railroads being the key to a new empire, the rails stretching west and north, bringing people and trade. He could hear the klick-klack of the wheels as they rolled through Chicago and west to LaCrosse. Maybe the rails will be my ticket to the future, he thought.

The train handed him off to the steamboat at LaCrosse. He recalled the exciting, boisterous connection the First Minnesota had made in 1861 when he and the other innocents had passed through to their great adventure. Happy Tony and laughing Shakey, affable Pudge, gritty old Sarge, and dependable, lovable Ox. What a bunch we were. Like thousands of others from Wisconsin, Iowa and Michigan and Maine and New York and Texas and Mississippi and Alabama and every other state in the divided Union. Young men full of excitement and hope and promise. One writer had called the Civil War the growing pains of a young nation, the adolescence of a potentially great people.

He saw again the imposing bluffs above Winona and farther along his eyes caught the first sign of those undulating prairies stretching west into the glorious spring sunset. Deep vees of returning geese and ducks activated a pink sunset background. He sat on deck and stared at the dimming horizon, bundled against the chill, hearing the pounding of the engine, the slap of the current and the occasional whistles and bells.

Just at daybreak he was awakened by the Red Wing call and got up to quickly breakfast and stretch on shore. He knew many men from Red Wing and of course Red Wingers Colonel William Colvill and William Shakespeare Cosgrove. They boarded again to begin the final stern wheel turns into Saint Paul.

Ben stood on the foredeck, feeling it now, an end and a beginning. His final port, at least for a while. His eyes roved the unfolding scene, as he caught the aromas of spring just emerging from the late grasp of stubborn winter. Ice chunks small enough to be non-threatening swept past, dissolving slowly into the swirling current. Streaks of soiled snow stubbornly survived in shaded areas. A few ambitious buds and blossoms rushed the season. Huge congregations of ducks covered the river's backwaters. He watched a winging threesome of frolicking, green-headed mallards as they banked to land. A crazy thought. Maybe they were the spirits of Pudge and Shakey and Tony coming home to Minnesota. He quickly chastised himself. Sentimental ass, he thought. But then he smiled and thought, what the hell, who knows? And just in case he threw the exuberant trio a quick salute.

As they churned on, his thoughts turned to Maurna and Ginny. He remembered three and a half years ago, their positions were reversed. He had been waiting on the dock for them to arrive. My God, the changes in that brief span. Six of us Irishers are now but four. The Sioux are dead or gone, hundreds of settlers killed, thousands of eager new ones already here or on their way, Saint Paul doubling in population, the war that disrupted thousands of families around the nation still relentlessly raging. Has any three-year period ever seen so much? We'll never be the same again as a country or a region. Lincoln said that we must be sure that these men shall not have died in vain. Will we carry out his resolve? Will men put aside their petty differences and focus on their similarities and need of one another? He knew he no longer possessed blind faith in his fellow man.

He saw the cliffs of Kaposia where Big Thunder and his heir Little Crow had reigned, then Pig's Eye Lake, and Dayton Bluff. And around the last bend on the east side of the broad Mississippi lay Saint Paul, no longer a village, but an impressive city. The depth and breadth of the settlement amazed him. Houses up the tiers and terraces and onto the slopes and elevations in the background. The set-back Capitol remained the centerpiece, but new churches sent steeples heavenward and additional warehouses and stores and shops crowded the commercial district. The crowd was sparse for the 9:30 A.M. landing. Many boats had preceded his this spring so the townspeople already were inured to first-boats-of-spring excitement.

His eyes picked out Maurna and Ginny as the vessel closed the last 100 yards. The steamboat whistle drowned out other sounds as they scraped the pier. Saint Paul. Would it be home for him?

Ginny in her bright red bonnet vigorously waved a kerchief. Always contained Maurna waved, too, but in a more dignified manner. Ginny, so grown, so pretty and bright-faced, such a glorious smile. Maurna, beautiful, composed, wearing a resplendent expression. He could feel his own mouth smiling, sense tears welling up. My people, my very own, no others can compare. They are me. I am them. Never doubt it. Oh, Dear God, it's so good to see them.

They tied up, and he was first one off and in their embrace. Joyful tears flowed as they walked slowly arm in arm to the street above. Maurna had hired a carriage, part joke, part tribute. They cantered slowly through the traffic. He was inundated with questions from Ginny and commentary from Maurna who pointed out the Campbell's store where she worked, the new Cathedral, and other landmarks. At last they pulled up before a small, neat two-story cottage, painted white with green shutters, with a low picket fence and a patch of grass and the upturned soil of a new garden plot on the side. Maurna announced proudly, "Our home." She quickly added, "Of course, we just rent, but will someday own."

They stepped onto the low-railed porch where the driver deposited Ben's small trunk. A settee and two benches furnished the south-facing porch. When inside, he knew for certain he was home, for the first object he spotted was the oak rocking chair with the shawl carefully draped over the high back. The whole house was Maurna, her taste, her sense of home. Then she sat him down while she made tea and the real catching up began.

Maurna interrupted Ginny's chatter. "Now, dear girl, slow down a minute and let your mother get a few important things said to your Uncle Ben. The reinterment service is scheduled for 3:00 P.M. at Calvary Cemetery. The funeral home will handle all of the arrangements, and a new, young priest, Father John Ireland, will officiate. You'll like him, Ben. He was a chaplain with a Minnesota Regiment that fought in Tennessee or Mississippi, I think. By the way, he asked me to tell you he'd want to be talkin' with you about the future. Well, anyway, I've purchased four burial plots for our family. Timothy will have the first one and I claim the one beside him. The others I would hope will not be used before mine, but they're there when needed. I'm so grateful to you, Ben, for seein' to bringin' him home to me. Tim belongs here, Ben. It's clear as glass to me."

"Can't tell you how good Bernard and Mary were to me, Maurna. They patiently listened to me rant on and on. So wise in knowin' how to live, those two. What a blessed marriage they have."

"Ah, yes, they have each other every day of their lives, the way it should be," Maurna said as she turned away to the teapot to keep from showing her brimming eyes.

Ginny had been repressed too long. "I go to school nearly every day, Uncle Ben. Want me to read for you?"

"Later, darlin', I'll be lookin' forward to it. Can you be doin' figures too, Ginny?"

"Oh, yes, but they're so dull to do. Apples must be added only with other apples. Can't mix in oranges with 'em. Mixes up the numbers," she said soberly.

He laughed and said, "I thought that gave you fruit salad when you mix them like that."

"No, Uncle Ben. Sister Marie Alice says it gives you a wrong answer."

The tea was ready and they chatted on. Not a word was spoken about the Sioux Uprising or the War. Maurna did mention that Pim had gone out ten days ago to the farm to prepare the soil for the seeding. He wanted to wait to see Ben but felt the timing too critical. Maurna told him that Ox had stopped by for a visit when he had passed through and was looking forward to seeing Ben.

"Maurna and Ginny, we'll go on out to the farm to see Pim in a few weeks after he and the Koukkari brothers get the seeds in the ground. We'll want to see the Lundes and the Rivards and others, too."

"Will and Rob have grown so tall, Pim says. Rose would be so proud of them. Ben, though I mentioned it briefly in a letter, I want you to know what Pim did to save Ginny and me. I won't speak of it now, but just know what a man he was when we needed him."

"I'm not surprised, Maurna. The makin's were there. Lot of Joseph. Did you ever see our older brother fail in somethin' that called for courage? Not Joseph, not Pim."

They talked the morning through, had a boiled chicken dinner and a fresh baked cake to honor their returning kinsman. It was such a glorious spring day that they strolled the downtown streets to familiarize Ben with some of the changes. The time sped by and they found themselves at the cemetery for the brief service.

Ben was re-acquainted with Angus, Iris, John, and Beverly Campbell who recalled meeting him in October, 1860. Two sisters of Saint Joseph, Ginny's teachers, also had come to witness the services.

Timothy's remains were reconsecrated in Minnesota soil. The others departed. Maurna and Ginny placed the first brave crocuses of spring on the grave. The stone was simple. Beloved Husband, Father, Friend. They stood for a few moments in prayer, not a tear from Maurna who was erect and dignified. She whispered solemnly, "Timothy and Joseph, two of the original emeralds gone, but they live in us and through us to ours and beyond. After all, dear brother, emeralds are forever, you know."

They made the sign of the cross and walked away arm in arm. Maurna was at peace. The circle was at last complete for her.

A quick supper and some inconsequential talk served to help them postpone issues they knew would have to be faced. They sat on the porch and enjoyed the colorful setting of the sun through the gorge that led to the Minnesota River Valley. Suddenly Maurna gasped. "Oh, Ben, forgive me, but it slipped my mind in the preoccupation with Timothy. You have two letters." She was up and away and quickly returned to place the letters beside him. "I'll get Ginny on to bed and be back, Ben." He glanced down eagerly but fearfully at the two envelopes. The top one was from Tom, stamped Alabama. Apprehensively he lifted it to uncover the other. Yes, from Washington, from Ellen. His heart jumped. Sent ten days ago while he was still in Harper's Ferry.

He wanted to be alone when he opened Ellen's letter, couldn't trust what his reactions might be. He'd open Tom's first, deal with that, then the other. He ripped it open and the first few lines spoke the gist. "I'll be coming to look over the much-bragged-about Minnesota. I thought it over, Ben. Be there around the first of July. The next day will be an anniversary of sorts for you and me. Old Purcell died six months ago and my Ma returned to live with her family. I'm free as a chicken hawk." He read it through, but what he wanted to know was already said. Be great to have you, Tom, he thought, just great.

Maurna returned and asked, "Good news, Ben?"

He replied, "Great news, my friend Tom Fuller is comin' to Saint Paul, Maurna. He may just be comin' permanent."

Maurna waited a moment for more. She noticed then the one unopened letter. She knew her brother, sensed his predicament, and began to move away.

"Don't go in just yet, sis. Sit a moment or two more with your just-returned-home little brother. I said home, Maurna, but I don't say it yet with the certainty that you do."

"Give it time, Ben. It's home to Ginny and me, and now to Timothy. From Cork to Virginia to the Valley to here. We feel it, Ben. I'll not seek another. Joseph found home in his beloved valley. You and Pim, not quite as sure, but you will be soon enough. Our roots are planted." She paused, gentled her emotions. "You've much to think about. I'll be here for you, and for Pim, you know that. Prayers do get answered, Ben. Believe me they do." She kissed him warmly on the cheek, touched his hand and whispered, "Welcome home, dear brother."

When she had gone in, he heightened the flame in the lamp, reached over for the letter from Ellen, opened it, and began to read.

> My Dear Ben,
> Forgive me for the delay in responding to your precious proposal. At the outset let me ask you to refrain from reading ahead to the end of this letter. I need to explain my answer in the sequence that it was determined. Your understanding of my conclusions will be more complete if you will indulge my request.
> First off, Julia informed me immediately after you departed on November 17 that she had told you the details of the tragedy in Kentucky. She said that she felt you had a right to know. I agreed. I then reviewed with her the discussion you and I had that last evening, and the beautiful proposal you honored me with. I suggested that if my feelings about the deaths of my husband and children were mere self-pity, I would have withdrawn completely; if they were anger, I could not have sustained them; if they were loss of faith, I would have sought things to replace them. No, I told her that what I truly felt was a suffocating feeling of guilt for having survived.
> I repeated your argument about having to risk pain in order to achieve joy, about living vitally in order to be truly alive. I shared with her my counter argument about respecting your special offer so much that I didn't dare not reciprocate with equal fervor.
> Ben, Julia just smiled, then tears filled her eyes and she said, "Child, can you not see past your arguments to the glorious tributes you are paying one another? Are you blind to the magnificent common denominator in your two points of view? His argument is real concern to help you, dear girl, not himself. Your point is concern about shortchanging him, not about yourself. Each of you is displaying the most essential ingredient of genuine love. Caring for the other more than oneself."
> She has eyes to see, Ben. But I had to be absolutely sure. I needed to take one dreaded step. In your words, Ben, I had to face up to it straight on. I made a three day visit to Cumberland in February. It was good to see my people again, and a few friends. It was pleasant. But the critical moment came when I went to the cemetery alone. I knelt at the three graves and let my feelings wash over me. Ben, I wept when I saw the three beloved names and let myself remember the beautiful, joyful, vital people who rested there. I remained for a long time. The tears seemed to cleanse me. And I prayed.

Before I rose, I had my answer, Ben, and yours. I again saw their zest for life as it had been, but this time I did not see it with pain, but with joy. That was when I knew that they would approve. Ben, *they would wish me life.* I looked down on them and smiled my gratitude.

My answer to your proposal of life together is an unqualified, resounding, yes. I will forever be grateful to you for persisting in your love, and for kindly waiting. I say yes, Ben Murnane, with true joy, with reclaimed vitality, and with genuine enthusiasm. To be Mrs. Benedict Murnane is my fondest wish and greatest good fortune. And next to me, the most happy person of all is dear, wise Aunt Julia who sends you her love and congratulations.

I'm so happy, dear Ben. You will have a wife who has no doubts about her ability to match her husband's ardor. As strange as it would have sounded before, I know that when I am there as your proud wife, Minnesota will become our loving home.

Vitally, gratefully, lovingly, eternally,
Ellen

Slowly he re-read the letter, savoring each precious phrase, overwhelmed by feelings of relief and joy. He rose, moved to the porch railing, and gazed westward up the Mississippi River gorge faintly outlined against a layered backdrop of lavender and crimson horizon. Through his mist-glazed eyes the scene appeared muted, mystical. Muffled night sounds and the fresh aromas of spring enveloped him as he felt elation gradually give way to humility and gratitude. Bowing his head he breathed, "Dear God, I vow to be worthy of your great gift."

Ellen's reference to home moved him deeply. He spoke softly, "Home." Maurna had emphasized that lovely word, a term of infinite warmth, that many believe connotes both the temporal and the eternal. "Dear Lord," he begged, "let me know again such comforting faith." He dwelled for a moment on the multitudes of homeless. Maurna lamented the Sioux, exiled on the arid hills of Dakota. And he recalled a newspaper columnist's portrayal of Negroes, "peering out of the dark cave of slavery, blinking in the bright, scrutinizing light of emancipation." And he remembered his own people, the vagabond Irish, and all the other immigrants flooding the continent. All seeking a home free of oppression.

He briefly mourned the cherished ones who had gone on. Uncle Tim, now near Maurna and Ginny. His brother Joseph and Rose Koukkari on their beloved hill. Ilsa, tranquil and safe in the glade, her sylvan sepulcher. Pudge, unmarked, near the Rappahannock River. Tony and Shakey at peace on Cemetery Hill among hundreds of First Regiment comrades and their Confederate brethren. He hoped that each and all were indeed home.

And he remembered those still traveling. Tom Fuller, Uncle Bernard and Aunt Mary, the Bauers, Julia Howard, Sarge, Ox and his brothers, the Lundes, and the Rivards. "Dear Jesus, guide their steps."

He whispered into the gentle breeze, "Yes, Ellen, my wife and my life, wherever we are together will be home. We'll be visited by hardships, conflicts, and vicissitudes, but together we'll stand up to their challenges. And how well we meet them will become our true measure."

Briefly he bowed his head, then straightened and wiped his eyes. Turning he strode to the open doorway and shouted, "Maurna, get up. You're not asleep yet, are you? I've got wonderful news. I've got a letter I want you to read. . . ."

Epilogue

August 18, 1942
Saint Paul, Minnesota

Aunt Virginia is gone. But not in passion and pride as had gone South Carolina. She gently passed on in grace and dignity at her Summit Avenue home in Saint Paul.

She had seen her last sunset from where David now stood, but had lived to give approval of Part I of the manuscript. She felt that the descriptions of her five emeralds, their friends along the Cottonwood, and the conditions leading up to the Uprising had been well portrayed, and she had penned the dedication herself. She was laid to rest beside her husband, Henry West, and within a few steps of her mother, Maurna, and her father, Timothy. To David, she was a superb representative of her formidable and energetic generation. In his mind she would always be the sixth emerald.

At first, David was disappointed and saddened that she had not lived to read and evaluate the finished book, but he soon realized that she had fulfilled her mission by commissioning and launching its pages and had departed fully confident it would be satisfactorily completed.

He was melancholy, but also satisfied and proud. He had kept his promise to his aunt and at this moment felt her abiding presence. As he gazed into her sunset and felt the gentle west breeze on his face, he whispered, "Together we have re-sounded a few 'mystic chords of memory.' Thank you, Virginia Russell West, for your inspiration and for many other gifts you passed on to us. You are not gone to us. For like the rocks, our heritage is forever. Good night, dear Lady."

NORMANDALE COMMUNITY COLLEGE
LIBRARY
9700 FRANCE AVENUE SOUTH
BLOOMINGTON, MN 55431-4399